Before the Truth: Book 1 of the Burden of the Innocent Rose Series

by

Mackenzie Childs

DORRANCE
PUBLISHING CO
EST. 1920
PITTSBURGH, PENNSYLVANIA 15238

Dorrance Publishing Co
585 Alpha Drive, Suite 103
Pittsburgh, PA 15238
Visit our website at *www.dorrancebookstore.com*

ISBN: 978-1-6853-7505-8
eISBN: 978-1-6853-7519-5

BEFORE THE TRUTH: BOOK 1 OF THE BURDEN OF THE INNOCENT ROSE SERIES

by

Mackenzie Childs

For everyone who struggled through the 2020 COVID-19 lockdown.

.

Character Powers Index

True Greer: Gunslinger Smoke: Can project and manipulate lethal, pitch-black smoke from skin, materialize copies of any gun touching body and manipulate bullet paths with wave of hands.

Eela Keilot: Hydroplane: Can manipulate water if touching a concrete base surface and damage any motor vehicle and/or machine with touch of palm.

Thomas Keilot: Hydro Manipulation: Can manipulate water with a wave of hand.

Stella Strickland: Spitfire: Can breathe red flames from mouth without damage to internal organs.

Cohen Barnett: Match: Can set skin on fire and cast out the flames. (Detail – flames naturally burn white; can change to red if angered.)

Fletcher Lockwood: Matter Manipulation: Can change an object's state of matter with the touch of a hand.

Camilla Streantest: Toxic Paint: Can produce paint and spray paint cans from palms that have twice the amount of toxins present in normal paint.

Maevis Anderson: Location Tracking: Can locate someone anywhere in the world if she has their full face pictured in her mind; can communicate with them through thoughts.

Randy Ramirez: Particle Manipulation: Can manipulate particles present in the air and multiply the quantity of particles touching the palm.

Ryth Navarro: Self Destruct: Can destroy anything touched from the inside out.

Stretch: Elasticity: Can extend arms and legs abnormally, similar to a rubber band.

Delta: Override: Can counter and destroy commands on electronic devices.

Bourbon Houston: Light Speed: Can move at the speed of light with no physical consequences.

Boss Harper: Heightened IQ: Wields an IQ significantly higher compared to the common human.

Cloudrix Terry: Dream Walker: Can infiltrate dreams of the sleeping and manipulate them.

Dusk Hudsun: Camouflage: Can make herself, others, and any object she touches invisible to the human eye.

Nicola Fowler: Emotion Projection: Can project emotions onto other people in point of view that distort the victim's mental state. (Detail – If overwhelmed, a wave of the emotion he feels is sent out in a violent manner, affecting everyone around him to feel the same way he does.)

Kumi Lyasu: Golden Glow Heal: Can breathe golden, glowing butterflies that can heal wounds on the physical human body. (Detail – Her own body turns to stone once the butterflies return to her after healing the injury.)

CHAPTER 1

LOWER-CLASS SECTOR, NEW YORK CITY...

Evil always finds a way to write itself into innocent life. Rain drizzled through the air as I walked through the backstreets of New York City with my head low, the water soaking my hoodie into my skin and making me squirm. Few people ran swiftly all around me, ripped umbrellas over their heads as they scrambled to the nearest stores to escape the oncoming storm. The uneven and soaked stones under my feet filled me with anxiety as they all sneered up at me, threatening to break under my weight. *Of course, the mayor leaves us lowlifes to rot in the decaying lower-class sector as he basks in perfect glory in the upper-class sectors of the city on the island.* I clenched my fists gently as I furrowed my brow down at the stones. *I hate how powers dictate how wealthy everyone is. These social classes disgust me.*

Old and rusting neon street signs flickered above me as I passed them, threatening to burst. Metal bars lining the windows of shops on the street trembled slightly as the ground shook below me. I narrowed my eyes at a flyer of the mayor's plans posted on an abandoned building door. *Great idea. Let's destroy the lower-class sectors to expand the middle- and upper-class sectors, forcing us lowlifes out of the city and deeper into the shadows.* I scoffed sadly, glancing up and seeing a group of people sitting in an alley to my left. *What's the point? Why are we all trying so hard to keep living if we're just going to be treated like we're dead anyways?*

Angry screams and curses pulled me out of my head from the store to my right. I paused and glanced up to see an old man behind the register being held at gunpoint by two younger men. The one furthest from the door looked past the man next to him and narrowed his eyes at me through the glass and tipped his head, signaling me to keep walking. I blinked at his annoyed glint in his eyes and sighed as I walked calmly towards the cracked glass door. Every step I took, the cashier shaking behind the register became more uneasy. I ignored the angry gaze of the man staring at me and looked down at the ground while I pushed the door open gently.

The shelves inside the store were all cleared and pushed over. Food strung the floor, and the freezers in the back had doors missing. Broken glasses of the drinks spilled down the old racks, creating puddles on the dirty tile below them. Cold steam raced the drinks as it hovered across the dark metal railings and disappeared into the air. The two men with the guns turned towards me with furrowed brows and widened eyes and stared at me for a moment. I blinked slowly at the cashier, who was staring at me as he shrunk down to the floor, and then I glanced up at the stained ceiling while I tucked my hands into my hoodie pocket. The two young men glanced at each other and shrugged before one of them raised their gun at me.

"You better get out of here," one of them snarled darkly, stalking towards me.

"Why?" I sighed softly. I turned swiftly to the destroyed store as I saw something dart across a walkway. "I just want to buy something. I won't interfere," I responded, monotone. *It wouldn't be a tragedy if you shot me; you'd be doing me a favor, actually. Go ahead.* "Hell, I'll give you two the money for what I get if you want—"

"Ah ha! You're the snarky type!" a third person suddenly snapped. A woman in bright red workout clothes darted across the fallen shelves and shoved me roughly into the rack of food near the window. She flicked a sharp blade open from her palm and held it to my neck as she stared up at me with a frown. Her angry eyes searched my face for something and only brought the knife closer to my neck when I stared at her with no response.

"Easy now…" I mumbled. "We wouldn't want anyone to get hurt right?" I whispered, bringing my hands up harmlessly.

"Leave!" the woman spat, getting in my face again. I winced, as her breath smelled heavily of alcohol and a strong perfume filled my nose. "You can get what you want once we're done here." she sneered, tapping my nose a few times with her sharp nail. I glanced over at the other two men staring at me with furrowed brows and frowned down at the woman. The cashier stared intently at me as he trembled behind the counter, blood running from his upper lip. I sighed and nodded once with a glance at the woman in front of me before I shoved her off me and left the store. *All of us are desperate I guess, but that was just pathetic...*

I glanced up at the cloud filled sky as I made my way down the street and inhaled slowly as I saw them part for a split second, revealing a clear sky filled with bright stars. My heart swelled in my chest as I paused my stride and stared in awe. Each star pulsed gently against the pitch-black sky. Some stars grouped together and pulsed brighter, while others were alone, dim and barely glowing. *Guess I'm not the only one then...* Loud glass shattering and yelling immediately broke my trance as clouds blocked the clearing in the sky. I closed my eyes for a moment and slowly looked down to the street in front of me. I continued walking and glanced over my shoulder with a sigh.

"We can't have any witnesses, right?!" one of the men from the store snarled. The woman and another man stood behind him with crazed smirks on their faces as the man in front of them raised his gun. The trigger was pulled, and bullet hurled towards me. A gentle click ran through the air as my vision blurred slowly, and I reached my hand out calmly. The bullet came into crystal clear view as it slowed to a complete stop in front of me. My vision steadied as the bullet fell helplessly to the ground, rolling in a puddle and hitting my foot. I blinked harshly and looked back up at the group with a furrowed brow. *Okay, that was just rude. I didn't feel like getting shot at this exact moment.*

"Really?" I winced pitifully, frowning down at the bullet. The three stood in the street with widened eyes and angrily glanced at the people staring out the store windows at us.

"His power is useless to guns!" the woman cried exasperatedly.

"Let's get out of here!" the man next to her yelled. The man holding the pistol dropped it and turned on his heel, running after the other two. *I don't have time for this...* I raised my brow and held back a smile. *Who am I kidding? I have nothing else to do.* I sighed as I turned to a trash can next to me. An old rope swung gently in the cold breeze as it stuck out from the side of the lid. I frowned as I slowly extended my pitch-black smoke from my palm and picked the rope up, pulling the trash can slightly around before it fully came out. I waved my hand, and the smoke tendril from my palm carried the rope down the street as it continued.

The rope flew down, tightening itself around nothing right in front of the trio. All three of them tripped and fell over the rope as angry curses filled the air. The smoke tendril quickly wrapped the rope in their legs and arms, before zipping to a light post and tying itself around it tightly. The store owner limped out from the broken door and stared with widened eyes at the group frantically trying to get away. He turned towards me with a gentle smile on his face as the smoke tendril from my arm faded away into the air while I put my hand in my pocket. The woman in the red workout clothes stared intently at me with angry eyes and her lip twitching. People then quickly leaned out of the stores around the street and stared at me with hopeful glints in their eyes. *No, I'm not an Elite. I don't have the money, motivation, or patience to be trained to work for the government; I'd help you all another way if I could.*

The glint in everyone's eyes dulled and burned out immediately as sirens filled the air. People retreated into the stores or deep into the shadows of the alleys as if nothing happened. No one around here could afford a run in with the police these days. Every passing day, they became more and more angry with the lower-class sector people, through no fault of their own but only through the influence the Elites had on them, fear. Each encounter only seemed to get more and more violent, regardless of the reason they were called. We were seen as dirty and worthless by the rest of society, a waste of time for those in the workforce. *One more reason why the crime rate is so horrible here. The police or Elites don't care most of the time, and when they do, it's for the wrong reasons.*

I tipped my head to the cashier and pulled my ripped hood over my head slowly. I kept my head down as I jogged to the broken sidewalk, my heart beating strong with worry in my chest. I sulked deeper into the shadows as I glanced up with only my eyes at the police cars powering down the narrow streets. The loud cars shot past me, their tires splashing up cascades of cold, dirty water all around me. I stopped walking and glanced over my shoulder as violent honks came from both cars. An arm flung itself out the passenger window and flicked me off.

"Don't walk so close to the damn road! You'll get yourself killed!" they snarled. I blinked calmly at the cars slowing down as they neared the stores and turned their sirens off. *Wouldn't that be a blessing…*

I shivered as loud yelling erupted through the air from the officers as they stepped out of their cars.

After walking a ways down a dark, empty street, I turned the corner of the local tattoo building into the dark alleyway next to it. Dumpsters and large piles of trash climbed the graffiti-filled walls as a single light sconce shone dimly above a light grey door in the back of the alley. *Lovely place to have a back door to an apartment complex. Perfect area to get robbed or killed... Jeez, I may get lucky tonight then.* I glanced up at the apartment building and sighed at seeing the cracked bricks and broken windows. I frowned, looked back down to the ground, and flinched as my body tensed.

An older man who looked like a skeleton laid against a dumpster, his clothes torn and soaking wet as his chest barely rose and fell with each rattling breath. My heart ached as I stared at him for a moment before I pulled a $20 bill from my jean pocket and dropped it in his lap while I passed him. The man yelped awake and thanked me repeatedly as tears filled his empty eyes. He tucked the money under his jacket, bowing his head and mumbling. *Anything to help another lowlife like me...*

I waved my hand out to the side and glanced at him in the corner of my eye, frowning as I saw him bow his head again with folded hands. I shook my head with a slight scoff and narrowed my eyes at the old building in front of me.

I roughly shouldered into the door of the apartment complex before it swung lazily open. *I forgot this wood swells when it rains.* I closed the creaking door as quietly as I could before I sighed and looked around the lobby room, the dirty teal walls begging for someone to clean them or repaint. I waved sheepishly at the clerk sitting at the front desk while I tensed. She flicked the newspaper in front of her and didn't acknowledge me at all. I sighed and lowered my head as I made my way to the old stairwell next to the broken elevator. *It's been a month... This still hasn't been fixed?*

After fighting with the seventh-floor door in the stairwell for a few minutes, I gently closed it behind me with a loud sigh. I shook my damp hair out of my face and tucked my hands into my pockets as I walked down the hallway. I passed rooms filled with quiet laughter, stern conversations, soft music, and silence. I slowly pulled up my sleeve to the key on my wrist and unlocked my apartment door at the end of the hall. I glanced over my shoulder to the door across from me near the window and frowned before pushing my door open roughly.

I ducked under the old door frame and mumbled as I locked the double locks I had installed on my door and shivered. I paused for a moment and stared at the broken wood next to the new hardware, feeling my chest tighten. I blinked my eyes quickly and turned to face the room with a frown. My one-room apartment looked emptier than usual as I stared at it through the dim light. My eyes drifted from the small kitchen in the back right corner of the room to my bed near the single window across the sunken step with the small TV on a shelf on the wall opposite of it. I scrunched my nose as the pungent smell of mold from the bathroom in front of me lurched through the air. It always made me feel like I was at least not living alone.

I hung my key on the hook next to the door and pulled my hood over my head, resting it on the small kitchen island. I gently stepped down into the sunken part of the room and sighed in relief. The old wooden floor creaked below me as I slowly walked to the window to the left of my bed. I leaned on the windowsill with shaking arms for a moment and glanced behind me at the box peeking out from under my bed. I took several shuddering breaths before I pulled the old curtain aside and stared out the window.

I had always loved to think I got lucky with this apartment. It was one of the only ones with a view of the rest of the city. The large, beautiful towers of upper-class New York loomed ominously through the pounding rain, only their silhouettes and lights visible. I grabbed a cigarette from the pack on the nightstand next to my bed and struggled to push the window open for a moment. Sharp pain shot up my arm as I winced and glared down at the small cut on my left hand with a frown. I held it up to my mouth as I searched for my lighter and climbed out onto my small balcony with a sigh. After lighting my cigarette, I sat and listened to the noises of the city. Loud cars, gentle music, and conversations of all kinds echoed throughout the air. Middle- and upper-class New York always had something going on. You only have to look a little further to the right and across the bridge to see the silent lower-class sectors.

As I began to drift off to sleep from the rain, I held out my cigarette and let the rushing water put it out. I threw it off the balcony and slowly climbed back into my apartment, reaching blindly for the towel near the windowsill. I dried myself off gently, threw the towel back on the shelf, and sat roughly on my bed. I stared at the blank wall for a moment and felt everything drain from my body. I sat in complete silence: no thoughts; no emotions, nothing. The old, cracking paint and the loud thunder from the window was the only thing around me that I could hear. The moment I reached down for the box under my bed, a gentle knock came from the door. I gasped, taking several deep breaths as I held my face in my hands. *Ugh...*

Tears filled my eyes as I leaned on my knees and stared at the box in anger. I quickly wiped my eyes while I hesitantly creeped across the room and glanced through the peephole as I held my breath. I opened the door to a cheerful familiar face with his daughter by his side.

"Good evening Mr. Keilot," I sighed, my voice wavering. I smiled gently down at his daughter peeking at me from behind his hand, and she giggled, ducking out of my view.

"You seemed to walk a little slower down the hall than normal today," Mr. Keilot whispered softly. "Looks like I was just in time," he grinned, tipping his head to the box sticking out from under my bed. I frowned and flicked my hand towards my bed. The box immediately shot out of sight, hitting the wall roughly.

"I came to say hi, and give this to you," Mr. Keilot chuckled, pulling an envelope out of his back pocket. I took the piece of paper and frowned at it in my hands for a moment, glancing back up at him. "A friend of mine said you helped stop a robbery today?" he tried, raising his brows expectantly at me. "Good job staying close to your name, True," he giggled softly. His daughter, Eela, also giggled into her arms as he turned around and ruffled her golden hair on her head. I tensed slightly as I saw her dart out of his hand's reach and come running back to him, roughly shouldering into his side.

He grunted and picked her up quickly, swinging her in a circle before setting her back down again with a sigh. "It's a food stamp and some cash." Mr. Keilot smiled. "Take care of yourself, True. Your ribs are starting to show again." He frowned, glancing up and down at me.

I nodded, bringing my arms around myself and leaning against the doorway. He reached towards me and rested his hand on my shoulder and ducked down to look me in the eye. I flinched at his touch and kept my gaze away from his warm eyes. My arm began to tremble under his hand.

"You look sad today, True," Eela whispered softly. Mr. Keilot closed his eyes briefly and frowned down at her as he slowly took his hand away from my tense shoulder. "Can I take that sadness away?" she asked hopefully. I blinked a few times and nodded with a slight smile at her. Eela suddenly leapt up at me, wrapping her arms and legs around me in a tight hug. I widened my eyes and put my arm around her as she purposefully started to fall backwards, giggling into her hand. I breathed hard as she buried her face into my shoulder and mumbled a song softly. Her small heart beat strongly and proudly in her chest as she tightened her grip on me slightly. My own heart skipped a beat as she took a deep breath with her face in my shoulder.

Mr. Keilot's tired eyes softened as a warm grin spread across his face at us. I felt my legs begin to tremble under me and my chest tighten as my breaths became quick again. I then sat her down awkwardly and waited for her to let go of me. A gentle nudge from Mr. Keilot was all it took for her to give in and lean into his side. I trembled, wrapping my arms around myself as I smiled hesitantly up at Mr. Keilot after staring at Eela mumbling with her eyes closed in front of me.

She shook her entire body and clapped her hands once.

"BOOM! You're happy now!" Eela beamed proudly.

"Thank you, little one, I needed that," I chuckled, my voice wavering. I rubbed the back of my neck slowly as Eela began to mumble a different song while hugging her father's leg tightly.

"You always have me across the hall, True," Mr. Keilot whispered gently. I nodded and leaned back into my apartment slowly. "You know where my shop is, too!" he chuckled, pointing at me roughly.

I grinned at him and tipped my head before waving slowly at Eela furiously shaking her hand towards me. I watched the two of them walk into the apartment across the hall from mine and sighed before I stared down at the envelope in my hand.

Loud yells and bangs suddenly echoed through the stairwell, sending a jolt of panic into my chest. I scurried inside and closed my door roughly, locking the double lock and flicking the lights off. I darted across the room, using a smoke tendril to place the envelope on the kitchen island as I leapt into my bed. I laid in silence for a moment, my heart screaming out of my chest in panic. Loud bangs knocked against my door as I flinched and closed my eyes, my heart beating out of my chest.

"No lights! Come on next door!" an angry voice snarled. My breaths quickened as I immediately recognized the voice.

There was a group who came to the apartment complex every month. They would go apartment to apartment, stealing anything they pleased on "Mayor's orders." The first time they came to my apartment, they busted up my face and locked me in my bathroom. They wrecked everything, took my old pistol and all the money I had in my drawer. Any and everything else they took wasn't important enough for me to remember. I was too hyper focused on strangers being in my home and destroying things. I closed my eyes tighter as I heard multiple people yelling from one of the apartments on my floor. The distant memory of the break-in that took my parents loomed in my mind, making my heart spike in my chest with panic. I then fell asleep, drowning in my anxiety-filled thoughts.

I jolted myself awake from a nightmare as loud yelling filled the apartment complex. The old walls of the building groaned as the entire building shifted slightly. My old cabinet doors in the kitchen swung open and slammed shut as my lamp fell off the nightstand next to my bed. I leapt off my bed, waving my hand at the box under it and ran across the apartment, unlocking the door with shaking hands. The box slid out from the bed and quickly followed me across the room, hiding behind the wall at my fingertips as I leaned my head out into the hall.

The other people on my floor were also standing out in the hall, all angrily asking what was going on. Old paintings lining the dark green walls fell roughly to the ground, making everyone flinch. I turned my head to the window outside Mr. Keilot's room and widened my eyes. Mr. Keilot stood with Eela hiding under his scarred arm as he pointed out the window. I dropped the box to the floor inside my apartment and closed my door halfway before gently jogging over to him and peering out the window.

Loud cranes and machines roared through the fog-filled sky. Metal claws and large rods slammed into the building next to the apartment complex as a large group of people carried debris away. *What are they doing now?* The large machines groaned as they swung, breaking and shattering the old glass windows of the old bank next door. Violent cracks shot up the side of the building on one corner before the entire place crumbled in on itself and fell. Puffs of smoke and dust shot into the air, mixing with the fog and creating a horrible haze. I backed away from the window and darted back into my apartment.

I quickly fumbled for the remote in my bed sheets and turned the TV on to a news station with a racing heart.

"Mayor Maxwell has given the 'okay' to begin demolition a month early!" the reporter cheerfully exclaimed. I furrowed my brow as the old building shook around me. *Why weren't we told about a building demolition next to the complex? What if there were people in that old bank—*

"Finally, the lower-class sector of New York will be knocked away to make room for the quickly expanding middle and upper classes!" he beamed. "Maxwell has enough people and machines to have more than half of the wretched sector demolished before the end of this month," the reporter chuckled happily. *Maxwell really doesn't give a crap about us, huh?*

I shook my head in disbelief as I turned the TV off and sat roughly on my bed. I held my head in my shaking hands and stared at the old wooden floor below me with disdain. *I can't afford other apartments right now… this place is the nicest one I could afford in the lower-class sector…* I glanced at the old box next to my door and frowned, running my hands through my hair. *Screw whatever happens to me. What is Mr. Keilot going to do? I have to help make sure he gets Eela and him somewhere safe.* I grumbled as I stared at the powered down TV and waved my hand at the box at the door. The old cardboard bent slightly as something heavy inside hit the wall and pushed the box across the apartment, sliding under my bed again.

I sat in silence, waiting patiently for the loud rumbling of the construction machines to fade away. My heart ached in my chest at the thought of anyone being inside the old bank right before it was demolished. *They didn't check the building. No one even would have thought about someone living in an abandoned building…* I narrowed my eyes at my window and sighed. *Even if they did find someone, they would have just killed them for trespassing anyways. Not like anyone from the middle- and upper-class care about us lowlifes in any way possible.* I rubbed my forehead gently as I stood up with shaking legs off my bed. The wooden floor creaked under me as I stepped off it into the raised tile floor upper level of the room. I pulled my jacket on swiftly and flicked my hoodie over my head as I took my key from the rack near the door. *I'll go sneak around and see if anyone got hurt. If those construction people shoot me, oh well…*

I closed my door roughly and reached back down to lock it with a soft sigh. A gun suddenly was cocked behind me. I froze, my hand halfway to the doorknob with widened eyes.

"Open the door!" a woman hissed from behind me.

"H-hey. I don't have anything special in there—" I stammered weakly. The cold barrel of the gun was pressed into the back of my neck roughly.

"I said, open the door!" she snapped angrily. The same smell of strong perfume and alcohol filled my nose as I coughed. I nodded and pushed the door back open with a furrowed brow. The woman behind me kicked me violently in the back, sending me into my apartment floor with a yelp. I pushed myself against my bathroom door as the woman slammed the front door shut, locking the double lock. She kept her back to me for a moment before she pulled the hood off her head and glared at me. I shivered and widened my eyes as I recognized her face. *It's you.* She stepped towards me quickly, bringing her pistol up towards me.

"You got my boys and I arrested," she hissed, pointing her shaking hand at me roughly. "I was able to bail myself out, but my boys are *stuck* there for a few months…because of *you*," the woman stated.

"I wasn't trying to get anyone in trouble," I croaked weakly, keeping my gaze away from her angry eyes.

"I don't give a *damn!*" the woman screamed, stepping towards me again. She glared at my apartment with disdain and smiled wickedly down at me. "What I do give a damn about is taking away your freedom, too!" she laughed maniacally. "Even though it doesn't look like you have that much anyway…" Before I could react, she pulled the trigger.

A loud gunshot echoed through the air as violent pain shot up the side of my head from my ear. My vision blurred, and my ears rang painfully loud with high pitched screaming. I clutched my head as I fell over onto the ground, wincing in pain. Violent crashes filled the room around me in the distance, echoing around my skull. Through my blurred vision, I saw the TV shatter into the floor and my shelves hurl themselves across the room. I gasped for breath as my chest tightened with panic, and I closed my eyes. I felt myself shrink down further into the ground as I covered my face. Memories of my mother's lifeless eyes came flooding back into my mind. More loud crashes echoed around me as my door was forced open. A second gunshot echoed through the air before glass shattered, and everything became silent.

CHAPTER 2

A SMALL APARTMENT IN NEW YORK CITY...

A horrid memory quickly came rushing back to me. "For the last time, Margret!" my father's voice screamed from the other side of my closed door, making me shiver. "I told you I will do whatever it takes to keep our *son*, our seven-year-old son, safe from *you!*"

"How am I a threat to him, Jonathan?!" my mother's raspy voice asked with annoyance.

"You're a threat just by breathing in the same house as him!" my father responded quickly. "He's scared out of his mind of you! Don't you see that?!"

I flinched as disturbing silence followed his question while I stared at the small book sitting on the bed next to me. *He's right. I am scared of you, Mom.* I blinked tears out of my eyes as my bedroom door gently opened, making me tense.

"I'm sorry, True," my father apologized, leaving my door open behind him as he stepped inside the room. I turned my gaze up towards his loving eyes and felt a wave of calmness wash over my tense body moments before he sat down gently on the bed next to me, the smell of cigarette smoke filling my nose. His scruffy, short beard tickled the side of my face as he kissed my cheek multiple times, making me giggle and push away from him with a grimace. His burly hand then ruffled my short, dark hair while he leaned out of my reach when I raised my hand to do the same to him. I then shivered as I saw my mother stalk past my bedroom door with a malevolent glare on my father before she disappeared into the kitchen, making me move my hand back down into my lap and my face fall emotionless.

"I won't let her interrupt our reading time again, okay?" my dad whispered, holding me tightly under his arm. I nodded and reluctantly grinned up at his exhausted eyes and bruised face moments before he flipped open the book to the page we once were on before he began arguing with my mom. I stared at the bruise near his eye and the cut on his lip from my mother for a moment before I turned my gaze to stare blankly at the book in his hands. My heart beat strongly out of my chest as I leaned into my father's side and rested my head against him to hear his own. My breaths seemed to slow as I focused on his racing heartbeat rather than the words he whispered quietly to me. *I want to help you, Dad, I really do. I just don't know how when it's Mom that's doing this to you...*

I flinched fully awake from a dozing off state and tensed as loud banging echoed through the apartment from the front door. I grabbed my dad's arm tightly in my bruised hands and shook him awake, glancing into the living room. Several loud bangs echoed around the apartment once again, followed by angry yelling.

"Open the door, or we're coming in on our own!" someone screamed.

"Dad!" I whisper-cried, tightening my grip around his arm as he stood up next to my bed.

"I'm not going anywhere," he calmly chuckled, moving my hand while he tipped my chin up towards him. I stared into his tired green eyes that widened with the presence of my mother hovering outside my room.

"Aren't you going to get the door?" my father asked, turning to face her.

"It's *your* house anyways, right?" he hissed, his voice becoming lined with anger.

I warily leaned around my father's side and immediately locked eyes with my mother's glare staring directly at me. Her dark eyes were emotionless yet lined with so much hatred while she stared blankly through the screen of smoke hovering in front of her from her cigarette. Loud banging on the door broke the silence, making me flinch behind my dad once again as my mother sighed loudly. My father mumbled under his breath and carefully sat down next to me once again as my mother opened the front door.

"Who are you?" my mother asked sharply, her voice wavering in anger. Panic shot through my chest while a violent *smack* echoed into my room as my mother screamed in pain. My entire body froze in terror as I watched my mother stumble backwards across my bedroom doorway and hit the shelf next to the wall.

"Hey? What are you doing in here?!" my father ordered, lunging up off my bed and storming angrily out of my room. I watched my dad protectively kneel in front of my mom, who was laying on the floor crying, as he stared angrily at the front door. The moment his face fell into horror, I knew something was wrong. My father immediately turned towards me with tears filling his eyes.

"*Hide!*" he cried, seconds before a burly man wearing all black punched him violently in the face. I sobbed in panic as I scrambled backwards across my bed, leaning heavily against the wall while I watched my dad get pulled off the ground, screaming in anger. "Get your hands off my wife!" my father ordered, struggling in the man's grasp before he was shoved down onto the glass table in the living room, shattering it easily. My mother's screams of panic and pain sent waves of helplessness down my body as I watched several people pull her off the ground while she desperately kicked and struggled to get away. A large group of people dressed in all black began pouring into the apartment and began breaking everything they searched, not paying attention to me sitting in my room.

I stared helplessly at my father getting pulled off the glass table and shoved violently onto the ground as he cried out.

"*Hide!*" my father screamed as he angrily pushed himself up towards the shotgun being held at his chest. I gasped quietly in grief as the loud shot from a shotgun echoed through the apartment, and my father immediately fell to the ground behind the table, a screaming silence filling the entire apartment. I felt every weak spark within me burn out. My mother begged for her life as she sobbed uncontrollably on the floor on the other side of the table while another shot was fired down towards my dad. *Why is this happening?*

I then flung myself across my bedsheets and landed roughly on the carpet in my room before scrambling underneath the bed while holding my hands over my mouth. Silent tears streamed down my face as my vision was blurred while I watched the people standing over my mom begin beating her with bats. Her cries of agony gurgled into silence as the people continued to beat her while others stormed the apartment and continued to destroy everything. My heart roared in my ears, and I stared at her lifeless eyes looking at me from the living room floor through the blood lining her face. The people all stepped away from her, breathing hard in triumph.

A soft sob escaped my mouth, and my body trembled uncontrollably, making the people in the apartment freeze. Panic shot through my chest as I exhaled quickly repeatedly, struggling to push myself deeper under my bed. Several people immediately darted across the main room and violently forced my door fully open to make the handle break through the wall. I held back a cry of panic as I watched their dark boots stomp around my room, hearing them snicker and push over my dresser and shelves. Another sob escaped my mouth when one of them threw a picture of my parents and I on the ground and shattered it with their foot. Panic coursed through my body as the people in the room froze and collectively turned towards my bed.

Immediately, a hand slammed down onto the carpet in front of my face next to my bed, making me scream. My voice broke in panic as the people in the room all moved towards my bed, quickly lifting my mattress up while one of them violently latched onto my wrist. I continued to scream as they drug me out from under the bed on my back, making a broken wooden beam on the bed frame snag my lip. I kicked and flailed as I was dragged across the room with tears rolling down my face, feeling the carpet rub harshly on the bruised skin lining my body. I was then quickly dropped in the center of my room, the bitter taste of blood filling my mouth and pain throbbing across my lip.

I sobbed in panic as I pushed myself away from the group of people staring down at me, backing into the shelf next to the broken picture. Pain shot up my arm as I felt glass on the carpet stab into my palm while I held myself up on my trembling hands, staring up at the people in panicked silence. The group of people all turned towards one another without speaking before they all walked out of the room, leaving the entire apartment completely. I exhaled slowly as I kept my gaze away from the lifeless eyes of my mother staring at me from the living room floor. Tears rolled down my face while I suppressed any noises of grief, making me tremble uncontrollably. *Why...*

CHAPTER 3

SEVERAL HOURS LATER...

I weakly opened my eyes and blinked several times to steady my vision, squinting as I looked around the inside of Mr. Keilot's apartment with a racing heart. *What...?* I pushed myself up from the couch, gripping the rough cushions below me as my breaths quickened. Eela looked up from the corner of the room with widened eyes, turning her gaze away from me with a frown. Violent pain shot across my head from my ear as my vision blurred again. I held my face in my hands and grimaced as the steady feeling of nausea built in the back of my throat. *Where is she? Why am I here? What's happening—*

"Easy there, True!" Mr. Keilot's gentle voice winced, making me flinch. "Everything's alright!" he promised. He jogged across the room and knelt in front of me, holding his scarred hands out to me gently before moving my hands away from my face. "Slow your breathing down." He frowned, furrowing his brow in sympathy. My shuddering breaths only quickened as I leaned away from him with widened eyes. I glanced behind him, blinking my eyes several times and saw Eela staring at me in confusion. My heart ached in my chest as I whimpered and shrunk down into the couch, wrapping my arms around myself. "I know break-ins are hard on you," Mr. Keilot sighed, slowly sitting next to me and putting me under his arm.

"I heard a gunshot after that woman yelled, True," Mr. Keilot continued gently, keeping his arm around me tightly. "I knew something was wrong when I heard you open your door but not lock it or walk down the hall, so I had to come check on you." He frowned, staring intently down at me. I nodded, keeping my gaze on the table in front of us as I rested my head on his shoulder. Eela then scrambled up from her chair in the corner of the room and darted into the kitchen, talking softly to herself. I closed my eyes and listened to Mr. Keilot's heartbeat in his chest and felt my own begin to ache, remembering my father's constantly fast heart. *Why didn't I use my power to stop that woman... Was I just too scared? Typical...*

Eela suddenly jogged in front of me, holding out a glass of water. Her large green eyes stared intently at me filled with worry as I slowly took it from her hands.

"I scheduled an appointment for your ear to be properly treated. And for your mental health, True," Mr. Keilot softly explained, waving Eela away. I widened my eyes as I lifted the cup of water to my mouth.

"What! Why?" I cried, my voice distorted from the cup. "That's too expensive!" I exclaimed, waving my hand around quickly. Eela giggled and fell over onto her large bean bag in the corner of the room as Mr. Keilot chuckled with a warm grin down at me. He shook his head and smiled proudly at Eela, laughing as she rolled off the bean bag and laid on the floor. Her hands quickly searched the table in front of the chair as she pulled a book off it gently. She yelped as the book fell directly onto her and then began laughing harder.

"I recently got a new job, so I can afford it easily, True," Mr. Keilot assured me gently. "Why do you ask? I care about you like you're my other kid," he grumbled suddenly, making me flinch. "It hurts me too much to see a beautiful soul like you in so much pain," he whispered softly.

My heart leapt in my chest as I slowly looked up at him with widened eyes. Mr. Keilot stared down at me with a gentle smile on his face before he got up and slowly walked across the room towards the kitchen, my body tensing as I saw his right arm wrapped in bandages. *Did that woman do that to him? Where did she even go?*

Eela suddenly waved at me from across the room, making me turn to her with just my eyes as I took a sip of water, watching her scurry onto the couch with me, smiling sadly.

"I'll take your sadness and pain away again, okay?" she whispered hopefully, leaning towards me. I nodded once, bringing my hands into my lap and frowning at the glass of water. Eela hugged me again, resting her head into my shoulder. My heart and chest swelled with something again, making me uncomfortable as I shifted away from her slightly. My entire head pulsed with a violent headache as pain sang loudly from my right ear, a loud ring still buzzing around inside my mind. Eela's hug slowly became less and less tight as she also began to lean away. Mr. Keilot sighed with a smile as he walked up to us.

"Can I talk to True for a little bit?" he asked hopefully, crouching down with a grunt in front of us. Eela nodded, squeezing me one last time and standing in front of me for a moment, tapping her fingers together.

"I hope I took all of it away this time," she mumbled, frowning at my tired gaze at her. I grinned softly and tipped my head to her, shivering as Mr. Keilot sat next to me on the couch. Eela slowly backed away as Mr. Keilot smiled gently at her and sat in the corner of the room to read her book while sitting in her large beanbag. I watched her for a moment and sighed as I looked back down to the glass of water in my hands.

"I think this entire building is going to be next," Mr. Keilot mumbled softly, glancing at Eela. "The front desk workers were handing out letters from the mayor shortly after the police left here," he frowned. "That letter states that we're receiving an eviction notice, but it could be cancelled at any time, it's unbelievable..." he spat, clenching his fist momentarily. I blinked a few times and felt my heart begin to race in my chest as I took a long sip of water.

"Basically, what I'm hinting at is," Mr. Keilot continued quickly, "where are you going to end up?" he asked, his voice wavering in hesitation. Eela glanced up at us for a brief second and frowned down at her book while furrowing her brow. I shook my head, unable to answer him for a moment.

"I haven't thought about that yet, but I'll figure something out..." I winced, touching the side of my pulsing head gently. Mr. Keilot waved my hand away from my patched ear and sighed as he furrowed his brow. His scarred hands twitched for a moment before he started tapping his knee quickly.

"I'm getting a two-bedroom home," Mr. Keilot began. I sat up quickly and frowned at him. "It's far into the middle-class sector! Maybe—"

"No!" I hissed, setting the cup down on the table roughly. "I'm sorry, but I can't!" I growled, clenching my shaking hands. "I can't interrupt and mess up you guys' lives more than I already have—" I cried, my voice breaking as I wrapped my arms around myself.

"You can help me out though," Mr. Keilot offered, raising his brow at me. "I'll need someone to watch Eela as she does her homeschool work while I'm at my new job," he explained. I shook my head and held it tightly in my hands as I leaned on my knees.

"You don't even have to watch her if you don't want to," Mr. Keilot chuckled, gently nudging my arm. "I'll have my sister come over and help most of the time, but you can stay with us as long as you need," he whispered, slowly taking my chin and tipping it up to him. I stared into his love-filled eyes and frowned with a slight nod. "Eela and I are going to pack all our things today and leave for the home tomorrow, if you want to come with us?" he offered slowly.

I sighed after taking a deep breath and rubbed the back of my head gently.

"Sure…" I mumbled, staring at the ground.

After I had limped back to my apartment, I stood in the doorway silently. I looked at the destroyed room blankly as anxiety began climbing back up my chest. I glanced at the large bullet hole in the bathroom door, shivering at the stain of blood on the tile and wall behind it. I looked around the even smaller room with a frown and sighed at the letter resting on my kitchen island. My legs trembled as I stepped around my destroyed TV and into the sunken part of the apartment and kneeled on the glass-filled floor with a wince.

I reached under my bed with closed eyes and felt around the dark for a moment. As my fingers brushed the cardboard box, my heart leapt in my chest. I quickly grabbed the damp box and pulled it out in front of me with a sharp breath. I peeked inside and sighed with relief, resting my forehead on the old lid. *It's still here…* I winced as I stood up, wiping my jeans of the dust and glass sticking to them with a frown. I glanced around at the room and bit my lip in annoyance as I saw nothing missing; everything just broken. I turned around quickly and looked at the nightstand next to my bed. I clenched my fists and laughed sadly for a moment as I pulled the drawer open and shook my head. *Really. You took my cigarettes and lighter but left the money? Prick.* I spent the rest of the day cleaning the apartment as best I could, in silence.

CHAPTER 4

THE NEXT MORNING...

I took one last look at my small apartment and sighed. The place I had lived most of my life out of the orphanage was now on the road to be destroyed. I pulled the old box off the floor and frowned at the bag of clothes in my hand, glaring at the bullet hole in the bathroom door in front of me. I then closed the door, locking it gently, and stood still for a moment. A chill ran down my back as I rested my hand against the door before I slowly pulled myself away, wearily glancing behind me before I jogged down the hall after Eela and Mr. Keilot with their bags.

As we walked into the main lobby, I pulled the key around the bracelet on my wrist off and set it down on the counter of the front desk. Eela called for me as she ran out the front door, Mr. Keilot mumbling under his breath and darting after her. I stepped forward towards the door and flinched as the woman at the front desk suddenly stood up. I turned towards her with widened eyes as she stared at me for a moment. She held up her hand and then crouched down behind the counter, fumbling with a set of keys before pulling open a filing cabinet. The woman flicked her dark hair out of her face as she scrambled around the desk, taking my key off the counter and holding it out to me with an envelope.

"It's half of the money that woman took," she sheepishly explained, pushing it closer to me. I gently took it from her and nodded, dropping the envelope in my bag and held the key out in front of me. "I know how much this place means to you. It won't be here much longer, so I have no use for the key..." she chuckled sadly. "Keep it." I stared at her in shock for a moment and grinned slowly at her. *That's the longest sentence you've said to me in all the years I've lived here...*

"Thank you." I sniffed, attaching the key to the bracelet on my wrist again. She nodded and waved at me before she backed away towards the desk again. I lifted my hand at her and slowly looked down before walking out of the building.

I flicked my hood over my head as I walked down the street. People scurried out of my way with slight head nods as I stared at the ground. Many faces, most familiar, some new, all stared hopefully at me. I glanced at all of them, keeping my head down and sighed. *Stay safe you guys... If I could do something to help you all I would.* I clenched my fist tightly around the bag and box in my hands and bit the inside of my cheek. *I hope you all find purpose in your lives and get on the right path, unlike me...* A few acquaintances I had made over the years leaned towards me with sad glints in their eyes as I ignored them and continued down the street. *I'll be back one day... To help you. All of you. I promise.*

Anxiety filled my chest as we passed through the guarded posts of the social class merging area. The boundaries between each social class were the most dangerous places anyone could be. Regardless of which sector you belonged to, if you were spotted hanging around the boundary, you'd be arrested or killed with no questions asked. The social classes were not to interact on unofficial matters under any circumstances. Lowlifes like me were rarely allowed to even pass through the guard posts, but once we did, we had to act fast and make a stern decision. Middle- and upper-class citizens were allowed to go where they pleased. If you were from the lower class, you had more restrictions placed onto you since you come from the worst part of the city.

I kept my head down, ignoring all the people walking around the middle-class neighborhood. Everyone stared at me and shot me ugly looks before scoffing in disgust and turning their heads away from me. I glared at them in the corner of my eye as I sighed and shrunk deeper into my hood. *Yea, yea... A hooded figure following a man with his daughter looks totally not suspicious at all.* I shivered as a young man walked towards me with a furrowed brow, making me shy away from him and jog up closer to Mr. Keilot. *I know I'm just a worthless piece of scum who shouldn't be here.*

Mr. Keilot turned the corner of the street and jogged calmly across the intersection road, Eela sitting on his shoulders as she rested her chin on his head. He crouched down in front of a red brick home and coughed as Eela jumped off him and ran to the front door. I walked across the street without looking either way and sighed as he turned around, smiling happily at me. I stood on the sidewalk and glanced around at all the nice houses lining the street and shivered. Mr. Keilot slowly made his way along the walkway leading up to the front door and opened it as Eela yelled happily and darted inside, leaving her bags on the ground. He sighed and nudged them inside before he set his own down.

I stood on the front porch, watching families or lone people on the street, listening to music or jogging with each other, not a care in the world. I narrowed my eyes as a group of teens skated around the corner of the house, loud music blaring through the air. Several of them glared at me in disgust and stuck their tongues out before continuing down the street. *If you would have done that in the lower-class sector, you would have been shot on sight kid…* I rolled my eyes as they quickly powered through another group of teen girls walking down the sidewalk. I then held back a smile as the groups exchanged words with each other, glancing at me watching them over their shoulders.

"Well?" Mr. Keilot sighed, grabbing my shoulder and turning me to face him. "What do you think?" he asked hopefully, pulling me inside. He closed the door gently and stood with his arms crossed as he gazed at the home in front of us. The living room loomed happily in front of the kitchen in the back. Glass sliding doors behind the curved island revealed a small backyard with a newly built swing set. On either side of the large, open room were two hallways with various doors at the end of them. I smiled gently and looked at him for a moment and nodded.

"This is nice," I whispered softly. "Gives me some kind of hope for my own future," I mumbled, turning my gaze down to the dark floor below us. Something in my mind suddenly shifted, clawing its way closer towards me, making me shiver and roll my shoulders out. Mr. Keilot gently pulled my hood down off my head and smiled at me for a moment.

"Your future is going to be amazing, True," he beamed. "I see it in your eyes; you're going to be something great," he explained, resting his hand on my shoulder. My heart leapt in my chest as I widened my eyes slightly and felt my face flush. I looked away from him, shying towards the couch and sitting down slowly. He sighed, picking his bags up and walked across the room, disappearing into the left hallway.

Eela screamed happily as I heard Mr. Keilot growl playfully before a large thump echoed through the home. Eela darted around the corner of the hallway from the room they were in and raced across the room into the other hall. I held back a smile as she came running back out of the other hallway with a pillow and ran into Mr. Keilot walking out of the hallway.

The two of them laughed with one another as Eela struggled to keep the pillow in her hands while he pulled on it. Mr. Keilot picked then picked her up and spun her around in a circle before setting her back down. She then jogged across the room, breathing hard, and dragged her bags away from the door to the hallway on the right side of the home. Mr. Keilot ran his hand through his hair for a moment and coughed into his arm before he walked calmly to the kitchen island filled with boxes. I sighed, quickly jumping off the couch and walking across the room to help him with the boxes.

The two of us worked for an hour or two, washing and putting away all the dishes into the cabinets in silence. Both of us listened with gentle smiles to Eela singing loudly in her room and playing her favorite songs repeatedly. As I was putting away the last plate onto the shelf, I shivered and blinked several times. Mr. Keilot looked up from having his head down at the small dining table behind me and sighed. I closed the cabinet door and turned to bring the boxes off the kitchen island as Mr. Keilot shook his head at me with a small chuckle.

"What was your new job?" I asked softly, glancing at him as I dropped a box on the floor.

"I'm a construction manager for the middle- to upper-class merging zone," he sighed, rubbing the back of his head. I widened my eyes and nodded thoughtfully as I placed more boxes into each other on the floor. Mr. Keilot looked at me expectantly before turning back to the table and holding his head in his hand for a moment. *I'm sorry I'm not talkative. This is the longest I've been around you the entire time we've known each other...*

"What do you plan on doing?" Mr. Keilot asked expectantly, letting his scarred hands fall to the table below him. "I can always ask around and see where businesses are hiring?" he offered happily. I widened my eyes as I lifted my foot to crush the cardboard boxes under me. I frowned and stepped roughly onto the boxes and remained silent. *I don't know what I'm doing; I never planned to keep myself alive this long anyways.* Mr. Keilot mumbled under his breath and stood up from the table and walked over to the kitchen island.

"Have you looked into the Elite's power training school?" he asked, raising his brow at me. "With a power like yours, I'd think you'd be a great asset to the company—"

"I don't have *any* interest in becoming an Elite!" I hissed sharply.

Mr. Keilot flinched and widened his eyes at me as I clenched my fists and leaned on the counter, raising my leg out of the box. "I'm not looking to get rich off of stepping on those in the lower-class sector and others by bullshitting my way to a job I don't deserve!" I spat.

Mr. Keilot frowned at me and crossed his arms slowly.

"You know not all the Elites are like that," he gently sighed.

"Yea?! Well, I guess I just got the bad end of the stick with them then!" I snapped, looking up at him quickly. "Where the hell were they when those people broke into my childhood home and *murdered* my parents in front of me?! Huh?" I asked angrily. "Where were they when I walked the streets every day and saw people dying of hunger and lack of shelter?" I continued, my voice rising.

"True, I'm sorry—" Mr. Keilot growled.

"I have no interest in joining those bastards! All they do is steal money right out from under the lowlifes of the city, people like *me!*" I snarled, flicking my hands to myself.

"*True,*" Mr. Keilot suddenly snapped, making me flinch. "That's fine that you don't want to be an Elite. It's not for everyone," he calmly explained, waving his hand at me. "But you still need to at least apply for their training school. It's a requirement for everyone to go through at least a portion of it on power control."

I narrowed my eyes at him and moved the boxes over with my foot while shaking my head.

"What would a fancy school like that want with someone like me?" I asked "I'm 24 already. Aren't I a little old for them?"

Mr. Keilot rolled his eyes and frowned at me.

"No. The program is designed for anyone of any age to go through it. Most people just do it when they're in high school," he smiled gently.

"If you have the power control course under your name, jobs will be more likely to hire you," Mr. Keilot explained after we stood in tense silence.

"I think I have plenty of control over my power..." I mumbled, leaning against the island gently.

"Listen kid," he sighed. "I'm just trying to help you get back on your feet." He frowned, walking around the counter and nudged my arm gently. "I know you're used to doing what you want and having no one to tell you what to do. Just take my advice and judgement with a grain of salt." He smiled, backing away and walking around the corner to the hallway.

"What are you doing?" I asked, rubbing my forehead gently.

"Pulling up the online application, so you can send it in tonight," Mr. Keilot responded haughtily, holding his laptop in his hand and glancing up at me with a raised brow, his mischievous grin growing.

"Wait, tonight?" I yelped, my voice breaking.

Eela giggled loudly from her room while she mocked me. Mr. Keilot held back a smile as he set the computer on the table in front of him.

"Yes. Tonight," he chuckled. "The quicker you get this sent in, the quicker you can start the classes and get back onto your feet!" he beamed, smiling happily at me over his shoulder. I huffed in annoyance and nodded, slowly pushing off the counter and walking over to the table. I peered at the screen over his shoulder with a frown. *Like I was ever on my feet in the first place...*

I held my head in my hands as I sat at the kitchen table, staring at the screen filled with unchecked boxes.

"This is pathetic. They're not going to accept me..." I mumbled softly, scrolling down the questions I was asked.

"Of course they will! It's there to help anyone!" Mr. Keilot chuckled warmly from the living room. I glanced over my shoulder and sighed with a small smile as I saw Eela trying to pull him off the couch towards me. I turned back to the screen and shook my head as I stared at the contact information boxes being empty. *I don't even have a phone number to give them...* I put my head down and mumbled under my breath as I felt Eela scurry next to me and lean on my back gently.

"This is really random," I began slowly, lifting my head up. "But can I cook dinner for you guys?" I sheepishly asked. "You've done so much to help me, and I don't have anything I could possibly repay you both with yet." I frowned, staring at the table below me. Eela looked over at her dad walking slowly across the room towards us with a large smile, making my heart leap out of my chest. "I promise I'm a better cook than I look like," I snarked, bringing my hand to my face.

Mr. Keilot scoffed into his hand as Eela giggled and darted back towards the living room.

"You don't have to do anything to repay us True, but you can cook if you'd like," he beamed. "Let's see what you got," he snarked, winking at me as I rolled my eyes and held back a smile.

After I had cooked a recipe my mother made me when I was little, the three of us sat at the table and ate. We talked and laughed all our worries away and stayed smiling. Years of regret and cold nights alone were slowly being pushed away by the warmth of love from Mr. Keilot and Eela as they argued playfully back and forth with each other. Once we had all finished eating, Eela began to explain one of the books she was reading to the both of us. Every now and then, I'd make a snarky comment at her, making her narrow her eyes and smile at me as Mr. Keilot would laugh into his arms. When her stories were done, Mr. Keilot carried her to her room and stayed with her as she played music.

I sat at the dining table alone in silence as the music eventually was turned off. "I haven't eaten dinner with another person in over five years," I mumbled, glancing at the now empty seats next to me. "Or laughed that much in a long time," I whispered, bringing my arms around myself as I shrunk into the chair.

"I'm glad my daughter and I brought it back then." Mr. Keilot chuckled warmly from the hallway, making me flinch. He shook his head with a smile at me and calmly walked across the room, taking the plates off the table. I kept my arms wrapped around myself as I took a shuddering breath. My heart began to beat out of my chest as I watched Mr. Keilot wash the dishes with a happy smile on his face.

"Thank you," I whispered softly, staring intently at him. Mr. Keilot dried his hand on a towel on the counter and looked up at me with raised brows. "For taking me in and *caring* so much about me," I continued, my voice breaking as tears filled my eyes. Mr. Keilot widened his eyes and quickly walked over to me, sitting in the chair next to me and holding his arm out. I leaned into his side as I trembled and closed my eyes. A memory of me sitting on a counter of my father's pawnshop under his arm flashed through my mind, sending a wave of grief through my chest. Mr. Keilot wrapped his arm around me slightly tighter as he rested his head on mine and sighed.

"Everyone is born with the ability to be kind, always," Mr. Keilot breathed softly. He then patted my shoulder and slowly stood up, walking down the hall to his room. I sat still for a moment and kept my arms wrapped around myself as I glanced around at the home. I frowned as I turned the lights off and slowly made my way across the room to the couch on the wall. I easily melted into the soft cushions and closed my eyes gently, drifting off listening to the sound of my heart roaring in my ears.

Lightning flashed violently through the sky. Brief moments of bright light illuminated the entire room, casting shadows to race along the walls. Rain pounded down relentlessly on the window above me as I laid still for a moment. My heart began beating out of my chest as I slowly sat up and rubbed my eyes sleepily. I looked over my shoulder and moved the dark curtain over to see the rain draining perfectly down the street. I furrowed my brow and closed the curtain, turning back around and held my face in my hands. *The lower-class sector is probably flooding horribly. Everything leads to the lower-class sector anyways. All this water is just being pumped onto the backstreets, and no one cares how much damage it's doing to the people who live there...*

A small noise from the kitchen pulled me out of my head as I flinched and looked up. Eela stood at the corner of her hallway to her room, wrapped in a blanket and holding a small stuffed dolphin. Her soft eyes were filled with worry as she glanced around the home.

"Hey... It's okay," I awkwardly whispered, smiling gently at her as she began to shake while staring at the window behind me. Lightning cracked through the sky again, making her yelp and dart over to me. Eela leapt into my lap and hid under her blanket in my arms as she trembled. I froze with widened eyes in panic as I stared at her for a moment, holding my breath.

I suddenly blinked a few times as something within me gave in, a sigh escaping my mouth. I immediately began whispering to her softly about all the wonderful things of a storm. As her trembling body began to calm, the storm around us became still. The harsh wind and rain died down to a slight breeze and gentle drizzle. The small drops of rain echoed off the roof peacefully, filling the silent home.

Eela fell back asleep in my lap, holding her stuffed dolphin gently. I smiled down at her peaceful face and ran my shaking hand along her head as I slowly leaned my head back on the couch and closed my eyes. *I don't know where any of that came from… I don't necessarily like or care about kids but… She's different.*

Warm sunlight slowly began flowing across my face, pulling me out of a dreamless sleep. I fluttered my eyes open and lifted my head, glancing at Eela still asleep in my lap. I turned my head and winced as the sunlight struck me in the eyes. The creek of a door opening across the room filled me with panic as I lifted my head up fully, blinking away the spots in my eyes. I held my breath as Mr. Keilot stumbled down the short hallway, rubbing his eyes and yawning loudly. His fluffy, dark-grey hair fell messily in front of his face as he stretched his arms and ran his hand across his forehead. His sleepy warm eyes met mine as I tensed with a slightly furrowed brow. I held back a smile as he did a quick double take at me with widened eyes.

"She got scared with the storm that rolled in last night," I explained softly, keeping my eyes away from him as he walked across the room. He smiled proudly at me as he gently lifted her off my lap and strung her over his shoulder.

"See? You do have a soft spot," Mr. Keilot teased. I rolled my eyes and glanced up at him as I gently picked up Eela's stuffed dolphin from the floor and held it in my hands for a moment. As I lifted the stuffed animal to give it to Mr. Keilot, he was already halfway across the room. I widened my eyes and drew myself back with a small sigh and felt myself shiver. I stared down at the soft, light-blue and grey dolphin in my hands and smiled gently. My rough thumb slowly began to glide across the soft fur. *I don't remember the last time I held a stuffed animal.*

Mr. Keilot huffed softly after rolling his shoulders out as he walked back into the main room.

"Did the lightning wake you up last night, too?" I asked softly, fumbling with my bag next to the couch, pulling my knife out and tucking it under the inside hole in my hoodie sleeve. Mr. Keilot yawned loudly and shook his head at me as he turned the coffee machine on.

"Nope," he scoffed. "Slept through it like a brick!" he cheerfully explained, laughing embarrassedly. I smiled at him and nodded thoughtfully with a small sigh. I held the dolphin in my hands as I weakly stood up and walked across the room towards him. Sharp pain struck me in the back of the head as I moved too quickly, making me grimace. Mr. Keilot glanced warily at me as I rolled my neck out.

"Want some coffee?" Mr. Keilot offered, tipping his head to the hissing machine behind him. I shook my head and placed the dolphin on the counter, rubbing the back of my neck.

"What are your plans for today?" I asked softly, glancing up at his tired eyes. "Does Eela need anyone to watch her?" I sheepishly continued. Mr. Keilot chuckled warmly, making my heart spike in my chest.

"I'll be here the entire day sorting the final touches out on this place," he beamed, pouring himself a cup of coffee. "You should explore," he snarked, taking a long sip of the coffee. I widened my eyes at him and furrowed my brow slightly. He scoffed softly into the cup and laughed into his hand as it echoed in a distorted way. "You know, go make some friends?" he chuckled.

"Friends?" I echoed softly.

"I know there is someone out there who needs you as much as you need them," he beamed. I trembled and nodded slowly, looking away from his gaze. *Who would need me? I'm just a waste of time.*

CHAPTER 5

SEVERAL MINUTES LATER...

Anxiety shot through my chest as I kept my hood over my head. The early, sun-filled morning drew everyone out from their houses as I walked through the neighborhood, inward to the center of the middle-class sector. All the people around me walked carelessly, faces buried in phones and warm smiles on their faces. *You all are so unused to danger... you wouldn't last a day in the lower-class sector streets.* I clenched my fists as I sighed softly, shaking the angered thoughts away. I nervously glanced at all the people again and winced. I stuck out like a sore thumb, wearing a dark hoodie against all the lively colors.

After exploring the market and other parts of the middle-class center district, I wandered further back towards the lower-class merging zone. The downtown plaza was a large series of intersections on the edge of the middle-class sector. Buildings were slightly less formal and more weathered. Dulled, bright-colored shops and cheerful faces of the people disregarded how close they all were to being outcasted to the lower-class. *Is it normal to not worry about your safety all the time here? No one is paying attention to anyone else or the alleys they pass...*

The main street of downtown was lined with even older-styled buildings. Shops, restaurants, and small apartments made up most, if not all, of the space along the small, clean street. Gentle music hummed through the warm air as I glanced up at the cloudless sky above me for a moment. Groups of people walked past me on the sidewalk, shooting friendly glances and grins at me as I kept my head down, my gaze on the concrete below after keeping my head up at the sky for too long. *I guess you've all found comfort in the uncertainty. Wish I could do the same.* I glanced away from the sidewalk, up at sudden bright colors that sang loudly in the corner of my eye.

I paused my stride and stopped, slowly turning around to the shop behind me. *Old Museum* was painted rustically into the top metal canopy above the pristine glass windows. Large canvases rested in the display window with small lights shining down on them. I shivered at seeing my own reflection in the clean glass. My gaze rested inside the museum to pillars of small sculptures and walls lined with paintings. I blinked up at the building for a moment and frowned as I glanced around at the mostly empty street. I inhaled to take a step towards the museum and felt my heart spike in my chest as someone began yelling.

"Hey!" a gruff, raspy voice screamed. I widened my eyes and turned to an older man stumbling down the other side of the street. "Are you planning on stealing those paintings!" he ordered slyly, raising his fist towards me. I widened my eyes in shock as his entire hand and arm were covered in burn scars. "Huh?" the man demanded, tripping over his own foot into a fire hydrant. *He's drunk…*

Inside the museum, a young woman glanced at me and furrowed her brow at the man yelling at me as she ran to the door. My heart leapt out of my chest as I quickly backed away to continue walking down the street. I shook my head at the man's fiery, pride-filled gaze as my breaths quickened, my entire body tensing.

The door to the museum flung open roughly. A blonde-haired woman stepped out of the building, screaming at the man across the street, flames coming from her mouth. The corners of her eyes glowed brightly as it seemed like fire filled them.

"Get lost you asshole! He wasn't doing anything wrong!" she snarled, flicking her hand at me. The old man yelled back at her as he waved his hand and stalked angrily down the street. People walking in the street paused with widened eyes and snickered under their breaths as they glanced at the woman standing in front of me. She breathed hard, smoke puffing from her mouth as she furrowed her brow and clenched her fists, her eyes following the man stumbling away from the intersections.

"Hey! It's okay! You can come in if you'd like!" she suddenly exclaimed, turning to me. All anger immediately left her face as her light eyes suddenly widened while she stared at me. I froze, widening my own eyes and feeling a chill shoot down my back as we stared at each other intently, my heart spiking in my chest. The woman grinned warmly at me as she tipped her head to the museum next to her with a hopeful glint in her eye. I blinked quickly, looking away from her gaze and nodded once, warily stepping towards her. A group of other people pushed past me roughly, making me flinch. The woman glared at the smug faces looking at her as they passed, and a sad glint filled her eyes. I frowned and inhaled slowly to calm my heart and followed her inside the museum.

"I haven't seen someone dressed like you in a while!" the woman giggled, glancing slyly at me over her shoulder. Her sharp grey eyes sent a chill down my back again. "All the people I've seen wearing dark and mysterious clothing are from the lower-class sector, you know?" she continued, glancing at the people in the back of the museum. "I had some friends from there a few years back. They all moved though, no clue where any of them went," she chuckled, rubbing the back of her neck and turning towards me. I nodded and kept my gaze on the paintings around the room. Light-tan carpet lined the floors as grey walls loomed around us. The low, dark ceiling seemed to be a night sky as bright lights hung from above, shining brightly on every art piece.

"I'm Stella!" the woman beamed, flicking her long blonde hair over her shoulder. "I'm one of the four workers here at the downtown museum!" she announced proudly. A group of people in the back of the room groaned, rolling their eyes and mumbled under their breaths. A young, curly haired man standing next to a painting narrowed his light eyes angrily at Stella as she tipped her chin up at him. I glanced at the name tag on his shirt before my eyes wandered even further to the back of the museum. *Avin, huh…* An older woman, also with a name tag, glared at us through the mirror on the wall.

"What's your name?" Stella asked, leaning towards me and smiling happily. I froze, looking back at her intently. "Hello?" she scoffed, holding back a laugh.

"Stella! Leave him alone already!" a raspy voice snapped. A silver haired young woman peeked her head out from behind the counter in the top right corner of the room with narrowed eyes. "If he doesn't want to talk to you, don't force him," she growled, hitting something under the desk. The other people inside the museum snickered under their breaths as the corners of Stella's eyes began to glow slightly while she stared at the woman at the counter.

"Well sorry," Stella spat. "I just want some friends,"

"True," I bluntly stated. Stella and the woman at the counter widened their eyes, switching their angry gazes off each other towards me. "My name, True…" I whispered, sheepishly cowering away from the cold eyes of the woman behind the counter.

"Oooo!!" Stella exclaimed, her face lighting up again. "Mysterious and pretty! I like it!" she giggled, smiling proudly at me. The woman at the counter rolled her eyes and stood up, roughly pushing a drawer closed with a growl of disapproval.

Her body was lean and muscular, a tattoo covering most of her shoulder up to her neck. The back of her head was shaved into a buzzcut with her short, silver hair falling from under a black bandana on her head. She narrowed her eyes at Stella as she stalked across the room towards us. Stella tensed, backing slightly away as the woman stood next to her, crossing her arms at me with a frown. Her cold eyes stayed glued to me like a viper as I tensed under her gaze. I glanced at the nametag tied around the red checkered jacket around her waist and shivered. *Egret… Everyone seems scared of you…*

"Feel free to look around," Egret spat calmly. "This is obviously not the main museum of New York, but I guess we have some pretty cool stuff." she gruffly continued. Egret grabbed Stella's arm and roughly pulled her away from me as I nodded, watching her intently. She waved her hand at me as she brought Stella to the counter, mumbling angrily under her breath.

The older woman at the back of the room glanced at the young man with the group and smirked before turning back to the boxes below her. I frowned as the man met my gaze and immediately looked away. I shifted my gaze to Egret towering over Stella with a sour expression on both their faces and furrowed my brow.

How are you so happy with everyone here hating you? Why are they treating you like this? My heart ached slightly in my chest after I felt it spike as Stella glanced over at me. I shook my head and slowly walked to the painting that caught my eye from the street. It was a small painting, hung by itself away from all the others on the wall. A bright, dark blue, neon-yellow, and fiery-red sunset with silhouettes of the city in the foreground strewn out perfectly along the canvas. Light and dark clouds filled the corner of the painting as a crescent moon slowly appeared, the sun fading away on the other side of the picture.

"That's one of my favorites, too," Stella suddenly sighed. I flinched and yelped softly as I turned around to her standing behind me. She furrowed her brow as I widened my eyes and took shuddering breaths. "You don't seem like you're used to being around people, are you okay?" she asked gently, frowning slightly at me. I shook my head, waving my hand to her, and stared at the floor below us as my heart raced in my chest. Egret grumbled from across the room as Stella glared over her shoulder at her.

"Stop asking him so many questions!" Egret snapped in a low voice. "You know *you* are the entire reason why we get so little people coming in here right?" she explained bluntly. "Always annoying everyone by *constantly* running your mouth!" Egret hissed. I narrowed my eyes at Egret as she darkly glanced at me. The corner of Stella's light eyes flickered for a split second as she blinked at Egret staring at her. *What is this woman's problem? You didn't do anything wrong, Stella.*

"Please, don't fight. I'll leave if I'm causing trouble," I whispered, backing away slowly.

"Why would we fight?" Stella chuckled, all anger gone from her face. She glanced at me intently with a worried frown before trying to smile at me. Egret stood up from her seat next to the desk and narrowed her eyes.

"You're from the lower-class sector, aren't you?" Egret suddenly spat, stalking towards me. I widened my eyes and shrunk away from her as she glared at Stella and stared down at me.

"Explains a lot," Egret sniffed gruffly. "I was born there because my parents were lazy pricks," she growled. "That place is rough, and I know somewhat of the things you've gone through then," Egret gently explained. "I didn't spend as much time there as you probably have because I moved out and made a life for myself here instead of living in pity with my sorry excuses for parents…" she spat. "I know everything here is confusing, and you're asking a lot of questions in your head. You'll be fine. Just keep your head down for a while and slowly acclimate yourself to not living in fear," Egret offered, her cold eyes softening. Stella stood with widened eyes and an open mouth as she stared at Egret looking at me.

"Since when did you get the ability to be *nice?*" Stella hissed with a snarky tone. I nodded, glancing up at Egret for a moment before shivering under her gaze. I glanced at the painting on the wall and at Stella one last time before I swiftly turned and jogged across the room toward the door.

"Hey! Where are you going—?" Stella began worriedly. I pushed the glass door open gently and quickly walked down the street back the way I came. I flicked my hood back over my head and shoved my shaking hands in my pockets as I kept my head down. People's worried glances at me sent anxiety up my chest as I breathed hard, keeping my gaze intently away from everyone.

As I turned the corner of the street towards the beginning of the neighborhood, someone roughly grabbed my hood. I was yanked backwards gently as I yelped and stumbled over my shaking legs. I fell harshly to the ground and held my trembling hands over my face.

"I'm sorry! I'm sorry!" I cried, my voice wavering.

"For what?" a confused voice gently asked. I breathed hard as I blinked and stared up at a police officer standing over me. "Sorry friend. I didn't mean to scare you or make you fall," he chuckled embarrassedly, holding his tan, lanky hand towards me. The officer pulled me to my feet and grinned warmly at me. His light eyes and tan skin began to glow as the setting sun hit him through the buildings behind us. A long scar rested across the base of his nose as he furrowed his brow at me slightly.

"Oh, my goodness!" he suddenly exclaimed. "What happened to your ear?" he asked worriedly, reaching towards my head. I flinched away from him and pulled my hood over my head again as I trembled.

"Break in,"

"Where? Did you report it?"

I shook my head as I struggled to gather myself. My heart raced quickly in my ears as sharp pain echoed around my head.

"Lower-class sector," I whispered. "I moved here yesterday," I explained, keeping my gaze away from him.

"Ahhh, makes sense." the officer chuckled sadly, glancing down the street. "I was called over for a 'suspicious character' hanging around, but you're nothing to worry about," he explained. I furrowed my brow slightly as my heart spiked in anger. "Do you want a ride back to the place you're staying? I'd be happy to help, especially since I made you fall earlier. Sorry again for that,"

I shook my head, keeping my gaze on the ground.

"No, thank you, I'm going to walk." I gently explained. "I've caused enough discomfort for others today anyways,"

The officer frowned and stared intently at me before he nodded.

"Make sure you get your ear properly treated. It looks infected. Get home safe!" he beamed. I tipped my head with an awkward grin at him as I quickly turned and walked away.

My heartbeat roared in my ears as extreme discomfort and pressure spread across my head. The ground below me wavered as I struggled to walk in a straight line. My vision blurred horribly, making me pause, leaning heavily onto the brick wall to my left. I held my head in my hands as I began shaking, glancing around at the dark alley around the corner. *I can't…stop here.* I pushed myself away from the wall as a surge of anxiety filled my chest, making my heartbeat quicken. I turned quickly to the alley with a furrowed brow. *Was that someone standing there? What the hell is wrong with me right now?* As I turned to continue, something cold slammed into the side of my head. Everything went black.

I felt myself being dragged. Cold concrete scraped painfully against my side as I blinked to steady my vision. I frantically tried pulling away, but the person dragging me had me firmly in their cold grasp. Panic surged through my chest as I blurrily made out the image of someone in a light grey cloak, dragging me by my leg. I furrowed my brow and flicked my arm out. The knife in the hidden tear on the inside of my sleeve slid into my palm. I quickly opened it and shoved myself off the ground, slashing the arm of the person dragging me. The person let me go immediately with a hiss of pain as I rolled to my feet and held the blade to them breathing hard.

The person turned towards me calmly as I widened my eyes as blood soaked through my left sleeve. *What?* A small, dark gas mask covered their face, and most of their body was hidden by the cloak. Suddenly, pitch black smoke erupted out from the fabric towards me. I flinched, activating my own smoke with a wave of my hand. Both smoke columns collided violently, immediately filling my mind with loud screeches. My smoke was forced away as I held my head in my hands, stumbling over from the shock of the screams. The smoke from the person shot towards me again, wrapping around me tightly, and slammed me into the brick wall behind me. I coughed hollowly as my chest ached in pain, my knife clattering to the ground.

My vision steadied as the person walked over to me and stood directly in front of me. I trembled as I locked eyes with them through the dark glass on the mask. Their eyes were pure white and filled with angered curiosity. The smoke tightened around me as I gasped for breath weakly. I clenched my fist and shivered as I felt blood run down my left arm into my hand. *How did I cut them and make myself bleed? Why aren't they bleeding? Is that their power or something?* The smoke tendril wrapped around me suddenly loosened before disappearing entirely. I fell roughly to the ground and immediately tried jumping back up to my feet.

The person immediately slammed the back of their gloved hand into my face, forcing me back to the ground. I grimaced at the bitter taste of blood in my mouth and narrowed my eyes. Every action I made, they countered it with ease, as if they knew I was going to make it. The person suddenly lunged down towards me, pinning me to the ground with their heavy boot on my chest. They slowly pulled out a pistol from under their cloak and leaned towards me, bringing the gun towards my neck. I furrowed my brow at the pistol and at recognizing the design on the handle. *Wait—how did you get my pistol? Are Mr. Keilot and Eela okay?*

"Who are you!" I demanded hoarsely, struggling to push their heavy foot off my chest. Smoke seeped from under the cloak onto my side, making my skin hiss in pain. The person's pure-white eyes narrowed as if they were smiling down at me, sending a violent chill down my back. Pressure formed in my head, and my vision blurred as something else—something powerful—filled my mind.

"*Who you were meant to be,*" they whispered inside my head. I panicked as his dark laugh filled every inch of my thoughts, sounding exactly like me.

The man holding me down suddenly had everything pulled away from him, revealing a pure, pitch-black smoke figure standing over me. Smoke columns shot towards me from the man, latching roughly onto my neck and face. I screamed in panic and agony as a burning sensation filled every part of my body. The man's dark laugh only got louder and closer to me inside my head. Violent pain erupted inside my skull as I kicked the air around me. The pressure formed even more inside my mind, making it feel like it was going to explode. I yelled in discomfort as everything suddenly went silent and still.

I opened my eyes weakly to see a bright, white tile ceiling shooting past me. My vision wavered in and out as I glanced at two nurses standing next to me, worried expressions on their faces.

"Hey buddy," one of them gently smiled.

"You're going to be okay," the other groaned, sending a shiver up my back. I tried sitting up but was immediately held down by a tight strap across my chest. I widened my blurry eyes and looked around at a doorway passing over me. *What's going on?*

"Can someone tell me what's happening?" I gasped, violently trying to pull my arm up. The nurses on either side of me tightened the straps holding me down even more, making me cough. Neither of them responded as they began hooking me up to various machines. One of the nurses brought a needle to my arm as I flinched away from her. The needle pierced my skin roughly, and something violently cold shot up my arm. Something within my head screamed in panic and laughter as I trembled. *What are you!* I screamed back at it in my head. I gritted my teeth as my entire left side of my body went numb.

"Don't fight it." the nurse ordered. My vision faded away as the thing inside my head chuckled amusedly.

I flinched myself awake from the recurring nightmare I've had my entire life. I blinked away tears as I took deep breaths to calm my racing heart. Memories flashed through my mind of seeing both my parents die and me unable to help them.

"Calm down, True," Mr. Keilot's voice distortedly echoed. I coughed hollowly as my vision steadied. He walked stiffly across the room with his arms held out to me. *What's wrong with you?*

"What happened?" I cried, weakly. Mr. Keilot's eyes darkened as he stared at me for a moment. "He's up!" he yelled over his shoulder. He then stalked closer stood at the bedside silently, his gaze down at me filled me with unease.

"You tried killing yourself *again*, True," Mr. Keilot spat. I flinched and furrowed my brow at him.

"What?" I snapped. "That's not—"

"An officer you talked to followed you after you left and saw you throw yourself into an alleyway," he began explaining coldly. "He wasn't able to get to you in time before you stabbed yourself in the neck again,"

"I didn't—" I cried, running my hand along my uncut neck.

"Liar," Mr. Keilot snarled darkly. Panic climbed up my chest as something pulled my hand away from my neck as I looked down at restraints suddenly on my wrists.

"I was attacked! I promise!" I angrily explained, roughly trying to pull away from the straps.

"He's lost it," a cold voice growled. A tall man in a white lab coat inched into the room holding a clipboard with a disgusted expression.

"Please! Listen to me!" I pleaded, my voice wavering. "Someone else did that to me—"

"He's going to be out of it for a little while. True, you gave yourself a seizure," the man in the lab coat grumbled.

"I'm not *out of it!*" I snapped angrily. *Why aren't you listening to me!* Mr. Keilot and the man in the lab coat suddenly froze, still as statues. Their cold gazes rested on me intently.

I breathed hard and glared down at the straps holding my hands down. I narrowed my eyes as the straps slowly faded into my own smoke. The heart monitor connected to me began going off rapidly the more I struggled. The entire room suddenly trembled, the lights going out. Mr. Keilot and the man faded away into the shadows as I desperately tried following them.

"Wait!" I cried, my voice echoing loudly around me. The lights flickered back on as a cold, smoke hand grabbed my wrist tightly. I froze in fear, staring down at the hand and blinked several times.

"Tell anyone about this and I'll make sure you're dead," the same voice from the alley hissed into my ear. A smoke tendril extended across the room, pulling a door with a mirror on it closed. I stared at myself in shock as a gas mask was suddenly melting into the side of my face. The same cold, white eyes from the man in the alley narrowed in delight as a wicked smile crept across his distorted gaze through the mask. I screamed in panic and agony as I tried pushing myself away from him.

The glass on the mirror shattered, filling the other side of my face with the smoke figure's face instead. Everything suddenly faded into darkness, everything leaving as quickly as it had come. A distant, frantic voice filled my mind as warm hands grabbed my shoulders and shook me.

I opened my eyes quickly and gasped for breath. My chest tightened as anxiety wrapped itself around my neck. I glanced around frantically through blurry eyes. *I'm back at the alley?* I turned and saw the same officer I had run into earlier with his gun raised, the light-grey cloaked figure running down the alleyway and disappearing into the shadows. The cloak slowly floated to the ground, melting into the concrete. I pushed myself off the ground and sat against the brick wall, holding my head in my hands tightly as I suddenly couldn't breathe. I quickly grabbed my neck and ran my shaking hands across my wrists as I coughed.

"Kid?" the officer's voice cried. "Are you okay?" he asked worriedly, jogging over to me. The man fell to his knees in front of me, his hands outstretched slightly. "Easy now," he gently explained, his brow furrowed. "10-52. Code 8! I repeat! 10-52. Code 8!" he ordered into the radio on his shoulder. "Look at me," he softly ordered, tipping my chin to him. My eyes were wide and filled with tears as I frantically gripped my head and stared at him. The smoke figure's words, '*Who you were meant to be,*' raced around in my mind as I coughed hollowly into my arm again, pitch black smoke coiling around my fingers. I began to sob fearfully as the same voice echoed in my head, laughing darkly. The officer gently stood up and crouched next to me, holding me under his arm as I cried.

CHAPTER 6

SEVERAL MINUTES LATER...

"That was a low-level villain," the man explained softly to me after I'd calmed down. I sat with my knees to my chest and my chin resting on them, my heart racing. He stood protectively over me with his gun in hand as he watched both sides of the alleyway intently. "He hasn't killed anyone yet, but he's done and said some messed up stuff..." he explained warily. "You're the first person he's physically hurt," the officer croaked, glancing at my bleeding arm. "We have a spotting on S-Mask. Heading east to the lower-class sector," he growled gruffly into the radio on his shoulder.

"Did he say anything to you?" the officer asked hesitantly, his grip tightening on his gun.

"I just asked him who he was...he gave an..." I trailed off. "Interesting response," I whimpered, tightening my grip around my legs. Something chuckled darkly within my head as sharp pain struck me in the neck, making me grimace. The officer widened his eyes as he stared down at me after glancing at my bloody knife on the ground. I frowned at him and shook my head. "I cut him, and the wound appeared on myself..." I spat, pulling my knife back into my sleeve.

A single, loud siren echoed down the alley as I saw an ambulance park on the street. The officer in front of me furrowed his brow and intently stared at me.

"What did he say to you?" he asked darkly. I widened my eyes and looked at the people jogging down the alley towards us.

"Who you were meant to be..." I hesitantly replied.

"Has he been to a doctor to get tested for ICD?" one of the people from the ambulance worriedly asked. I shook my head as all of them backed slightly away from me.

"I don't know what that is. I haven't been to a hospital or doctor in years," I spat. Everyone standing over me glanced worriedly at each other before turning back to me with furrowed brows.

CHAPTER 7

MIDDLE-CLASS SECTOR, MR. KEILOT'S HOUSE...

I frowned down at the wrap on my arm as the officer opened the back of his car door. I glanced up and felt my heart spike in my chest as I saw Mr. Keilot jog down from the house towards us.

"He's physically, mostly fine. He's shaken up mentally," the officer explained, holding out his hand to him as I stepped out of the car. "He needs to be back at the station after he's calmed down for questioning," he grumbled. Mr. Keilot held my face in his rough hands, staring at me with tear filled eyes. I felt my own eyes fill with tears at seeing the glint of love in his warm, worried face, and shivering at the memory of the cold glare he had towards me in my nightmare. *That wasn't him... It couldn't have been! That was fake!* A laugh deep within my head disagreed.

"Questioning? What did he do?" Mr. Keilot ordered, holding me gently under his arm.

"Nothing. He's not in any trouble," the officer sighed, blinking slowly. "I recommend you both do some research on ICD. It will help him when he's questioned by us. Someone will be back in an hour or so for him once he calms down," he spat.

I nodded, frowning at him slightly.

"When you get to the station, ask for Officer Lopez. Okay?"

Mr. Keilot frowned and tipped his head at him as he stepped back into his car and drove off. I immediately melted into his grasp as tears filled my eyes again.

"I don't know what's happening," I whimpered.

"We'll figure this out, together," Mr. Keilot gently whispered, slowly bringing me towards the house.

CHAPTER 8

AN HOUR LATER...

"Imposter Clone Disorder, also known as ICD, is a hereditary yet rare problem," Mr. Keilot said softly. I rested my forehead on my arm as he sat across the table from me, reading on his laptop. "In more recent years, the disorder has become incredibly more dangerous. Higher stress levels in the population of a city can lead a person with this disorder to pass it on to their children, by choice or accident," he continued, raising his brows in disbelief. I frowned and stared at the dark wood in front of me. *One of my parents gave this to me?* "With the classes getting stricter in recent years, I guess you fit into this category," he mumbled.

"ICD is self-explanatory," he began again. I scoffed loudly into my arms as he chuckled sadly, resting his hand on my arm. "It's when a 'clone' or 'altered' version of the host is born in solitary at the same time they are, living a very similar life to their host," he continued, wearily. "This altered version of the host has free will and the ability for speech. *It* does not have the ability to feel real human emotions unless connected to or in contact with their host," Mr. Keilot growled. I shivered as something in my mind shifted again, peering closer in curiosity.

"Regardless of what choices the clone makes, depending on when the host goes through the same situation, and possibly makes different decisions, the clone's 'reality' is immediately affected. Meaning, if the host has a rough life with bad decisions, the clone also will have the same life, even if they make choices first or differently," Mr. Keilot trailed off. I lifted my head slowly and glanced up at him worriedly.

"The darker the host's life, the more likely the clone is to turn and distort into something evil and difficult to control," he whispered, looking intently at me. Panic surged through my chest again as I took several shuddering breaths.

"There is no known cure for this disorder and must play out its course naturally by the host and clone merging in an event," Mr. Keilot explained coldly, his eyes going back to the screen. "The chances of the host themselves changing and adopting the clone's aggressive and evil habits depends entirely on them…" He frowned. I held my head in my hands and sighed, holding back a sad laugh. "The goal for the clone is unknown but likely to take the place of their host and take over their lives," he whispered. Mr. Keilot's face darkened the more he read on silently. *Why would either of my parents give this to me? Which one of them had it—?*

Mr. Keilot suddenly stood up and walked away from the table, his hands on the back of his head.

"I don't want to hurt anyone," I tried softly, intently looking at Mr. Keilot with his back to me. "Even if I 'merge' with this stupid clone, I wouldn't let myself harm anyone," I hesitantly explained.

"Well, how do you know that for sure?" Mr. Keilot snapped. My heart lurched in my chest as he glared over his shoulder at me. "If you have the ability to hurt yourself—"

"What does that have to do with anything?" I hissed, hitting my hand on the table and standing up. Mr. Keilot stepped away and frowned slightly at me. Something within my head shifted, giggling darkly. I gripped the sides of my head as my legs faltered. "Shut up," I growled softly through gritted teeth. My breaths quickened as I turned over my shoulder and stared at the box under my bag.

I can't stay here. I don't know how long I have…what if I hurt you guys? I shoved myself away from the table and quickly ran across the room. I slid to my knees and began gathering everything back together.

"What are you doing?" Mr. Keilot asked warily.

My heart spiked in my chest as I shook my head quickly.

"Leaving!" I snapped. "I don't want to put you or Eela in danger," I cried, my voice wavering.

"Wait a second!" Mr. Keilot sighed angrily, jogging over towards me. I ignored him, lifting the tattered lid of the old cardboard box and shivering at the sight my pistol laying calmly inside. I blinked tears out of my eyes as I stared at the design on the gun being the same as the one in the smoke figure's hand. I quickly shoved my bag inside the box and closed it, picking it up and stepped towards the door.

"True! Stop!" Mr. Keilot yelled. I dropped the box onto the couch as I flinched away from him and held my hand over my face. The memory of my mother screaming at me after she choked my father filled my mind, sending a jolt of panic up my chest. "I'm sorry." He apologized softly, resting his hand on my trembling shoulder gently. "Read this damn email. Please?" he pleaded, glancing at my tear-filled eyes behind my hand with a frown. He roughly turned his computer around towards me and held inhaled softly.

I widened my eyes as an acceptance letter was placed on the screen.

"They accepted me?" I asked, astonished.

"Your case is different from most people's... With recent information from the police under your name, the company wants to help," Mr. Keilot explained proudly. I shook my head in disbelief as my legs began to tremble. "You can start the classes as early as tomorrow!" he beamed. My heart ached in my chest as the thing in my mind stalked closer to me while I stared at Mr. Keilot.

"Okay, sure. I'll start," I spat. "I can't be around Eela. I'm going to hurt her on accident and then—" I cried, reaching for the box. Mr. Keilot grabbed my wrist tightly and pulled me towards him, setting the computer down on the couch behind him. "I'll get paid to do these classes, right?" I asked hesitantly. "I'll use that money to get my own place. Away from here. I can't put you in danger—" I whimpered, leaning towards the box. Mr. Keilot's grip on my wrist tightened as he leaned down towards me as tears streamed down my face.

"Listen to me, True," Mr. Keilot whispered. "My wife...Eela's mother...had this disorder," he explained. My heart fell as I widened my eyes in shock. "Her life before she met me was horrible. Much like yours but with bad relationships and family problems," he softly said. "She was on the road to merge with her clone soon, who was violent and angry—until Eela suddenly came into the picture," he smiled, tears filling his eyes. "She was fine for a long time! Her clone had calmed down some, and we were all *fine*," he chuckled, his voice breaking. "Or so I thought,"

"My wife hid so much from me," Mr. Keilot grumbled. "She hid how much pain she was still in because of various circumstances in both of our lives, lied to me, and…" He trailed off. I tensed, reaching for his hand as he pulled away from me. "One night, on her way back from work, in a storm," he continued softly, "her clone found her and killed her during the merge," he whimpered, closing his eyes as tears fell from them. My heart ached in my chest as I kept my hand out to him. He brought his hands to his face, rubbing it gently. "No one knows if it was intentional or not, but there's a reason I care so much about you, True," he breathed, wiping his face.

"I knew something was wrong when I met you for the first time; these things give their host a certain feeling to them that I can't explain," Mr. Keilot cried softly. "I had a gut feeling that you had this as well because you gave off the same feeling as my wife did when I met her," he whimpered, looking directly into my eyes. Tears streamed down my face as I wrapped my arms around myself. "That's why I invited you to places, came to check on you…" he explained, shaking his head slowly. I slowly crumbled to my knees and sat on the floor, breathing hard as I held my head in my hands. Something laughed deep down in my head, making me grip my head tighter and growl in anger.

"So, this thing is going to kill me no matter what," I hissed. "Why not end it now and save everyone the struggle?" I cried angrily. I stared up at Mr. Keilot standing over me with tears streaming down both our faces. He stepped down towards me quickly and roughly pulled me to my feet. Mr. Keilot shook me several times, both hands on my shoulders.

"Don't you *ever* think about that!" he snarled, tightening his grip on me. "You may think you're alone in this world and that no one cares! But it's a lie!" he snapped. "*I do!*" he pleaded, tipping my chin to him as I looked away.

"I care and I love you so much, True." Mr. Keilot cried. "I know I met you, so I could heal myself and also do *more* to heal and help you!" he growled. "I'm *not* giving up on you even though you've given up on yourself time and time again!" Mr. Keilot angrily explained, shaking me gently again. "We're going to overcome this, *together*," he whispered. "I'll make sure you get through this, no matter what it takes from me. Do you understand?" he harshly snapped. "Do you *understand!*" Mr. Keilot hissed, tightening his grip on me.

I looked into his tear- and pain-filled eyes for a moment. I nodded slightly, tears filling my eyes again. Mr. Keilot pushed me back as he turned and walked across the room, closing his bedroom door gently. I blinked several times and slid down to the floor trembling, waiting for the officers to come for me with a racing heart.

CHAPTER 9

THIRTY MINUTES LATER – THE MIDDLE-CLASS POLICE STATION…

"These cases are pretty rare, but we may be able to help you, True…" Officer Lopez explained gently. I nodded, keeping my gaze down at the metal table below me, avoiding the watchful eyes of people around the room. Several other officers and people with clipboards surrounded me, staring intently at me with cold, uninterested eyes. *How can we change the future if it's already decided? So far, the only way this ends is if I give into the clone and let it kill me.* The thing inside my head shifted in protest, sending a wave of pressure across my skull.

"How many times have you come into contact with the clone?" a man with a clipboard asked sharply.

"Once?" I hesitantly answered.

"What is proof that you actually have this disorder?" another man snarked.

"You could be faking for all we know—" another continued.

"Enough! I saw the clone with my own eyes!" Officer Lopez argued. "I saw this poor kid almost get suffocated by it!" he hissed, narrowing his eyes at the disapproving faces staring at me. A young woman widened her eyes swiftly with a nervous glance at me.

"You've only come into contact with your clone once?" she asked nervously. "Why is it so violent towards you already?" she winced.

I blinked slowly and stayed silent.

"How am I supposed to know? I only found out about this a few hours ago. I still have no idea what's going on!" I snapped softly, clenching my fists.

"He has an interesting health record," the first man with the clipboard snarked. "Orphaned at age 7, runaway at age 16, attempt of suicide at 19, prescribed antidepressants after it failed. Still taking those?"

I frowned at him and shook my head.

"Couldn't afford them anymore," I spat. The man tipped his chin up to me and scribbled into the clipboard.

"Listen, sure he's had a rough life, but with other cases, the clone doesn't start forming a relationship with the host until after they've met!" the young woman cried.

"Maybe this time it's different." Someone else grumbled.

"So much is still unknown about this disorder, for crying out loud! What the hell can we do to even help this poor man!" another snapped. I rolled my eyes and slowly brought my head down, resting my hands on the back of my neck. *What do you want from me? I don't have anything possibly useful to you.* The presence in my mind stayed silent as it shifted again. I had waited for a response but eventually gave up. The loud, frantic arguing around me drowned out any possible question I could have asked myself.

CHAPTER 10

INTERLUDE

Every day after the police questioned me, I felt myself changing. The clone kept getting stronger, more demanding. Its voice became louder and louder, more powerful, and more aggressive towards me. The stronger it became, the sicker in the head I felt. The classes from the training school helped me stay distracted from it most of the time, even though I still struggled. Mr. Keilot did his best to help, even though I didn't see him every day after I had moved into an apartment near the main campus of the school. Stella, even knowing little to nothing on what I was going through, also did her best to help. She was there for me through every time the clone became too loud within my mind.

CHAPTER 11

TWO YEARS LATER…

I had just dropped Stella off at the downtown museum and finally finished the classes from the training school after working tirelessly. I sighed down at the small envelope in my hand and fixed my backpack strap on my shoulder with a deep breath. *I can't wait to show Mr. Keilot and Eela. I think by the time I get back to my apartment, she should be done with her homeschool work. I'll probably stay with them for a few hours and just relax…* I smiled softly as I began walking down the street after waving to Stella in the museum. I inhaled deeply and stared up at the bright blue sky as my heart pounded in my chest. *What am I supposed to do now?*

I shifted uncomfortably as I realized the clone had been silent in my head all day. My phone began going off in my pocket, making me flinch. *An unknown number?*

"Hello?" I softly sighed into the phone.

"Is this Mr. Greer?" a voice solemnly asked. I furrowed my brow and shivered.

"Yes, this is him?" I half laughed. *Probably someone from the school to settle some paperwork…*

"I have some terrible news for you," the woman gently whimpered through the phone. My heart spiked in my chest as I stopped walking, glancing over my shoulder at the museum. Stella was looking worriedly out the window at me with a furrowed brow. "Thomas Keilot was killed in a work accident earlier this morning…"

I blinked several times. My chest tightened as my vision began to tunnel. *No...* Time slowed down around me as I slowly brought the phone away from my face and stared at the ground.

"The building collapsed on the entire crew during inspection to damages that had been done last night... There were no survivors," the woman continued, her voice far away and echoing. "I'm deeply sorry for your loss..."

I took shallow, short breaths as I heard Stella call out for me worriedly.

"Mr. Greer?" the woman asked hesitantly. My phone fell from my hands as I crumbled to my knees, dropping my backpack on the ground.

My entire body trembled violently as my breaths suddenly quickened. I clutched my stomach and slowly leaned forward towards the concrete. My entire body had felt like it was crushed. I closed my eyes as I screamed in agony and grief into the ground. Stella's frantic voice was distant as her arm was wrapped around me, shaking me gently. Her worried voice soon became angry as she started yelling for help, her voice echoing. Stella shook me again and tried pulling me to my feet before she kneeled next to me with widened eyes. She roughly picked up my phone on the ground and held it to her ear as Egret and other people on the street gathered around us.

Every hard moment I had gone through in my life flashed through my mind. Each and every time after I had met Mr. Keilot, he was there. He was there for me, right by my side, the entire time. Each time I planned to kill myself, he appeared at my door, checking on me with his warm, gentle smile...

"You walked a little slower down the hall today, so I came to check on you... Seems like I came just in time, huh?"

"I care and love you so much, True!"

"I am not giving up on you!"

"We'll figure this out together..."

His loving voice yelled in my mind. Many worried voices surrounded me as I felt myself being pulled away. The small, fighting light inside...went out, *again.*

CHAPTER 12

SEVERAL HOURS LATER...

I had been sitting alone in a hospital room in silence, constantly being monitored by doctors and nurses on a suicide watch. Noises from the hospital wavered in and out of my ears, echoing around my skull. Everything around me felt numb, as if I wasn't even in my body anymore. I kept my head down, my gaze resting on the white tile below me intently. My heart switched between racing and slowing down drastically as I realized I was in the same hospital room from my nightmare a few years ago. My clone stirred in my mind slightly, leaning down towards my neck. I coughed hollowly into my arm, pitch black smoke shooting violently from my mouth.

The room around me darkened as the blinds on the window were quickly pulled shut. The heavy door was roughly slammed, the lock turning forcibly. Loud, frantic voices began yelling as people began pounding on the door, struggling with the handle. Something dark in the corner of the room shifted and grew, gently inching towards me. A cold, pitch-black hand of smoke slowly reached in front of me, grabbing my chin and tipping it up. I stayed emotionless as I stared into my clone's white eyes, narrowed down at me. The door was roughly slammed into, making my clone's attention dart away from me. A pistol loomed out from the smoke figure's side and floated across the room gently, the barrel of the gun clicking against the glass as it hit it. The nurses on the other side backed away with raised hands and quickly darted out of sight. The pistol was then violently slammed into the glass, cracking it so horribly that you couldn't see through it. My clone slowly retracted the pistol as I stared blankly up at it.

"Finally…" it hissed darkly. "You're weak enough for me to come out again," it beamed, tightening its grip around my chin. "Give in to me, True…" it ordered, the voice distorting. "You know you can't take anything anymore!" it laughed. I blinked up at my clone as it smiled mischievously down at me. "Life has chewed you up and spit you out time and time again…" the clone growled, wisps of pitch-black smoke reaching out to me. "If you give in to me, I can make that all go away… You can get payback and justice for yourself!" it proclaimed, raising its other arm up proudly.

"What if I don't want justice for myself?" I snarled coldly, waving my hand up at the clone's arm. The skin on my hand stung horribly as it passed through the clone's smoke arm while it narrowed its eyes. My eye twitched in pain as I pulled my chin away from it and kept my head down.

"You're only saying that because you've lost someone—" it began, leaning down at me. "Never mind! Well, what about others? *Screw yourself* then!" it changed slyly. I froze as my heart leapt in my chest. "Aha…" it chuckled darkly.

"What about Stella?" it sneered. "Poor girl, so scared and worried for you, and all that's being told to her are lies and insults on how she's too emotional, how she needs to shut up. Always talking and running her mouth—" the clone began rambling. "Eela! She's lost her father! Poor girl doesn't know what to do with herself anymore, and she's blaming everything on her. She's wanting to give up in school because everything just keeps getting worse,"

"Shut up!" I hissed, clenching my fists.

"What about all those people down in the lower-class sector? Dying alone without any help from others around them because every single one of them is struggling and cannot afford to help anyone else but himself because of the Elites! Oh, you can do so much for those bastards. Prying the Elites of their pride and sense of comfort from stealing money out from your people's mouths!" it screamed, the voice distorting violently. The clone lifted its head and cackled loudly into the air as I glared up at it with a frown.

"So, what if you don't get justice for yourself. But you are in a position now to help others that you deeply care about," my clone snarled coldly, grabbing my neck violently in it's cold hand. I quickly grabbed its smokey arm and narrowed my eyes at it. The clone's prideful eyes widened at my hands holding and not falling through. "You're already liking the idea..." it chuckled. "Whadda'ya say?" it asked sharply, tightening its grip on my neck. The itch that had been inside my head for two years was finally revealed. It stood front and center, proclaiming itself to the world, begging to be set free. "Now, these plans won't be easy. But if you don't accept me now, I'll make sure you die before you even leave this damned building, you and those two pretty girls you care so much about..." it hissed darkly, smiling wickedly down at me. I frowned and nodded once, narrowing my eyes at it.

The smoke figure holding onto my neck slowly let its smile fall into a peaceful grin. Moments later, violent pain shot through my neck as the smoke latched onto it tightly, pain then spreading to the rest of my body. I screamed in agony as the clone tightened its grip around my neck, causing me to cough and gasp for air as I fell to the ground. I clutched my neck and clawed at my skin as I screamed, the lights flickering on and off above me. Dark laughter filled my mind as the pain surged into something worse. Immense pressure built inside my head as my vision blurred and I stared at the flashing lights above me. Everything suddenly went silent and still. My vision restored slowly as the pain throughout my entire body subsided.

I gasped deeply and coughed hollowly into my arm, rolling onto my elbow. My entire body felt restored and healthier than I ever had been. I took deep breaths as I held my face in my hands for a moment, staying on the floor. *I don't feel anything different than before, other than I'm not numb...* I winced as I slowly stood, using the side of the bed to help me up. I held my head and looked around at the room warily. My gaze landed on the door's window as I saw groups of desks outside my room abandoned through the shattered glass. I frowned as I looked myself over and sighed, walking across the room hesitantly.

I gently tried opening the door and grumbled at the broken lock. *Thanks for breaking that...* I bit my lip and slowly nudged the broken glass window with my elbow. The glass immediately shattered, falling roughly to the floor. I felt around the other side of the door and struggled with the lock for a moment, mumbling under my breath. I stepped back, glancing at my elbow with a frown before I sighed. I then held out my hand to the doorknob and braced myself slightly. My pitch-black smoke gently seeped from my palm towards the door, making me shiver. With a few small clicks, the door was unlocked.

I slowly pulled the door open and leaned my head out into the deserted hallway.

"Hello?" I called out hesitantly. My voice echoed slightly, sending a chill up my spine. *Are they that scared of me to go into hiding?* I waited patiently for a response from my clone in my head and rolled my eyes when I got nothing. *Guess you're gone then. How nice of you to talk me into this and leave no directions on what to do afterwards.* I widened my eyes as the stairwells on either side of the hall suddenly filled with loud, angry voices.

Both heavy metal doors were flung open, armed guards barreled through the doorways with large guns raised at me. I quickly lifted my hands with a furrowed brow as they closed in towards me.

"Step down, you imposter clone! We know who you are!" an angry voice demanded. I tipped my head, holding back a growl of disapproval and frowned.

"I'm not the clone… It's me, True," I gently explained.

"Liar!" the same voice snarled. I narrowed my eyes at the guards standing tense all around me. *You said this was going to be difficult! I didn't think you meant this kind of difficulty with having to deal with biased Elite guards!* "I won't say it again!" the same voice ordered. "Step down!"

"What does it look like I'm doing!" I hissed darkly, leaning forward slightly. Several people began yelling, their grips on their guns tightening fearfully. "You don't need to be scared of me; I promise!" I laughed offendedly.

"Funny story *clone!*" a voice from the group of guards on my right laughed.

"I'm not a clone!" I snarled coldly. "I have my hands up, and I'm not being violent! What else do you want me to do!" I asked sharply, glaring at both groups of guards. "Arresting me is unnecessary!" I snapped, stepping back slightly as a guard pulled out handcuffs. I inhaled to speak again when a loud gunshot echoed through the silence. I gasped, stumbling into the doorway as I gripped my side with gritted teeth. Sharp pain and heat shot up my leg and pulsed from the blood running down my hands. Loud yelling came from the guards as they all widened their eyes in panic. The same guard raised their gun and quickly darted forward at me again. I took a shuddering breath as I narrowed my eyes, glaring up at the man charging towards me.

Without thinking I suddenly shot two smoke columns from my palms. The smoke tendrils hissed with glee as they collided with the officer, tightening around him dangerously and lifting him into the air.

"True! We made a mistake! Calm down!" another guard cried.

"*Mistake!*" I snarled, tightening the smoke around the guard.

"We know it's you now, True! Put him down!" another frightened voice cried.

I shook my head, holding back a smile as I glared at the guard struggling in the smoke tendrils. *I guess if I was really the clone, I wouldn't have started bleeding after being shot. They aren't human after all.* I nodded, faking a smile and sighed.

"Oh sure, I'll put him down," I grumbled, feeling the heat from the bullet in my side pulsing. The smoke tendrils violently shot up, slamming the man's head into the tiled ceiling above then back down into the tile with the same force. I held out my hands to either side of me as guards began firing their guns again. My vision tunneled and focused on every bullet being fired at me slowing to a stop and dropping helplessly to the ground. Guards cried out in horror as their bullets kept getting stopped by me. My smoke tendrils shot from my back, knocking the guards behind me to the ground, and from my palm to the guards ahead of me. I quickly wrapped myself in the pitch-black smoke, feeling bullets ricochet off the smoke armor as I sprinted down the hallway to the stairwell, ignoring the flaring pain from my bleeding side.

I burst through the hospital's front doors after letting my smoke armor disappear and jogged out onto the busy street, immediately merging with the crowd. I flicked my hood over my head, keeping pressure on my side with gritted teeth and gasping breaths. Loud sirens echoed through the air and were drowned out by the loud conversations of the city. Upbeat music pulsed through the air, competing with the voices of everyone walking the streets. *Why am I such a big deal now? No one cared who I was until this clone and I merged.* Sudden yelling from behind me sent a jolt of panic into my chest.

"Everyone freeze!" a demanding voice boomed. People in the streets yelped in panic, immediately stopping and raising their hands. I pushed past them roughly, glancing over my shoulder at Elite guards filtering out from the hospital doors. I shoved an older man out of my way and tried turning into a dark alley.

"What are you doing, kid? You're going to get yourself shot!" he hissed, glaring at me angrily.

"I'll shoot back then," I spat, stopping and staring directly at him. The man widened his eyes warily as he stepped away, keeping his hands up towards the yelling guards. I narrowed my eyes slightly as I clenched my fists. *It's you again? The man who yelled at me on the street.*

"Man in the black hood! Put your hands where we can see them!" another voice from my right snarled. "We will open fire!"

I stopped and turned towards the police officer standing in the street with guards from the hospital coming at me from the left. To my right, more Elite guards and a few Elites were storming through the crowd. *Only in it for the paycheck. Just because you use your power for the government doesn't make you entitled to treat normal civilians like crap.*

"Careful now!" I yelled hoarsely. "We wouldn't want any of these innocent people around me to get killed, right?" I snapped. The people around me nervously stepped further away from me with widened eyes. "That would look worse on your part if *another* innocent civilian were to get shot by the same group of Elites and their guards on the same day, huh?" I laughed angrily, glaring at the Elites stalking through the frozen crowd at me. I tensed my body as I locked eyes with a well-known and trusted Elite. His warm eyes were filled with worry as they stared intently at me.

"You have five seconds before you're going to regret refusing police orders!" the Elite snapped, raising his hand from his sides. I glanced at the badge on his chest and frowned. *Of course, they send an Elite with his kind of power. Always used to violently capture anyone the police deemed untrustworthy.* Several more police cars pulled up around the guards moving people out of the way. The civilians around me scurried out of my reach as I glanced at all of them slowly. And *of course, they send this many guards. They want to make me look like the villain, like they are the great little saviors of the day…anything to protect their pathetic and tattered Elite reputation.*

I suddenly lunged at the man who had snapped at me. I violently pulled him next to me, wrapping my arm around his neck tightly. I closed my eyes briefly and materialized my pistol from my apartment into my hand. I quickly raised it the man's head as he frantically tried escaping my grasp.

"I'm not going to kill you," I whispered softly to him. "Don't go around yelling at people like me. You have absolutely *no* clue what could be happening to them," I warned dangerously, glaring down at him in my arm. He nodded furiously as he helplessly tried prying my arm away from him. I materialized a second pistol floating in the air above my head and frowned, keeping an intent gaze on the officers surrounding me on the street. *I have so much better control than before…*

"You all just have to let me go on with my day, and I'll let this poor man go! If not…" I announced loudly, "I'll kill him!"

"Hey now!" an officer nervously chuckled. "Calm down, sir…" they winced, holding their hand out to me.

"Wouldn't want this to get violent again, *right?*" I darkly asked, glaring at the Elite staring at me. He narrowed his eyes as his fists clenched, his face going pale as the civilians around him nervously backed away. *You know exactly what you've done. You're lucky the police and government help you hide it and seem innocent.* I smirked calmly at him and glanced at the guards and police surrounding me.

The policeman in front of me suddenly stepped towards me, sending a wave of panic into my chest. I suddenly fired the pistol floating above me, dropping the old man to the ground. I immediately covered him in my pitch-black smoke, holding out my hands in front of me as loud gunshots from the surrounding guards echoed through the street. Each bullet slowed to a stop, hovering in the air in front of me in a large circle. Yelling and screaming filled the air as the shots rang out, silencing the city for a moment. The gunfire ceased as the Elite suddenly darted down the sidewalk towards me.

I quickly waved my hand in an arch, shooting every bullet floating around me back at the guards. Each and every one of them getting hit by the bullets I sent back. I then lifted my own pistol and shot at the Elite lunging towards me. He yelped in pain as both bullets struck his bullet proof vest, sending him to the ground. I stepped back, glancing behind me at the alley and widened my eyes. A singular gunshot suddenly echoed through the air from the civilians in the crowd, making me flinch. The bullet grazed the side of my face as I turned back to the people around me. I widened my eyes in disbelief as I saw Egret standing with a pistol aimed at me, her brow furrowed with worry. I locked eyes with her and shook my head slowly before wrapping myself in my pitch-black smoke again, heat pulsing across my cheek. Smoke columns shot from my palms, slamming into anyone in their way as I darted to the alley. More gunfire echoed through the street as bullets hit objects all around me. *I guess sometimes the world doesn't need another hero. What it needs is someone with their heads not in the damn clouds.*

CHAPTER 13

SEVERAL MINUTES LATER...

After running a few blocks from the hospital through the alleys, I collapsed to the ground. I breathed hard, my heart roaring in my ears as I listened to distant sirens and helicopters searching for me. I sat against an old building wall, holding my side tightly with gritted teeth. I glared down at the blood on my hands with a grimace and frowned. *What the hell are you doing?* I closed my eyes tightly as I pressed down on my bleeding side harder and bit my lip, holding back a cry of pain. *Where am I supposed to go? Back to the lower-class sector? No one would waste their time and go looking for me there.*

I inhaled sharply to begin walking as a loud bang echoed through the alley. I froze, pressing myself against the wall even more and dragged myself behind a large dumpster, grimacing in pain.

"True!" Stella's voice called worriedly. I widened my eyes and furrowed my brow as my heart spiked in my chest. "I'm not working with the police or anyone else!" she announced softly. "I'm not armed, and I'm alone…." She continued, her voice becoming softer. My breaths quickened as I slowly peered around the dumpster at her standing in the alley with her arms around herself. "I don't even know if you're listening, but," she began again, "I want to join you!"

I raised my brow and held back a laugh as she brought her hand to her face and mumbled under her breath.

"I meant, whatever you're planning!" she chuckled. Her gentle eyes were slightly glowing around the edges as she gazed up at the old buildings around us. *It's dangerous for you to be out here by yourself… Why come this far to look for me? Shouldn't you fear me?*

"I think you're a crazy *lunatic* for pulling those stunts with the police and Elites, but I'm not scared of you!" Stella sighed, looking down sadly. "You're not even here to listen," she mumbled, turning on her heel to leave.

"Whatever I'm planning? I wasn't planning anything…" I gruffly exclaimed, forcing myself to stand using the wall. Stella flinched with widened eyes as her face lit up, and we locked eyes again. The same chill shot down my back as I turned away from her gaze and frowned. I materialized two pistols floating above my shoulders, bringing them towards her as she slowly stepped forward.

"Why risk the perfect life you have to join someone like me?" I asked hesitantly. Stella scoffed and rolled her eyes.

"*Perfect?*" she echoed. "I've been told to shut up my entire life… I talk too much, I'm too blunt, I'm just too extra and over exaggerating everything…" she snapped. "Pretty perfect," she hissed, narrowing her eyes. My heart ached in my chest as her eyes began glowing for a split second before dulling down again. Stella kept her gaze intently at me for a moment before she yelped with widened eyes.

"Oh my God, you're bleeding!" she cried, stepping towards me. I quickly stepped back, bringing a pistol closer to her as I grimaced. Stella paused, glaring at the gun and furrowed her brow at my blood-stained hands and clothing as my legs trembled below me. "Listen, I know we've only known each other for two years, and we still know nothing about the other," Stella spat slowly, "but I think with both of our minds put together, we could do something great!" she announced proudly, stepping into the pistol floating in the air. I quickly waved it away as she smirked slightly and turned her gaze away from me.

My mind flashed back to what my clone offered me back at the hospital.

"I know how screwed up the Elite system is, and I also know from you briefly mentioning a few times, that you have a strong distaste for them…" Stella gently winced. "Don't you have something planned to fix that?" she asked expectantly. "You wouldn't have fought so hard against those guards if you were going to sit in a cell and *rot* for the rest of your life…" she scoffed. "You must have something? Anything?"

I shook my head, frowning at her and waved the other pistol away.

"That's fine, we'll think of something soon. But before that..." Stella groaned. "Mind telling me why those people are looking for you and why you're currently bleeding?" she spat. I chuckled softly and winced as my side flared in pain.

"Long story that I'll explain with something else once we're in a safe place..." I mumbled. I widened my eyes suddenly at the words 'safe place'. *Eela*— "I need to get someone, come on!" I breathed, turning on my heel quickly. Stella darted after me without another word.

CHAPTER 14

MIDDLE-CLASS SECTOR, MR. KEILOT'S HOUSE...

My heart roared in my chest, and tears swelled in my eyes as I limped up the walkway towards Mr. Keilot's home. I lifted my shaking hand up to the door as Stella sided up next to me, worriedly glancing at me for a moment.

"What are we doing here?" Stella whispered. I waved my hand at her and shivered as footsteps came close to the door. "Oh—" she breathed, bringing her hand up to her face. I rolled my eyes and blinked away the sharp ache in my chest with a frown. *I think I've talked about Eela with Stella before... I guess she knows why we're here now...* I clenched my fists slightly. *Her aunt should be here with her... I've only met that woman a few times, but—*

The door suddenly swung open as I reached to knock again.

"Can I help you?" the woman at the door gruffly sighed. Her sorrowful eyes widened slightly as she stared at me. "True..."

"I'm looking for Eela." I snapped, ignoring her sympathetic look towards me. The woman frowned at me and closed the door slightly behind her.

"Why would you need to see her?" she hissed defensively.

"Is Eela at the house right now?" I asked, ignoring her question. Stella tensed next to me as the corners of her eyes flickered. The three of us stood in awkward silence as annoyance began to bubble up in my chest. *You know me. Why the hell are you pretending like you don't?*

"True!" Eela cried, shoving her aunt out of the way. She ran roughly into me, falling to her knees as I struggled to hold her up with widened eyes. I knelt in front of her, wrapping my arms tightly around her as she whimpered in grief. I widened my eyes at the memory of her cowering under my arms during a thunderstorm flashed through my mind. I then frowned up at Eela's aunt staring disapprovingly down at me as I tightened my grip around her. My eye twitched in pain as my bleeding side flared. *Please don't freak out if you see that…* I winced as I glanced down at Eela leaning into me.

"She's coming with me," I growled slowly. Her aunt raised her hand to protest as I materialized a pistol in front of her silently. My own pistol shifted in my hoodie pocket as I shivered under Stella's glare. Eela's aunt closed her mouth with widened eyes and nodded backing out of the doorway. "Go get your things…" I whispered softly to Eela, slowly standing up and pulling her to her feet. I waved my pistol away as I slowly shuffled into the home, Stella closing the door roughly behind us. "I'm going to take care of you… Your father would have wanted me to," I gently continued, wiping the tears of Eela's face as she stared up at me. She nodded, backing away from my reach with a nervous glance at her aunt. She then turned and scurried across the room, her shaking arms wrapped around herself. I glanced at Stella, materializing a pistol in front of her to take as I walked across the room.

I gently pushed Mr. Keilot's bedroom door open and shivered with grief. The entire room felt empty and cold as tears formed in my eyes again. I slowly crouched down at his desk on the left wall and rummaged through the drawers for a moment. My heart spiked out of my chest as I pulled open a small secret slot and an envelope fell out. *Thank you for leaving this for me to get for Eela and myself if anything happened to you.* I gently took the envelope from the drawer and tucked it carefully in my back pocket, wrapping my arms around myself. I closed my eyes and stumbled backwards, sitting roughly on his bedside.

I leaned forward and bit back a cry of grief as my heart lurched in my chest. *I promise you; I'll take care of her. I won't let anything happen to her.* I inhaled deeply, quickly wiping my face and held my head in my hands for a moment. I slowly turned my gaze up to a picture on his desk as tears filled my eyes again. A silver framed photo of Mr. Keilot, his wife, and Eela as a small baby rested safely on his desk side. I stared at Mr. Keilot's cheerful smile down at his wife and Eela and felt my heart leap in my chest. I shook my head and forced myself to stand on my trembling legs as I gently took the photo and held it in my shaking hands. I furrowed my brow and frowned as I tucked it inside my hoodie pocket and walked out of the room.

Eela was leaning into Stella's side as they stood in front of the door. Eela's aunt had a dark glare in her eyes as she watched me like a hawk from across the room.

"You can't do this!" she hissed, narrowing her eyes at Stella and Eela.

"Watch me." I smiled calmly. Stella grinned mischievously and opened the front door with a glance at me. Eela's tear filled eyes looked worriedly at her aunt as Stella guided her out the door. Eela's aunt stood up and jogged across the room as I followed them. My heart leapt in my chest as she grabbed my wrist and violently pulled me towards her.

I turned and stared directly at her with a furrowed brow, glancing calmly at my wrist in her hand.

"You're not going to get away with this, you can't just take her from me!" she hissed angrily.

"Well, you're doing a bad job at stopping me," I spat, slowly leaning away from her.

"You're going to get in so much trouble once I call the police!"

"Go ahead. Call them." I laughed, ripping my wrist away from her. "Good luck trying to explain what happened." I smirked, glancing at Stella and Eela waiting for me. I pushed the door slightly more closed with my foot as I materialized a pistol in front of her aunt's face, slamming it roughly into her nose. I quickly darted out the front door, slamming it shut as she yelped in pain to help drown out her cry.

"Where are we going, True?" Eela asked softly, clinging to my arm as I passed her. Stella took the suitcase from her shaking hands with a gentle grin down at her and followed me.

"We're going back to my place… It's near the training school." I sighed, bringing my arm around her and glancing down warmly at her. Eela nodded, keeping her gaze on the ground with a worried frown. My heart spiked in my chest as I tightened my arm around her, glancing at Stella's intent gaze with a frown.

Don't look at me like that—

Stella smiled into her hand as she slowly looked away from my concerned expression at her.

CHAPTER 15

THIRTY MINUTES LATER...

I rubbed my face gently as I walked through the building complex's doors.

"Hey True!" Katie, the woman working the front desk, announced. I waved at her and gently encouraged Eela towards Stella as I walked towards the counter. "I need to finish paying for my old apartment and get one of the suites on the 11th floor please." I sighed, fumbling for the envelope of money. Katie nodded, grinning down at the monitor in front of her and quickly pulled her glasses on. Her dark mahogany hair fell over her shoulders as she leaned down and started typing into the keyboard.

I glanced over my shoulder to see Stella's smug expression with a raised brow at me. I rolled my eyes and glared at her before turning back to Katie at the desk. Eela giggled softly into her arm as Stella mumbled something to her. Katie amusedly glanced up from the keyboard at Stella and Eela then at me for a moment before she continued typing. *I'm glad you're on the same level of thinking as me, Katie. I know regardless of what I do, you won't say anything to authorities if they come looking for me.* I shifted slowly and shivered as I pushed my pistol further into my hoodie pocket. Katie took the envelope in front of me off the counter as she leaned down and handed me the new room key.

"There you go." Katie grinned. I tipped my head to her and sighed at Stella's gaze at me as I walked towards the elevators.

After bringing my things from my old apartment on the lower floors, Eela and Stella helped me unpack and organize things in the new suite. Every time Stella noticed Eela or I becoming distracted from organizing and thinking about Mr. Keilot, she would begin teasing me. Stella would bring up embarrassing stories from our hangouts at the museum and at the café's downtown, making Eela and I laugh each time. Stella eventually put on music and danced with Eela around the suite and around me, purposefully knocking into me when I refused to dance with them. Once we'd put everything away and ate dinner, Eela went to her room to begin setting up while Stella and I sat on the balcony of the suite after she cleaned the wound on my side.

Cold wind swept across the balcony as I struggled to light my cigarette. Stella stood leaning on the glass railing, staring at the upper-class buildings towering in the distance. Loud car horns echoed through the lively city over the bustling music and echo of conversation weaving its way through the buildings. Thin clouds passed swiftly overhead, blocking most of the dim stars shining down onto the city. My heart swelled slightly in my chest at remembering the moment of peace I felt in the backstreets of New York. Seeing the groups of stars pulsing with light through the clouds filled me with a new sense of hope for myself. Stella glanced at me over her shoulder and sighed, bringing her hand up to her face.

She took my cigarette swiftly and blew a short spurt of flame onto it, lighting it easily before handing it back to me with a raised brow. I widened my eyes as I glanced at the lit cigarette in my hand and turned away from her smug gaze down at me as she sat down. I blinked away the spike in my chest with a frown as I sighed, looking down to the balcony tile below us. Stella shifted in the seat next to me as she stared at the bright lights of the city skyscrapers in front of us with a small grin. I glanced at her in the corner of my eye as the stern look in her grey eyes faded into something calm.

"So, since we're living together basically..." Stella began softly. "Does that mean we're dating now? Are you like my husband or something?" she snarked playfully, glancing mischievously at me. I widened my eyes and looked at her with a furrowed brow as she snickered into her hand.

"What? No!" I awkwardly laughed, shaking my head at her. "You're just a friend who agreed to work under me with whatever I decide to do with myself to help others..." I mumbled softly.

"Oh? So, you're a top?" Stella slyly asked, elbowing me roughly. I groaned as I brought my hand in front of my face, holding back a smile as Stella playfully narrowed her eyes at me.

"I think we should get to know each other, you know, not as simple acquaintances," Stella sighed after a few minutes of silence. "Sure, we've known each other for two years, but I still know so little about you," she whispered, nudging my arm. I frowned as I kept my gaze on the buildings in front of me. "You're still the awkward, quiet, kind guy I met on the street." She giggled softly, glancing slyly at me again. I held back a smile as I shook my head. "Yes, I still called you awkward even though you currently have the Elites and police looking for you—" she groaned playfully.

"That has nothing to do with me being awkward—" I began, looking at her sharply with a smile.

"You obviously know more about me because I run my mouth sometimes," Stella chuckled, running her fingers along the side of her face for a moment. The corners of her eyes flickered slightly as she furrowed her brow. I widened my eyes slightly as I saw small puncture scars lining around her lips. She sighed and shook her head, blinking the light in her eyes away as she hopefully turned to me. "What about you?" she asked softly. "What caused you to be so…down? So quiet and drawn back?" she continued, her brow furrowing with worry. I narrowed my eyes slightly as I frowned and put my cigarette out, blinking away the smoke being pushed into my eyes.

"I can't name a single thing in my life that was good and made me happy except for brief moments with my father, Mr. Keilot and his daughter," I softly snapped, crushing the cigarette even more. "Everything else is demented and not worth me explaining," I spat, my voice wavering.

"Please, I want to help." Stella sighed. "How can I work with someone I know nothing about?" she tried, nudging my arm gently. I closed my eyes and rubbed my forehead softly as I shook my head. *I don't understand why you want to waste your time on me. You could be doing things much greater and meeting people better than me… Why choose to stay with a nobody like me?*

"I've been an orphan since I was seven," I began slowly, keeping my gaze away from Stella. "I watched both of my parents get killed in front of me, and I couldn't have done anything to help them," I scoffed, my voice wavering. I flicked my hair out of my face and narrowed my eyes down at the tile floor as I held back a growl of annoyance. Stella's eyes were wide as she looked intently at me, her brow furrowed with worry. I bit my lip slightly as I shook my head, clenching my fists.

"Skip a few years down into my life from living on the streets, and you find me trying to kill myself," I half laughed, feeling my face flush with embarrassment. I pulled my hoodie collar down slightly, revealing a scar on my left collarbone as I kept my eyes down. Stella tensed as she frowned at me. "The details aren't worth wasting my breath on. You get the gist of how screwed up my life has been," I growled, clenching my fists. Stella nodded, looking at the buildings in front of us for a moment. *It's fine if you leave. I wouldn't want to deal with someone like me either.*

"I'm proud of you," Stella suddenly whispered. I flinched and widened my eyes, turning to her quickly. "I knew you were going through or went through something rough when I met you, but," she trailed off. "I'm glad you're still here and breathing, and I'm glad I've met you, especially with what you're currently going through, so I can help," she explained, staring intently at me. My heart spiked out of my chest, as Stella's eyes were filled with worry. I nodded, looking away from her and inhaled sharply to respond. The glass sliding door behind us suddenly was pulled open.

Stella stood up quickly as I tensed and looked over my shoulder with widened eyes. Eela was standing in the doorway, tears in her eyes as she looked at me.

"So that's why my dad always came to check on you," Eela admitted softly. Stella sighed, bringing her hand to her face as she turned away from Eela's hurt tone. "I remembered you were always tired and quiet… I never understood or thought of why though," she continued. I stood up and slowly walked to her, holding my arms out. "It's *stupid* to think about now since I'm older, but did my hugs not help as much as I thought they did?" Eela asked, her voice breaking.

My heart caved in my chest as I pulled her into a hug while she crumbled to her knees in front of me.

"No, no, they helped. More than you could ever imagine," I quickly explained, my voice wavering. Tears filled my eyes as I tightened my grip on Eela. She began crying again, hugging me tighter.

"I can't lose you, too…" she whimpered through her cries.

I widened my eyes, taking deep breaths as my heart quickened in my chest, pounding stronger than it ever has before.

"I promise you, Eela," I breathed softly, blinking away tears in my eyes. "I will never try doing that to myself again. I will never leave you. Ever,"

CHAPTER 16

A FEW ROUGH MONTHS LATER...

Through determination and hard work from the three of us, we had finally gotten back onto our feet. Being forced even further away from the glory of the light in the upper class, Stella and I turned to the shadows for those looking to help. Every day, we scouted the streets, peering around in the "Underworld" for those who would be interested in changing the way things have been for hundreds of years. Money and power dictated everything about your life, those determined to not be worth anything useful to the government after having their mandatory evaluation would immediately be sent to the lower class. No one really knew what they were looking for in each person. Those who were accepted were forced into silence.

Many people forced into the shadows grew a strong liking for my plans, immediately spreading the word themselves. With how quickly my plans spread through the shadows, those peering in from the light even had their interests sparked. Powerful people of the Underworld working in secrecy in the basking light of the upper-class even reached out, eager to help. It didn't take long for applications to start piling up either. I accepted very few and only those who I knew I could trust with this delicate operation. Most of the Underworld, working businesspeople, or lowlife scavengers like myself, wanted in and wanted a change. My plans had finally given hope to those who had been lost for so long on the fault of the Elites abusing their privileges with the government.

When word of my plan spread through rumors to the mayor of New York, the entire city slowly began changing. The once ignorant and selfish people of the media began watching their backs, flaunting their successes less and less and speaking more carefully in public. Everyone in power began becoming weary of everyone around them, fearing that they were working for my plans. The civilians who had been fighting against them for so long had started to band together, pressing on further in places my own people couldn't reach. Finally, the rest of the city had begun to taste their own medicine: *fear.*

The lower-class sector had been dropped completely from being controlled by Elites and officers at merging guard posts. The mayor wanted nothing to do with us underdogs. The lower-class sector fell into control under me and my thought process. After influence from the Elites being forced away, the lower-class sector flourished. The people living in the Underworld began to work together against the greater evil. I had changed the lower-class sector to a place where people no longer had to walk with their head down in fear of being killed or attacked by the Elites prowling the streets looking for trouble.

The whole continent knew my name and my plans. I was labeled as, '*True Leader,*' the country's most dangerous and powerful villain, and I was proud of it. Cities across the country began to grow wary of the tensions rising in New York because of my ideals. Unrests sparked across every city, regardless of population or the social classes. The Underworld had begun to unite as one under me after years of turmoil. Together, my group of anxious three had grown into a strongly knit Agency, even extending beyond my home's walls. The shadows of society finally had enough of being forgotten and were beginning to take back their place.

In life, you either die a hero or you live long enough to see yourself become the villain.

I suddenly shuddered myself awake with a small gasp. My breaths were quick as I held my chest tightly in my shaking hands. I blinked my blurry eyes several times before I rubbed my face gently with a wince. The suite was completely silent as dim light filtered through the curtains from the glass door to my left. Faded silhouettes of the skyscrapers lined the floor and walls of the room as I stared at the ceiling for a moment with a frown. I inhaled slowly as I gently pushed myself up on my elbow, gripping my aching head in my hand. I shook my head gently as I glanced over my shoulder at Stella sleeping peacefully with her back to me. *That…totally shouldn't have happened…* I groaned slightly as I sat up and gripped the side of the bed for a moment.

I stood up, wincing as I knocked into the nightstand next to the bed. I fearfully glanced at Stella as she shifted slightly. I held my hand out to the lamp with a frown before I fumbled around the side of the bed to my desk in the front of the room. My shaking hands patted the cold wood before I grabbed my hoodie off the chair and pulled it on swiftly, turning back around to the bed. I briskly walked towards the nightstand, taking a cigarette and my lighter from the drawer. I turned to the glass sliding door and paused with a slight frown, shaking my head and walking away from it. *It'll make too much noise.*

My bedroom door gently groaned as I pushed it open and stepped out into the main room. I flinched at seeing Cohen sitting on the couch with crossed arms. His dark hair stuck out messily from under the beanie on his head while his sleeve-tattooed, burly arms shifted slightly at my presence. I kept my gaze away from him as I silently walked across the room, sliding the glass door to the balcony open with a sigh. Cool air smacked me in the face as I shivered, tipping my head away from the breeze as I slid the door shut. The noises of the lively, waking city filled my ears as I slowly walked across the balcony, lighting my cigarette. Loud conversations and distant car horns lined the crisp air, echoing throughout the buildings as I sat in a chair, my face resting in my hands, tuning out the noise.

"Sorry if I woke you up, sir," an anxious voice suddenly apologized. I flinched, standing halfway up and bringing my arm out in front of me with widened eyes. "I'm sorry!" Fletcher cried, stepping away from me and holding out his shaking hands.

"Don't do that," I growled, rubbing my forehead. "I could have shot you!" I hissed, narrowing my eyes at him. I slowly sat back down, ignoring my heart racing in my ears as I shook my head and stared at new sunlight beginning to reflect off the buildings in front of the balcony. I glanced behind me to see Fletcher kneeling on the floor on the other side of the balcony with a small bag of tools next to him.

"I was fixing the outlet…" Fletcher mumbled softly. "You scared me when you came out here, but I guess you didn't see me," he chuckled, rubbing the back of his neck. His warm, brown skin began to almost glow from the vibrant sunlight reflecting off the glass buildings onto us. I shook my head and sighed as I closed my eyes from being blinded for a moment by a sunray.

"Next time don't stay silent, please. You almost gave me a heart attack," I spat, holding back a smile at his worried expression. Fletcher nodded quickly, glancing worriedly at Cohen, who was shaking his head at him through the glass. Once Fletcher went back inside and I finished my cigarette, I heard Stella and the others slowly begin waking up.

The glass sliding door behind me opened gently, making me shiver as my heart spiked in my chest. I glanced behind me as Stella stepped out from the room with a small grin at me. I furrowed my brow slightly as she nudged my shoulder with her hand, leaning down towards me.

"You're tense, even more than last night," Stella sighed, rubbing my neck gently as I closed my eyes briefly. "I know you're nervous about today," she mumbled. "Try and think positive! I think we'll get a lot done today," she beamed proudly, shaking my shoulders gently. I held back a smile as I brought my hand to my face. I nodded slightly as Stella turned and walked back inside.

Everyone's voices from inside the suite continuously became louder as I sat in silence on the balcony, watching the sky become brighter and brighter. Eventually, everyone's conversations from inside the suite were drowned out by the awakening city. More and more music began to beat heavily through the air as the sound of cars filled the streets, echoing throughout the buildings. Cool wind swept across the balcony, sending a shiver down my spine as I pulled out my phone. I grinned down at the screen with pride as I checked the headlines on the news.

"Breaking News: The northside Elite headquarters has been attacked for the second time this month. The raging riot outside the main doors escalated from a protest within a matter of seconds as more people showed up chanting True Leader's phrase: 'Justice Reversed.' The people outside the doors became more and more violent, giving no time for the guards outside the building to follow safety precautions. Several arrests have been made with zero fatalities as of this morning," the news reporter groaned. I clicked away from the video with a sigh as I shook my head.

"Of course, they blame my followers," I mumbled, frowning down at the images taken for the headline. *We'll pay this place a visit to calm things down then.*

I pushed open the sliding door into the suite and immediately felt a headache form on the sides of my head. Eela and Cami were in the kitchen cooking with Fletcher as Randy and Maeve argued from the dining table. Cohen and Stella sat across from Randy and Maeve, watching amusedly as Randy did most of the talking in the playful argument. Randy's curly, brown hair fell in front of his eyes as he brought his hand to his face after Maeve's disapproving scowl met his gaze. Maeve glared at Randy with a quick glance at Stella before she shook her head and rolled her eyes, looking back down at her phone. Randy nudged her gently with his foot to get her attention as he grinned. Maeve immediately reached for her knife on the table next to her. Stella quickly slid it away from her grasp with a frown as Maeve glared up at her through her dull red hair. *What's the crazy guy rambling about today, huh?* I held back a smile as Maeve shot me an annoyed glare while I walked towards everyone as Randy giggled into his hands.

"Are you all up to 'calm down' a riot disturbing the Elite's northside headquarters?" I sighed with fake empathy. Everyone shifted with excitement as they turned towards me leaning on the kitchen counter. I grinned softly down at my hands as everyone's eyes filled with mischief, and they slyly glanced at each other. Eela smiled happily at me from the sink as Cami shoved Fletcher out of her way with a small giggle. Cami's blonde hair contrasted the light freckles on her face, making her nose ring glint in the low lights from above. Fletcher yelped with disapproval as he knocked into Eela, and the three of them began playfully arguing.

After everyone ate, Randy, Cohen, and I stayed behind at the suite while Stella took the others on a quick scouting mission to view how serious the riot was. I sat with my arms crossed on the couch, listening to the news as Randy and Cohen sat on the balcony, peering down at the busy streets below. I glared at the reporters talking quickly on the screen, showing select images of the Elites and police officers being the victims and my followers being the antagonists. *Bullshit. I have video proof from some of my scouts of a whole different side of this event.* My heart spiked out of my chest with worry as I turned the tv off as the subject changed.

I furrowed my brow for a moment before quickly turning the TV back on, clenching my fists slightly.

"A new trio made their debut action today here in New York City! These three are the top three retired Elites coming back to help during this time of chaos," the reporter beamed. I tipped my head slightly as I furrowed my brow. *Top three Elites, my ass. Those three have horrible records of abusing their government-granted access to hurt innocent civilians. Why the hell are they back now?* I narrowed my eyes as the reporter continued to explain as I leaned down to the table in front of me for a pen. I quickly threw it at the glass sliding door to the balcony, making Cohen and Randy flinch and turn towards me. I flicked my hand at them and glanced at the TV with a furrowed brow as they stood up and jogged inside.

"Officials haven't been able to get a strong hold on the three to speak to them, but their actions are louder than their minimal words!" The reporter chuckled. "In the alleyways, graffiti and posters idolizing True Leader and his horrid morals have been destroyed or painted over with the Elite symbol. Evidence of burned piles of missing posters have also been found throughout the city's garbage dumps," they continued. Randy clenched his fists as he narrowed his eyes at the screen while small flickers of white flames came from behind Cohen's ears.

"What is this about?" Randy snarled, waving his hand at the TV. I shook my head in disgust as more images were placed onto the screen. Cohen's face stayed emotionless as he glanced at Randy radiating with anger next to him.

"We advise you all to steer clear of these three for now. Their actions may be helpful to us, but they are still violating code and could be dangerous," the reporter warned. I mumbled under my breath as I muted the TV.

"Those three are the least of this city's worries," Randy hissed, turning towards me expectantly. "We'll deal with them when we cross paths." I growled, rubbing my forehead. Cohen stared at the screen, staying silent with no expression as Randy began pacing back and forth across the living room.

"Why do you seem so calm about this?" Randy asked, roughly pushing Cohen's shoulder. Cohen rolled his eyes with a quick, fiery glare at him before they both turned to me staring at the ground. *Don't start breaking down on me now...*

"Do you lack confidence in me that I won't fix this?" I asked bluntly, standing up slowly. "Do you not remember who took down the most powerful and corrupt Elites in this city with only a wave of their hand?" I growled, leaning towards him with clenched fists. Cohen shifted uncomfortably as my gaze at Randy darkened. Randy's amber eyes were wide with worry and anger as he stared at me through his shaggy curls. "You shouldn't worry about anything this damned city throws at us," I glowered. "You only worry if I'm dead. While I'm alive, *nothing* will be able to stop my plans," I snarled. "These three will not be a problem to us, I'll make sure of it,"

CHAPTER 17

Nearing the Elite Northside Headquarters...

Echoes of the riot around the deserted street corner weaved around the air like whips. Wind ripped violently through the concrete jungle all around us, sending packs of trash and debris below us as we slowly made our way through the broken buildings. Glass crunched roughly under our feet as we stepped over fallen signs and streetlights. Slight haze hung over the roads; the sun's rays visible through beams of light breaking through the building's corners. Angry voices and chants drowned out the distant noises of the busy city surrounding the nearest blocks. The looted buildings towering over us groaned in grief with every gust of wind.

I ran my hand gently along the outside of the gas mask around my face with a small grin as I glanced over my shoulder at everyone else trailing behind me. A prideful chill shot down my back as Stella's light eyes met mine through the pristine glass of her mask. *Once I have better control over my smoke, we won't have to use these anymore...* I glanced down at my hand with a slight frown as pitch-black smoke weaved its way between my fingers. *Too much of a risk for any of you to inhale this after I've covered you all to protect you.* I shifted uncomfortably at the distant memory of my mother's smoke wrapped around my father's neck after suddenly ducking into an alleyway.

I shook the thought away as I carefully peered around the old brick building, my heart beating out of my chest. A large crowd of angry people stood gathered around the Elite headquarters. Rows of armed guards lined the destroyed building front with sour expressions.

"Justice Reversed! Justice Reversed!" the people chanted angrily; their voices lined with indignation. Cami's voice gently echoed the chant through the intercom system on the inside of my gas mask as I grinned at her over my shoulder. *Your phrase caught on well with my followers.* I inhaled sharply as my heart spiked in my chest from seeing an armed guard shove someone down. *I'm glad you all are on the same page as me. Get rid of the fake Elites, no questions asked.*

I lifted my hand slowly to Randy, waving it in an arch to an old ladder mounted on the brick wall across from me with a quick glance at Fletcher. Randy trembled with excitement as he leapt up the ladder, mumbling quickly to himself.

"Once we have the guards' attention, I'll have Fletcher help us keep the upper hand." I ordered sternly, turning to everyone looking expectantly at me. "We need to try and keep the guards distracted, so we can attempt to make it inside the building." I grumbled, glancing up at the tall skyscraper looming through the haze. "If things get too heated and we get shot at, wait for me to take care of the bullets,"

"Cami, Cohen, Stella, you will create a fire screen for us to escape if needed," I sighed with a small chuckle. "Eela, Maeve, stay near Randy on the ladder and keep watch if back up troops make their way down the block," I continued, turning back to the chanting crowd.

"What if that trio shows up?" Cohen asked gruffly. I blinked slowly as I leaned away from the wall.

"If they show up, we'll just have to show them how our 'Justice Reversed' works," I beamed darkly. *The moment I step out into the street that trio will come. I know they will. So hungry for attention that they're stupid enough to attack my agency and I head on.* Everyone shifted in pride under my sharp gaze as I waved my hand to the street and stepped away from the cover of the alley.

The crowd gathered outside the towering building immediately roared with delight at my appearance. The two-word chant only became louder and filled with more passion as I slowly stalked across the street towards them. Armed guards at the doors tensed, raising their guns in my direction as I harmlessly held out my hands to my sides, smirking at them from under my gas mask. *What will you decide? Focus on me and risk letting them inside? Or ignore me, and let my agency and I have some fun?* A chill shot down my back as the crowd began to roar with noise again as they suddenly pushed forward.

The ground below everyone suddenly shifted. The once jagged concrete was softened into a Jell-O state, rippling like a wave. The ground bent over on itself before snapping back into place like a whip. Buildings down the street groaned as they rose and fell with the wave of the sudden moving concrete. I glanced to my left to see Fletcher with both his palms on the ground, his gaze intently on the headquarters entrance. The crowd yelped in panic as they all were thrown off their feet. Their panicked tones immediately faded as multiple of them helped others back up and darted towards the fallen guards.

"Randy! Now!" I ordered harshly into the gasmask radio, wrapping Fletcher carefully in my pitch-black smoke.

"Hell yea!" Randy's adrenaline filled voice beamed.

The sky above us shifted as I glanced up to see a cloud of pristine glass particle specs. The small shards grouped together as an illusion of one large pane of glass before breaking away into millions of small shards, glistening like dangerous diamonds in the sunlight. The armed guards stumbled in the warped street, yelling angrily at the rioters charging towards them as the glass shards from Randy knocked them back to the ground with cries of pain. Guards from inside the headquarters slid past the rest, ignoring the harsh glass rain.

I held out my hands slowly as gunshots began to violently echo through the tense air. The shots ripped through the cleared streets, weaving their way all throughout the concrete jungle surrounding us. My vision tunneled on each individual bullet as they slowed to a stop in front of me, floating harmlessly in a dome around me. The rioters pushing past the fallen guards yelled in delight as they made it inside the building. The few stragglers, startled by the gunfire, simply turned and fled down the street. My heart spiked in annoyance as armed guards shoved people to the ground inside the main lobby of the building. *Too risky. They have their defenses up higher this time than last month.* I frowned slightly as I waved my hand quickly, and the gunfire ceased. The floating bullets around Fletcher and I were suddenly fired back directly towards their source.

"We'll have to wait! Defense is too high! Let the rioters keep trying; we'll get a report in a few days!" I ordered calmly into the gasmask.

Several small shadows shot across the street as spray paint cans slammed into the building. The spray paint cans rolled calmly, knocking into the armed guards' feet as a slow hissing sound began to howl. The armed guards stumbled away in a panic as I smirked pridefully at their terrified faces behind their helmets. I turned away quickly, grabbing Fletcher's shoulder as I darted across the street. The spray paint cans suddenly burst, sending clouds of yellow, pink, green, and blue into the air, hindering everyone's view.

Confused yelling from the guards and remaining rioters sounded roughly through the tense air. The gasmask around my face worked tirelessly to filter the paint from coming into the mask. As I ducked into the alley, all particles of the paint were suddenly lifted away from us. I glanced up at Randy leaning halfway off the ladder with his hands out, a mischievous grin on his face. *Nice touch.* Moments later, a single spark of white flame shot from Cohen's fingertips into the particle filled street. The spray paint hovering in the air surged away from us as powerful flames ignited, rolling towards the building. Guards yelled in panic as helicopters above began screaming orders, the blades holding them up became slightly more distant from shying away from the flame filled air.

Come on! Where are you? I clenched my fists tightly as I stared at the armed guards patting the fires on their armor out quickly. The remaining rioters were restrained on the ground, guns to their prideful expressions towards us.

"You can't hide or escape, True Leader!" the voice from the helicopter above snarled.

"Who says I'm doing either of those!" I snarled back, pressing on the side of my mask to let my voice be projected.

"What are you doing?" Maeve hissed angrily, nudging my arm. I glared at her over my shoulder as Stella narrowed her eyes slightly.

"Drawing that stupid Elite trio here. I'm not leaving until they understand I'm not *fucking* messing around," I snapped. Eela and Cami snickered softly as Maeve rolled her eyes and jogged down the alley mumbling.

"Come to think of it!" I yelled again, clenching my fists as I turned back to the street. "Shouldn't the Elites be the ones running and hiding?" I asked proudly. The restrained rioters screamed in angry agreement as the guards holding them down ordered them to stop talking. "Hasn't there been thousands of videos with proof of Elites abusing their government granted power?" I snapped. "Maybe you haven't seen them yet because the media hides the *ugly truth!*" I laughed darkly. Cohen and Stella shifted behind me angrily as Cami and Eela glanced at one another. The armed guards scanned the street with raised guns, with worried gazes at the other.

"You all know it! You're working for a corrupt system!" I beamed darkly. Sharp pain struck me in the right side of the head as I shivered.

"*We have company!*" Maeve warned inside my head. "*SWAT teams are surrounding the block on every side. That Elite trio is making their way here now, but I only see two of them and can't find the other,*"

The pain faded out through the left side of my head as I chuckled softly. *Knew it.* I glanced behind me, signaling with my hand to keep a sharp eye out. *You pathetic guards better back away. I won't feel bad if any of you get injured with this trio here.* I clenched my fists slightly as I furrowed my brow and stepped out from behind the cover of the alley.

The armed guards released the rioters immediately as I walked towards them. The wind ripped through the streets, howling like a pack of angry wolves. The rioters all gazed pridefully at me with large smiles before they all chanted as they backed away peacefully, shooting dark glances at the guards. The remaining guards backed away, lowering their heads and guns as I continued walking across the street. *Finally got the hint. Guns don't work on me.* A chill shot down my spine as I suddenly turned around with a frown.

"I knew you would show up!" I yelled loudly. "Want to prove you're not all bark and no bite?" I laughed, raising my hand to the duo stalking around the corner of the building.

"It's over, True Leader!" one of the Elites chuckled coldly. The rusted Elite badge on his chest shimmered slightly as the sun caught the metal peering out from under the corruption.

"Is it now?" I asked. I glanced down at myself and raised my hands calmly. The duo paused with furrowed brows at me as I smirked slowly. "It's over; you caught me," I sneered at them. My gaze glanced at my Agency watching me worriedly from the alley. *Don't worry. I know what I'm doing.* I inhaled sharply as I began wrapping them all in my smoke.

My heart spiked out of my chest as a figure in the corner of my eye moved. In a broken window of the skyscraper to my left, a gun scope suddenly loomed out of the darkness. My eyes widened as I turned to Randy climbing higher up the ladder. *Quit moving away! I can't reach—*

"Randy!" I snarled, stepping sideways towards them. A loud gunshot suddenly echoed through the air. My vision tunneled too slowly as a thin bullet fired from the barrel of the narrow gun. Randy yelped as he leaned away from the ladder, lifting one of his hands. The thin bullet violently struck his other wrist gripping the metal tightly as my heart fell from my chest.

"GAHHH!" Randy howled. Eela and Cami yelped in panic as Cohen tensed up at him. The ladder dented inwards from the bullet grazing it snapped under Randy's weight. My heart spiked out of my chest again as I watched Randy's legs get forced out from under him as he gripped his wrist in pain and slid roughly down the ladder. He fell helplessly through a red and gold canopy covering the entrance of a shop to my right, landing roughly onto the concrete below. Dark laughter filled the air as Maeve rounded the alley corner with widened eyes and joined Cami in dragging Randy behind the cover of the wall.

I narrowed my eyes, materializing a pistol in the air in front of the window. The figure shrieked in surprise as the pistol fired several times at them, sending them to the ground, their gun falling from the window. Quick and sudden gunfire from the fallen gun sounded through the air, piercing the cracked glass panes of the buildings around us as I ducked my head away. The Elite duo charged across the street towards me as Cohen suddenly sided up next to me, grabbing my wrist. We flinched as we darted away to the alley while another spray paint can suddenly exploded directly in front of the Elites.

Yells of confusion filled the air as I saw Cami and Eela bolt across the street through the cover of the bright red paint. Water suddenly surged up from a broken fire hydrant, shooting up into the air like a fountain. As the water gathered on the street below, the concrete warped slightly, creating several pools buried within the smoothed corners. I smiled in pride as I watched Eela crouch to the ground. Moments later, the pools of water came to life. The water shot up from the pools, animated in the air beautifully as it rose higher and higher into the paint and drizzle filled air.

Water suddenly surged all around us in an animated tidal wave, weaving gracefully through the air, avoiding us perfectly. The Elite duo and all the armed guards were violently slammed into the ground by the rushing water. I gazed up as bright blue figures filled the warped concrete below from the sunlight travelling through the water. Though it seemed peaceful as it surrounded Cohen and I, frozen in the street, behind the calm mask was a tsunami force of pressure built up, waiting to slam into anything that touches it. The water walls around us slowly moved in a pathway for us to follow as I stared at the two Elites struggling against the water, lying helplessly on their backs on the cracking concrete.

Cohen pulled me into the alley as the water wall surged shut behind us. Maeve carefully detached Randy's cracked gas mask off his head as Fletcher held his bleeding wrist tightly. Randy coughed hollowly as he gasped in pain with narrowed eyes. I furrowed my brow down at them as Stella glared roughly at me from under the water splattered glass eye holes. *He moved too far for me to reach.* I glanced over my shoulder up at the tall water wall bristling with force under the surface with pride as I found Cami and Eela's warped images on the other side of the street through the stream of floating water. I clenched my fists as I frowned back down at Randy before I stepped towards the street again.

"Going back out is stupid!" Cohen gruffly snarled, grabbing my wrist tightly. I ripped my wrist away from him as I turned sharply back at him with a furrowed brow. "You can't go alone," he spat after a few moments of tense silence. The water wall behind me suddenly slammed to the ground, sending a small wave of pristine water below our feet as Cami and Eela ran swiftly across the street.

"The two Elites and the SWAT teams surrounding the block are currently hindered," Cami explained.

"Perfect," I grinned, glancing one last time at Randy grimacing in agony as blood dripped from his wrist. *This trio is learning what 'Justice Reversed' really means. Right now.* I nudged Cami and Cohen forward as I walked swiftly back out from the alleyway. "We'll catch up with you soon. The rest of you, head back to the suite. Stay out of sight!" I ordered. Stella nodded once, pushing Eela forward gently as Fletcher and Maeve helped Randy stand.

Cohen, Cami, and I walked calmly through the flooded street as cascades of water flew from the broken fire hydrant. My gaze rested intently at the two Elites, helplessly lying in the flooded ground. Cohen glanced up around the intersection with a frown as the SWAT teams slowly gathered themselves back from the rushing water. I stared down at both Elites with a frown as the "leader" of the once trio glared darkly up at me. My heart raced in my chest as I slowly leaned down towards him with a small grin.

"You really think you three retired Elites could take down the most feared man in New York City?" I sneered calmly. The man's exhausted eyes widened in pure fear as I stared down at him.

"True—" Cami gasped. I flinched as Cohen was suddenly struck by a powerful jet of cold water. He struggled against the water for a moment, boiling rage breaking through his once calm expression.

"You all don't give up, do you!" I snarled coldly as the water stopped. Cohen trembled with anger as he clenched his soaked fists, weak flames spurting from behind his eyes while he rubbed his short beard with the back of his hand. My heart ached slightly in my chest as I remembered him explaining to me his past. Images of him being blasted with cold water in the prison he once was in filled my mind as I frowned at his slowly calming expression. I glared across the street to the firemen holding a hose tightly in their shaking hands with armed guards surrounding them.

I wrapped Cohen and Cami in my smoke gently as I materialized two pistols in the air, aimed down at the two Elites.

"You're surrounded!" an angry voice snarled from down the street.

"And?" I yelled angrily, firing both pistols several times. SWAT and police officers shifted uncomfortably as my gaze darkened up at them while I turned to face the three ways we were surrounded. *You all know you can't stop me. Bullets have no use on a man with a power involving guns.* I glared down at the two Elites on the ground still for a moment before I waved my hand and turned on my heel. The SWAT and police officers watched helplessly, lowering their guns as we calmly walked away.

CHAPTER 18

AN HOUR LATER...

I burst through the backdoor of the building complex with a grumble.

"Get Dr. Briner up to the suite, now!" I snarled, waving my hand at Katie sitting at the front desk. I held the door open for Maeve and Fletcher as they struggled to keep Randy on his feet. Katie widened her eyes at the sight of Randy's bloody wrist as she nodded quickly, dialing something on the phone in front of her. I shook my head in annoyance as everyone filtered through the narrow door, heading straight for the elevator across the room. Katie frowned slightly at me as she began typing on her computer again.

"He's coming." she sighed, putting the phone down gently. I grinned quickly at her, shutting the door roughly before jogging after everyone.

"You're lucky Dr. Briner was available!" I snarled, slamming the front door to the suite. Dr. Briner shuffled quickly across the room as Fletcher sat Randy down in the center of the main room. Randy laughed angrily, flicking me off with his good hand as he glared at me through his shaggy curls. I held back a smile as I ran my hand through my hair and sighed as Dr. Briner crouched next to Randy's bleeding wrist with a frown.

"Just by looking at it, I can tell he'll be fine. It grazed the top of his wrist and not the direct joint." Dr. Briner gruffly mumbled, glaring darkly at me in the corner of his small eye. Everyone sighed in relief as Randy grimaced, closing his eyes tightly as Dr. Briner lifted his wrist. I furrowed my brow slightly at his glare and shook my head with a frown.

CHAPTER 19

Thirty minutes later...

Stella and Cohen sat on either side of me on the balcony. Cool wind gently raced along the streets, creating a slight hum in between the bars of the railing in front of us. Helicopters swarmed the city as loud car horns blared aggressively at one another. *Looks like our little stunt this morning didn't faze many people.* I clenched my fists as I shifted in my seat. *Of course, it wasn't going to be talked about. The officials backed away and gave in, letting us leave. Can't broadcast a loss against me, huh?* I glanced over my shoulder with a slight sigh as I frowned. Maeve sat next to Randy, who was sleeping on the couch, her cold gaze intently on his pain filled face. *If only I was faster—*

"Don't blame yourself, True." Stella sighed gently, nudging my shoulder. I blinked slowly as I turned back towards her saying nothing.

"Why? I didn't get him in my smoke fast enough,"

"That was the crazy bastard's own fault," Stella scoffed, waving her hand at the sliding door. "He moved out of your range willingly knowing he could be at risk." She frowned. Cohen nodded, keeping his silent gaze on the towering buildings in front of us. I shook my head as I rubbed the back of my neck before frowning down at my hands. Pitch black smoke slowly seeped from my palms as I shivered, clenching my fists tightly, drowning the smoke away.

"We accomplished nothing today," I spat. "We wasted time and left with one of us injured,"

"Quit being so dramatic," Stella groaned playfully. "We fueled your followers by showing them you're not afraid of the officials!" she explained proudly. "Hell, you even stopped that retired Elite trio easily!"

Cohen's dark eyes glanced over at Stella with amusement as she continued to try and hype me up. I shook my head and nodded, holding back a smile at her playful gaze. I inhaled to respond as violent rumbling filled the air.

The building complex trembled in agony as the three of us gripped our chairs tightly, warily looking at one another. Car horns blared louder from the street below as the skyscrapers surrounding our complex groaned angrily. Yells of confusion filled the street as distant police sirens began to weave their way through the trembling buildings.

"What is that?" Cohen asked sharply, standing up slowly. Stella and I carefully jogged to the railing, glaring down at where Cohen was staring. We furrowed our brows in confusion as people frantically ran out from the building's entrance from across the street. Stella gasped quickly, gripping my arm roughly.

The giant glass panes of the skyscraper were violently cracked along the street edge. I widened my eyes as people scattered in the street, pointing at the damaged building. A chill ran down my back as the cracks slowly climbed up the first few floors. A loud groan of agony from the cracking building echoed eerily through the tense, silent air. Stella glanced at me slowly as Cohen furrowed his brow, all three of us staying still. *Why is the building collapsing...?* I widened my eyes as the two front corners of the building suddenly shifted inwards.

Violent cracks raged up the glass panes of the building as an eerie screech of agony wailed through the air. Glass panes shattered as the metal beam frame of the building broke from the inside out. The metal corners of the building immediately gave in to its own weight. Stella, Cohen, and I watched in horror as the tall building suddenly began falling inwards on itself. People screamed in panic as they began sprinting away from the collapsing building. The two skyscrapers on either side of the falling building had their walls nearest to it shattered, clouds of glass swarmed the sky.

The three of us yelped in pain as a cloud of debris, dust, and glass was shot up from the street from the fallen building. Cohen coughed violently into his arm as he turned and quickly darted for the door. I grabbed Stella's arm, pushing her forward to the open door as I covered my face with closed eyes. My skin pricked with pain as small glass shards brushed against me. More and more dust and debris were flung through the air as we stumbled inside, coughing hollowly into our arms.

Cohen leaned his arm against the glass as he clutched his chest, grimacing in between coughs. Maeve and Randy warily stared at us as I shook my arms roughly, glass shards falling to the floor below us. Stella coughed into her arm as she breathed hoarsely, fumbling for the remote on the glass table in front of the couch. Eela, Cami, and Fletcher's heads peeked out from the hallway in concern as they widened their eyes as the room darkened from smoke, dust, and debris covering the light outside. *What just happened?* My heart spiked in my chest with worry as I imagined the people inside who didn't make it out in time. My chest ached painfully as Mr. Keilot's warm smile flashed in my mind.

"The downtown business district experienced another fallen skyscraper this afternoon," the news reporter on the TV groaned sorrowfully. The man on the screen fixed the messy papers on his desk as he worriedly stared at the camera as images were brought up onto the screen. "This is the third fallen building this month," the man growled. "Investigators are still stumped as to who or what is causing these collapses," he continued. "Rumors have begun to spread through the media of 'True Leader' being the one behind these tragedies, seeing as only large name business buildings relating to our Elites are being affected," I clenched my fists angrily as everyone shifted uncomfortably behind me.

"Has True Leader finally begun his line of action?" the man asked. "Has the most feared man in the city put his foot down after months of dangerous preparation?" he continued. "Are our Elites in danger?" he asked sharply. *They sure are…* The reporter began to go back to reading the reports on his desk as Stella turned the TV down slightly with a frown. We all glanced at each other for a moment with narrowed eyes before Eela pointed quickly at the screen behind me.

"Zoom in! There's someone on the building!" a quiet voice from the TV ordered. I turned over my shoulder as a helicopter camera panned over to a separate building rooftop slowly. "Is this the person behind these buildings collapsing?" the reporter cried. "Authorities are investigating this mystery person now—"

The channel suddenly glitched. We all shifted uncomfortably as I furrowed my brow at the screen. Stella changed the channel to a separate news station that also was capturing the image of the person standing on the rooftop. *That was weird...*

"Maeve, try and see if you can figure out who this is," I said softly, tipping my head to the person in all black crouched on the rooftop. Maeve jumped up slowly from the couch, squinting her dark eyes at the screen for a moment. The person crouched on the roof, pulled down their black mask for a split second before immediately turning away from the camera.

"Got her," Maeve beamed, closing her eyes slowly. *Why would she do that? Does this girl know about Maeve and her tracking ability?* The cameras zoomed in on the girl running across the rooftop and panned away before she disappeared behind an old billboard.

Maeve's brow furrowed as she held her head tightly in her shaking hands. Stella turned off the TV as Randy weakly darted across the room and caught Maeve as she stumbled over. She grimaced in pain as her breaths quickened.

"Maeve," Stella growled slowly as I crouched next to her. Randy gritted his teeth in pain as he used his wrapped wrist to hold her up.

"She knows you were watching, True..." Maeve breathed weakly. "She wants in... Meet her at central park," she explained, holding her head tighter. Everyone shifted uncomfortably again as Maeve's body jerked before she opened her eyes and gasped for breath.

"The kid's mind..." Maeve cried softly, moving her shaking hands away from her ears. I widened my eyes as a trail of blood ran down the side of her head, soaking into her hands. The bright blood proved how dull red her hair really was as it mixed against her light tan skin. "Constant screaming..." she whispered, frowning at her hands.

Eela slid to the floor next to Maeve, gently giving her a tissue before dabbing the side of her head. Maeve hissed in pain, leaning away from her touch with narrowed eyes. Eela frowned at her as Cami pulled her away and sighed at Randy holding Maeve. Stella and I worriedly stared at each other for a moment before I sighed and nodded.

"I'll go find her,"

CHAPTER 20

SEVERAL MINUTES LATER...

I merged into the frantic crowd with Cohen on his skateboard behind me. We slowly continued further and further down the street, away from the destroyed building surrounded by police and firefighters. I flicked my hood higher up on my head to hide my face as I pushed through the curious crowd watching. Cohen did his best to keep up with me, accidentally knocking the edge of his skateboard into the people's ankles around him. Dark and dirty looks were cast at both of us as he frowned, keeping his gaze on me, ignoring everyone around us. I rolled my eyes in annoyance as the street blocks around the fallen building seemed to be continuing normally with their day. *Proof no one cares about anyone but themselves…*

After Cohen and I walked through the park, searching for the girl for almost an hour, we both became annoyed at not finding her. I glared through the trees at the setting sun behind the towering skyline with a frown.

"This kid better not be wasting my time…" I growled, rubbing my head slowly. I sighed as I saw Cohen grab a tree branch to swing himself around towards me, pushing forward on his skateboard quickly. He grinned playfully at me as he circled me for a moment before stopping in front of me with a frown.

"If we can't find her, we'll just have to wait for Maeve to be able to speak to her again…" Cohen shrugged, seeming uninterested in her. I shook my head, gazing around at the people enjoying the evening at the park with a sigh.

"I don't know," I mumbled. "Maybe the kid has been trying to get my attention with the other buildings, but we only turned the news on with this one."

Cohen rolled his eyes and stepped back up on the skateboard, mumbling under his breath.

"She knows she doesn't have to just destroy things for attention, right?" he scoffed. "You have countless messengers and scouts throughout the city for new recruits," he sighed. I nodded and shook my head again.

"That's too easy," a shaky voice suddenly snapped, followed by a disappointed laugh.

Cohen and I flinched as we warily turned over our shoulders with furrowed brows. Cohen grabbed my wrist tightly as he stared angrily up at the tree towering above us. Gentle flickers of white flame shot from behind his dark eyes as he narrowed them up at the waving branches. I calmly pulled my wrist away from him and turned up to the tree with no emotion as my heart began to beat roughly out of my chest.

The girl from the news was kneeling up in the tree with narrowed eyes down at us. A sleek, armed bow rested in her trembling hands as she aimed it directly at me. Her long dark hair fell in front of her face as she scrunched her nose at us disapprovingly. I shivered as I stared into her ice-colored eyes for a moment and saw a glimpse of how much pain she was in. *Maeve wasn't kidding... What's wrong with this poor kid?* The three of us stood in tense silence as the girl leaned closer at me with a frown. Her scarred wrists peeked out from her dark sleeve, sending a spike of empathy into my chest.

"What are you doing?" I sighed, staring intently into her eyes and ignoring the arrow being aimed at me. The girl frowned as she lowered her bow slightly. Cohen leaned closer to me as he grumbled under his breath, making the girl tense again, lifting the bow to him.

"I can easily kill you, too, flame boy," the girl hissed. "True can't stop arrows, if I remember correctly." she scoffed. I raised my brows and nodded slowly as I tucked my hands into my pockets.

"Seriously kid," I growled. "What are you doing here? Why cause so much destruction for my attention?" I snapped, trying to mask the annoyance in my voice.

"Name's Ryth. Not *kid*," she hissed. I closed my eyes briefly as she brought back the tense bow, tucking the arrow into the older resting on her back. "I caused all of that destruction, for *you*," Ryth breathed pridefully. I widened my eyes slightly as she slowly lowered herself from the tree and landed roughly on the ground in front of me. "Am I strong enough for you now?" she asked sharply. Cohen and I glanced at each other for a moment before he rolled his eyes and backed away from her glare.

"I'm sorry," I chuckled. "I don't have any idea what you're talking about... Have we met before?" I sighed. Ryth narrowed her cold eyes and nodded.

"You turned me away when I applied to get into this Agency," she snapped. I widened my eyes slightly as my heart ached in my chest. "I still remember you turning down a man with an ice power before I came to you," Ryth haughtily explained. I shook my head and frowned at her. "I don't remember anyone from the tryouts who didn't make it. I have who I need," I sighed coldly. Cohen nodded once, narrowing his eyes at Ryth.

"Do you now?" Ryth scoffed offendedly. "Okay then. How are you going to get rid of the Elites if you can't make it into one of their buildings?"

"Watch it—" Cohen snarled darkly, stepping towards her. I held out my arm, shoving him away as Ryth tensed, stepping towards him as a bloody knife slid from her sleeve and into her shaking palm.

"Calm down, both of you," I sighed, rubbing my head gently. "She has a point..." I admitted, narrowing my eyes slightly at her. "Whatever reason I turned you away for, I don't remember, but I apologize." I sighed. "I should have seen your potential, and I guess I didn't at the time,"

"Cool, thanks. Does that mean I'm in?" Ryth excitedly smiled. Cohen rolled his eyes as she narrowed her own at him and I shook my head.

"Not yet," I sighed tiredly. "Sure, you're powerful but, what's your motive?" I asked. "What's driving you to want to join my Agency?"

"The drive to hurt those who've wronged me sounds pretty great right now," Ryth sneered. "Sounds familiar to you, huh?" she scoffed. I narrowed my eyes as Cohen turned away and mumbled under his breath. "I hate the Elites just as much as you do. They never showed when I needed them either!" she snarled. I blinked down at her as she began trembling with anger as her eyes hardened up at me. "Just imagine how much faster I can help your operation move if we can just take down the *buildings* of corrupt Elites!"

"Why are you so persistent on joining us?" Cohen asked gruffly.

"Because True is the only man with the drive and resources to succeed in his plans to take down the Elites. The rest have no spines!" she snapped. "I also agree with him the most out of the rest of lowlifes trying to make a change," she chuckled. "I think everyone stuck in the dark deserves a chance to be in the light instead of being shoved further from its reach," she snapped, clenching her shaking fists as her smile fell. Cohen stared intently at me with no emotion before he glanced at Ryth and sighed at her dimmed expression.

"People are just so horrible sometimes," Ryth whimpered, narrowing her cold eyes to the ground. I stared into Ryth's light eyes intently and shivered. I had seen a glimpse of my past-self inside her. Someone who was lost in their dark mind and had nothing left to keep them going the right direction. Someone who was pleading for help and receiving nothing in return, left alone and left behind. My heart began to beat out of my chest as something inside me snapped again like it had with Eela. *I can't leave you.* I frowned for a moment before I hesitantly stepped towards her, holding out my shaking hand. Ryth tensed as I slowly wrapped my arm around her and pulled her close to me. Her trembling body melted into my grasp as her breaths quickened and muffled cries escaped her mouth as she leaned into my shoulder. "You're in. I won't let anything happen to you," I whispered softly, closing my eyes as tears filled them.

Ryth clung to me tightly, keeping her head buried in my shoulder as Cohen followed me to an exit of the park. The setting sun casted golden rays and dark shadows from the buildings onto the ground below as people slowly made their way out of the park behind us. Cold wind swept across the park making Ryth shiver in my grasp as I slowly tightened my grip around her. Cohen frowned worriedly at her before he turned his gaze back to the path below as he pushed on, skating ahead of us.

"Is that girl alright, sir?" a sharp voice suddenly snapped from behind me. My heart spiked out of my chest as I continued walking, glaring at Cohen's glance at me over his shoulder.

"Yes, sir." I beamed softly, turning to the old man limping towards me. "She's fine. Tired, that's all," I sighed, grinning harmlessly at him. Cohen skated up beside me, his dark eyes narrowed at the old man glaring at us. His white flames flickered from the corner of his eye as he stared at the man for a moment. I nudged his shoulder roughly with my elbow as I saw his hand slowly reach behind him. *Don't you dare. Let me handle him.*

"She looks a lot like the kid from the news earlier...and you also look quite familiar!" the older man challenged. I narrowed my eyes at him and sighed while shaking my head.

"I don't know what you're talking about, sir. If you excuse me, I can get her home where she can rest properly," I calmly explained, my smile becoming faker.

"How do you know this girl exactly?" the man challenged.

Several people walked past us, shaking their heads in disappointment at the man bothering us with helpless glances of empathy at me.

I sighed gently and quickly linked my hand with Cohen's at his side, my eye twitching in pain from the harsh heat coming from his palm.

"She's our daughter, asshole," I lied, tipping my chin up at the old man. The man recoiled slightly as he widened his eyes and frowned at us.

"I apologize..." he grumbled softly. I huffed as I let go of Cohen's hand and nudged him forward, glaring at the man over my shoulder as we turned the corner to the sidewalk of the street. People around us snickered at the older man as he began to limp over to other people leaving the park.

After we walked for a few minutes in silence, I turned to Cohen and smiled playfully. Cohen's brow furrowed as he slowed himself on his board down.

"3...2..." I slowly began. **BAM!** A loud gunshot echoed through the once peaceful street. Screams of horror filled the park as I heard a man cry out in agony. "Tada," I scoffed, smirking down at the ground. Cohen smiled into his hand as he shook his head and glanced behind us at the people fleeing from the park. He shifted himself on the board by waving his arm as he knocked into a dip in the sidewalk.

"Was that the only thing you could have thought of back there?" he asked softly, raising his brow at me. I rolled my eyes at him and chuckled as Ryth snickered sleepily into my shoulder as she tightened her grip on me.

"Sorry," I sighed. "I needed to come up with something for him to leave us alone. Ryth needs to rest," I explained gently. Cohen nodded, staring at the police car shooting past us down the street.

"Nice touch," he sighed. "I didn't know you had your pistol with you," he winced.

I half laughed and shook my head.

"When do I not have it with me?" I scoffed. Cohen nodded with a playful nudge to my shoulder before he skated out of my reach.

CHAPTER 21

THE SUITE...

I closed the spare bedroom's door at the suite after I had laid Ryth down for her to rest. I turned and flinched at Eela standing behind me.

"Sorry," Eela giggled, bringing her hand to her face. I shook my head and pulled her towards me as I slowly walked into the main room. "Is she going to be okay?" she asked worriedly. I sat on the couch as Eela nestled next to me with a worried glance at the room in the beginning of the hallway. I nodded with a gentle grin down at her.

"Now that she's with us she will be," I sighed, rubbing Eela's shaking shoulder gently.

"She's scary...but powerful," Eela beamed, frowning down at her own hands.

"She may be both of those things, but she's also lonely and scared," I chuckled sadly. "Ryth is going to love you, Eela. I know you both will get along," I beamed, smiling down at her.

Eela nodded and grinned slightly.

"Knowing how you are, is she my new sister now?" Eela giggled. Stella and Cohen snickered from the kitchen as I glared at them over my shoulder with a playful frown.

"Sure," I admitted softly, hugging Eela tightly as I rested my chin on her head. I kissed her forehead gently before I stood up and walked across the living room to my bedroom.

I flinched awake as sharp pain struck me in the side of the head. I confusedly looked around my room and frowned at the dim light filtering through the curtains on the balcony. I fumbled for my phone on my nightstand and winced at seeing the time. I rubbed my head gently as I frowned and turned over my shoulder to see Stella asleep next to me. *Did I fall asleep that quickly? I hope everyone got along with Ryth while I was out...* I shook my head, blinking my eyes several times before pulling off my dark hoodie as I weakly stood up and shuffled to the door.

The bedroom door groaned slightly as I pushed it open, and I peered around the door. Cohen sat alone at the dining table on the computer with his chin resting on his hand.

"You missed dinner," Cohen gruffly whispered. I rolled my eyes and closed my bedroom door gently as I scoffed at his glance at me.

"My bad," I sighed, rubbing the back of my neck. "Was Ryth alright?" I asked slowly, fumbling with the pack of cigarettes in my back pocket. Cohen nodded once, glancing at the cigarette in my hand with a sigh. I turned on my heel and walked back across the living room towards the sliding door and stepped outside with a shiver.

I sat outside on the balcony in silence as I lit my cigarette and stared at the night sky fading in. I frowned as a chill ran down my back at seeing the building in front of the complex gone. *How did she even get the building to collapse? Is that her power? Destruction?* I sighed as I rubbed my pulsing head for a moment, and I stared down at my lap. Car horns echoed weakly through the chilly air as music thumped softly, both being drowned out by the wind. I widened my eyes as my phone suddenly buzzed in my pocket. I waved the smoke in front of my face from the cigarette away as I stared down at the screen. I sighed, coughing softly and shaking my head as I set my phone down and closed my eyes.

I forgot I have to go see her *tomorrow. Things should start picking up and go smoother with her as the name I'll be working for.* My mind raced with worry at all the possible ways this meeting could go wrong. *Boss is the leader of the Underworld for a reason. No one double crosses or messes up when her name is involved—*

A gentle knock on the glass behind me made me flinch. I turned over my shoulder with slightly widened eyes as I saw Cohen pull open the sliding door for Ryth to come through. He glanced down at her with worry in his dark eyes before he slowly slid the door closed behind him and sat on the other side of the balcony.

"Hey Ryth," I smiled softly. She waved sheepishly at me, tucking her long dark hair behind her ear before she limped over towards me. "Sorry I missed your first dinner here," I sighed, glancing down at her sitting on the tile floor next to me. She shook her head and grinned, leaning slightly closer to me.

"It's okay. Everyone was really nice," she mumbled, glancing warmly at Cohen staring at his phone. He glanced at her with a slight grin before his eyes darkened back at his phone as he turned it off and set it roughly in his lap.

"I just wanted to thank you," Ryth softly whispered. She looked slowly up at me with tears in her eyes making my heart spike out of my chest, "for accepting me with little to no questions like anyone else here had to answer to get in…" she continued, looking down.

"You're different from them, Ryth, in a good way," I sighed, shifting my chair to face her. Ryth shook her head and laughed sadly into her hand.

"I am different, but it sure isn't a good different," she spat, her voice shaking. I frowned down at her as Cohen turned worriedly to us from Ryth's voice wavering.

"What kind of person has such a twisted mind like me?" Ryth growled. "One twisted enough to try and end their own life," she spat. My heart roared in my ears as I stared down at Ryth shrinking in on herself, pulling her dark sleeves over her scarred wrists. I inhaled slowly as tears filled my own eyes.

"A person like me, Ryth," I gently chuckled. Ryth's gaze met mine as her eyes widened in shock. A flicker of white flame shot from behind Cohen's ears as he furrowed his brow at me before turning his gaze back to the ground in front of him slowly. I sighed, waving the burst of smoke from my mouth and the cigarette as I slowly reached up and pulled my dark shirt's collar down slightly.

"I was in your exact same shoes at your age, Ryth," I sadly smiled. Ryth's cold eyes filled with more tears as she stared at the ragged scar across my left collar bone and up the side of my neck. Cohen's eyes widened as he stared intently at me with clenched fists. "I understand what it's like to be cast out from everyone else just because of how dark your mind is," I gently explained, turning my gaze up to the star filled sky. "The look in your eyes matched my own from a few years ago. I knew I couldn't refuse you again once I saw that…" I frowned, intently staring at the bright stars pulsing against the dark blue sky night sky.

"Even if we don't accomplish *anything* with the Elites, everyone here is a family before anything else. We take care of one another," I explained. "A family different than most, but we make it work," I chuckled, glancing warmly at Cohen as he rolled his eyes and smiled. "I'm glad you're here with us, Ryth. You are welcome and loved here whether or not you know us or if you feel like it," I whispered proudly, leaning down and resting my hand on her shaking shoulder. Ryth nodded, wiping the tears streaming down her face. She quickly stood up and wrapped her trembling arms around me in a hug as I rested my own around her and closed my eyes.

"Thank you," she whispered as she leaned away. I smiled at her as she turned and limped back inside. My heart spiked in my chest at seeing an ugly, open gash on the back of her heel.

After sitting in silence for a few minutes as I finished my cigarette, Cohen stood up and walked towards the sliding door. He paused and turned over his shoulder at me slowly.

"That's what the scar is from?" Cohen asked gently.

I frowned and nodded, pulling my shirt up to cover it again. Cohen worriedly started at me with a furrowed brow as he stood with his hand on the door.

"I was just a little older than Eela when I gave it to myself," I chuckled sadly, blinking away the tears forming in my eyes.

"I wish I was around you sooner than now. I could have helped you," he frowned, his voice rasping slightly.

I waved my hand at him and shook my head.

"Just be glad all of us are here now to help," I sighed. "Co," I laughed softly, smiling warmly at his worried gaze. He closed his eyes at me as he shook his head and nodded before stepping inside without another word to me. I took a deep breath as I turned back around in my chair and stared at the star filled sky.

My mind drifted back to Cohen and I's first time meeting the other. He was the first one Stella and I found to help us form the agency. Cohen had been by Stella, Eela, and I's side from the first day he joined us. He was one of the most loyal ones we've found, no questions asked. I smiled gently as I closed my eyes and rested my head on the back of the chair. *Even after knowing him for only a few months, we're already great friends… Everyone here is. That's a blessing.*

A quick knock from the glass behind me pulled me out of my head. I turned and saw Stella's raised brow at me before she shook her head down at the chair. I rolled my eyes at her and quickly stepped towards the sliding door into the bedroom.

CHAPTER 22

THE NEXT MORNING…

Cohen, Randy, and I swiftly walked down the crowded street. The day was unforgivingly cloudy as a cold mist lathered the air all around us. I shifted uncomfortably as my dark suit stuck to my skin from the water streaming lightly through the air. People scrambled up and down the street as we brushed past them, keeping our gazes down. Cars honked and music blared loudly through the city as the noise of conversation fought for the spotlight over them. My heartbeat roared in my ears the closer we made it to the meet point. *If any of us screw up we're all dead… Boss doesn't mess around.*

I gently pushed through a large, spinning door and blinked several times to adjust my eyes to the dim light. Lantern antler chandeliers hung sternly from the large, A-framed, dark ceiling above. Dark accents lined the walls and decor of the mostly open lobby space. The front desk strewn itself out in the right side of the room, allowing the rest of the room to be a sitting area. People talking into microphones on their shoulders scurried around the room, holding clipboards as they spoke to various other clients. Cohen nudged Randy's arm roughly as a mischievous glint filled his eyes. Cohen frowned at him as I snickered at them while we walked towards the front desk.

"How can I help you?" the woman at the front desk asked sharply. Her gaze stayed glued to the screen in front of her.

"True," I gruffly responded. The woman paused her typing as she darted her gaze up towards the three of us. I tensed slightly as she stared with no emotion at each of us individually.

"Boss will allow access in a few minutes," the woman snapped, returning to her typing. I tipped my head to her and guided Randy and Cohen away towards the golden elevator in the center of the back wall of the room, surrounded by guards in formal attire.

After waiting patiently at the elevator for a few minutes, the doors opened with other Underworld clients walking briskly out, paying no attention to the three of us. I shivered violently as a tall man with half his face hidden by a black, metal mask and dark gloves stormed passed with another man angrily following behind him. The guards on either side of the golden doors tipped their heads to the elevator, keeping their gazes on the others walking across the lobby. *Those two looked like they had a rough time.* I shivered slightly as the second man glared at me over his shoulder before turning quickly back around. Randy shivered as Cohen nudged him forward after me once I stepped into the elevator. The three of us stared down at the gold intertwined in the marble floor below us as more guards stared intently at us. My heart spiked in my chest at the elevator immediately going down once the doors closed instead of going up. *I forgot the meetings are held underground. Harder to infiltrate and more escape routes...*

The elevator doors opened gently to reveal a pitch-black room. Red velvet carpet strewn itself out in a path from the elevator as I glanced down at the dark room with a shiver. A small lock extended out from the side of the wall, placing itself around the elevator doors and keeping them open.

"One at a time," an armed guard inside the elevator growled, pushing me forward. I glared at him over my shoulder, worriedly glancing at Cohen and Randy as they tensed. I shook my head at them as I shivered and stepped out onto the red carpet.

A red laser immediately was activated, pointed directly at my chest. The laser widened itself until it reached the width of my shoulders and traveled up my neck. I blinked quickly as the laser passed over my eyes, temporarily blinding me for a moment with a wince. The laser then quickly scanned the rest of my body with small flashes of green intermittently going off between the red. The laser became fully green as it powered down at my shoes before it slowly disappeared. Small, white lights lining the ceiling following the red-carpet path slowly powered on a few strides away from where I was standing. An eerie chill shot down my back as I glanced around at the pitch-black room surrounding me as I walked towards the lit area.

Once Cohen and Randy were scanned, the armed guards inside the elevator escorted us down the path. Cohen continuously glared over his shoulders at the dark room on either side of us as Randy's eyes darted quickly at any light that powered on in our direction. *I've never been to a meeting area of the Underworld like this. Normally there isn't a single shadow in sight...* I clenched my fists slightly as I frowned at the desk looming from the darkness.

The guards escorting us suddenly held out their large guns, forcing us to stop walking as we reached the end of the red carpet. Cohen and Randy were moved roughly to either side of me as we tensed from a door opening in the back corner of the room. The moment Boss walked into sight from the bright light behind the door, the entire room seemed to shift. Respect and reverence lined the air as the armed guards behind us drew themselves inward, their heads bowed solemnly as Boss continued across the room towards the desk in front of us with the chair's back facing us.

Boss suddenly spun around in the large chair with folded arms. The dark blue suit resting against her dark skin shimmered dangerously in the lights as they dimmed around us. Golden accents lined the suit, matching the golden bobby pins on the sides of her head, pinning down her sleek, black hair. Boss slowly lifted her hand, sliding her golden glasses down her nose to reveal her piercing, ice-blue eyes. My heart spiked out of my chest as her gaze immediately struck my soul with authority. She intently studied each of us individually before she closed her eyes for a moment.

"That was quite a show you put on yesterday," Boss chuckled darkly. "You impressed *lots* of people with your bravery." she beamed, raising her brow triumphantly. Boss' gaze drifted away from my own to the cast peeking out from Randy's suit as she sighed. "Speak," she ordered calmly, bringing her hands to the desk in front of her. Cohen and Randy shifted uncomfortably as Boss' gaze continued to strike all of us with fear. *There's a reason you've been the Underworld main leader for so long. You know exactly how to intimidate people the right way.*

"We've come today to discuss action forward for my plan, ma'am," I gently explained, tipping my head down slightly. Boss flicked her hand up at me and raised her brow as my gaze drifted away from her own. I blinked as my heart spiked in my chest as I quickly locked my eyes with hers.

"You're the man who plans to take down the Elites?" Boss asked, a curious glint flashing through her eyes. I nodded once, taking a deep breath as she relaxed slightly with a prideful smirk at me. *Good thing you like this idea with no explanation. Let's hope this stays this way…*

"My end goal is to rid all the Elites in the system who abuse their government granted access to use their powers on civilians," I explained sternly. "Too many lives are lost and ruined by fault of the Elites overusing, or using, force when it is not necessary," I spat. "Too many Elites have the government saving their asses by hiding all their mistakes and shifting blame to people like me, the lowlifes of society who are already struggling enough as it is," I continued, my voice filling with more passion. Boss' gaze filled with more pride the more I explained. Slowly, a genuine grin spread across her face.

"Elites abusing their powers against civilians ruins too many lives," I explained, my voice wavering. "So many people are forced to hide in the shadows, left to fend for themselves and die alone with no offerings of help," I growled, clenching my fists. "Too many lives are lost due to this, and no one deserves to live a life of constant pleads for help but receiving absolutely none," I breathed, my voice lined with grief. Cohen leaned slightly closer towards me as Boss shifted in her seat and waved her hand towards me.

"I like you, kid," Boss exclaimed proudly, smiling sharply at me. "You have the right amount of passion to get this job done, with the drive and motivation to succeed." She sighed, glancing down at her hands for a moment. "I rarely do this, but," she began, "you'll be receiving 'special' forces and treatment from my operations," she chuckled, bringing her hands together on the desk. The rings lining her fingers reflected the dim light into my eyes sharply, making my heart spike in my chest. "I haven't seen someone with your drive for this topic in a long time," she sighed sorrowfully.

"I'm all in," Boss hissed, hitting her fist on the table and leaning towards me. I exhaled softly in relief as Randy and Cohen grinned pridefully at me for a moment. "There's something about you, True," she chuckled, shaking her head. "You're no ordinary man with an ordinary goal of any kind," she explained. "You're more than you think you are." Boss sharply breathed, leaning back in her seat as her voice slightly wavered. I widened my eyes slightly as I tipped my head down respectfully. Boss spun slightly in her chair as she held her chin in her hand for a moment before she took a deep breath. "Let's get this change going," Boss beamed, raising her hands proudly to her sides.

The agency celebrated Boss accepting my goals that night with a meal from our favorite restaurant, followed by drinking games back at the suite. Everyone laughed, danced, and sang happily to the music Eela kept putting on in between games. As the night went on, the rest of the details turned into a blur. Our competitive family side had come out, and we all became focused on beating the other at whatever game that was brought up by Ryth and Eela. Cami and Fletcher helped keep the games running smoothly when things got too heated.

CHAPTER 23

3:00 AM…

I shifted uncomfortably in bed as I closed my eyes tighter with a frown. My heart suddenly spiked out of my chest, driving me to sit up. *Something's wrong…* I furrowed my brow as distant sirens echoed into the suite from the lively night city. I fumbled weakly for my phone on the nightstand and quickly skimmed through news headlines through blurry, tired vision. *Nothing is obviously wrong. Why is my gut telling me that something is though?* I set my phone down and rubbed my head slowly, grimacing as a headache formed on my temples.

My smoke suddenly shot from my palm, shoving my head away from my hand. I flinched and widened my eyes at the pitch-black smoke slowly retreating towards my skin. Severe pain began to form under the concentrated smoke in the center of my right palm. I yelped as I held my wrist, struggling to get out of bed. My vision suddenly blurred even worse as I stood up, my head becoming light. I shook my hand as I gritted my teeth tightly and breathed hard before stumbling across the room to the bathroom.

I flicked on the lights and blinked quickly as my vision blurred again. I brought my palm closer to my face and shivered at a faint burn mark left from the smoke. I frowned down at the burn and slowly ran my hand under cold water as I shook my head. After drying my hand, I glanced at the mirror quickly. My heart spiked out of my chest, making me have a double take at myself. I widened my eyes in horror as I thought for a split second, I saw someone else staring at me through the mirror, something dark hovering over their shoulder.

I backed away from the mirror as my breaths quickened, gasping softly as I backed into the wall behind me. I squinted at my reflection for a moment as a violent chill shot down my back. I rubbed my eyes roughly as I stumbled forward to look back at myself. I blinked confusedly at my eyes being warped in the mirror, the normal dark brown now a pale, eerie grey color. I narrowed my eyes, thinking there was something wrong with the mirror as I reached out to brush my hand against the glass.

My vision suddenly went black as nausea hit me like a truck. For a split second, I saw myself worriedly staring at the mirror from the other side. Strong claws dug into my left shoulder as severe pain formed around my face. I flinched violently as I was back in my normal body as I fell to the ground, a violent crack shooting from the mirror where my hand once was. I coughed hollowly into my arm as I stayed laying on the bathroom floor, gasping for breath. I lifted my hand and widened my eyes as I saw light grey and my pitch-black smoke around my palm. I blinked several times and shook my head before I waved the smoke away and brought my hands to my face.

"True?" Stella mumbled softly from the doorway. "What are you doing?" she scoffed.

I kept my hands in my face as I shook my head with a groan. *I definitely had too much to drink.*

CHAPTER 24

AT NOON...

Distant, excited voices rang through my ears as I was shaken awake. I opened my blurry eyes to see Ryth and Eela leaning over me, smiling widely. I shook my head as I groaned and sat up on my elbow.

"True!" Ryth laughed, shaking my arm as Eela giggled. My hearing spiked in my head before going back to normal, a headache pulsing through my skull.

"Yes?" I hoarsely asked, rubbing my blurry eyes.

"It's noon! Get up!" Eela groaned, pulling my arm towards her.

"We have something to show you!" Ryth excitedly beamed, shaking Eela's shoulder. I nodded and waved my hand at them as I let my head fall back to my pillow. Stella's sigh from the doorway made Eela and Ryth flinch before giggling again and darting out of the room.

"They've been patiently waiting for you to wake up for a while," Stella scoffed softly, leaning against the door frame. I sighed and blinked slowly at her gaze at me with a shiver. "I think you'll like what they want to show you, it's in their room." Stella tipped her head to the main room with a smile before she turned on her heel and swiftly walked away before I could protest. I frowned at her leaving the door open before I weakly sat myself up and held my face in my hands. I shivered again at feeling the burn on my palm raised more than it was last night. I widened my eyes down at my burned hand and frowned before I clenched my fist, wincing in pain.

I glanced up at the brick wall on the other side of my bedroom and sighed at all my guns mounted calmly. *I need to find time to clean those soon.* I rubbed my head as I heard Stella come in the room again and yelped as Stella brought a hot mug to the side of my face.

"You are the worst morning person I've ever met," Stella teased, handing me the cup of hot coffee.

"I'm not a morning person at all," I spat, sipping the coffee with a sly smirk at her. "I don't even like waking up," I continued softly. Stella roughly hit my shoulder after rolling her eyes at me giggling at my own statement. My heart spiked in my chest as Stella stared down at me for a moment with a small grin before turning her gaze to the door.

"I'm coming you two!" I groaned, grabbing a pillow and throwing it at Eela and Ryth from across the room. The two of them laughed softly as they ran into one another before turning and darting across the living room. *I'm glad Eela has helped Ryth come out of her shell in such a short time.* I winced as the burn on my hand flared in pain at touching the hot cup as I stood up. *Behind all Ryth's pain, she's such a happy girl... I can't believe no one has helped her until now. No one should have their happiness held out of their reach by no fault of their own.* Stella glanced at my hand for a moment before she turned and guided me out of the room in silence.

I set my cup of coffee down roughly on the table in the living room as Ryth and Eela began pulling and pushing me across the room. I glanced around the suite confused on where everyone was.

"Guys, what's wrong?" I laughed, purposefully leaning backwards onto Eela. She punched me roughly in the side, making me double over with laughter as Ryth struggled to keep pulling me. I reached behind me for Eela as she darted away from my hand and joined Ryth in front of me to pull me forward. I stumbled into the doorframe, laughing into my hand as Ryth and Eela giggled while Stella rolled her eyes with a smile behind us.

"Cami and I had been working on this for a while, but Ryth helped us finalize a lot of things," Eela nervously explained, glancing at an art stand with a canvas covered by a blanket over it. Cami sat in the corner of the room, her hands stained with paint and a bright smile on her face towards me. Stella leaned against the doorway as Ryth pulled me to the ground next to her, trembling slightly. Eela smiled excitedly at Ryth and Cami before she pulled the blanket away from the hidden canvas.

I widened my eyes in shock as I gasped softly. Before me was a dark silhouette of myself with Ryth and Eela on either side. The silhouettes faced the rising sun with the outline of the New York City skyline in the distance. Vibrant blue, yellow, and red sprawled across the canvas; the faint words of the night sky were being pushed away by the sun. "Pain, depression, loneliness, suicide" were the words that caught my eye first. Each word was being drowned out intently by a ray from the sun as it reached into the night sky, forcing it away from us. On the same ledge as Eela, Ryth, and I were the rest of the agency, all sitting pridefully with outlines of smiles on their faces towards one another. My heart began to beat out of my chest with pride, and tears swelled in my eyes.

"This is beautiful," I whispered softly, my voice breaking.

"I hope you like it," Ryth mumbled, resting her shaking hand on my shoulder. Eela nodded nervously next to Cami as they hopefully stared at me.

"I love it," I breathed, blinking the tears out of my eyes as before closing them. Ryth whimpered slightly as she leaned into my side, and Eela knelt in front of me, leaning into both of us. I held them both in my shaking arms as more tears filled my eyes and my heart raced in my chest. *Thank you.*

"We all have been trying for months to come up with the design," Maeve sighed proudly from the doorway. "We wanted to have something as a 'thank you' gift for you to have," she chuckled.

"You were someone in the darkest place a human could possibly be mentally, and yet," Stella began, her voice wavering, "you still stayed in the dark. Pushing us all into the light before even doing a single thing to help yourself first." She beamed, resting her hand on my shoulder, Maeve doing the same. My heart caved in my chest as I leaned slightly forward. I began shaking.

"Society left us all to rot in the shadows, but you stopped and pulled us along with you on your way to the light," Randy added softly from behind me, his trembling hand resting on my other shoulder.

"You put up with all of us, no matter how much we anger you," Fletcher chuckled, resting his hand next to Randy's. Everyone snickered softly as Cami rested her head on my shoulder next to Ryth. Cohen's hand was the last one I felt; his silence said thousands of words to me.

"You put everything on the line to help us all," Stella softly whimpered.

"You gave everyone here a second chance before you even tried saving yourself," Ryth added, leaning into my side as she trembled.

"You've created such a tight knit family aspect between everyone here," Cohen suddenly explained, his voice wavering. "Those are the bonds that propel us all forward to continue trying every day to be better," he continued. My chest ached with pride as I nodded and felt tears stream down my face.

"Look closer," Eela whimpered, nudging my arm. I looked back up at the painting through my tears and widened my stinging eyes. A faint silhouette of Mr. Keilot stood behind me with his hands on Eela and I's shoulders. I gasped in grief as I leaned over fully, bringing my arms around myself. I let out a quiet sob as I covered my face in my trembling hands. Everyone behind me leaned closer to me as we all were overcome with emotion.

We all sat in silence, listening to everyone else cry. *I hope I'm raising your daughter the right way, Mr. Keilot… I wish you were here to help me…* I gasped again as I could almost feel his own hand rest on my shoulder. *Just one more time. One more chance to thank you. One more moment with you…*

CHAPTER 25

A WEEK LATER...

My heart raced in my ears as the Agency trailed behind me, darting through the alleyways between buildings. The streets all around us were filled with roars of angry civilians and honking cars. *Should I have let Eela and Ryth stay alone back at the suite? What if the authorities find the room and take them?* Stella nudged my arm roughly, pulling me out of my head as she tipped her head at me. I blinked several times with a frown before I glanced at everyone jogging behind me silently. *This organized riot by Boss seems too forced, too soon. The Elites will see through the acting crowd.* I clenched my fists slightly as a glass shattered from the intersection to our right. *Why even waste our energy on this place? The files we need aren't even in this headquarters!*

A second bottle clink echoed eerie through the alley. I slid to a stop as I held my hand out to the side, signaling everyone to stop. We all breathed hard as we listened to the sirens weaving through the streets with pride. A chill shot down my back as I quickly turned around, narrowing my eyes at the dark alley. Cami and Fletcher worriedly glanced at each other before turning over their shoulders to the alley with furrowed brows. Randy and Cohen stared intently at me as Maeve rolled her eyes and waved her hand at me.

"Why are we stopping?" Maeve grumbled. I waved my hand at her roughly as I looked up quickly. Dark clouds covered the sky, creating silhouettes and shadows of stairwells and balconies lining the buildings above us. The same chill shot down my back as I scanned the broken and opened windows lining the brick walls with a furrowed brow. I inhaled sharply as I slowly wrapped everyone in my smoke, shivering at seeing my pitch-black smoke graze against their gas masks.

"Don't you all feel that?" I asked softly, gathering myself slowly with a frown. Everyone shrugged as they warily looked around for a moment.

A chill shot down my back, making the hair on my arms stand on end. A small *click* of a trigger suddenly pierced the weirdly silent air. I narrowed my eyes angrily as I immediately turned in the direction of the noise, and I held my hand out quickly. My vision tunneled as it focused on a sleek bullet flying through the air from one of the balconies above. The bullet slowed to a stop directly in front of my mask as I sighed. With a wave of my hand, I sent the bullet directly back the way it came. A loud yelp of pain suddenly sounded through the air as someone fell over on a metal balcony above.

"What was that?" Randy snarled angrily, stepping towards me. A large gun suddenly slipped over the edge of the metal railing as I stared at it, falling roughly to the ground next to me. Everyone froze behind me as we all stared up at the person struggling to stand on the balcony. My heart roared in my chest with panic as I watched him lean over the railing, holding his arms weakly out for us to see. The person breathed hard as I squinted my eyes to try and see their face, hidden by a dark hood and white mask.

"What do you want?" I ordered calmly, clenching my fists.

"A paycheck, pal," the voice sneered happily. "No wonder you have such a large bounty over your head! There is a great reason why you've been deemed as the most dangerous man in the city," the man continued slyly. I narrowed my eyes at him as one of his arms suddenly extended out from his body, wrapping around the railing like a rubber band. Moments later, the man suddenly launched himself off the balcony, his arm extending and turning into an almost liquid state as he lowered himself in front of me, keeping his free hand visible to me.

Randy quickly darted to my side, picking up the man's gun and holding it to him with narrowed eyes as I frowned. The man kneeled in front of me with a bowed head as blood dripped from his left shoulder before he slowly tipped his head up to me with a soft chuckle. The white, metal mask on his face sent a chill down my spine. His right eye was the same cloudy white, a nasty gash through the middle of it. *Being half blind, you still have a damn good shot.*

"Who are you? Why did you try shooting me?" I asked, leaning slightly closer to him.

"Like I said, you have a pretty good price tag over your head." The man beamed, winking at me proudly. I blinked slowly at him as he winced and adjusted himself more comfortably on his knees. "Who I work for has no concern regarding you. Hell, we're closer than you might think," he slyly explained, gazing intently at everyone standing behind me.

"I don't know you at all," I gruffly spat.

"Call me Stretch then," he spat back. "There! You know me now,"

"True, we can't keep wasting time here," Stella warned softly, nudging my shoulder. "The rioters can only keep up the act so long before the Elites see through it!" she hissed. I nodded, backing away from Stretch kneeling on the ground. Randy quickly pried the magazine off the gun in his hands before throwing it roughly back to him as he sighed offendedly. I waved my hand at the agency, worriedly glancing around before I stepped towards Stretch with a frown.

"Don't try shooting me again," I warned, calmly turning on my heel away from him. "It pisses me off when people forget guns have no effect on me," I sighed, materializing a pistol in the air in front of Stretch. I fired the floating pistol once, striking his other shoulder. He cried out in pain as he doubled over, breathing hard. "Don't waste my time either," I snarled, waving the floating gun away.

I narrowed my eyes as Stretch slowly looked up at me again, staring directly at me with an angry glint in his seeing eye. I shook my head at him as I quickly darted down the alley after the rest of the Agency.

CHAPTER 26

A TENSE HOUR LATER...

"Ugh, I told you!" Stella roared through the gas mask intercom being drowned out by the steady rain slamming into the ground. "We wasted too much time!"

"It's too dangerous, True! The Elites have this headquarters guarded in every direction we look!" Randy angrily explained through the channel.

I narrowed my eyes at the armed guards struggling below my column of smoke as I breathed hard.

"It wasn't *my* idea to even come to this place! Boss forced it onto me!" I snarled, waving my hand quickly. My pitch-black smoke column tightened around the guards before throwing them violently back to the ground. The crowd pushing towards the building yelled angrily as more guards filtered out through the doors with raised guns.

"The fake riot only pissed them off even more—" Cami yelled through the channel, her voice getting cut off abruptly as one of her paint cans exploded down the street. The paint flowed through the air for a split second before getting drowned out by the raindrops. *Not a protection screen but a distraction to run...*

"Fine then! We'll just leave!" I spat. "I'll get chewed out by Boss but, we can't keep pushing against this! It's an uphill fight!" I continued, laughing angrily as I ducked behind a car as bullets flew towards me. Cohen, Fletcher, and Maeve all rolled to the ground in front of me, breathing hard with narrowed eyes.

"Why would Boss force this onto us so quickly? Wouldn't she know it would be too much too soon?" Cohen angrily grumbled. I waved my hand at him and shook my head as Maeve mumbled angrily under her breath, glaring at her switchblade in her palm.

I inhaled sharply as I stood up and wrapped Cohen, Fletcher, and Maeve with my smoke. I held out my palms with narrowed eyes as more bullets fired through the air towards me, slowing to a stop in a dome around me. I then wrapped the car in front of me in my smoke.

"Fletcher! The ground!" I ordered quickly, waving my hand to send the bullets back.

Fletcher lunged forward, gripping the soaked concrete with his palms before the ground under me shifted. The concrete warped violently inward on itself as I pushed the car slightly away from me with the smoke column. As I let my smoke fall away, the rippling ground carried the car easily, violently slamming into the armed guards charging towards us. I waved my hand as I darted down the street, glancing over my shoulder to see Stella, Randy, and Cami following us.

The rain only continuously became stronger as we weaved quickly through the traffic. Cars honked as angry voices of panic competed over the rain as we ran through them in the street. Gunfire echoed through the air, causing cars worriedly to try pulling out of line as bullets struck their metal. *Are these guards idiots? Why are they firing directly into traffic!* I glared over my shoulder in panic at seeing everyone else further behind me than I thought they were. *What's going on? Why are they lagging behind so much?* I shook my head and slammed a car door shut on an angry old man who tried climbing out towards me and continued sprinting towards the sidewalk.

As I passed through two large charter busses, something shot between the gap of the cars. I was suddenly tackled to the ground from above my right as a large arrow slammed into the 18-wheeler trailer where my head once was. I widened my eyes in panic and shock as Stretch held me to the ground. For a moment, as he kneeled over me, he talked angrily into a mic on his shoulder. He stood up quickly and lunged up at the 18-wheeler trailer, pulling himself to the top before extending both his arms across the street as I fumbled to my feet. I held back a laugh as I saw his hands wrap around an Elite with an armed bow and launch them into the glass building behind them.

The rest of the Agency yelled worriedly towards me. They'd caught up to me using the alleyways on the edges of the buildings. I turned over my shoulder, seeing Stretch in the corner of my eye as I saw the Agency charging towards me. I frowned and looked back up at Stretch as my heart spiked in my chest. He was completely gone. I gazed around in confusion for a moment before Cohen shouldered into me, pulling me towards him as the rest of us ducked back into the alleyways. *Where did he even go? First, he tried shooting me and now he's helping! How is he even using his arms after being shot in both?* I widened my eyes in angry realization as I held back an annoyed grin. *Don't tell me this prick is someone from Boss' team she was sending to help us.*

"True! These people that are following us now aren't with the Elites!" Cami angrily explained, throwing her broken gas mask to the ground as she sided up next to me.

"Didn't you see how they were firing directly into traffic at civilians?" Fletcher cried. I nodded and inhaled sharply as I slid around the alley corner.

"Who are they then?" I snarled, clenching my fists.

"I have no clue! But they aren't too pleased with us!" Maeve laughed slyly.

"Obviously!" Randy snarled playfully at her as he punched her arm while he jogged up next to her.

"Guys! We have company!" Cohen yelled worriedly, sliding to a stop next to me. We all breathed hard as we backed into one another, our eyes wide in panic. We stood weakly around each other as we stared at the three alleys meeting at the open space we occupied. Each alleyway was filled with people in all-black clothing; everything but their eyes covered as they charged towards us with raised guns.

"How are they tracking us so easily?" I angrily asked, covering everyone in my smoke. "We have to go back out to the street. We can lay low at HQ for a bit until things calm down! Boss will help protect us!" I breathed quickly, glaring at the groups stalking towards us.

I turned on my heel and ran directly down the alleyway leading back to the brightly lit street as my heart raced in my ears. I glanced behind me to see Fletcher warp the ground down the alleyways as Cami threw spray paint can bombs each direction. I widened my eyes slightly in panic as someone from one of the groups suddenly leapt from a broken window of the building next to us directly at Randy. *Crap!* My legs faltered under me as I slipped on the sleek concrete with a huff of annoyance. I stumbled forward, falling slightly into the street before I turned halfway back around to help.

Through the crowd of frantic people running through the streets from more gunfire echoing past the rain, a louder, singular gunshot fired. Civilians screamed in panic as they all fell to the ground, covering their heads. My heart leapt out of my chest as my vision tunneled in on a bullet flying directly towards me. I raised my hand too slowly, as I was caught off guard and locked eyes with a person standing among the civilians on the ground. Their cold brown eyes sent a chill up my spine as they looked exactly like the man's from Boss' lobby. His right hand holding the pistol towards me was completely metal, matching the dark mask hiding his face. *Wait*— Violent pain suddenly struck me in the side of the head, sending me to the brick corner of the building next to me.

I slammed into the wall, sliding helplessly down to the slick ground as I gasped in shock. Immense pain shot up the side of my head as my gas mask blared warnings loudly in my ears. My vision blurred horribly, the glass eye holes becoming shattered. Loud ringing filled my ears, drowning out the screaming crowd and roaring rain as I laid helplessly on the water filled concrete. Through the bursts of my vision returning, I saw Stretch lunge over me, extending his arms down the alley as he yelled. His voice echoed loudly in my mind as my Agency's cries of panic sent anxiety clawing up my neck. Stretch knelt over me, glaring at someone in the street before waving his hand at everyone in the alley. Everything became silent as my heart faltered in my chest, darkness clouding my blurry vision.

CHAPTER 27

SEVERAL HOURS LATER...

Quiet voices filled the room around me as pain radiated across my skull from the side of my head. My neck and body ached horribly while I gritted my teeth, closing my eyes together.

"Someone's waking up…" Stretch chuckled softly. *Oh great. You're still around…* "You were beginning to worry me, True," he sighed. Gentle footsteps echoed across the room as I felt someone's presence hover over me. I lifted my hand quickly, knocking someone away from me as I groaned, struggling to pick my head up. My heart began to beat out of my chest as I slowly opened my eyes, squinting at the blurry room. I glared up at Stretch's smug gaze down at me as I rubbed my forehead slowly.

"Is everyone okay?" I asked hoarsely. Stretch nodded calmly, glaring at the other two people staring at us from across the room.

"They're all fine," Stretch sighed, seeming bored. "Fletcher took a pretty good beating from the armed guards at the Elite building. Everyone else is something not worth talking about," I narrowed my eyes up at him as pain flared across the side of my head.

"Of course they're worth being talked about—" I hissed quickly.

"Cool your jets. They'll all be fine," Stretch groaned, turning on his heel and walking calmly away from me. The other two people snickered under their breath before they slowly left the room with sly glances at me.

"You know who's been acting a little off though," Stretch mumbled, glancing at me over his shoulder before extending his arms up to the sliding door. "Randy? Is that his name?" he scoffed. "Destroying things in his room, laughing at nothing," he began explaining. My heart spiked out of my chest as I widened my eyes at him.

"Oh no," I breathed, holding my head tightly. *Randy… I'm fine.* I threw the covers off me and quickly forced myself to stand.

"Woah! What are you doing?" Stretch gasped, waving his hands at me. I shoved him roughly out of my way as I weakly stumbled across the room.

Once I pushed my bedroom door open, everyone's cries of worry rang loudly through the air. I ignored all of them with an aching heart as I quickly limped across the main room and opened Randy's bedroom door. I immediately ducked as a large knife flung itself from the doorway, slamming into the wall behind me. I blinked slowly as I stumbled into the room towards Randy sitting on the floor, trembling violently. I nudged the door closed roughly, hitting Stretch as he tried coming into the room. His scoff of disapproval was silenced by Stella and Maeve yelling at him.

I crouched down in front of Randy, holding his shaking, lean shoulders in my hands as I stared into his eyes.

"Hey," I gently smiled. "I'm okay. I'm here," I explained, leaning closer to him. His amber eyes were wide with fury and panic as I brushed his shaggy curls out of his face with a gentle grin at him. Tears filled his eyes as he quickly shook his head and began mumbling quickly to himself in Spanish. I slowly pulled him into a hug as I frowned at the destroyed room around us. Randy immediately melted into my gasp as he began trembling again. "I'm okay," I whispered softly as I carefully pulled myself away from him. He nodded, bringing his arms around himself as he began staring at the floor in silence.

I closed my eyes tightly after I closed Randy's door with a sigh. Stretch gently guided me back across the main room as my legs began to tremble under me. The other people who were in the suite working under Stretch roughly shoved everyone away from me as I kept my gaze on the ground.

"Why can't we talk to him and ask if he's okay!" Stella snarled angrily, shoving the person's arm off her.

"Who do you think you are, Stretch!" Maeve asked harshly as he moved me into my room.

"An asshole who knows his job," Stretch responded coldly, glaring at her over his shoulder. I shook my head with a frown as I closed the door behind me, leaving Stretch and Maeve in a screaming match.

My entire body throbbed in discomfort in waves from the side of my head as I stumbled around the room towards the bed. I flinched as the door was roughly pushed open behind me, and Stretch gave a final snarky comment towards Maeve. Stretch grumbled under his breath as he pulled a silenced, ringing phone out of his pocket with a sigh. He held it out to me with a raised brow as I blinked at him for a moment. *What?* Stretch held back a smile as he waved the phone at me as it stopped ringing. He scoffed softly before forcibly giving the phone to me.

"Boss has been trying to get a hold of you," Stretch slyly explained.

"Well, why didn't you just tell me that first thing?" I hissed, quickly calling back the recent number. Stretch shrugged apologetically with a mischievous glint in his seeing eye down at me before he pulled his black hood off his head.

"Your gas mask is the only thing that kept you alive," Stretch winced, pointing to the side of his head with a slightly worried glint filling his seeing eye. I shivered gently as I touched the side of my head with a frown. *Why did that man shoot specifically at me? Was he the one organizing those people who were coming after us?* My eye twinged in pain as a headache began forming on the back of my head. *Wasn't he the same man from Boss' place?*

"True!" Boss' voice suddenly exclaimed loudly. I flinched, bringing the phone away from my ear with a wince as I turned the volume down. "You scared me!"

"Sorry, ma'am,"

"Anyways, not the main reason I called," Boss interrupted. "I really wish I didn't have to say this, but," she hesitantly continued. My heart spiked in my chest as Stretch furrowed his brow slightly at me, "someone hacked into my files and sent you on that mission. You were set up, True, and it wasn't by me," Boss hissed angrily, a gentle thump coming from her side of the phone. Stretch shifted uncomfortably as he turned away and glared out of the glass sliding doors at the busy city around us.

"What do you mean someone got into your files and set me up?" I asked slowly, my voice wavering. "Who has an ability to get into the

Underworld leader's files?" I scoffed angrily. Stretch shifted again as he frowned with a glance at me. I furrowed my brow up at him, making him turn his eye away again with a sigh.

"I'm not sure but I may have a few ideas," Boss snapped softly. "Stretch reported to me that you were shot at and hit. Is that accurate, True? Are you alright?" she asked, quickly changing the subject.

"Wait, Stretch works for you? Actually?" I said sharply. Stretch giggled under his breath as he adjusted the white metal mask around his face. Boss sighed dramatically. "Sadly, he does,"

"Hey!" Stretch hissed offendedly, narrowing his eyes playfully at the phone in my hand.

"To answer your question, yes," I sighed. Boss grumbled under her breath as she began typing quickly. "Did you by chance see who fired the shot at you?" she hinted. I furrowed my brow as Stretch scoffed and turned towards the bedroom door.

"Yes. It was someone I saw leaving HQ before I went in for the interview with you," I explained softly. An angry fist hit the desk from the other side of the phone, making Stretch and I flinch.

"Okay. Thank you," Boss sighed angrily. "Stretch may be a pain in the ass, but I trust his judgement. He'll guide you and your Agency through this mess while I try fixing this," Boss chuckled after a few moments of silence. I frowned as Stretch's eyes narrowed as if he was smiling at me. "Try your best not to kill him if you can help it,"

"I'll try," I groaned, narrowing my eyes at Stretch. He rolled his own as he began walking towards the bedroom door again, flicking his black hood back over his head.

"I'm sorry this happened, True." Boss apologized softly. I widened my eyes as Stretch turned sharply over his shoulder at me. "I've never had one of my clients put in so much danger on a fake mission before," Boss explained angrily. "I'll make sure this doesn't happen again. I'll talk more tomorrow," she sighed. "For now, get some rest. I'll have someone else sent over who can help you and your Agency recover soon,"

"Thank you." I winced slowly. Boss hung up the phone without another word. I sighed as I set the phone down on the bed next to me with a frown up at Stretch's dark eye staring at me over his shoulder.

"I'd get some rest if I were you," he mumbled, pulling open the bedroom door softly. I flinched as he closed it roughly behind him, not allowing me to respond.

What's his deal? He seemed to get so offended or worried when Boss and I brought up the man who shot me? I clenched my fists tightly as I winced from resting my head on the headboard behind me. *Does he know something he isn't telling Boss and I?* I suddenly widened my eyes as my heart leapt out of my chest. *How did you even find me on the street?* I furrowed my brow as I stared at the phone laying on the bed next to me and a chill shot down my back. *I need to tell my Agency to be careful around you... You're giving me too many mixed signals for me to trust you, even if Boss sent you.* I shook my head with a frown as I gently closed my eyes, pain pulsing through my head with every beat of my aching heart.

After failing to fall asleep for a few hours, I hesitantly tried sitting up again. Dim light filtered through the curtains from the sliding glass door as I blinked my eyes to adjust to the low lighting. I frowned as pain immediately shot up the side of my head while I slowly swung my feet over the edge of the bed. I scoffed slightly at seeing my cracked phone charging on the nightstand next to me. "*Are you guys up?*" I slowly typed to Stella. I blinked quickly as my vision blurred from a sharp stab of pain into the back of my neck while I winced.

"*Yes,*" she replied. I shook my head as I slowly stood up and stumbled to the living room.

I widened my eyes as I met the worried gazes of my Agency gathered in the living room with one another.

"Yay, you didn't die," Maeve sarcastically beamed. I rolled my eyes at her as everyone snickered under their breath. I slowly sat on the couch next to Stella.

"What even happened to you?" Stella asked sharply, the corners of her eyes glowing. My heart spiked out of my chest as I wavered in my seat.

"Who is Stretch? Why does he think he's in charge?" Cami hissed.

"I want to know who was able to shoot *you!*" Randy glowered angrily.

"*Guys*—" Cohen suddenly snapped. Everyone silenced themselves immediately under his fiery glare. "Give him a second to breathe," he grumbled. I sighed as I grinned worriedly at their anxious expressions.

"Stretch is with Boss," I answered quietly. "He's acting like he's in charge because he is,"

"Oh you're kidding me!" Maeve snarled softly, making Randy giggle into his arm.

"Why him? Out of all people, Boss puts an idiot in charge over you?" Stella grumbled.

Everyone held back their laughter as I brought my hand to my face and sighed.

"I know he's a pain, but he supposedly is going to help us for a bit," I frowned. "Earlier Boss called me and explained that she wasn't the one who sent us on that mission,"

Everyone shifted uncomfortably as they glanced at one another.

"Someone was able to hack into her computer files and send out a fake mission for us to follow," I continued, keeping my gaze away from Stella's.

"Well, that's fantastic, hm?" Maeve hissed. Cami hit her arm roughly as Stella's angry gaze landed on Maeve's cold glare towards me.

"It's not her fault. It's never happened before," I sighed.

"Of course, shit hits the fan when you come along though," Randy frowned. I laughed sadly and nodded, shying away from Stella's annoyed glance at me.

"Where's Fletcher?" I asked softly after a few moments of relieved silence. "The girls?" I continued, glancing around the dark main room.

"Fletcher's resting in our room," Cami frowned softly.

"The girls are sleeping. They were worried about you, True," Randy hesitantly explained, pushing his shaggy curls out of his face. I nodded and rubbed my face gently, wincing as my finger brushed against the wrap on the side of my head.

"I'm sorry I couldn't keep you all protected after I was hit," I grumbled. Everyone sighed as Stella shook her head quickly.

"We shouldn't have to rely on you to always keep us safe," Stella sighed. "I think we can handle ourselves just fine," she grinned. Cami and Maeve raised their brows unbelievingly as they both glanced at Randy.

"What the hell—" Randy angrily laughed, bringing his arms to his face to muffle his laughter. I shook my head as I smiled at Randy angrily bickering with Maeve under his breath in Spanish. Cami and Stella giggled at one another as Cohen held back a smile and stared worriedly at me. After our laughter subsided, we all anxiously glanced at one another, our smiles falling.

"Something isn't right about this situation, True," Stella suddenly breathed. "Everything from Boss' files getting hacked, you get shot, Stretch being put in charge…" she began explaining, waving her hand around in the air as her eyes began to glow slightly. "Something's off," she hissed.

Randy and Cami nodded furiously, and Cohen's gaze fell away from mine as he frowned. Maeve narrowed her eyes as she stared at the glass table in front of us. I waved my hand around and shook my head as I winced while sitting straight up. Stella quickly looked at me with a furrowed brow as I gritted my teeth.

"We'll figure it out…" I gently chuckled. I winced again as my voice sounded the least bit confident. *She's right. Something's wrong…*

Stella suddenly stood up and glared down at me briefly, making everyone tense. She frowned slightly before leaning down and gently holding my face in her hands for a moment. My heart leapt out of my chest as I stared into her light grey eyes as they filled with worry. Without saying a word, Stella let go of my face and stood up, walking silently to our room. I widened my eyes and blinked at the bedroom door for a moment as I furrowed my brow. *What was that about?*

"Ooooo," Randy suddenly snickered. Cohen's dark eyes narrowed as white flames flickered from behind them as he leaned towards Randy. Maeve's hand swiftly smacked Randy in the chin as she rolled her eyes and held out her hand towards Cohen. I held back a smile as Randy yelped, rubbing his chin softly as Maeve pulled him up roughly from the couch. Cami giggled at them with a worried glance towards me before she disappeared into the hallway after Maeve and Randy. Cohen sighed as he let his head fall back on the couch cushions behind him as I rubbed my forehead.

"You scared us today, True," Cohen suddenly admitted, making me flinch.

"I'm sorry," I sighed, frowning down at my shaking hands. "I don't know why I didn't stop the bullet," I grumbled. "I was just caught too off guard." I chuckled, shaking my hand as my pitch-black smoke began seeping from the burn on my palm. I closed my hand quickly as I saw Cohen's eyes darken at my hand. I nervously stared at him for a moment as he sat up and rested his elbows on his knees at me. Cohen's calm expression masked the anxiety hidden in his eyes towards me.

"I know you're figuring something out alone and not telling anyone," Cohen whispered softly. His gentle eyes hardened slightly with worry and disappointment as he stared at me intently. I widened my eyes as he slowly stood up and disappeared down the hallway, saying nothing more to me.

I winced as sharp pain struck my clenched palm. Light grey smoke forced my hand open as my pitch-black smoke hovered in the center of my palm angrily surrounded by the light grey smoke. My arm began to tremble as I stared at the two smokes combining in my palm. I furrowed my brow as the smoke changed to an unnatural dark grey color, seeping perfectly into the burn on my palm. I widened my eyes as I recognized the symbol. *Where have I seen this before?* My eye twitched in pain as the light grey smoke suddenly disappeared, leaving only my pitch-black smoke hovering worriedly in hand. I shook it away quickly and rubbed my aching head before I limped towards the bedroom.

CHAPTER 28

THE NEXT MORNING...

I rubbed my head tiredly as I shook my damp hair out of my face and glared at the crack in the mirror. My entire body shivered at seeing the concentrated shattered glass where my hand had reached. I frowned at the burn on my palm with worry, as it had become more defined overnight and darkened in color. I blinked several times at my reflection, making sure my eyes were their normal dark hue as I sighed. *Did the mirror burn this into my hand? How would a mirror do that though?* I rolled my eyes as I pulled my shirt collar up to hide the scar on my collarbone before I gently placed my towel in the hamper in the closet. I glanced at the deep gash on the side of my head with a frown before I slowly walked out of the bathroom.

A chill ran down my spine at the suite being weirdly quiet as I stood in the bathroom door frame for a moment. I furrowed my brow slightly as I shuffled across the room and opened the bedroom door. I sighed, seeing Stretch balancing on Cohen's skateboard on one foot with various items in his hands, a simple black bandana across his face.

"Where is—?" I began tiredly.

"Your flame boy is out on the balcony, my friend," Stretch beamed. I furrowed my brow slightly as I scrunched my nose at him.

"Don't call me friend," I groaned, shaking my head. Stretch mocked me softly as I turned my back on him and slowly walked towards the glass sliding doors.

Hot air smacked me roughly in the face as I stepped out onto the balcony, closing the door roughly behind me. From inside the suite, Stretch yelped followed by a loud thud. Cohen grumbled under his breath as he calmly glanced at me gazing at him.

"You okay?" I asked softly, sitting in the chair next to him. White flames flickered from behind his ears as he frowned at the phone in his lap.

"Rough phone call from my mom," he mumbled softly. My heart twinged in my chest as I bobbed my head thoughtfully, looking out at the bright skyscrapers towering above. "I just needed to be alone for a little bit," Cohen sighed, rubbing his forehead gently.

"I guess Stretch wasn't helping?" I winced, grinning playfully at him. Cohen grumbled as white flames flickered from behind his eyes, briefly turning red.

"He's driving Stella up the wall," he spat, holding back a laugh. I held my hand to my face and nodded, glancing at Stretch on the phone with someone in the main room.

"I could imagine that. Where are the others?" I asked hesitantly, turning back to Cohen.

"Stretch sent them a few rooms down to some healer Boss had brought in," he mumbled.

"Why didn't you go with them?"

"Leaving you here with Stretch?" he harshly snapped making me flinch. "I almost set that prick on fire earlier, I don't trust him," he growled roughly. I sighed and frowned at the burn on my hand before turning it away from Cohen.

"I don't understand why Boss trusts him," I whispered. "He doesn't seem to have an ounce of respect in his body..." I continued softly. Cohen nodded, glaring over his shoulder as the sliding door opened.

"Since sleeping beauty finally woke up, both of you need to come with me," Stretch snarked, glaring at Cohen darkly. I shivered at seeing the two of them tense as they met each other's eyes.

"I've been awake. I just didn't move," I mumbled, slowly standing up. Stretch mocked me softly again making me narrow my eyes at him. I extended a column of my smoke and shoved him roughly inside, making him yelp in amusement before darting across the main room. Cohen rolled his eyes as he followed closely behind me, staring intently at Stretch holding the front door open for us.

The three of us walked in silence down the long walkway on the side of the building. Stretch ran his fingertips along the dark railing to our right, mumbling softly to himself as Cohen and I glanced at each other. Cohen leaned slightly over the railing, gazing disappointedly at the busy street swarming with people below. Stretch's dark eye caught my attention as he glanced at us over his shoulder before turning quickly back around. Cohen furrowed his brow as I sighed and shook my head, my fingers brushing against the pistol handle in my hoodie pocket.

When we reached the end of the walkway next to the elevator, Stretch pulled a keycard out of his ripped black jacket. The old door on the very edge of the building slowly creaked open as Stretch held it for us to walk through.

"Ladies first," Stretch snarked, raising his brow at Cohen next to me. I held my arm out as Cohen stepped angrily towards him before I violently shoved Stretch inside the room. He yelped as he scrambled away from me walking towards him on the floor.

"Hey now," Stretch worriedly chuckled, holding his hands up to me. I stepped over him, ignoring the panic in his eyes as my heart spiked in my chest. *Woah. Haven't seen that emotion on you yet*, I blinked several times at the dark room as Cohen coughed hollowly into his arm. I waved my hand around the smoke hovering in the air and frowned at Cohen. I glared over my shoulder at Stretch extending his arm like a rubber band, closing and locking the door from the floor, turning away as he looked hopefully at me.

"You two get comfortable," Stretch sighed, pulling himself to his feet quickly. He turned and darted down the hallway branching off from the front door as Cohen and I glanced at each other again. The room was lined with old wooden floors that groaned with the slightest bit of weight on them. The air was heavy with smoke as the damp walls seemed to lean towards us, threatening to collapse. Cohen coughed hollowly again, making me look intently at him for a moment. *I forget you can't handle smoke in general. Your Asthma is to blame for that.* I sighed as I held back a smile. *Yet you have a power that produces smoke when you use it...*

Cohen and I sat down on the old couch in the center of the room facing the broken TV mounted on the wall loosely. I glanced up at the ceiling and frowned at the smoke detectors being broken. *I didn't know there were still rooms like this in the complex. I thought Katie had every room renovated with the grant she received.* I shook my head and frowned worriedly at Cohen intently scanning the old room in silence. I shivered slightly at remembering my childhood home smelling exactly like the heavy air around us and felt my heart leap out of my chest. *I'd never go back, even if my parents were still alive...*

"Good morning, gentlemen," a deep voice suddenly chuckled. Cohen and I flinched as we stared at a tall man in a dark green, ripped suit stalking across the room towards us. A lit cigarette rested in the corner of his mouth as he grinned happily down at us, running his scarred hand over his buzz cut, golden hair. *How ironic. A person with a healing power who smokes.* I frowned slightly as the man glanced over his shoulder at Stretch, who was leaning on the hallway entrance with crossed arms.

"You're the guy they call 'True Leader,' yea?" the man asked calmly, crouching down in front of us. My entire body squirmed with unease as the man's voice became oily and sly. I shifted slightly in my seat and nodded once as he blew smoke directly at me. Cohen grumbled under his breath and coughed into his arm with a glare at the man.

"Boss got lucky with you," the man chuckled, turning to Cohen and holding out his hand. I shivered at seeing freshly healed scabs covering the man's skin.

"Oh, this?" the man grinned, noticing my worried expression. "Backlash of my healing power," he grumbled, moving the cigarette to the other side of his mouth as he held Cohen's arm in his hand gently. "I get whatever I heal," he frowned, holding his hand over a burnt patch of skin on Cohen's arm.

"I've never heard of a healing power doing that," I mumbled softly, wincing as the side of my head flared in pain. The man shivered as the burn mark on Cohen's arm slowly faded away. His own arm trembled as he pulled up the dark green, ripped sleeve and showed the exact patch of burned skin resting against his own arm.

The man blew smoke away from Cohen with a glare up at him as he stood up and moved over towards me. My heart began to race in my chest as the man leaned down and turned my head to the side roughly.

"You need to calm down," he mumbled, glancing at me worriedly. "I can't do this properly if your heart is stressed,"

"Oh, don't worry about that, Heal," Stretch called haughtily from across the room. "That's just him in general,"

I rolled my eyes as I materialized a pistol directly in front of Stretch and glared up at Heal standing over me. Stretch shifted, glaring at the pistol in front of him as he slowly leaned away from it.

"Take the gun away from the kid, and I'll heal this," Heal spat, glaring at Stretch. "This one will hurt more than normal," he chuckled. I sighed and waved the pistol away as Cohen stared intently at Heal's firm grip on my head. His fingers were uncomfortably rough against my skin, like sandpaper as he held my chin tighter, hovering his hand over the gash on the side of my head. Violent pain struck my skull as my vision blurred, causing me to grip the couch gently below me. Heal chuckled darkly as he blew smoke into my face, making me sputter a cough. "Told you that you had to calm down," he snickered, leaning away from me.

I blinked slowly as the pain slowly melted away from the side of my head and winced while the same gash appeared on the side of Heal's head. Blood ran down the side of his head, trailing down the tattoo on his neck before hitting the dark green suit.

"Thank you," I mumbled, touching the now normal side of my head. Heal nodded once and turned around, pulling a bloodied rag from his pocket and dabbed the side of his head gently. "Where's everyone else?" I asked sharply, standing up slowly.

"Ask the kid. He moved them somewhere," Heal mumbled, glancing mischievously at Stretch.

"Oh come on!" Stretch cried, holding his hands out to me as I turned my gaze to him. I quickly pulled my pistol out of my hoodie pocket, stalking quickly across the room towards Stretch with narrowed eyes. I materialized a pistol floating in the air directly in front of Heal as Cohen jumped up from the couch, shoving Heal into the shelf next to the TV. Stretch backed away from me quickly, stumbling over onto the ground with a frantic glint in his eye.

"Well?" I snarled, bringing the pistol towards him.

"They're all at the suite next to yours," Stretch nervously chuckled, his voice wavering. I glanced over my shoulder to see Cohen holding the pistol I made at Heal with narrowed eyes then turned back to Stretch and shook my head at him.

"You need to stop acting like this Agency belongs to you just because Boss put you in 'charge' of us!" I hissed darkly, tightening my grip on my pistol. Stretch glared up at me, staying silent as Cohen calmly walked past us with a sharp cough. I sighed as I lowered my gun and followed him out the door, slamming it roughly on Stretch as he tried following us.

I gently pushed the door of the suite next to mine open as my heart raced in my ears. *Why would Stretch take them here and not back—* The door opened to a mostly dark room with everyone sitting at a table facing a dark TV screen. I sighed in relief as I quickly stepped into the room. Immediately, several barrels of guns met me through the darkness as I slowly froze and held my hands up. I narrowed my eyes as Cohen also had guns raised towards him. Stella and Maeve glanced worriedly at each other as they stared intently at the people surrounding Cohen and I.

"It's True. Calm down," I grumbled coldly. The guns immediately were brought away as the armored people stepped back with tipped heads. I rolled my eyes as we slowly walked across the room towards everyone sitting at the table. Eela and Ryth's faces lit up as I grinned softly at them while I sat down at the end of the table.

"She left for a moment, but—" Maeve softly explained.

"True! Ahhh! There you are!" Boss' voice suddenly boomed, making me leap out of my skin. Everyone in the room flinched as we all looked up at the dark TV looming ominously above us.

"I'm glad my healer babe found you! You're looking good!" Boss exclaimed proudly. I scoffed softly, rubbing the back of my neck as I shook my head at Maeve's raised brow at me. *Boss is old enough to be my mother. No Maeve.* Stella kicked Maeve's leg roughly as the two of them giggled at my worried expression at her. "Sorry if Stretch caused any worrying thoughts about him moving your Agency around, my dear," Boss sighed hesitantly. I blinked away the spite that filled my chest as everyone grumbled under their breaths.

"Knowing him, he didn't explain why I had him bring them here, right?" Boss growled.

"No, ma'am, he did not," I answered calmly, masking my anger.

Boss sighed and mumbled under her breath before the TV flickered for a moment. Boss' sharp blue eyes suddenly pierced my soul once more as her figure appeared on the TV screen, a bright smile on her face at us. Everyone gasped softly as she scanned each of us individually.

"You have a powerful group, young man. I like it." She beamed, pulling down her golden glasses and waving them at the camera with a raised brow. I tipped my head and sighed as Boss squealed softly and set her glasses down excitedly.

"Get me the info!" Boss suddenly snarled, glaring at someone in the room with her. She raised her hand confidently and kept her sharp gaze away from the camera as her smile immediately left her face. I shivered at seeing her pitch-black hair slicked back into a bun on her head, shimmering red as if it was doused in blood. Her white suit lined with red accents made her bright blue eyes pop even more against her warm, dark skin. Her hand moved slightly in the air as she frowned before a file was quickly placed into her palm. Boss squealed happily again as she moved the toothpick in her mouth to the other side and quickly opened the folder.

"Now, I know the last mission 'I' sent you guys on didn't end too well," Boss began softly, laughing sadly. "This next one is going to be a real challenge, but I think you'll be fine," she beamed. Boss became silent as she quickly flicked papers up as she skimmed them all intently. I glanced over my shoulder at the opening door and shivered at seeing Stretch's angry gaze resting on me before he glared down at his bloody hand and sniffed angrily. Cohen glanced at him over his shoulder before turning back and intently looking at Boss searching through the folder of papers.

"You all are going to have to trust me on this one," Boss sighed. "I have a perfect plan for us to follow that is going to save me money and lower the risk of you all getting injured by a significant amount,"

"Lovely," Maeve sighed. Randy winced as Boss' gaze glanced up at us, making Maeve shiver.

"I'll be sending you the detailed instructions later tonight, True. For now, I'll verbally tell you what you're going to do," Boss grinned, pulling out a single sheet of paper.

"I'm sending you to the Elite's main headquarters here in New York City tomorrow," Boss bluntly beamed. Everyone shifted with worried glances at me as Stretch began laughing softly behind me. "This sounds like a big deal, but it will be quite simple if Stretch keeps his head screwed on right and his people placed where I tell him to,"

"We have to trust this guy with something this important?" Maeve snarled, waving her hand at Stretch. Everyone in the room snickered as Stretch narrowed his eyes at her.

"I think you'll be fine. He's a good troop leader, eight out of 10 times," Boss quickly continued. "All the details will be sent to True soon. He'll fill in all holes I left open for wiggle room, depending on how you all do things as a group." she sighed, snapping her fingers at someone in the room with her. "Your main goal at the headquarters is to get all names of Elite's on file. Maeve, your wonderful tracker and best hacker on your team will then find anything she can on every Elite," she continued. Maeve's dark eyes filled with mischief and pride as she smirked up at Boss on the screen. "Once she has all of them, True and I will deem all who we need to eliminate. From there on, True will be back in the main control with me on the sidelines providing anything I can to help,"

"Hardest part of this is just *getting* those files in the first place," I chuckled worriedly.

"You'll be alright. Stretch knows where he needs to have his people to ensure everyone's safety." Boss warmly grinned, setting the paper down and folding her hands in front of her. "I expect the files to be brought to me before you even do any digging on them, Maeve. I need to make sure they're legit and not fake, so we don't waste time," Boss growled, pursing her lips at all of us for a moment. "That's all for now. Pay attention when True explains everything." Boss beamed. Boss winked with a smirk at all of us before she saluted her hand quickly as the TV screen went dark again.

"I still hate that we have to work with this idiot!" Maeve snapped, glaring at Stretch walking towards us.

"Well, I don't get to choose who I get assigned to," Stretch sneered calmly at her.

"Enough," I spat, rubbing my forehead slowly. "He's not with us permanently, so you two will just have to put up with each other until we get this finished," I grumbled, standing up slowly. *This doesn't explain why you tried shooting me in the alley. Boss wouldn't send someone to try killing me before they helped me. Unless it was a final test to make sure I was worth Boss' time.* "Let's just get back to the suite,"

"What's everyone's opinions on Stretch having such a large responsibility with us right now?" I asked calmly, sitting on the couch inside my suite. Eela and Ryth sat on the floor next to each other, worriedly watching everyone else sitting to my left on the couch.

"I hate him," Maeve spat.

"We can tell," Stella mumbled, making a face at Maeve. The two of them smirked angrily at the other before they turned to everyone else. Cohen stared intently at the front door with a frown, staying silent.

"He's so rude. Especially to you, True," Randy grumbled softly, clenching his fists as he trembled with anger.

"He is disrespectful, but he knows what he's doing," Cami sighed hesitantly. Fletcher nodded, rubbing his wrists gently with a frown.

"He treats Eela and I like toddlers who are in the way all the time," Ryth grumbled. Eela nodded, narrowing her eyes as Cohen grumbled softly next to me.

"You know my opinion on him already," Cohen whispered softly, crossing his arms and closing his eyes as white flames flickered behind them. I nodded and looked expectantly at Stella next to me.

"This response was expected, but I still think he shouldn't be too much of a problem," I sighed.

"He's useful with that power of his though!" Randy exclaimed suddenly, raising both his arms.

"It's disgusting," Stella spat while crossing her arms and shaking her head. I inhaled to continue as a series of quick knocks suddenly came from the front door. Everyone rolled their eyes as I stood up and jogged across the room, opening the door slowly. Stretch smiled calmly at all of us with a raised brow and mischievous glint in his seeing eye.

"I'm glad you all *adore* me so much," Stretch beamed. I rolled my eyes and let the door go as I turned on my heel. Stretch caught the door roughly and pushed it open, stepping into the suite after me. "I know I can be a pain in the ass, but I'm pretty useful!" he chuckled, sliding onto the floor next to Eela as I sat back down on the couch. Eela frowned at him, scooting closer to Ryth as I mumbled under my breath. Everyone glared at Stretch's smug expression as I shook my head. "You'll miss me when this mission is over," Stretch giggled.

"Sure, we will," Stella growled.

"I'll miss the fact that I didn't get to kill you myself." Maeve snapped.

"Oh! I feel so honored," Stretch beamed, clutching his chest.

"No one is killing anyone yet, calm down." I sighed. Ryth and Eela giggled as Stretch scoffed offendedly with a worried glance at Maeve's smirk, making everyone snicker under their breaths at him. *I feel like once everyone gets to know you, we'll be fine... Behind the mask and asshole comments you seem like a loyal guy...*

CHAPTER 29

EARLY NEXT MORNING...

I really have to trust Boss on this one... I squirmed uncomfortably as I leaned away from people walking briskly past me in the crowded street. Side-eye glances from the civilians towards me sent a chill up my spine. *You all better not be stupid this mission, Boss didn't allow us to bring our gas masks, so I can't use my smoke to protect you guys.* I frowned slightly, adjusting the black, disposable, mask covering my face as I saw someone knock shoulders with Maeve in front of me. Maeve's cold, brown eyes immediately darted towards the man as he kept walking while I shook my head at her. *You don't have to kill or want to stab everyone you mildly dislike.*

Randy's anxious gaze met mine before he quickly took Maeve's arm and darted into a store. I sighed as I turned and slowly followed them inside, Cohen and Stretch trailing closely behind me.

Warm smiles and welcoming gestures from the employees filled my eyes as I glanced worriedly around the store. I scanned the racks of clothes before I spotted Randy and Maeve examining jackets near the back wall of the store. *Sure, Boss didn't let us have our gas masks and we can fare just fine without my smoke protection, but...* I clenched my fists as I turned over my shoulder at Cohen and Stretch arguing. *Splitting us up into two uneven groups?* I furrowed my brow before I rolled my eyes and half smiled under my mask at an employee worriedly watching Cohen shove Stretch into a rack of clothes. She widened her eyes before turning away and quickly went back to stacking shoe boxes.

"Knock it off!" I hissed, waving my hand roughly at Stretch.

"I didn't even do anything!" Stretch began.

"You're definitely lying!" Cohen growled, stepping towards him. I glared at the two of them before they both fell silent under my gaze. I tipped my head with a sigh as Cohen jogged up next to me while Stretch darted past us quickly, knocking shoulders with him.

"What did he do this time?" I mumbled, glancing back down at the white tiled floor below us.

"He was just annoying the crap out of me," Cohen spat, shaking his head and crossing his arms. I nodded with a sly glance at him in the corner of my eye, making him roll his eyes and turn away.

"How long are we supposed to stall for?" Randy asked quickly as Cohen, and I slowly walked to him. I shrugged and sighed at Maeve, who was looking at pieces of clothing by herself.

"Long enough to not draw suspicion?" I frowned.

"But we look normal!" Randy hissed. "No one recognizes us, so why are we wasting time!"

"Listen," I spat. "I'm just doing what Boss told me, okay?" I explained, masking the irritation in my voice.

"If you have a problem with this, why don't you go and talk to *her* about it?" Cohen snarked.

"She's scary! No!" Randy cried softly, bringing his lanky hands to his curly hair. Cohen and I giggled at his remark as Maeve even scoffed from behind us. A loud crash from the back of the store made the four of us flinch.

"What are you doing!" an angry voice yelled from across the store. Employees in various places around the store all widened their eyes with worried glances towards the direction of the voice.

"Are you kidding me, Stretch," I hissed through gritted teeth as I quickly turned around. Randy snorted into his arm as Cohen and Maeve rolled their eyes. *Do you really have to cause trouble wherever you go?* I quickly jogged through the racks of clothes, scanning the store for any signs of Stretch as I mumbled under my breath. *If he screws something up, Boss can't blame my Agency and I. She's the one who assigned him to us.*

I shook my head with a frown as I furrowed my brow at seeing a burly man pinning Stretch to the tiled ground, his jacket collar firmly in his hand.

"Excuse me, sir," I suddenly growled, tucking my hands behind my back. Stretch and the man flinched, turning their wide-eyed gazes up to me. "I apologize if my friend caused you any trouble." I sighed, glaring darkly at Stretch as he chuckled nervously at me.

"Who are you, pal?" the man growled, tightening his grip on Stretch's collar slightly.

"None of your business," I spat calmly. Stretch winced under the man as he narrowed his eyes up at me.

"Why the masks?" the man snarked. "Are you both sick?"

"Sick in the head," Stretch beamed, giggling softly under his breath. I closed my eyes with a sigh as the man roughly pulled Stretch up from the ground before pushing him back down to the tile. *What did you do this time, Stretch?* I tipped my head slightly as a young woman frantically came jogging towards us with a store employee behind her.

"Let him go, he didn't do anything!" the girl nervously pleaded, glancing at me quickly.

"Sure! He did *nothing*," the man responded harshly, making the girl flinch. Stretch and I furrowed our brows as the girl shied away from the man's angry glare towards her. "So, a random dude flirting with you is nothing!" the man snarled.

"He wasn't flirting with me!" the girl hissed, clenching her fists slightly. *Are you kidding me?* I sighed softly as I shook my head down at Stretch's offended glare up at the man.

"How did I flirt with her by giving her the shoe size she was looking for?" Stretch scoffed softly. "I helped her more than you did, you prick—" he snarked. I tensed as the man holding Stretch quickly forced him to his feet, tightening his grip around his black jacket.

"Just let him go, *please*," I snapped, stepping towards them slowly.

"Sir, let him go," the employee standing behind the girl gently sighed, holding her hand out towards me. "I'm going to have to ask you to leave the store," she frowned, glancing worriedly at me staring at the man.

"Why do you want us to leave?" the man snarled. "I haven't done anything wrong!" he laughed angrily. The young girl quickly took the employee's arm as she quickly stepped away.

I suddenly lunged forward, roughly grabbing the man's shoulder and forced him backwards into the shelf as I pulled Stretch towards me.

The man swiped for Stretch as I stepped between them, narrowing my eyes at him. Stretch mumbled angrily as he began walking towards the man again.

"Drop it," I grumbled, grabbing his jacket hood roughly. I rolled my eyes at the man glaring at us as I began to turn back towards the entrance of the store.

"I legitimately didn't do anything!" Stretch mumbled to me, fixing his jacket with a glance at the man over his shoulder.

"I don't give a crap," I hissed. "If you screw this mission up, Boss will kill you!" I whispered.

"Nah, she likes me. I think I'm good," Stretch giggled. I rolled my eyes as I frowned at him.

"I'm not done with you yet!" the man's angry voice suddenly snarled from behind us. I flinched, turning around quickly with widened eyes. A dark snake violently flung itself from the man's arm, hissing wildly. Stretch's extended arm immediately came between the snake and I as he shouldered me out of the way. I slid to the floor with a yelp as Stretch gritted his teeth in pain while the snake's fangs dug into his skin. I quickly wrapped a small knife inside my pocket in my smoke and shot it towards the snake as Stretch flailed away from it. The knife's pristine edge sliced the body of the dark snake as it continued across the aisle before striking the man in the shoulder.

Stretch's arm slowly went back to normal as he held the puncture wounds on his arm with gritted teeth. Blood coursed down his arm, dripping onto his bleached jeans as he stared at me in shock. The man cried out in agony as he stared at the smoke covered knife sticking out of his shoulder, waving his hand towards me. People inside the store worriedly cried out in confusion from the noise as I scrambled to my feet towards Stretch. I gently pulled him to his feet and glanced down at his bloody arm before narrowing my eyes at the man staring fearfully at me. I frowned, pulling my half-fallen mask backup my face as I retracted the smoke column with the blood knife towards me.

"That power…" the man breathed. "I know…" he hesitated. "You are," the man gritted his teeth in pain as he gripped his bleeding shoulder. "I know who you are!"

"You do?" I asked slowly, tipping my head slightly. "How strange." I beamed, narrowing my eyes at him. I glanced disapprovingly down at the cut-open snake laying on the floor before I quickly grabbed Stretch's good arm and jogged quickly to the exit of the store. Employees and other customers frantically scrambled out of my way from my glare as I tightened my grip on Stretch and I mumbled under my breath. *Great. Now we have to move quickly.* I scoffed as I angrily glanced at Stretch. *Screw staying hidden. We're getting this done my way.*

"We're here to see Mrs. Fey!" Maeve explained happily, leaning her elbows on the Southside Elite Headquarters' front desk.

"Mrs. Fey isn't having visitors today, ma'am," the woman at the front desk sighed.

"Oh, come on," Maeve chuckled, darkly glancing at everyone staring at her from behind the front desk. "You don't remember me?" she asked, pulling down her mask with a smirk. I shivered as the team members behind the front desk all froze with widened eyes as Maeve smiled happily at them. "Let us in." Maeve beamed, twirling her switchblade in her hand calmly.

The five of us stood in tense silence as we watched the elevator number on the side of the wall slowly climb higher and higher.

"How long has it been since you've seen any of them?" Randy asked softly, glancing at Maeve.

"Since I mixed the files a few years back and stabbed Mrs. Fey on the way out," she responded calmly.

"Wait," Stretch gasped, his eye twitching in pain as he knocked his puncture arm against the wall. "You worked for the Elites at some point?" he asked, exasperated.

"Not my brightest choice in my life, but screwing up things for them was a *joy*." Maeve sighed, slyly smiling at the broken camera staring down at us. *I forgot you used to work here at the Elite headquarters, how ironic that you're working to destroy them now.*

"You all stay out of sight of the guards at the entrance. Come inside only if I tell you to," I ordered, pressing down on my earpiece.

"Be careful, True, the place is swarming with police out here already!" Stella growled through the channel. Maeve giggled softly, swiping the bloody switchblade on her jeans with a smirk before staring intently at me.

"Thank Maeve for at least getting us in," I sighed.

"You're welcome." Maeve smiled. Stella grumbled under her breath before she began yelling at Fletcher before cutting off. *You all need to be extra careful. We'll be quick: Get the files and get out.*

The elevator doors pulled open peacefully, revealing the main computer room. The desks lined the glass walls, filled with books, computers, and people sitting at their desks, speaking into microphones. A woman wearing a bullet proof vest and a golden badge on her chest stood in the center of the room, her back towards the elevator as she stared out at the city. *I'm guessing that's Mrs. Fey, head manager of the Elite headquarters of New York City.* Two guards in dark suits turned quickly towards the elevator as I calmly stepped out.

"Hey, you all can't be here," one guard snapped, pointing roughly towards me. I suddenly materialized two pistols in front of each guard and shot them to the ground, keeping my gaze on Mrs. Fey. Shrieks of horror filled the room from the gunshots as I materialized pistols at every person sitting at a desk.

"Everyone put their hands where we can see them, and no one else will get hurt," I ordered boldly. I glanced over my shoulder at Cohen, Stretch, and Randy before tipping my head to the elevator. Maeve quickly darted past me, shoving a man out of his seat and spinning around happily in the chair before she began typing on the computer.

Mrs. Fey turned around calmly; her brow furrowed with worry as I slowly walked across the room towards her. Loud rumbling noises echoed through the panicked air as the elevator's cables snapped. Horrid screeching noises and booms filled the stairwell as the elevator violently slammed against the metal shaft, falling all the way down the building. As the huge metal doors closed, the echoes of the crashes became muffled, sending a chill across the entire room. I kept my pistol in hand aimed up at Mrs. Fey as she stared disapprovingly at me. *I dare you to try anything.*

"True Leader," Mrs. Fey spat slowly, tipping her chin up to me.

"Good afternoon, ma'am." I beamed insincerely, narrowing my eyes at her.

"I see you've recruited one of my best employees," Mrs. Fey growled, glancing at Maeve typing on the computer.

"Oh shut up! You hated my guts, and everyone knew it!" Maeve snarled, glaring darkly up at us.

"Focus. Ignore her," I snapped, glancing over my shoulder at her. I rolled my eyes as I saw Cohen and Stretch shove each other around as they took the people sitting at the desks' weapons away. Randy smiled awkwardly at my glare before he widened his eyes.

"True!" he cried. A loud gunshot echoed through the silent room, making everyone scream. I immediately turned around and glared down at Mrs. Fey laying on the ground, clutching her chest and gasping, her own gun inches from her fingertips.

"You really think that trying to shoot me was going to work?" I asked. I waved my hand at the gun laying on the ground as a column of smoke slowly extended from my palm, wrapping tightly around it and snapping it in half moments later. Mrs. Fey whimpered slightly as I dropped both pieces of the gun directly next to her and frowned.

"Maeve, can you hurry up!" Cohen suddenly snarled. "There's people coming up the stairwell!" he hissed. I turned over my shoulder with widened eyes. Stretch darted across the room, picking up staplers and books from the desks, extending his arm towards Cohen and tossing them to him. Cohen angrily launched the objects into the stairwell as loud snapping noises echoed through the concrete shaft. Moments later, Cohen flicked both his arms past the doorway as a wall of his white flames shot down the stairwell.

"I'm trying!" Maeve snarled back over her shoulder.

"What are you trying to accomplish!" Mrs. Fey snarled up at me. I sighed as I turned calmly towards her and leaned slightly down.

"You know exactly what's wrong with your company," I chuckled.

Mrs. Fey's angered face immediately fell. *Exactly. Try and protect the Elites. All these people in this room will watch you make a fool of yourself if you do.* Mrs. Fey narrowed her eyes as the people around the room worriedly glanced at one another, keeping their hands up.

"You should thank us, you know!" Stretch suddenly laughed.

"We're fixing the things everyone is too scared to talk about!" Randy snapped, smiling wildly at Stretch's smirk.

"I have them!" Maeve called, quickly standing up and tucking a USB into the pocket inside her jacket.

"You're a traitor Maeve!" Mrs. Fey snarled angrily. "You're all villains!" she hissed, sitting up weakly towards me. Maeve, Stretch, Cohen, and Randy all began laughing softly with sly glances at each other as the people around the room shifted fearfully. I rolled my eyes and fired a second round into her shoulder, making her scream in agony.

"You think we didn't already know this?" I grumbled, leaning down towards her.

I fired several bullets into the giant glass pane in front of us as I roughly grabbed Mrs. Fey by her shoulders and forced her to her feet in front of me. A knife flung itself violently past us, grazing the side of her neck before shattering the glass completely. I glanced over to see Maeve staring at Mrs. Fey with narrowed eyes, her hand frozen in the air. One of the muffled sirens suddenly became painfully loud as the cold wind filled the tense room. The people sitting still at their desks cried out in panic, pleading for their lives towards the four staring at them.

"This is for every innocent person your Elites screwed over," I darkly spat, staring directly into Mrs. Fey's eyes. I materialized several more pistols floating around me, firing them all at once. The bullets struck Mrs. Fey roughly, knocking her back closer to the open window. She fell to the ground, screaming in agony on the ledge as I slowly walked towards her. Her eyes were wide with pain and anger as she stared up at me, gasping for breath while blood spilled from her body. I frowned slightly as I gently nudged her backwards with my foot. The small push from me sent her tippling over the edge, disappearing from the window.

The people sitting at the desks screamed in fear as I turned around and jogged across the room, staring at them.

"I'd suggest not helping this crooked system anymore!" I screamed. "Who wants to end up like her?" I asked loudly, roughly pointing to the ledge Mrs. Fey fell from. The people sitting at their desks stayed silent as they stared at me. "This is a warning that you're all going to spread once this is over," I snarled coldly, stalking closer towards the stairwell. "The people of the Underworld's silence isn't weakness or proof that you all have won," I snarled softly. "It is merely the beginning of our revenge." The entire room shifted; eyes filled with horror staring back at me before I waved my hand at the stairwell door.

After pushing through countless rows of armed guards lining the streets and getting briefly separated, we regrouped together in an abandoned warehouse a few blocks away from the Elite headquarters.

Sirens blared through the streets as helicopters swarmed over the city. We all breathed hard, staring at each other in proud silence. I glanced over everyone and sighed in relief at not seeing anyone too badly injured. My heart spiked out of my chest at seeing a deep gash across Stella's shoulder, her light eyes wide with worry as she stared at Ryth and Eela sitting next to me. I frowned slightly as she glanced up at me and narrowed her eyes before I turned over my shoulder to Stretch sitting away from everyone.

Stretch laid on his back, breathing hard as he clutched his side. His white metal mask had been broken on one side completely, revealing a patch of scarred skin on the edge of his jaw. I widened my eyes as I saw his hands covered in blood as it seeped through his dark shirt.

"Are you okay, Stretch?" I asked worriedly, breaking the silence. Everyone shivered as we turned to him worriedly. Stretch said nothing, nodding quickly as he kept his gaze on the ceiling. I flinched as I saw dark bruises forming on the side of his neck. *When did he get those?*

"Can you get a hold of Heal?" Cami asked softly, kneeling behind Fletcher and frowning slightly. Stretch scoffed, weakly reaching into his pocket and pulled out his phone in multiple pieces, dropping it to the ground next to him.

"I don't think so," Stretch spat.

"Use my phone then," I sighed, slowly taking mine out of my pocket and shuffling over towards him. Stretch stayed on his back, bringing his bloody hand to his mask to hold it on as he gently took my phone with a furrowed brow. We all waited in anxious silence as he began trying to call Heal, receiving no response each time. I frowned and shook my head as I took the phone back from him.

"He normally answers…" Stretch mumbled, sitting up with a grimace. He held his bleeding side tightly in one hand as he held up his broken mask with the other.

"Maybe he just doesn't recognize my number," I sighed.

"No. He would at least answer once," Stretch grumbled. Cohen's gaze immediately shifted over to Stretch while he knelt next to Randy and Maeve, keeping his arms on the cold concrete as steam rose from them. I sighed and frowned down at my cracked phone in my hand with unease. As I was about to tuck my phone back into my pocket when it began to ring. Everyone flinched as they looked towards me expectantly.

"It's Boss," I sighed, bringing the phone up to my ear.

"True!" Boss cried. "Thank goodness you're alright!" she breathed, clearing her throat.

"Is everything okay?" I asked, frowning at Stretch as he rolled his eyes.

"Well…" she hesitantly responded. I widened my eyes and put the phone on speaker, holding it out to everyone in my shaking hand. "Is everyone with you alive?" Boss asked nervously.

"Yes ma'am. We're all here and listening," I gently responded, grinning softly at everyone.

"Heal has been found dead," Boss suddenly growled, her voice wavering. Everyone inhaled sharply as we widened our eyes. Stretch bowed his head slowly, resting his shaking elbow on his knee as he held up his mask, a blank expression on his face. "Authorities with armed guards and Elites chose rooms at random in the complex building, looking for you all," she explained. "You're all not badly injured, right?" Boss asked nervously.

I glanced around slowly at everyone and sighed with relief.

"Nothing life threatening, I think," I mumbled softly, staring intently at Stretch's bleeding side with a frown.

"You all stay put and out of sight from the streets until I can get someone over there to transport you all back to the complex," Boss chuckled angrily. "That complex is a dangerous place to be, True. It's already a top tier target as a suspect for your presence," she spat. I closed my eyes and fought back a snarky comment towards her. "It's going to be awhile before the complex becomes safe again and everything else around you guys calms down. Sit tight, I'll be working on something for you all, but I'm here if you need me," Boss explained, voices of people becoming more prominent around her. Moments later, she hung up without another word.

Fletcher slowly stood up and shuffled next to Stretch with a concerned grin on his face. His shaking, lanky hand gently reached up and rested on his shoulder as Stretch's expression darkened slightly while he blinked quickly with a furrowed brow.

"Do we at least have what we need from that place?" Stella groaned.

"Yep," Maeve beamed, reaching into her jacket pocket. "Names of every single Elite and their records, hidden from the public or not, are on this USB,"

"Good. Cause I'm not definitely doing that again," Cohen grumbled under his breath, frowning at his sizzling arms. Everyone giggled slightly with relieved glances at each other before we fell into a grateful silence.

CHAPTER 30

BACK AT THE SUITE, SEVERAL HOURS LATER...

Warm, relieved laughter filled my ears as I sat at the dining table next to Maeve typing quickly on her computer. My head throbbed in my hand as I watched her search through each Elite profile, taking notes of every crime under their name. *Finally, getting closer to change...* I glanced up away from the screen and sighed, holding back a smile at Fletcher and Cami tickling Ryth and Eela on the tile floor. My heart spiked in my chest at seeing Ryth's genuine smile across her face as Fletcher picked her up and fell over. Cami and Eela's laughter turned into silent wheezing as they covered their faces against the tile.

Maeve sighed, holding back a smile as she shook her head at Randy giggling softly under his breath from the couch. His bright, amber eyes glanced mischievously up at Maeve, making her scoff and turn her attention back to the computer. Stella smiled up at my glance towards her as she wrapped Cohen's steaming arms with cold, wet rags in the kitchen. I winced slightly as Cohen gritted his teeth as more steam flew up from his arm under the rag. Stella sighed with a nervous grin at his annoyed glare before looking back over towards me. My heart swelled in my chest under her gaze before I shook my head and turned back to the computer screen in front of Maeve.

I inhaled to ask Maeve a question as Stella suddenly cleared her throat. Maeve's cold, dark eyes glared up at Stella from over the computer screen before the two of them narrowed their eyes at one another playfully. I looked up at her with raised brows before she frowned at me and tipped her head across the living room. The laughter in the room immediately subsided under Stella's glare. I shivered slightly as the room seemed to shift as Stella tipped her head across the room again. I furrowed my brow at her and slowly leaned over, gazing behind Fletcher holding Cami in a headlock on the tile. My heart began to ache in my chest as I frowned at Stretch sitting alone on the balcony.

Eela and Ryth's gazes met mine as they worriedly glanced at him before turning to me with a hopeful expression. I shook my head and stood up slowly, waving my hand at them as I slowly made my way across the room. Fletcher quickly pushed himself backwards with his feet, dragging Cami with him as they both held back their laughter towards one another. My heart began beating out of my chest the closer I got towards the balcony doors. I glanced over my shoulder, looking at everyone intently before I sighed and pushed open the sliding glass door.

Cold wind immediately smacked me in the face, making me grimace slightly as I closed the door behind me. Stretch kept his back towards me as he stared out at the lively skyscrapers shining brightly against the night sky. I frowned as I tucked my hands inside my hoodie pocket and sat silently in the chair next to him. The cold wind brushing against my skin made me tremble as I frowned at Stretch not wearing his jacket that he always had. *I don't even know what to say to him; I've never seen him like this.* I glanced softly at him in the corner of my eye and sighed before turning my gaze back to the stars shining dimly in the sky. I bit my lip softly as my heart spiked in my chest before I inhaled sharply and sat up in my seat.

"Are you alright?" I asked softly, my voice wavering. My heart roared in my ears as I tensed, waiting for him to respond. Stretch stayed silent, his cold gaze staring at the skyscrapers in front of us. I shivered softly at seeing the lower half of his face covered by an old, black t-shirt instead of his normal white metal mask or bandana. My eyes drifted across the side of his face as I blinked several times. A jagged scar coming from under the shirt slowly reached under his ear on his jaw. *That's not for secrecy. You're hiding something.* Stretch's bruised hand immediately reached up to the side of his face as he furrowed his brow, pulling the t-shirt tighter around his head, covering the small open patch of skin.

"Why would you want to know?" Stretch snapped softly, glaring at me in the corner of his seeing eye. I sighed, holding back a scoff of annoyance as I shook my head.

"You're part of this Agency, right?" I began. "It's my job to check on you guys," I mumbled, glancing over my shoulder at everyone gathered in the living room. Stretch tensed suddenly as his hand paused on the side of his head. His hand began to shake slightly as he narrowed his eyes towards me. He exhaled, dropping his hand into his lap and shaking his head slightly.

"That's never happened," Stretch spat.

"Excuse me?" I sighed, furrowing my brow slightly at him.

"Someone actually checking on me," he sadly laughed. "I wasn't exactly around people who *cared* for a pretty long time," Stretch grumbled, flicking his bruised hand to the glass door behind us. I frowned and nodded, turning my gaze back to the city. *Neither was I.* The cold air around us gave one final gust before it became still. The once chilly air slowly warmed, allowing both of us to sigh softly in relief.

"I'm guessing people who didn't care did that to your face?" I suddenly offered, inhaling sharply. Stretch tensed, darting his suddenly angry gaze over to me as he clenched his fists, sitting up in his chair.

"Why would you—?" Stretch began angrily.

"You're obviously hiding it for a reason," I spat, interrupting him. "Why would you care so much about me seeing that one scar near your jaw? Hm?" I asked him gently. Stretch's blind eye was blank, sending an eerie chill down my back; his dark seeing eye was filled with distress and concern. I grinned softly as he stared intently back at me, saying nothing. "I notice the little things about people." I sighed gently. "Things people hope no one sees or cares to ask about," I continued. "Things people wish they could get rid of…" I whispered, my voice wavering. I trembled slightly at remembering my father hiding the bruises on his body from my mother as I blinked tears out of my eyes. "I see it. All of it," I mumbled, glancing at him slowly with a small grin as I furrowed my brow. Stretch's intent gaze softened slightly as he gently relaxed, leaning back in his chair. He closed his eyes, resting his head on the back of the chair as he shook his head.

"You really want to know?" Stretch grumbled. I nodded once, turning back to him and grinning gently.

"It's my job to know about you all, the pretty and the ugly," I beamed. "I wouldn't be a good leader if I didn't know and care for each of my troops," I chuckled, waving my hand to the glass door behind us. Stretch's eyes slightly narrowed as if he was grinning, and my heart spiked out of my chest.

"I see why Boss chose to put so much effort into you now," Stretch sighed. I raised my brow at him slightly as he shook his head and pushed himself up in his seat, his face going blank.

His bruised hands slowly reached up towards his face as he turned fully towards me. The black t-shirt hiding his face gently was pulled down, resting around his neck. I widened my eyes slightly as I inhaled. The lower half of his face was covered in faint, jagged, scars, some running down his neck. Mixed under the scars were patches of burned skin that made me shiver. I furrowed my brow as I clenched my fists and blinked quickly. Stretch frowned, sighing deeply and turning his gaze back to the city. *I can see why he wants to hide that, but he doesn't need to. Not with us.*

"I know. It's bad," Stretch mumbled. "I've lived with my face covered up and being half blind for a little over two years now," he sadly smiled. "When I was 19, my older brothers had their friend group from school jump me in a back alley, and they left me to die," he growled, his voice becoming cold as his eyes darkened. I shifted slightly in my seat with a frown as I looked at him intently. His seeing eye was narrowed, anger dwelling beneath the surface, while his blind eye stayed mostly emotionless. His fists clenched slightly as he turned his dark gaze to the tile floor below us as he frowned and bit his lip.

"I tried asking for help, and no one cared." Stretch snapped angrily. *You and I are more similar than you may think...* "Until one of Boss' scouts found me and took me in," he sighed, his voice wavering. Stretch took a deep breath as he shook his head and slowly lifted his shaking arm up towards me. "Boss gave me a second chance at life," he frowned. "I owe her everything," he whispered, quickly pulling the black t-shirt back over his face while I stared at the Roman numeral II tattooed onto his skin. I nodded slowly and turned my gaze back to the skyscrapers in front of us. My heart beat out of my chest with pity as I glanced at Stretch next to me several times while we sat in silence.

"You can sleep here tonight instead of going back to your suite if you'd like," I offered slowly. "I can understand not wanting to be in the same room that you lost someone you cared about in," I mumbled, rubbing the back of my neck quickly as I stood up. Stretch's dark eye caught mine, making me shiver, and I turned away from his gaze, my heart spiking out of my chest. Stretch narrowed his eyes slightly and furrowed his brow as he crossed his arms. I rolled my eyes and pulled the sliding glass door open.

"Don't play tough with me," I growled over my shoulder at him. "I can read people better than you think I can." I smiled. My smile fell slightly as Stretch scoffed and rubbed his head slowly. "I know you're hurting, Stretch." I sighed. "But you don't have to face that pain alone anymore. We're all here," I sternly explained. Stretch tensed slightly as he turned his gaze around towards me. We stared intently at one another for a moment before I relaxed my face and tipped my head inside. He looked down at his shaking arms for a second as he stood up and nodded, keeping his eyes away from mine.

"Sleep in my room, Stretch," Cohen offered softly from inside. "I'll sleep on the couch," he sighed, waving his hand to the couch behind him. Stretch narrowed his eyes as flames flickered from behind Cohen's as they stared at one another. Cohen blinked without saying anything else as he calmly walked down the hall and turned into his room. Stretch glanced at me with a furrowed brow as I shrugged at him and waved my hand to Cohen leaning into the hallway waiting for him. I sighed in relief as Stretch finally began walking silently towards him while I turned and went into my room.

CHAPTER 31

THE NEXT MORNING...

Distant, frantic mumbles filled my ears as I was shaken awake. I blinked quickly, sitting up with widened eyes as Stella shook me.

"Boss has been calling you!" Stella hissed, shoving the phone into my hands. I sighed and shook my head as I stared at the several missed calls from her with a frown. Stella waved her hand at the phone in my hands before she rolled her eyes and walked back into our bathroom mumbling under her breath. My fingers shook gently as I began to read all Boss' messages towards me. As I was going to call her back, the phone began buzzing again in my hands making me flinch. *Jeez, you're persistent.*

"True! There you are!" Boss' loud voice chuckled, relieved.

"Sorry, ma'am, I didn't mean to—"

"Anyways, now that you're here, I wanted to ask for another favor!" Boss snapped, interrupting me. I widened my eyes and shook my head as I frowned. "Make sure you send the list Maeve makes as soon as she's done with it," she admitted. "I need to double check everything, and if we disagree on whether or not someone is staying on the list or going on the list will be discussed in person, okay?" she beamed proudly as a keyboard clicked away from her side of the phone.

"Yes, I'll get that to you as soon as possible," I winced, clenching my fist as the burn mark on my palm flared in pain.

"Great! Thanks!" Boss exclaimed, hanging up without another word.

"How often does she do that to you?" Stella chuckled softly from the bathroom. I scoffed into my hand as I shook my head and rubbed my eyes.

"There hasn't been a single phone call where she didn't end it like that," I mumbled. Stella giggled softly and whispered something under her breath as I frowned slightly over at her. Her light eyes immediately met my gaze, sending a chill down my back as I turned away and rolled my neck out. My phone buzzed a few times in my hand, making me roll my eyes and set it down roughly on the nightstand next to me. *It's too early to read those scout reports.*

An uneasy chill suddenly shot down my back as I leaned down to take my pistol from my desk across the room. I widened my eyes and frowned at the hair on my arms standing up on end. A series of quick buzzes from my phone made me quickly pull on my hoodie and jog across the room with a furrowed brow.

"Is that still her?" Stella scoffed.

"No, it's some of the scouts," I replied, picking up my cold phone in my shaking hands. My heart began to beat out of my chest as I quickly skimmed all the past reports from the most recent months, ignoring the new scout reports on purpose. The same chill glided across my skin as the burn on my palm hissed in pain as my pitch-black smoke slowly drifted from it.

I furrowed my brow, shaking the smoke off my hand as I read the most recent article sent by a scout. "Who is this man and why is he more dangerous than TL?" an article headline spat directly in my face. Stella shifted uncomfortably from the bathroom as I heard her grumble of disapproval. My heart continued to beat out of my chest as I scrolled through the website with a furrowed brow. Every picture of the man in the main topic of the article was blurry and low quality, sending another spike of unease down my back. I shook my head quickly as I sat down on the bed behind me and squinted at the best quality picture from the website.

The man's face was hidden by a black mask under a loose dark hood. I shivered violently as I stared into his cold brown eyes, and I widened mine. *The man from HQ...*

"Wait a second," I grumbled softly, zooming in more on the picture. My heart leapt out of my chest as I saw the same half metal arm peeking out from the ripped jacket. *This is the bastard who shot me in the street...*

"Is this man the future and savior of our society from TL and his goals?" I narrowed my eyes as a grumble of disapproval escaped my mouth. Stella inhaled to speak after staring at me from the bathroom intently as a loud yelp and thud came from the silent living room. I widened my eyes as Stella paused doing her makeup and turned towards the door with a furrowed brow. I quickly leapt up from the bed, turning my phone off and jogged across our room, pushing open the door roughly.

I widened my eyes as I saw Cohen laying on his stomach on the floor, holding his head tightly in his hands.

"Woah, Are you alright?" I asked quickly, walking over and crouching down next to him. Cohen's shuddering breaths answered my question as he stayed silent, keeping his gaze on the floor below us.

"Bad dream," Cohen hissed softly, shaking his head and slowly leaning up onto his knees. White and red flames flickered quickly from behind his dark eyes as he kept his gaze away from mine, his brow furrowed. I widened my eyes slightly as the red flames were quickly drowned out by the white. *You only have normal fire when you're in a rage. What happened?*

Cohen hissed in pain as he bumped his sizzling arm on the coffee table next to us while he struggled to his feet. My heart spiked out of my chest as wisps of flame spurted from the burned patches of skin on his arms.

"You need to ice them again," I frowned, quickly standing up.

"No, True, I'm fine—" Cohen sighed. I ignored him as I jogged into the kitchen and leaned down below the sink, grabbing the two rags before running them under cold water. Cohen mumbled under his breath as he sat himself up slowly on the couch, frowning at the steam rising from his arms.

My hands stung from the cold water as I gently draped them over Cohen's arms. Hisses of annoyance sprouted from his skin as more steam rose through the rags and Cohen gritted his teeth in pain.

"I don't understand why my arms are like this," Cohen mumbled, shying away from my hand as I reached to adjust the rag. "My arms are used to my flames," he frowned. I sighed and nodded, yelping softy as my hand brushed an uncovered part of his burning arm.

"You overused your flames for too long." I admitted. "I shouldn't have pushed you so hard to keep using them."

Cohen shook his head as he frowned at me.

"You're my boss," he sighed. "It's my job to listen to your orders," he sneered, elbowing my shoulder roughly. I rolled my eyes as I sat on the couch next to him and rubbed my red hand with a frown while Stella walked out of our room.

"Did you ice them last night like I told you to?" Stella spat gruffly.

"No," Cohen mumbled, leaning slightly away from her glare.

"Of course not," Stella snapped, shooting both of us a sly glare with an annoyed smile as she walked towards the kitchen. Cohen and I snickered under our breaths for a moment before I began moving the rags on his arms.

"We may have another lunatic trying to screw with us," I mumbled after a few minutes of silence, glancing up at Cohen's dark eyes for a moment. He furrowed his brow at me as white flames flickered briefly from behind his ears and eyes while he looked at me. I gently pulled out my phone from my hoodie pocket and opened the article back up. I scrolled quickly passed all the commentary and assumptions on the masked man before I found the best quality picture the website had.

Cohen's eyes widened suddenly as he grabbed the phone. Normal flames shot from behind his eyes as he stared intently at the phone in his hands.

"What?" I hesitantly asked, leaning away from the heat around his head.

"This man was in my dream!" Cohen snapped. "He was warning me to tell you to stay out of his way, or…" he trailed off. My heart spiked in my chest as I waited for him to continue.

"What even is he?" I asked sharply, waving my hand at his metal limbs. Cohen shrugged as he frowned and handed the phone back to me. "Maeve! Come here!" I called out loudly, frowning at the screen as I scrolled up to a picture that showed his face more.

Maeve yawned sleepily as she stumbled out from the hallway next to the couch and furrowed her brow at me.

"What?" she rasped softly, clearing her throat before standing over me disapprovingly.

"Can you figure out who this guy is?" I asked softly, turning my gaze away from her cold, tired eyes. Maeve sniffed as she took the phone and stared at the screen blankly. Her dull red hair fell gently from her head as she flicked it out of her face and squinted at the phone. I glanced behind her and saw Stella's gaze resting intently on me with a furrowed brow. I shivered slightly and narrowed my eyes as Cohen playfully nudged my shoulder after seeing me look away from Stella's gaze.

"I can't figure out who he is," Maeve suddenly admitted. "This isn't his full face," she sighed, rolling her eyes and frowning at the phone.

"Who are you trying to have her find?" Stella asked loudly.

"Some idiot who thinks he can ruin True's plans," Maeve spat gruffly, glaring over her shoulder at Stella jogging towards us. Stella quickly took the phone from Maeve's hands as they playfully narrowed their eyes at the other before Stella stared at the screen intently. I shifted slightly in my seat as the corners of Stella's eyes began to glow with her brow furrowing.

"This is the man who slashed my arm," Stella snarled darkly. I widened my eyes as my heart spiked in my chest from my looking at the tight wrap around Stella's shoulder. Cohen and Maeve worriedly glanced at one another as we all patiently waited for Stella to continue. "I had Ryth and Eela with me as we were running through the crowd away from the Elite headquarters," Stella slowly began, her eyes slowly going dim. "Fletcher and Cami were somewhere behind us, but I knew they were fine," she sighed, clenching her hands around the phone for a moment.

"As we were running past a deserted shop, I saw something move in the broken window," Stella snapped. "I had to trip Ryth and push her over to stop the blade that extended from the darkness from slicing her throat," she continued softly, her voice wavering. My heart spiked with anger in my chest as I clenched my fists. Cohen and Maeve grumbled softly under their breaths. "Ryth was able to force the knife from the person's metal hand and break it as we both stared at someone huddled in the shadows of the shop," Stella explained slowly. She shook her head as she handed the phone back to me gently.

"He didn't have the mask around the bottom half of his face," Stella continued. "Just a weird glass helmet thing over his eyes that had some kind of light set up that almost made a face," she spat. "His lower jaw was metal," Stella shivered, rubbing her arms slowly as her eyes became filled with worry.

"Why would he try killing Ryth?" Maeve snapped.

"She's a child!" Cohen added angrily.

"He's the man who shot me," I gruffly snarled. The three of them flinched and fell silent as they tensed under my gaze. We all shifted uncomfortably as we stared at the image of the man glaring over his shoulder at the camera. *Who are you?*

CHAPTER 32

UNKNOWN POV – NORTHSIDE CITY POLICE STATION...

"Aren't you the man who was able to shoot True Leader?" the officer asked me sharply. I blinked calmly at him and remained silent as more officers warily came from the office behind him, their hands hovering near their guns on their sides. "Holy crap, that is him!" one of the other officers cried softly, stepping back.

"I am here to assure you that I am not the enemy here," I gently grinned, lifting my hands out harmlessly. The metal from my right arm glinted sharply into my eyes from the bright LED lights above me as I stared at the group of police officers standing in front of me.

"Who exactly are you?" The first officer asked warily.

"Someone who is going to fix a lot of things True Leader has screwed up," I replied calmly.

"No, your name, genius," the officer half laughed, tensing slightly as I narrowed my eyes at him.

"Why does a name have to be stated in this conversation?" I chuckled. "I'm only here to let you all know that True Leader and his group of goons are going to be off their guard and weak from the attack on the Elite Headquarters." I explained. "I know exactly where some of them will be in precisely three hours, and I'm giving you a friendly *hint* on where that location is," I gruffly stated, bringing my hands behind my back slowly and leaning towards the officers.

"The police stations around the city are next in line to be attacked by True and his delinquents, and I know exactly how to stop him,"

The officers standing in front of me all worriedly furrowed their brows as they glanced at one another.

"How do you know this for sure?" one of them asked warily.

"If you question me or show hesitation in believing my words, I will promise you, everything will hit the fan *very* quickly for a lot of officers in the force!" I sharply snarled, stepping towards them roughly. My metal boot hitting the tile floor made the building tremble all around us as the officers stepped away from my glare. "You are all questioning me currently, and that is not a good sign," I began sternly. "All of you are wondering who I still am and how I have access to this information on True and his Agency," I continued. "Now you are all beginning to become worried about how I exactly know what you all are thinking about right now as I'm quickly explaining everything to you,"

The officers all tensed, their hands slowly gliding towards their guns as their eyes filled with fear stared up at me. I laughed softly as I relaxed myself and glared around at other people inside the police station worriedly watching us.

"I want to warn you all that I should be the least of your worries," I spat. "True has every single file of all the Elites in New York City and is working towards killing most of them," I snarled. "If you don't want that to happen, I suggest you listen to my every word and make sure you do exactly what I say when I tell you to do it, okay?" I sneered calmly. "If you all want to keep having an easy job and leave all the hard work to the Elites, I suggest that you go and tell your chief exactly what I've said," I continued. "Unless you just want to have an overloaded amount of work again with most of the Elites saving you to be *dead.*"

CHAPTER 33

TRUE'S POV – THREE HOURS LATER...

"I don't understand why several of my scouts would have wanted us to go to this location..." I grumbled under my breath, frowning at the quick short messages on my phone.

"Maybe they found something having to do with that guy Maeve wasn't able to find?" Randy asked hesitantly, shying away from her sharp glare at him. Ryth trembled next to me slightly as I pulled her in front of me while a group of rowdy teenagers skated past us full speed. I shrugged and tucked my phone back into my pocket, glancing warily up at the crowded street. A cold gust of wind made the four of us tremble as it brushed passed us roughly.

My heart spiked out of my chest as a fiery red-haired woman suddenly darted out of an alleyway, knocking Randy roughly to the ground.

"What is your problem?" Randy snarled angrily from the ground as Maeve tensed.

"My bad," the woman gasped, glaring at Ryth and I for a moment. "The scouts are this way. Too many police up ahead, they'll recognize you," the woman explained. Maeve pulled Randy up from the ground and tightly held his arm as he tensed and stepped towards the woman with his amber eyes wide with anger. I narrowed my eyes and frowned at her sharp gaze at me for a moment.

"Why would the scouts not tell me themselves that they changed locations?" I asked calmly, masking the worry in my voice. The fiery-haired woman raised her brow and frowned at me for a moment before my phone went off. She smirked at me slowly before she glared at the people walking past us and turned and walked swiftly down into the alley. Randy mumbled angrily and quickly under his breath in Spanish as his body trembled with anger. He glanced over his shoulder at me. I waved my hand at him and glanced at Ryth under my arm and sighed before we hesitantly followed the woman.

"What exactly have the scouts found?" I asked sternly after walking in silence for a few moments.

"Traitor scouts giving our information to police and Elites," the woman in front of me replied sharply. "They have the known ones contained, but there could be more," she explained, glancing over her shoulder at me.

"How come I've never seen you before? Who even are you?" I asked softly. The woman chuckled under her breath and shook her head, turning her gaze away from me.

"I'm from Stretch's group. Boss reassigned me a few days ago," the woman pridefully spat. I furrowed my brow as Maeve and Randy looked quickly at me and Ryth shivered. *Stretch or Boss would have told us something about a new person being assigned to us, right?*

The pit of unease only grew more in my stomach the longer we walked away from the busy street. The buildings towering over us slowly became more rundown and abandoned as the ground below us deteriorated in quality. *This is near the merging border to the lower class… Why did they move so far away from the original location?* I clenched my fists as my heart spiked in my chest from Randy kicking a glass bottle and it shattering against a metal dumpster. Maeve roughly hit his arm as he sighed and shook his head, running his lanky hand through his curls falling into his eyes.

"I don't like this, True," Ryth mumbled softly, leaning into my side. I nodded and gently lifted my arm over her shoulder as I glanced down at her. "Why are your scouts suddenly being all weird and secretive?"

"They have to change their communication with me to declare how important or serious something is," I explained calmly. "If they're all blunt and open about something, it means that it's low threat, and I can be mostly off guard." I continued. "If they become secretive, quiet, and shady like this, it means that there is a problem arising that needs to be taken seriously," I grinned. Randy and Maeve nodded, warily glancing at the woman walking in front of us. Ryth frowned and glared sharply at the woman as she ran her shaking fingers over her scarred wrists.

"How much longer are we—" I harshly began.

The woman walking in front of us suddenly disappeared. The four of us froze with widened eyes as we stared intently at where she once stood. My heart began to beat out of my chest as I watched the air ripple slightly as something moved away from us.

"What the?" Maeve snarled softly, flicking her switchblade open from her sleeve quickly and turning towards me. Randy lifted his arms and let them fall to his sides as he mumbled under his breath and glared up at the destroyed buildings all around us. I took a deep breath and frowned at the broken street sign dangling from an old light. *I guess we're at the place we needed to be then.*

"True, I think we need to leave," Ryth whimpered softly, tightening her grip on my arm making me grit my teeth in pain.

"Everything's fine, Ryth," Maeve growled as gently as she could. "The new scout is just being a pain in the *ass!*" she yelled angrily, her raspy voice echoing through the broken buildings. Randy snickered under his breath as he nodded and dusted off his maroon turtleneck sweater sleeves. Ryth shook her head and leaned away slightly with a worried glance behind me. I furrowed my brow as I watched her dull blue eyes become filled with fear. *What's scaring you so much?*

"Guys, I think she's right—" I whispered, my heart spiking out of my chest. The abandoned buildings around us violently trembled, interrupting me. "Down!" I snarled, immediately pulling Ryth forward and shouldering into Maeve. A loud gunshot fired through the tense air, the bullet ricocheting off a light post behind me. The light post groaned painfully as it snapped in half. The old, rusted metal immediately gave in on itself and lunged down towards us. I quickly extended columns of smoke from my palms, wrapping it tightly and gritting my teeth in pain as I barely was able to hold it up. The metal groaned again as more weight was added onto it from something above. My entire body trembled as I lay on my back, my gaze intently focusing on the light post trembling above us.

"Hands in the air! You're surrounded!" a loud voice through a megaphone suddenly snarled.

"It was a set up!" Randy roared angrily, pulling his pistol out from his side and firing it several times over the dumpster. Police officers and people dressed in all black appeared out of thin air on every side of us in the alleyway with raised guns. *Where did they even come from?!*

"True!" Ryth cried worriedly as I shifted the light post away from the three of them and hovered it over me. With one swift motion and a cry of pain, I launched the broken light post over me with the smoke column.

The smoke forced the light post down the alley as it screamed in agony. The large metal light post knocked roughly into the police officers and people dressed in all black that were charging down the alleyway towards us. Cries of pain erupted in the air as guns fired at random, bullets shattering windows along the buildings surrounding us as they were hit with the rusted metal. I gasped in relief as I quickly pulled myself up and casted out a wall of my pitch-black smoke down the opposite alley. My heart beat out of my chest as I brought my sleeve to my face and glanced worriedly at the three behind me on the ground.

The three of them quickly brought their sleeves in front of their faces as my wall of pitch-black smoke lunged down the alley. The officer's cries of agony were silenced abruptly as the wall of smoke passed them quickly, giving them no time to react. All of them immediately fell to the ground limp, dropping their guns roughly to the ground. My lungs stung painfully in my chest as I coughed violently into my arm and my legs faltered. *Sure, my own smoke isn't deadly to me, but this still hurts like hell!* My breaths became raspy as the smoke wall down the alley faded up into the sky while I quickly reached down and pulled Ryth to her feet with Randy and Maeve right behind her.

Bright, fiery-red hair suddenly appeared out of thin air next to me as sharp green eyes glared into my soul. The woman who led us here quickly ripped Ryth's arm away from me as she forced me to the ground. Her hand grasped something invisible as she swung it down at me. I panicked at not being able to materialize a pistol and widened my eyes as my pistol suddenly appeared in her hands. The loud gunshot echoed loudly in my ears as the stone next to my face was suddenly shattered, and pieces of the stone slashed the side of my face.

My pistol was thrown violently across the alley as Maeve collided with the woman above me. The two of them wrestled with one another on the slick stone, bright red hair and dull red hair in a frenzy as they cursed one another. More people in all-black clothing suddenly appeared out of thin air as the buildings trembled violently.

"Randy! Get Ryth out of here!" I yelled angrily over my screaming ears. I rolled onto my stomach and held out my hand as I focused on my pistol lying next to a drain leading down into the sewers. In the corner of my eye, Randy grabbed Ryth as she began screaming something, and they disappeared around the corner of the abandoned buildings.

The woman screamed in agony as Maeve slashed her sharp switchblade across her side, and the two of them fell into an old, glass panel, shattering it easily. One of the people in all-black clothing stepped roughly on my pistol as I narrowed my eyes. The pistol violently slid out from under them, sending them to the ground. My heart lurched in my chest as sparks flew out from under the metal gun as it slid across the broken tile towards me. Once my fingers brushed the pistol, I immediately materialized multiple around me and fired at the people charging towards me.

An angry yell echoed through the buildings as they trembled. A tall, burly man in all-black suddenly appeared standing over me. His rough hands violently grabbed my neck and threw me to my feet before he punched me roughly in the chest, sending me back to the ground. I coughed and gritted my teeth in pain as I kicked him in the knee and forced myself back up, knocking into him roughly. My smoke spilled from my palms and wrapped itself around my arms as I struggled to get the tall man away from me.

The man suddenly disappeared from in front of me as the walls trembled. I quickly turned around, searching for him as my heart beat out of my chest. He appeared directly behind me and kicked me roughly to the ground, making me gasp in pain. *Whatl kind of power is that!* The man violently picked me up by my shoulders as he grabbed my pistol lying on the ground next to me. He lifted the gun to fire as a switchblade suddenly flung itself towards us. The blade sliced through his arm easily, making him cry out in agony before disappearing, the buildings trembling.

Maeve ran over to me and breathed hard as she quickly picked up her blade from the ground and helped me to my feet. I grabbed my pistol as I gritted my teeth in pain, and we both darted back down the alley.

"What is happening!" Maeve snarled angrily as we ran.

"I don't know!" I gasped weakly, clutching my chest in pain. The buildings all around us continued to tremble as more angry voices echoed through the tense air. *Who organized this attack? How did they get so many troops?* Our footsteps echoed painfully loud over the voices surrounding us making us both wince. "We can't go to the main street! Police will be waiting there!" I hissed angrily, forcing myself to not get dragged by Maeve anymore.

"Where do we go then!" she asked, shoving my arm off her with narrowed eyes.

"True! Maeve!" Randy's worried voice suddenly yelled. We both turned and saw him leaning around the corner of an abandoned warehouse with widened eyes and a scuffed face.

"We'll have to hide for now!" I growled, darting forward towards him. "I'll contact Boss and tell her to send help!" I laughed angrily, holding my chest tightly as I ran.

"How was our communication hacked again!" I snarled sharply into the phone.

"I don't know, True!" Boss snarled back. "Whoever is behind this sure is *extremely* persistent!" she hissed, slamming her fist on her desk. "You all need to keep moving!" she ordered quickly.

"Move where? We're practically surrounded!" Maeve laughed angrily.

"Go to the main street, I know it sound like a stupid idea but trust me!" Boss growled.

"The main street!" Randy cried, clenching his fists.

"We'll immediately get killed if we go out to the main street! Police are surrounding this entire area!" I angrily spat.

"I promise you; I'll have someone there to help, just go!" Boss pleaded, hanging up immediately. I clenched my fists angrily as I waved my hand in the air and coughed hollowly into my arm.

"I'm not going out to the main street to have my head blown off by the cops!" Maeve hissed, stepping towards me roughly.

"Well, we'll have our heads blown off either way at this point, so let's just say screw it and go!" Randy snapped, wheezing into his bleeding arm afterwards. Ryth giggled slightly behind me as we all began to jog towards one of the doors of the building as Maeve and I held back our laughter.

"Try and hide your faces if you can!" I breathed tiredly as we approached the main street. "Act normal!"

"Oh, so we have to act like we totally didn't almost just die? Okay," Randy mumbled. Ryth and Maeve snorted into their arms as I rolled my eyes and smiled at him for a moment. I glanced at all of them and frowned as my heart spiked out of my chest. *We're going to stick out like a sore thumb regardless of what we do. Boss you better know what you're doing, cause at this point, I'm questioning my Agency's safety with working under you.*

The four of us merged into the crowded street, receiving wide eyes glances from the people all around us. *Come on...* My heart only beat louder and louder out of my chest as police cars shot down the street in our opposite direction with Elite vehicles following swiftly behind them. I widened my eyes slightly as I glanced up from the ground and locked eyes with a familiar face. Egret was walking directly towards me, her eyes wide with fear. I inhaled sharply and turned my gaze away from her again, quickly speeding up my stride. Egret darted out of my sight, making my heart leap out of my chest. *You better not think I forgot you trying to shoot me a few months ago...* My fists clenched at my sides as my heart spiked out of my chest again. The memory of my clone threatening me in the hospital overtook my mind as anxiety clawed its way up my throat.

My vision suddenly tunneled as a loud gunshot echoed through the street. My eyes focused on a bullet gliding through the air towards me. I quickly waved my hand to my side as people all around us screamed and fell to the ground. The bullet slid to a stop in front of me before I shot it back with the same force. A well-known Elite suddenly fell to the street, blood gushing from her chest as civilians all around us screamed in panic. My gaze darkened to Egret, who was kneeling on the ground next to the Elite as her cold gaze met mine again. Randy and Maeve quickly grabbed my shoulders and shoved me forward as I materialized a pistol in front of Egret and fired.

Police sirens filled the air loudly as helicopters swarmed the sky above us. We quickly darted into an alleyway, all of us breathing hard.

"Who the hell was she!" Randy hissed angrily, shoving my shoulder into the concrete wall behind me. "Why did she try getting you shot!"

"She looked like she recognized you," Ryth whispered softly.

"Because we used to be friends." I snapped, holding my chest tightly. "When I first merged with my clone a few months ago, she tried shooting me herself in the street. She's on the Elite's side." I gasped, struggling to breathe for a moment. The three of them worriedly looked at each other before we all flinched at a voice yelling at us from the street.

"Justice Reversed!" A small voice cried out angrily. I leaned slightly out from the indention in the building we were hiding in with slightly widened eyes. An older man holding a young boy's hand looked fearfully at my gaze as he was being dragged forward.

"I can help you!" the boy pridefully called, glancing back at the man behind him. Randy immediately lifted his gun towards them as Maeve flickered her switchblade out. Both paused their stride, lifting their hands. "Please sir!" the boy exclaimed. "I can help you all escape!" he pleaded, holding his hands out to the wall next to him.

"How?" Maeve snarled coldly. The shaking hands of the boy began to glow slightly as his gaze rested on the wall. Slowly, a small bright ball of light formed on the stone and began expanding with bright pink flurries around the edges. "I can make portals that can transport things! Just tell me an address!" he cried, glancing fearfully over his shoulder at the man behind him. Ryth widened her eyes up at me as Maeve and Randy tensed.

"Justice Reversed…" I sighed, nodding to him.

CHAPTER 34

SEVERAL HOURS LATER...

The four of us sat in silence in the middle of the old warehouse with worried glances at the large door in the back of the room.

"What are the chances of that?" Randy asked softly, turning over his shoulder at me and Ryth.

"Of what?" I replied, rubbing my aching chest.

"Well, one," Randy began, "us somehow not dying from that attack; and two, a kid with a portal power finding us and helping us escape to here?" he continued. Maeve scoffed into her arm softly as Ryth nodded up at me. I sighed and shook my head with a grin.

"I'm not sure," I whispered, my voice rasping horribly.

"Now what are the chances of Boss hurrying up the transport she said she was sending for us?" Maeve spat.

"Give her some time," I frowned, wincing slightly as my chest flared in pain. "She's waiting for things to calm down around the city before she sends anyone to come get us," I growled.

"Are these people coming for us going to try killing us, too?" Maeve snapped.

"At this point I have no clue," I admitted.

"Perfect!" Maeve beamed sarcastically. Randy fell over giggling into his arms as Ryth trembled with soft laughter next to me. I sighed softly at the three of them, smiling as I kept my gaze on the cold concrete floor below me. A fierce, loud knock on the door suddenly made all of us leap out of our skin.

"Boss's transport! Hurry up!" a booming voice yelled.

My heart beat out of my chest as we passed rows and rows of police cars lining the streets of New York. I glanced at the man next to me in the driver's seat and shivered at seeing a resemblance between him and one of the people I fought in the alley. My chest suddenly lurched in panic as I saw a wrap of bleeding bandages peek out from under the tight jacket around his arms. I turned over my shoulder to the three in the back and caught Maeve's dark gaze on it as well. Ryth was leaning into Randy's side as he rested his chin on her head and held her under his arm protectively, his gaze staring outside the window at the chaotic city surrounding us.

I narrowed my eyes as I kept seeing Boss' number come up on the car's radio screen but the driver ignoring it each time.

"Aren't you going to answer that?" I worriedly asked. The man tensed as his grip tightened on the steering wheel in front of him. Boss' number came up once again, making us both flinch. I reached my hand towards the dashboard to answer as the driver declined the call, shoving my hand out of the way.

"You can speak to her when you're back at the suite. It's too dangerous to discuss things out in the middle of the streets over the phone," the drive snarled softly. I widened my eyes as I leaned away from him as he glared darkly at me in the corner of his rage-filled eye. Maeve and Randy shifted uncomfortably as the man's gaze met theirs through the rearview window, and he pulled into the back alley behind the complex.

We all walked silently through the back door with a small sigh of relief. I widened my eyes as Katie waved her arm roughly at me for my attention. She shook her head now with a quick glance to her right behind the wall. I furrowed my brow at her as the car outside the complex violently sped away.

"Hide!" Katie mouthed frantically, smiling nervously at the wall. I quickly grabbed Ryth's arm and pulled her down to the ground as I ducked behind one of the couches. Randy and Maeve darted across the lobby and slid behind the old vending machines, their switchblade and gun in hand with widened eyes.

My heart beat out of my chest as I peered around the couch's edge as the same woman from the alley glared around the corner wall. Her face was covered in horrid bruises and scuffs as she narrowed her sharp green eyes and flicked her fiery-red hair out of her face. I quickly brought myself further behind the couch as I widened my eyes. *Uh oh…* Ryth trembled next to me as she held her hands over herself and shook her head quickly. A loud glass suddenly shattered against the tile as I heard Katie yelp. My heart fell in my chest as I slowly looked over the couch with a furrowed brow.

"Why are you hiding something from us!" a young, unfamiliar voice snarled.

"I told you I don't know what you're talking about!" Katie hissed angrily. A man with bright teal hair suddenly stepped out from behind the wall and glared down at Katie sitting at her desk with clenched fists. "He's never been to this building!" she continued. I flinched as the man roughly grabbed her by her shoulder and neck and pulled her out of the chair. "Then why has this building been marked as a location where he could be!" the man grumbled.

"Enough," a sleek voice suddenly sighed. Ryth violently trembled next to me as she whimpered and leaned into my side. I widened my eyes and rested my hand on her shaking shoulder as my heart began beating out of my chest. "This was just a waste of our time then," the same voice cooed. I shivered in panic as I saw the man in the article step out from behind the wall and tower over Katie and the blue haired man. "We'll just keep looking," he chuckled calmly, waving his normal, left hand at the man holding Katie. He then roughly dropped her to the floor as the red-haired woman began stalking towards the front entrance of the complex building. Katie gasped for breath as she held her neck and stared fearfully up at the man from the article standing over her.

He then suddenly froze and turned over his shoulder towards us calmly. I immediately ducked behind the couch, focusing on my heart began roaring in my ears. His heavy metal boots made the room shake as he slowly made his way towards the door after the woman. Two more sets of footprints quickly followed him and disappeared under the loud noises from the open door exposed to the street. I slowly leaned out from behind the couch with a furrowed brow. Katie shook her head at me and flinched as the walls trembled.

The driver Boss had sent was suddenly standing in the middle of the lobby with his arms tucked behind his back. *How much of Boss' system has been compromised?*

"I apologize about Delta and the others ma'am," his booming voice suddenly admitted. Ryth trembled next to me again, tightening her grip around her head as I frowned at her. "He's a little stressed right now due to some work issues, we all are," the man sighed, glaring over in our direction with a frown. *Delta. Is that this man's name? Why did he look towards us like that? Are we the "work issue"? Who the hell are these people and why is Ryth so scared of them?* The lobby trembled violently as the man suddenly disappeared.

"All of you go up to the room, quickly!" Katie suddenly exclaimed, weakly pulling herself up to her desk.

"What do you mean Boss was compromised!" Stella roared angrily.

"Again?" Cami added sharply. I ignored both of their angry comments and questions as I nudged my bedroom door closed. Maeve and Randy had begun arguing with Cohen against Stretch from the main room as Fletcher and Eela tried calming everyone down. I set my scratched pistol down roughly on my desk as I grimaced in pain. I closed my eyes and bit my lip as I quickly pulled my ripped jacket and shirt off my scuffed shoulders. The muffled arguing from the main room became louder once more as the door slowly groaned open.

"True," Stella gasped softly from behind me. I turned over my shoulder at her with a frown as I stared down at my bruised arms with a sigh. "How bad was the attack?" she asked softly, jogging over and hovering her hands over the scrapes on my skin.

"Bad enough to screw me up a little bit," I mumbled, my eye twitching in pain as my side ached.

"I seriously am starting to doubt our safety with working under Boss, True…" Stella winced, stepping in front of me as I tried walking away. Her light eyes sent a shiver down my back as the corners began to glow after she glanced at me with a frown. I shook my head and brushed past her and quickly grabbed a new shirt.

"I'll just have to talk to her about whatever is going on," I gruffly spat, pulling the new shirt on slowly.

"Talk? You know she never lets you do that!"

"Well maybe this time I'll make sure she does!" I snapped. Stella flinched and turned away from me as I sighed and relaxed my tense shoulders.

"Look at you!" she growled, waving her hand to me gently. "What's going to happen to you next?" she asked worriedly. "How long are you going to let yourself get knocked around because Boss keeps screwing up?" she continued. I kept my gaze away from her as we stood in tense silence for a moment.

"True! Get in here!" Maeve suddenly snapped. I quickly jogged out into the main room as Randy turned the TV up with a shaking hand.

"Breaking news: Proof of violence from the most feared man in New York has been reported across several blocks. Northside Police station was given an inside hint on a location True would be heading and attempted to peacefully restrain him and the others with him. Somewhere along the line during the attempt for capture, violence broke out. Over a hundred officers from multiple stations around the city have been reported dead with the numbers still rising," the reporter on the TV explained.

"*Peaceful* restraining my ass!" I snarled quietly, making everyone shiver with a worried glance at my intent gaze on the TV. "Where is this 'inside' hint coming from!" I asked sharply. Maeve immediately turned to Stretch with narrowed eyes.

"The person who led us to the attack said she was with you!" Maeve snarled.

"I don't have any new recruits!" Stretch hissed, stepping towards her. Fletcher roughly brought his arm up, shoving Stretch back a few steps as he stood in between the two of them staring angrily at each other. "Boss brought all of my people back to HQ and only left me here with you guys. I'm not getting new people anytime soon, so whoever led you to the attack *wasn't* with me!" Stretch desperately explained, glancing at me worriedly.

"This just in," the reporter began again. "Our inside hint given to our police departments is being hinted at coming from an interesting character making new public appearances to the city," they continued. "Officials say this man currently has no name known to the public but has told that he is working towards keeping our Elites and city safe by stopping True Leader and his agency from carrying out their attack." Images of him slowly were brought on the screen. Ryth's worried gaze immediately left the TV as she trembled next to Eela on the floor.

"This man was in the lobby of this complex!" I snapped, clenching my fists. "I heard one of the people with him call him Delta,"

Stretch tensed slightly as Fletcher widened his eyes at him.

"He looks like that name fits him perfectly," Maeve grumbled, glaring at Stretch in the corner of her eye with a furrowed brow. Eela's worried gaze caught my attention from across the room making my heart spike in my chest. Ryth had completely shut herself down again and was leaning heavily into Eela's side. I frowned at them and narrowed my eyes as the news report continued. Quick low-quality videos of Delta were being projected onto the screen, showing him walking around and talking to police at the attack in the alley, his face blocked by a black metal mask and a glass helmet with LED eyes. As he glanced over his shoulder at the camera, the video immediately cut off, catching the news reporter off guard. *Who is this guy and why is Ryth scared of him so much? What is she not telling us?*

CHAPTER 35

DELTA'S POV

"Let's just start off with something short and sweet," I grumbled softly, turning the TV off swiftly. "People can do worse things than kill you," I grinned. "But I think a few of us here already know that," I sighed, bored, running my normal hand along my right, metal, prosthetic wrist. I glanced up at the four standing silently around me and frowned at them for a moment before I turned my attention back to my hand. "I personally believe this 'True Leader' character is just some moron who hates the idea of saving people and thinks he can get whatever he wants just because he's powerful and has Underworld leaders on his side," I explained softly.

I glared up at the three not paying attention to me and sighed at the one who was. Nicola, called Nerve, sat across the furnished area from me, picking the skin around his shaking fingers quickly. His fluffy, white hair trembled on his head as he mumbled softly to himself, keeping his eyes away from me. Dusk's scuffed face glared at Nerve sitting next to her as she twirled her fiery-red hair. Bourbon leaned next to the breaker box mounted on the wall next to the door with his eyes closed and a frown across his stern face. The once white wrap on his arm was now stained with blood as it ran down his dark skin and dripped to the floor below him. Clou's intense gaze rested on me intently as he furrowed his brow. His bright teal hair peeked out curiously from the dark beanie on his head as I rolled my eyes at him.

"Looks like you're all so *enthusiastically* listening to me," I spat, standing up quickly. Nerve shrunk down within himself as Dusk narrowed her eyes at me and Clou frowned at them. I glanced at Bourbon, who had one dark eye open and staring bored at me before I turned and stalked away from the furnished corner of the warehouse floor. My metal boots trembled the entire room as the floor groaned below me as I walked. Broken glass crunched sharply under me as I kept my gaze on the narrow windows on the back wall overlooking the merging area of the middle and upper class.

"I can clearly see multiple ways that simple attack could have gone," I whispered, glaring down at the flashing red and blue lights climbing up from the abandoned buildings a few blocks away. "Why be so violent and destructive towards anyone who tries to challenge your authority and plans?" I asked myself, narrowing my eyes at the memory of seeing True launch a broken light post at the officers. "Don't you all ask yourself the same thing?" I called over my shoulder. Annoyed silence followed my question as I slowly turned over my shoulder with narrowed eyes.

"Did you forget we all have *normal* human minds, Delta?" Bourbon's booming voice suddenly snarled. "You're the only ass whiz here, *genius!*" he hissed. Dusked laughed softly as Clou and Nerve snickered under their breaths with worried glances towards me.

"I didn't forget that, Flash on steroids," I snapped. Bourbon tensed as he leaned away from the brick wall with clenched fists and narrowed eyes towards me. "But that's the exact reason why I treat you all differently." I frowned. "To help you all become better and *fix you*—" I continued, my voice distorting sharply as my neck twitched.

I grabbed the box mounted on the back of my neck as I gasped in pain from a spark shooting out from it. I leaned heavily on the windowsill in front of me, gripping the cold, concrete ledge tightly in my metal hand. The concrete trembled for a moment before it cracked under my weight, pebbles of rock falling to the glass-filled floor. Bourbon snickered softly under his breath and mocked me from across the room as he shook his head at me. Dusk and Clou had begun angrily arguing with each other before they turned to Bourbon and began snapping at him.

"You need to stop doing that to him!" Dusk hissed.

"One of these days he'll snap and kill you!" Clou snarled, narrowing his eyes at Bourbon's amused gaze down at him.

"I'd like to see him *try!*" Bourbon spat, his voice rising.

"You know he'd easily beat you!" Clou snarked proudly with a glance towards my amused grin at them all. "He could beat all of us in this room with his hands tied behind his back!"

"Sure! But what about the kid!" Bourbon roared, pointing roughly at Nerve cowering next to Dusk.

"Guys! Please!" Nerve cried, his hands tightening around his head quickly. Dusk and Clou widened their eyes in panic as Bourbon's angered scowl turned into a smirk of amusement at him.

"Enough!" I snapped over my shoulder. The three arguing immediately fell silent and tensed under my glare towards them. My gaze darted over to Nerve trembling next to Dusk as a chill shot down my back. *Bourbon has a point though. Nerve can screw a lot of people over with his power; exactly why it's perfect for my plans.* "Obviously you all have a lot of things to work on," I sighed, leaning slowly away from the window.

"You know being vague about what we need to work on isn't helping!" Dusk grumbled.

"Ignore him. He's just used to thinking he's better than everyone and that everyone has some flaw that he can somehow fix with his *nonhuman* brain," Bourbon hissed. I narrowed my eyes at him as my metal limbs tensed.

"I'm going out. Do not follow me," I snapped, narrowing my eyes at Clou. He let out an offended scoff as I furrowed my brow at the four of them, and they glanced worriedly at each other while I stepped up onto the windowsill. The concrete cracked violently below my weight as I leaned over the edge of the warehouse building, gazing down at the deserted street below me. My metal arm tensed as I gripped the metal pipe along the inside of the room. I sighed and closed my eyes. Distant sirens echoed through the city as lights continued to flash up through the buildings surrounding the warehouse. Cold wind began howling eerily as I slowly opened my eyes and stared at the rooftop next to the window.

I inhaled sharply as I suddenly leapt from the windowsill, rolling over onto the rooftop of the next building. The weakened roof groaned in agony as my metal feet hit the shattered gravel. I kept my gaze intently on the skyline looming through the fog slowly rolling through the city. My phone repeatedly buzzed in my pocket as I sighed at the destroyed alleyway lit with police lights. *A lot of good people died today.* I narrowed my eyes slightly as I pulled my phone out, keeping my gaze away from the screen. *This is what happens when someone thinks they can get what they want by using violence.*

I glared down at the various messages reports from police and the scouts and shivered slightly at seeing a number I had become too familiar with for my liking. I quickly swiped all the messages closed as I searched in the complex building's address. *I'm not an idiot. I know True lives there and that he was in the room with me.* I narrowed my eyes at the website and slowly inhaled, the cold air stinging my throat. After several deep breaths, I gently placed my right metal hand over the phone's pristine screen. Severe cold deep within my chest began to bubble up as I began to concentrate intently on the words created by pixels.

Override.

My vision immediately went black before I appeared directly inside the website, scanning each pixel on the letters. Each one flashed red multiple times as I individually examined them all intently with a furrowed brow. Immediately, one flashed green a single time. I was violently thrown forward and sideways as my vision blacked out again. Loud ringing filled my ears as I kept my eyes closed calmly. Brighter and brighter light began to filter through my eyelids. The cold building up in my chest only became more violent the closer I got to the light luring me in. Sharp pain suddenly shot through my entire body as I grimaced slightly.

I rolled sideways in the air, slamming my metal boots down harshly into the blank white room. I blinked several times as I warily scanned the pure white looming around me. My eye twitched slightly as dozens of screens immediately appeared all around me, covering every inch of the pure white walls. I frowned at all the screens as they only showed financial history instead of what I was looking for. I mumbled softly under my breath as my right hand twitched, and the room around me was dragged away quickly. Darkness enveloped my vision as I focused on a small, dim, grey light coming from the end of a long tunnel that was surging towards me.

The doorway at the end of the tunnel shot over me, projecting me into a new room. The cold tile floor trembled with every step I took leading away from the door. The huge warehouse of a room slowly was illuminated by small lights along the edges of the ceiling. Immediately, rows of sturdy filing cabinets became visible by lamps lining the floors along the aisleways between each compartment of the metal boxes. I tipped my head slightly to the side in amusement as I stalked towards the shaking structures. As I neared one of the first columns of the cabinets, the drawers flung themselves open, shaking as the metal rollers holding them up strained.

I gently ran my metal hand along the digital folders resting neatly in each compartment of the filing cabinets until I found True's name. My index finger opened at the tip, revealing an intricate, small metal rod that forged to the file. A dim screen flickered in front of me for a moment as it struggled to pull the information out completely. I grumbled in annoyance as the screen faltered until it disappeared. I slammed my fist against the cold metal cabinet next to me, sending a roar of panic through the entire room. Cabinets opened and slammed shut, echoing eerily.

My chest suddenly began to ache as my breaths became rigid and painful. *Screw this.* I roughly latched onto the digital file clinging to the metal filing cabinet and violently ripped it away. The file surged quietly in my palm as my finger detached itself from the corner. I closed my eyes, running my hands along the four sharp edges of the file before swiftly pushing it in on itself, and turning both my hands in opposite directions. I felt the file twist itself and snap in my shaking hands as my skull began to tremble. The overwhelming sense of something else being present with me caused a sharp headache to form inside my head. In an instant, I was suddenly lurched backwards, everything becoming silent.

I opened my eyes and gasped for breath as I lay on my back on the rooftop. I coughed hollowly into my arm, cold steam shooting from my mouth and lingering around the gravel next to me before mixing with the fog surrounding me. I gripped the sides of my head as pressure formed at the base of my neck, causing me to gasp in pain. *I won't take that long again, I'm sorry!* I widened my eyes in panic as the pressure only became stronger, moving across my entire head away from my neck. I gritted my teeth as I pulled myself onto my elbow and shook my head quickly. Wisps of dark grey smoke fell from my shoulders as I shivered and glared at the small metal disk laying calmly in the gravel in front of me. *You're mine now.*

With a shaking arm, I slowly reached for the disk and sighed as it sent out a spark as my metal hand touched it. I pressed gently down on the middle of the disk, setting it down gently on the gravel. The middle compartment slid cleanly open, revealing a small teal light that then weakly projected a screen hovering in the air. I narrowed my eyes as I skimmed quickly through the information on True and his Agency. My gaze rested on Stretch's recently added profile as my heart spiked with anger and disappointment in my chest. *Remember idiot, you chose the wrong side and wanted to go against me this time. Let's just see how long you last there before I ask for a favor from you once more.*

CHAPTER 36

TRUE'S POV – THE FOLLOWING EVENING...

Angry curses from Stretch and Randy echoed loudly through the silent suite. The air radiated with annoyance and pride as the two of them were desperately trying to beat the other in a video game next to me on the couch. I glanced up at Maeve sitting at the dining table and held back a giggle at her scowl towards the two of them before she went back to typing on her computer. I sighed and shook my head as I glanced back down at my phone and shivered at more headlines about Delta appearing everywhere. *Why and how did you show up out of nowhere?*

Movement from out on the balcony caught my eye, making my heart leap out of my chest. I widened my eyes as I saw Cohen leaning against the railing with his head down, red flames flickering wildly from behind his ears as steam rose from his arms. Randy and Stretch glanced worriedly at each other before they both turned to me. I waved my hand at them and sighed as I stood up with a wince, holding my aching side.

"Why didn't you tell Stella to get you pain medication while she was out?" Maeve grumbled softly.

"Because I don't need it," I snapped, scrunching my nose as her brow raised in disbelief. "I wanted her to focus on Eela and Ryth with Cami and Fletcher. Those four needed a mental break from all my crap I've put them through," I frowned, ignoring the pain lingering in my chest.

I pushed the glass sliding door open slowly as I held my breath with a furrowed brow. Cohen kept his back to me as his shaking hands held his phone in front of him.

"Are you even listening to me!" an angry voice roared from the phone, making me flinch. "This is why you screwed everything up! You never listen to me—" the voice continued. I narrowed my eyes as he wistfully looked over his shoulder at me. *That voice sounds weirdly familiar...* Cohen's dark eyes narrowed as more bright red flames flickered from behind his eyes as he stared at the phone in his hands.

I gently took the phone from him as he frowned at me and turned his eyes to the skyline in front of us.

"I don't know who you are, but I would suggest you *stop* calling this number." I ordered sharply into the phone. The old man on the other side of the line mumbled under his breath as bottles clinked loudly against each other. I frowned at the phone and hung up, my eye twitching as my skin was caught on the cracked screen. My hand trembled slightly as blood began forming on the tip of my thumb as I sighed and set the phone down on the chair behind me.

"My father," Cohen whimpered angrily, keeping his eyes away from me as I leaned on the railing next to him. "He's somehow finding my new numbers and calling me, just to scream at me on how much of a failure I am to him," he grumbled, his eyes narrowing. I sighed and nodded, turning my gaze to the buildings looming through the fog. *He sounds a lot like my mother.* "He's blaming me for my mother's death." Cohen suddenly snapped, his voice wavering. I widened my eyes and turned towards him quickly.

"I'm sorry," I whispered softly, furrowing my brow at the rage building behind his dark eyes. *I've never seen you this upset.*

"He says that if I would have never hung up on her a few weeks ago, she wouldn't have overdosed herself," Cohen hissed. "I had nothing to do with her doing that! She probably did that on purpose, so she wouldn't have to deal with *him* anymore!" he snarled softly, his fists closing tightly around the metal railing in front of him. I frowned and nodded slowly at him as I trembled at seeing steam rising from his hands against the metal bar. "If I hadn't run off with my sisters, maybe they would still be alive," he mumbled. My heart spiked with anger in my chest.

"Don't blame yourself for the lies your father is telling you!" I snapped, harsher than I intended. "You tried doing what you thought was best for your younger sisters by keeping them safe and away from him," I continued more gently. Cohen's dark eyes softened as he shook his head and brought it down below his shoulders. "It's not your fault that they died," I whispered softly.

"Yea, but I'm sure I am partly responsible," he replied. "If I had only been able to keep them warmer for a little longer,"

"You were hurting yourself by forcing your flames to burn in the cold weather," I sighed. "You needed to take care of yourself, too," I frowned. Cohen shook his head as he raised it and stared down at the burn marks along his arms with a scowl.

I sat on the cold balcony with Cohen for a little while, listening to him ranting softly about his life before he joined the Agency. I made sure I kept silent unless he asked for a response. My heart swelled in my chest with pity and pride in how open and vulnerable he was with me. Hearing how scared he was for his sisters' safety from their father more than his own made my chest ache. He had done all he could to protect them from him, but he wouldn't accept it because of the lies his father had been forcing onto him. Deep within my mind, I tried my best to connect to anything he said with how my mother treated my own father and I as I was growing up.

Once he had stopped explaining, we sat in silence, listening to the noisy city around us. Cohen sat with his back against the concrete wall behind him, his forehead resting on his knees. Distant echoes of horns and music pulsed through the city, making the fog surrounding the building's stir. Dim, golden light from the setting sun cut through the passageways between skyscrapers, making columns of light appear floating in the air, illuminating each individual drop of water. I sat across from Cohen, my gaze staring intently on the white flames flickering from his palms as I rested my chin on my knees.

A series of gentle taps on the glass door to my right made my heart spike in my chest. I lifted my head to see Maeve smirking at me before drawing something in the air with her finger. I rolled my eyes at her smug gaze and turned back to Cohen with a half laugh. A harsh thud from the window made me widen my eyes as Cohen slowly looked up with a furrowed brow. I turned over my shoulder to see Maeve push away from the glass and flick her switchblade open at someone darting away from her reach. Stretch came jogging up to the glass with a nervous smile and a thumbs up before he turned and began yelling, darting away with narrowed eyes.

I turned back to Cohen, holding back a smile as he shook his head with a small grin and gazed out to the skyscrapers around us. I flinched as he suddenly grabbed my wrist and pointed to something with a furrowed brow. I grimaced slightly as his burning palm made the skin on my wrist turn red before he quickly let go of it. I frowned at my wrist and slowly turned over my shoulder, peering through the glass panel at the buildings down the block. My eyes scanned the buildings, looking for something out of the ordinary before I furrowed my brow at finding nothing.

"What?"

"There's a person," Cohen mumbled, pulling me towards him and turning my head where his finger was hovering. I widened my eyes and quickly pulled myself to my feet as I saw someone standing on the edge of a building with their back to the street below them.

"What the...?" I gasped softly. Cohen grunted softly as he pulled himself up and furrowed his brow at the person rocking back and forth on the ledge.

"Are they...?" Cohen trailed off slowly. I shook my head as my heart began racing in my chest and gripped the railing tighter. I quickly pushed away from the metal bar and darted back inside.

As I pulled open the door, I widened my eyes at Stretch desperately trying to keep Randy and Maeve apart from each other with two extended arms. Both angrily cussing the other out with annoyed smirks on their faces.

"I swear Maeve! I will throw you off the balcony if you cut me!" Stretch hissed.

All three of them began laughing softly as Stretch let his arms go back to normal, and he fell over. I rolled my eyes, holding back a smile as I pushed the door open to my room and quickly pulled on a hoodie, tucking my pistol into the pocket and starting towards the front door. I ignored everyone's questions towards me as I slammed it shut and darted down the walkway of the complex building.

I burst through the front door of the lobby out into the crowded street, pulling my hoodie swiftly over my head as people flinched with yelps of alarm at my entrance. I glanced up through the fog at the building where the person was and felt my heart leap out of my chest. *Oh no you don't.* I squinted and blinked my eyes quickly as drops of water clung to my eyelashes and I continued to jog along the street, pushing past people walking slowly down the sidewalk. *Where did they even go!* I widened my eyes in panic as I didn't see anyone standing on the building ledge anymore.

I darted towards the nearest sidewalk with a racing heart before I jogged quickly across the street towards the door of the building. I pushed the door open gently, flinching in alarm as I ran into a young man with white fluffy hair.

"Sorry! Sorry!" he cried, holding out his shaking, scarred hands to me and turning his gaze away from mine.

"It's alright," I chuckled softly, holding out my hand gently to him with a calm grin. The young man fearfully glanced at me before he brushed past me and ran out into the street. I stood in the doorway for a moment with confused glances at the other people in the lobby before I shook my head and walked across the room.

I pushed into the metal stairwell, my footsteps echoing loudly in the damp air. My heart only began to race louder and louder in my ears as I clenched my fists, skipping steps and using my smoke to hoist me up faster. I quickly brushed passed a teal-haired young man arguing quietly with a woman who looked familiar at first glance. Both stared intently at me as I continued forward, brushing the familiar aura away as I narrowed my eyes. *Please…* My legs began to ache as I grumbled in annoyance before I made it to the final flight of stairs in the complex building.

I slammed roughly into the door leading to the roof with a yelp of pain. I fell harshly on my elbow against the metal floor, as my yelp echoed eerily through the stairwell. I gritted my teeth in pain as I coughed and brought my hand to my face.

"Dammit," I rasped, grimacing at the taste of bitter blood in my mouth. I laid on the floor for a moment, catching my breath as I kept pressure on my bleeding nose with a furrowed brow. I shivered slightly as I weakly rolled to my knees and frowned at the blood covering my hand and hoodie sleeve with droplets below me. *How lovely…*

I pulled myself up with a column of smoke latching onto the metal railing in front of me as I narrowed my eyes at the heavy metal door. I roughly grabbed the cold handle in my free hand and shook the door as hard as I could. The large door only laughed at my attempts to open it as I frowned at the lock on the handle. *Come on…* I huffed in annoyance as I tried pulling the door open again once more before I leaned against the railing behind me. The huge door slightly moved as a small hissing noise came from the handle. My heart raced with panic in my ears as I stared at the door looming above me. *One last try…*

I pushed off the railing, turning my shoulder to the door and slammed into it once more. The metal door immediately flung open, sending me roughly down the concrete steps to the gravel covering the roof. I cried out in pain and annoyance as I gasped and blinked my eyes several times, slowly rolling to my knees and grimaced and I moved my elbow. I peered at the ripped sleeve, frowning at the blood and gravel pebbles seeping through the fabric. I rolled my eyes and held my aching side for a moment before I stumbled to my feet with a cough.

I limped quickly to the building's ledge as I continued to clutch my side with a furrowed brow. The gravel shifted and crunched quickly under my feet as I stumbled forward, gripping the concrete edge tightly. I peered over the edge of the building and felt my stomach drop as my legs wavered below me. *Out of all the ways, this is the worst one to choose.* I frowned at not seeing anything abnormal along the crowded street before I slowly pushed myself up and laughed softly at myself. *I don't know where you went, but please just make the right decisions and be safe…*

"That was hard fall, my guy, are you alright?" a sleek, familiar voice suddenly asked. I leapt out of my skin as I widened my eyes and turned to my left and I tensed. The person I had seen standing on the edge was sitting with their legs dangling off the side of the building, their back against a large transformer resting on the roof.

"I'm fine," I hesitantly responded, furrowing my brow at the person keeping their face hidden under a bright white hood. My heart began to beat out of my chest as I thought more intricately on why their voice was familiar to me. "I saw you on the edge from my balcony," I mumbled. "Are you okay? I didn't know if…" I trailed off, not knowing how to finish the sentence.

"Didn't know if I was going to jump or not?" the person laughed gently. I frowned at their lofty tone and shivered as they shifted closer to the edge.

"Why are you up here alone? Standing on the edge like that?" I asked sharply. The person chuckled while they sat up straight and stared at the buildings slowly becoming visible as the fog began to float away.

The person remained silent as they waved their light tan hand around in the air as if they were contemplating the reason.

"I wanted to feel what it was like," they responded coldly. "The fear of 'what if I fall?'" their tone shifted, sounding extremely robotic and forced. I trembled as I stepped away from them as they slowly pulled themselves up and stood on the edge, staring at the night sky climbing towards the city. We stood in silence as the person suddenly turned to glance at me over their shoulder. Cold, perfect eyes stared directly at me, sending a violent shiver down my back as I frowned at them.

"You made really good time, True," they hissed, turning away from me. My heart leapt out of my chest as I stepped back again, my hand brushing on the pistol resting in my hoodie pocket. I widened my eyes as the person suddenly turned around and faced me fully.

It was a man, whose cold, perfect brown eyes met mine again, this time filled with malice. The lower half of his face was hidden by a black, metal mask. He lifted both his arms, revealing a metal prosthetic on his right from the elbow down to his hand. My heart began to beat strongly out of my chest as I stared intently at Delta towering over me even from a distance.

"This meeting won't become violent," Delta chuckled mischievously at my worried stance. "I'm not *you*," he mumbled sharply. I narrowed my eyes as my hand tightened around my pistol handle and my heart spiked in my chest. "I want to have a simple conversation to see what you're really all about." Delta beamed proudly, stepping down from the ledge. The entire building rooftop trembled as his metal boots hit the gravel roughly, breaking the pebbles even smaller below him. "Don't try shooting me. It won't work," he suddenly hissed, his eyes darkening at my hand in my hoodie pocket. "Let's just keep all these tricks away and all hands *visible* while we have a civil *conversation* with one another like normal people. Hm?" Delta laughed angrily, his voice distorting slightly.

I nodded, frowning worriedly at him as my bloodied hand slowly fell to my side.

"That's better," he sighed, rolling out both of his shoulders as he scanned me up and down for a moment. My heart only began racing faster in my chest as he slowly walked towards me, his palms exposed harmlessly. I widened my eyes slowly as I saw the same symbol on my palm engraved into his own. Delta quickly closed his metal hand with a gentle smile as he stopped a few feet in front of me.

"I'm glad you're actually a caring guy," Delta whispered. "You always seem to put on a fake appearance for the public," he mumbled, slowly inching towards me again. I tensed slightly as he towered over me with a dead look in his eyes. *I can't shoot him and run; I have no idea what he's capable of, He'd catch me in the stairs if I tried getting away... Plus he could take me down with both hands tied behind his back with how tall he is. I'm a chew toy compared to him!* I stared up at Delta's gaze down at me as I shivered and blinked quickly.

"Analyzing the situation you're currently in," Delta began softly, making me flinch. "Weighing out the pros and cons, thinking whether or not to risk shooting me and running," he continued, his voice becoming slightly distorted. "While also thinking, 'But what will his reaction be? Would I even survive?' I find that cute," Delta hissed, making me widen my eyes. "You know, I kind of like you. I like the people who actually think and use their heads even when most of the time they look like an idiot," he chuckled, sending a wave of panic over me.

"Not too talkative huh?" Delta sighed. "This is because my presence is worrying you, hm? Yes, it is," he continued, quickly. "You are also worried about many other things at once right now," he snapped. "Wondering about what I'll do to you. Wondering what my power is and if it's mind reading—newsflash it's not!" Delta hissed through gritted teeth, his voice rising and becoming more forced. He suddenly leaned down towards me, making my heart leap out of my chest. "You know what. Enough of me talking. Time for *you* to talk."

"I have a question for you, True," Delta snapped calmly. "Why? Why do you want to change the world just by killing a few Elites? How will that change anything?" he asked harshly. I narrowed my eyes as I blinked quickly up at him. "To me, this just seems like a blind rage you've been suppressing from something that happened to you when you were little and disguising it as a perfect plan to change something that is already *fine* to begin with," Delta snarled quickly. I clenched my fists tightly as my heart slowed and pounded in my chest. *You're missing the point, but why are you making sense?*

"Let me let you in on a little secret, okay?" Delta laughed after staring at my falling face. "For the past month or so, you've been questioning everything about your plans, right? You're concerned if you really have your head screwed on correctly after you gave into that absolutely crazy disorder, which I think is a hilarious lie!" Delta breathed softly. "When you begin to figure stuff out, the people around you drag you back to square one and force you to start over. Right?" he continued. "Well, I know that struggle," he hissed, suddenly turning his back to me as his voice wavered slightly.

I stood in shocked silence as I stared blankly at Delta looking at the buildings surrounding us. He slowly turned over his shoulder towards me and began laughing softly.

"You caved that easily?" he spat. "Damn, you really must not have a single drop of faith in yourself!" he exclaimed sharply. "In that case, True," he continued, "let's just make this entire one-sided conversation a learning experience," his voice distorted again as he grimaced slightly, bringing his metal hand to the back of his neck and stalked towards me. I furrowed my brow at him as he slowly made his way across the roof. *What's wrong with you?*

Delta suddenly rested his metal, robotic arm on my shoulder violently. Sharp cold immediately pierced through my hoodie as his grip on me tightened, my skin screaming in agony. His metal arm felt heavier than a building as I struggled to hold myself up under it.

"If you don't have a reasonable, set-in stone, well-thought-out plan, it's a waste of time," Delta laughed coldly. "I don't care what you do from this point on, but," he continued, his voice becoming low, "stay the *fuck* out of my way." Delta's tone distorted his voice violently as all emotion was suddenly gone from his perfect eyes.

My heart leapt out of my chest as I stared silently at him. Something in his right eye shifted as it suddenly became a lighter shade of glowing brown honey in the setting sunlight. Wisps of a dark mist floated up from his eyes as he stared at me, not blinking. Delta suddenly brushed past me, flicking his normal, left hand up into the air. Dozens of sleek, dark cards flew up and fell gently down to the gravel below as he tucked his hands back into his white jacket pockets. The roof trembled as his metal boots walked along the gravel before he turned and disappeared down into the stairwell. The entire building suddenly shook violently, sending me to my knee as I exhaled slowly.

I frowned at the door humming softly in the cold wind as I blinked several times. I stumbled to my feet and took a card from the gravel and brought it closer to my face. *Have I really just been blinded this entire time? Does anything I've done make sense?* I stared at the sleek card lined with teal accents in my blood-stained hand before I tucked it inside my hoodie pocket. Blood began to run down my arm, dripping to the gravel below me as I grimaced from a gravel pebble pressing against my skinned elbow.

"Are you okay, sir? You're bleeding!" a worried voice asked from the front desk in the lobby while I limped from the stairwell door.

"I'm fine. I fell," I replied, walking faster out of the room. I flicked my dusty hood over my head as I kept my gaze down and winced at my blood drops hitting the white tile floor. A headache pulsed strongly around my head as I pushed through the front door and turned right, walking away from my building complex. *What just happened?* I blinked my eyes swiftly as tears threatened to from and I shook my head, ignoring my phone suddenly buzzing wildly in my pocket.

Eerie wind whispered frantically in my ears as I slowly pushed through the old iron gate at the cemetery on the outskirts of the middle-class sector. My entire body trembled with regret as I walked along the overgrown stone path with my head down. I turned and shuffled through the dying grass in front of the stone wall barrier before I roughly sat down, staring at a picture of a happy couple on a tombstone. I stared at both of their cheerful faces with no emotion as my chest began to ache. I blinked several times as a chill shot down my back, making me turn away from the woman's eyes staring at me through the stone prison.

I kept the picture of the couple in my peripheral vision as I stared at the grass below the stone.

"Dad… Mom…" I whispered softly, my voice rasping. A cold gust of wind shot past me, rattling small chimes on other graves throughout the cemetery. "Would either of you understand my plan and be proud of it?" I asked quietly. "Proud of me?" I continued, my voice wavering. I blinked away tears as I rested my elbows gently on my knees in front of me. Pain radiated down my arm from my bleeding skin as I felt blood begin to soak into my dusty jeans. "So many people are counting on me to make the right decisions now," I growled, clearing my throat. "How can I not let them down when I don't even know what I'm doing anymore?"

I took several rattly breaths as I glanced back up at their picture. I narrowed my eyes at my mother's smile on her face, knowing it was fake, and felt my heart lurch in my chest. I bowed my head and bit my lip as anger began to boil up deep within my chest. I roughly reached into my hoodie pocket and set my pistol down in the grass. *Why did those people have to break in and kill both of you? Why didn't I do anything to try and stop them? Why did no one show up to help after they left?* I inhaled sharply as I huffed and glared at the picture. *Dad, why did you let Mom hurt both of us? Why did you leave me with no one?*

I quickly stood up, ignoring the sharp pain in my side as I gritted my teeth. I clenched my fists as I stared at their picture intently. I blinked tears out of my eyes and shivered as I felt them run down my face and neck. I stood still, swaying slightly from the wind. I shook my head, wiping my face with a bloody sleeve as I rested my palm on the top of the tombstone as I closed my eyes.

"I'm sorry," I whispered softly. "Neither of you could control what happened that night, and I shouldn't blame either of you." My voice broke slightly as I sighed.

I slowly limped back through the tall grass and made my way across the small, concrete platform to another grave. My heart ached violently in my chest as I stared intently at the pristinely-kept tombstone. I couldn't hold back my smile as I looked gently at the cheerful, scruffy face of Mr. Keilot resting in the center of the stone. Beautiful flowers and small stuffed animals lined the tombstone with small notes rolled up and tucked into crevices along the side. I sighed gently as I sat down in the fluffy grass and leaned myself on my knees again, ignoring the pain shooting up my arm.

I closed my eyes and sat in silence in front of Mr. Keilot's grave and listened to the cold wind gusting through the cemetery. The old, iron gate groaned slightly in the wind as the trees clustered together whisked their leaves around. Small wind chimes rang beautiful in the breeze, creating a light, soft, and wistful tune that weaved its way through the rows of graves. In the presence of Mr. Keilot's grave, I slowly felt much more relieved as I bowed my head taking short, deep breaths. *Thank you.*

A loud thud and yelp from behind me pulled me out of my head as I had begun to fall asleep. I flinched, turning over my shoulder with widened eyes. A woman lying on her side along the stone platform rubbed her shoulder gently as she stared worriedly at me.

"Who are you? Why are you at my brother's grave?" she asked hesitantly. We both flinched as we recognized each other. We stared awkwardly at one another for a moment before I stood up and quickly jogged towards the iron gate. "Wait a second, you don't have to leave!" the woman cried softly as I continued.

I trembled slightly as cold wind surrounded me, and I slowly made my way back towards the lit-up skyscrapers of the city. People scurried quickly down the streets, paying no attention to me as I stayed near the building edge, hiding in the dim light with my dark hoodie. Sharp pain suddenly struck me in the right side of my head.

"True? Where have you been!" Maeve suddenly roared in my mind. I stumbled sideways, knocking into a trashcan as I yelped. People all around me flinched, turning towards me with a furrowed brow before continuing.

"I'm on my way back. Calm down," I grumbled.

The elevator doors opened smoothly after a gentle ding that rang in my ears for a moment. I stepped out into the cold, open space as I kept my head down. I flinched as something moved from the corner of my eye. I turned with a furrowed brow as I met a man with bright teal hair and dim light eyes. He leaned against the concrete corner next to the stairwell as he crossed his arms with a smirk at me. *Aren't you part of that group with Delta?* I stared at him for a moment as he looked blankly at me.

"Go on," he sneered, making me shiver. "Get a good night's rest in," he continued, his smirk turning into a wicked grin. I eyed him carefully as I stayed silent and slowly walked down the aisle with a racing heart. *I'll walk past the suite, so I don't lead him to the Agency...* As I passed the suite door, a chill shot down my back making me turn around. I widened my eyes as I saw dark arms suddenly loom from thin air around the young man. In a moment, he was gone, and the entire complex building trembled. I stared at the spot he once stood in shock before I shook my head and limped quickly to the suite's door.

I quietly pushed open the door and stepped inside with a sigh of relief. My heart roared loudly in my ears as I blinked quickly in panic. I hit myself in the stomach with a wince as I widened my eyes at not feeling my pistol in my hoodie pocket. *I left it at the cemetery—*

Two sets of footsteps suddenly echoed through the silence suite, pulling me out of my head.

"You're finally back!" Eela cried softly, her brow furrowed in worry. I smiled at Ryth as she followed silently behind her and sighed as they both buried their faces into my sides. I rested my arms along both of them and closed my eyes, focusing on their racing hearts as my own began to roar louder.

"Is everyone asleep?" I whispered quietly. Ryth nodded hesitantly and leaned away as Eela pulled herself in front of me.

"I think so, it's been quiet for a while, so I'd guess they're sleeping," Eela grumbled. Ryth snorted into her arm as I brought my hand to my face, knowing she was right.

"We just wanted to make sure you got back okay," Ryth suddenly whispered. "Maeve was freaking out for a while when she couldn't find you and you didn't respond to anyone's calls," she continued, looking away from my gaze.

I sighed and rubbed my forehead gently with a frown.

"You girls both go to bed. It's late," I grinned. Eela's light eyes darted to the blood on my hand before I tucked it calmly back in my pocket with a slightly furrowed brow at her. They both hugged me once more, Eela lingering longer into my side before they both returned to Eela's room.

I mumbled under my breath as I set Delta's card down on the countertop, resting my cracked phone next to it with a sigh. I grimaced and cursed myself under my breath as I weakly pulled my hoodie off. Pain shot violently up my arm from my elbow. I frowned at the rigid and gravel-filled gash on my arm before I bundled my bloody hoodie up and pulled off my ripped shirt. I glared down at the scrape along my side as I narrowed my eyes and tossed my shirt on the floor. My side and elbow screamed in pain as I crouched down and took a rag from under the sink and ran it under the cool water before dabbing my arm.

Something shifted in the corner of my eye, causing me to yelp.

"Stretch!" I hissed, shaking my head and holding back a smile.

"Sorry," Stretch chuckled, rubbing the back of his neck with a worried frown at me. "Are you okay?" he asked hesitantly. I raised my brow at him before I waved my hand at my elbow and side with a frown. "So, no?" he whispered, nodding his head. I scoffed at him as he slowly made his way around the counter towards me. I shivered as he reached his bruised hand towards the bloody rag in my hand. We stared awkwardly at each other before I gave it to him.

Both of us stayed silent as Stretch helped clean the gash on my elbow while I wiped down my side. Once we had cleaned them good enough, he wrapped my elbow in bandages, keeping his gaze intently on my arm. I leaned heavily on the counter in front of me as I gritted my teeth in pain while he tightened the wrap. Stretch winced with a nervous glance at me as I closed my eyes at him and turned to glare at the skyscrapers looming brightly against the night sky through the glass sliding doors across the room. *Why was he so persistent in shutting me down when he has never met me? Telling me to stay out of his way? Of what exactly? I know nothing about him.*

"I see you have Delta's business card," Stretch suddenly whispered, keeping his seeing eye on my elbow. I narrowed my eyes down at him and extended a column of smoke, moving my cracked phone completely over the card.

"I ran into him when I left earlier," I mumbled. Stretch shivered slightly, his dark eye darting up to my gaze before he ripped off the excess wrap from my elbow. "He threw them at me as he walked off." I frowned. Stretch looked intently at me for a moment, sending a chill up my back before he nodded and turned away. I furrowed my brow as the glint in his eyes changed before he stalked back down the hallway.

I sighed, glaring at my scraped side before I leaned down and grabbed my ripped and blooded shirt and hoodie with a frown. *What was that about?* I shook my head as I walked into the washroom behind the kitchen and dropped the bloodied towel into the washer and grimaced as I knocked my elbow on the metal door. I closed the door halfway before I limped back across the kitchen and grabbed my phone with Delta's business card and slowly made my way towards my bedroom. I glanced at Cohen sleeping peacefully on the couch and sighed with a gentle grin at him before I quietly made my way to my bed, melting immediately into the sheets.

I was suddenly sitting alone in a cold, dark room. A single light bulb on a wire hung lazily above me, illuminating only the area I sat. Light, metal tables lined the walls with dark glass panels that took up most of the space on the left wall.

"Finally, I caught you," a voice suddenly sneered, echoing loudly around the silent room. The same teal-haired man who met me outside the elevator quickly fell from the darkness above, standing with his arms crossed. A chill shot down my back as I stared up at the disapproving glare in his cold, light eyes. His brow furrowed as he looked around the room before he laughed softly at me. "You don't seem to be an interesting guy," he mumbled with a wicked smirk at me over his shoulder.

I shivered as two metal legs suddenly extended from the darkness in the ceiling and felt my heart leap out of my chest as Delta fell roughly to the concrete floor below me. The ground shook under his weight as he stayed kneeling on one knee in front of me before slowly standing up and sighing at my gaze at him. His normal, black, metal mask was gone from his face, revealing the cold, sturdy metal lower jaw he had that glinted dangerously in the low light. His normal, perfect brown eyes had a dark aura to them, as if something was clouding over his vision as he stared intently at me.

My right palm suddenly began hissing as light grey smoke melted from the symbol while my pitch-black smoke struggled to contain it. I frantically waved my hand around as I widened my eyes and cried out softly in pain. The symbol burned into my palm was more prominent and glowing slightly. My heart leapt in my chest as I squinted at the more visible symbol. A small, burning rose had been engraved fully into my palm. My breaths quickened as I recognized the symbol from Delta's metal palm, and I quickly turned my gaze up to him towering over me.

"I forgot to mention something, True," Delta hissed coldly, his voice distorting horribly and echoing away before becoming quiet. "You're not as safe as you think you are," he continued, his voice distorting again and becoming wildly familiar. I stared up at him with a furrowed brow as my heart roared in my ears. Delta's stance faltered as sparks shot from the back of his neck, and he grimaced, glaring at the other man standing next to me. *What was that?* Delta's breaths became rigid as cold steam floated away from his mouth before he stepped forward, pointing roughly at me.

Delta suddenly disappeared and reappeared directly behind me, holding a bloody knife to my neck as he roughly wrapped his arm around my shoulder. His metal arm stung my skin as I grimaced in pain, staring warily at the knife at my neck.

"Ryth," Delta breathed angrily. "Good luck trying to keep her safe from me," he hissed, his voice distorting horribly. Violent agony suddenly shot down my back as Delta removed the knife from my neck and forced it into my spine. I cried out in panic as I leaned away from him before everything around me turned to dust.

The dust-filled ground below me suddenly melted into boiling hot water as I continued to scream. I frantically swam up towards the surface, slamming my face into cold glass directly above the water, trapping me under. Blood spilled quickly into the water all around me from my back as it turned completely cold. I coughed violently as I inhaled the frigid water and gripped my neck quickly. I gasped as I felt something wrap tightly around my lungs while a burning sensation filled my chest. I looked quickly over my shoulder after hearing a distant cry of pain. I widened my eyes as I saw Ryth lying weakly on her side, blood spilling into the water around her, Delta's mask a dark void towering over her.

"Wake up!" I suddenly snarled in my head. A violent cry of agony filled my mind as I was suddenly lurched up from the water, shattering the glass above the surface...

I sat up in my bed, clutching my chest as I gasped for breath. My back screamed in distant agony at the memory of the knife piercing my spine.

"True?" Stella cried, sitting up quickly and reaching towards me. I pulled away from her as I threw the sheets off me and weakly stumbled out of my room. "True!" Stella hissed sharply as I jogged down the hallway and into Eela's room with a roaring heart, tears in my eyes. My vision doubled and blurred as I gripped the doorway and blinked several times before I fell to my knees next to the bed.

Eela flinched as she sat up next to Ryth sleeping beside her with widened eyes.

"True?" she whispered quickly with widened eyes. I rested my arm across Ryth's shaking side, holding my trembling hand on Eela's arm as I lowered my head and clenched my fist. "True! You're scaring me," Eela whimpered, grabbing my hand tightly in her own.

"I'm sorry," I cried softly, squeezing her hand as I felt tears fall down my face. "Just a bad dream," I mumbled, keeping my gaze away from Eela's confused eyes. My entire body trembled in anger, fear, and pain as I continued to kneel on the ground next to the bed.

"I'm sorry for waking you," I whispered softly, turning to Eela after I wiped all tears from my eyes. Eela nodded once, furrowing her brow at me before I weakly stood up. I leaned over Ryth, kissing her on the forehead before doing the same to Eela. I stared at them intently as my heart roared in my ears before I turned and left the room. I blinked quickly as I took shuddering breaths and limped down the hall. My heart spiked in my chest as I saw Stella push open our bedroom door quickly with narrowed, glowing eyes at me.

"What was that!" Stella hissed sharply.

"I had a bad dream, okay?" I replied, continuing past her as she tried stopping me.

"You woke up in a state of panic, True!" she snarled. "How is that just a 'bad dream'?" she snapped, her voice wavering as she shoved my shoulder roughly.

"What's going on?" Cohen gruffly asked, sitting up from the couch with squinted eyes at us.

"Nothing—" I sighed.

"True is what's going on!" Stella laughed, interrupting me. I shook my head at her as I held back a nasty comment.

"I'm fine," I mumbled, waving my hand at Cohen's furrowed brow. Stella grabbed my wrist quickly, staring at the burn on my palm before I ripped it away from her.

"What is that?"

"Nothing!"

"It's obviously something if you're hiding it from me!"

"Stella," Cohen snapped.

"What! I'm trying to see if he's alright!" she snapped back.

"I'm completely okay!" I sighed.

"No, you're not!" she snarked. I narrowed my eyes at Stella as her eyes began to glow even more and smoke floated from her nose.

"*Both* of you need to calm down!" Cohen suddenly snapped, standing up quickly.

Stella and I flinched, turning towards him as red and white flames flickered from behind his ears and eyes.

"Listen. It's too late for any of us to be arguing like this," he sighed in a gentler tone. "We can discuss this *calmly* in the morning," he offered slowly, holding out his hands towards both of us glaring at each other.

"True," Cohen began. "I know something's up. You're bad at hiding it," he snapped. I flinched at his harsh tone and turned away from him. "Stella," he continued. "I know you're worried about him, but yelling at him and demanding answers isn't how you figure him out," he gently explained, shifting slightly away from her glare. Stella's eyes immediately stopped glowing as she stared intently at me before turning and walking into our bedroom.

I rubbed my forehead slowly as I took several deep, shaking breaths.

"Thank you," I sighed glancing at his furrowed brow towards me.

"Stella genuinely cares about you, True," Cohen gently mumbled, sitting back down on the couch. "She just doesn't know how to get the right words out like she needs to," he sighed. I nodded, knowing he was right. "Try not to lose your head with her, okay?" Cohen asked softly. "She's just scared," he whispered. My heart spiked in my chest as I stared intently at his worried gaze up at me. I tipped my head to him and sighed as I turned and limped towards the bedroom.

"I don't understand why you need to hide things from me," Stella bluntly snapped as I closed the door. I widened my eyes as I looked at her lying on her side, facing away from my side on the bed.

"I don't hide anything from you, I just—" I began.

"Don't tell me things? That's the same as hiding it!" she hissed. I flinched and bit my lip before I sighed with closed eyes. I shook my head at her while limping over to the bed and hesitantly laid down next to her, my heart beating out of my chest.

"I don't know how to explain things to you in a way where you won't be worried," I mumbled.

"Worried?" Stella laughed. "True, you are you, of course I'm going to be worried," she sighed. I held my hand to my face, holding back a laugh as I smiled slightly. *Thank you for caring about me. I guess I'm not used to someone being so persistent on being concerned about me yet...*

CHAPTER 37

THE NEXT MORNING...

The news reporter droned through the daily topics with no life in their voice as I tuned it out and I poured myself a cup of coffee. *I need to go back to the cemetery and get my pistol*, I shivered and winced in pain as the hot coffee splashed onto my hand. *I hope it's still there.*

"Delta has been revealed as the name of the man who has stated that he plans to help protect New York from True Leader!" the reporter suddenly exclaimed. Cohen shifted angrily on the couch as he turned his dark gaze over to me while I glared up at the TV. I wiped my sore hand on a towel before I quickly walked across the room and stood next to Cohen.

"Here is the interview with Delta our journalists were able to start just a few minutes ago," they continued. The screen was enlarged to a camera pointing to Delta towering over another reporter standing in the busy street. Police officers lined the background, directing the civilians away from him as he blinked calmly down at the reporter talking to the camera.

"Tell us, who's side are you on?" the young reported asked in a lofty tone as she raised her brow at him.

"My own," Delta replied immediately, making the reporter flinch. Her worried glance at the camera sent a shiver down my spine.

"Are you going to be working alongside TL, or will you help defeat him?" she asked in a more serious tone. Delta's LED emotion glass helmet changed to a perplexed expression as he tipped his head sideways.

"I thought I've made it clear that I'm going to help protect the city from True," Delta chuckled. "This doesn't make us enemies at all! In fact, we're quite good acquaintances," he beamed, the expression changing to happy.

Cohen looked sharply at me as I winced and nodded slowly.

"When?" Cohen hissed.

"Yesterday evening," I frowned, turning back to the TV. The reporter raised her brow to the camera before turning back to Delta with a grin.

"Acquaintances?" she echoed. "So, you've met before?" she asked. Delta nodded calmly. "Was there any fight that went on between you two?" she continued. "Is True Leader still alive—?" the reporter asked harshly. Delta's mask glitched in and out of an angered expression, silencing the reporter.

"He's still alive, and no we did not fight," Delta snapped. "Our hierarchy with one another is still unknown but will be developed soon," he continued, turning slowly to the camera. I shivered as the LED emotion stared directly into my soul. I widened my eyes and stared intently at him. *You know I'm watching...how?*

"We're done," Delta suddenly grumbled, waving his hand to the camera. The screen glitched violently as he stepped away from the reporter. The camera crew and other reporters gathered around quickly, shouting questions towards him as he kept his gaze on the camera. The ground shook as burly arms wrapped around his shoulder before he disappeared into thin air. The camera and reporters searched the sky quickly as more questions were shouted out, echoing through the street. The main camera glitched once more before the audio cut out, and the video was minimized. The main news reporter came back onto screen.

Cohen turned off the TV quickly with a dark glance at the bleeding wrap on my elbow.

"When did you even have time to meet with Delta?" he snapped.

"Delta was the man you saw standing on the roof," I mumbled, limping over and sitting next to him as I sipped my coffee with a grimace.

"What even happened to you? Did he do this?" Cohen asked sharply. I shook my head and frowned at my elbow.

"I fell trying to get onto the roof," I chuckled. Cohen sighed at me and crossed his arms as he glared at the powered down TV in front of

218

us. I shivered as I rubbed my red hand along my sore leg before I turned to the balcony. "I left my pistol at the cemetery last night. I have to go back and get it," I sighed hesitantly.

"You went to the cemetery?" Cohen echoed softly.

I nodded, biting the inside of my cheek as I blinked my eyes quickly.

"Why did you go alone?" he asked. "You know it's dangerous to be alone on the streets, and plus going to the cemetery alone," Cohen trailed off under my glare towards him. *In the event that I'd kill myself out of sorrow there?* I closed my eyes and pushed the thought away quickly.

"I know but I needed to calm myself down," I admitted. "It was the only place I thought of to go," I mumbled, looking down between my knees. Cohen stayed silent as he looked away from me with a sigh.

"You're not going alone this time." He whispered.

My heart beat out of my chest as I pushed through the old iron gate with Cohen trailing behind me. He shivered as a cold gust of wind shot past us. I limped quickly through the tall grass and sighed in relief as I found my pistol laying gently in the dying weeds. I quickly picked it up and dusted it off before tucking it in my back pocket with a shiver. I purposefully ignored my parent's picture staring at me before I turned away from their grave. I blinked several times at not seeing Cohen anywhere but huffed in relief at seeing him crouched next to a grave in the middle of the field. *Might as well go see him one last time; I don't know when I'll be able to come back.*

I leaned down gently in the grass in front of Mr. Keilot's grave as I bowed my head and frowned down at myself. I glanced up to his cheerful smile and felt my heart spike in my chest with warmth and love immediately. My gaze drifted to the new decorations lining the grave. *His sister must have changed it last night.*

"I need you. I need your judgement and wisdom for my decisions right now," I whispered softly. "I know I'm asking for a lot, but I'm lost right now," I admitted, burying my face in my arm as my voice broke.

"Was this man your father?" A familiar voice suddenly asked. I flinched, standing up quickly and turning over my shoulder. The fiery, red-haired woman from the attack was leaning calmly against the tree behind me, her arms crossed and an amused glint in her eye.

"You…" I hissed sharply.

"I'm not your father, try again," the woman sneered. I narrowed my eyes at her as I clenched my fists.

"He was a close friend of mine," I snapped, turning back to face his picture. "Why are you even—" I began, glaring over my shoulder. I widened my eyes at not seeing her standing by the tree anymore. I gulped nervously as I glanced at Cohen still kneeling by the grave and sighed before I turned back to Mr. Keilot's tombstone.

A shiver ran down my back as sharp pain suddenly struck my arm. I yelped, flinching away from the grave as light grey smoke shot from my palm, slamming into something invisible next to me. Warm blood trickled down my arm as I grimaced and held it tightly in my shaking hand. My pitch-black smoke suddenly drowned the light grey smoke away quickly as a violent headache surged through my head, making me stumble and grip the tree to stay standing. I gasped for breath as my legs became too weak to hold me up. I shook my head with a worried glance at Mr. Keilot's picture before I stumbled quickly away back towards my parents' grave.

My heart leapt out of my chest as I stared at freshly cut red roses resting in front of the grave. *Did that woman leave those?* I shivered violently as I saw a note folded perfectly in between the thorn filled stems before I collapsed to the ground. I gasped quickly for air as I pushed myself through the dying grass, leaning heavily against the brick wall behind me. My head became too heavy to hold as my vision blurred and my heart spiked out of my chest repeatedly. The ground under me constantly moved, sending jolts of nausea through me. I closed my eyes, gripping the dirt below me tightly as I felt my heart falter in my chest.

"True!" Cohen's distant voice echoed. "What happened? You're bleeding!" he cried. "You don't look good; you're pale," he grumbled, his voice becoming further away. I weakly opened my eyes as he shook my shoulder gently and crouched in the grass next to me. Immense pressure formed inside my head as pain began to wrap its way around my neck. In an instant, everything shot back to normal. Loud ringing filled my ears for a moment as I blinked at Cohen. "What just happened to you?" he asked softly. I shook my head and grimaced as I frowned.

"Death is a complicated subject, huh?" a quiet voice suddenly chuckled, making us both flinch. "I know it's hard on you boys," an older woman smiled gently at us. "Especially at your young age, I know it's difficult for you." She frowned, staring warmly at the two of us as she limped forward using her cane. She leaned down slowly, pursing her wrinkly lips in concentration as she used the tombstone next to my parent's grave to help her sit in the grass. "I've just had to learn to accept that my loved one is happier," she beamed sadly, staring at the picture of an old man in front of her.

"My husband died in a construction accident a few years back," the woman explained gently. Cohen and I glanced at each other as my heart leapt in my chest, sending a wave of pain across my head.

"My friend lost a father figure in the same accident," Cohen gently responded, furrowing his brow at the old woman.

"Ahhh," she sighed. "I know exactly how he's feeling then," she chuckled, grimacing as she turned over towards us crouched against the wall. "Hatred? Jealousy? Vengeful?" she slowly began, my heart faltering in my chest each time. "I felt that way for a long time," she whispered, her voice wavering. "I was so angry at the court ruling the building collapse as an accident and closing the case not even three months into investigating," she hissed sharply, closing her eyes and taking a deep breath. "I know how much your heart is hurting young man," she continued, her voice becoming gentle again. "Grief is something you never get better at handling," the woman frowned. "Just know that you're not alone and trust the people around you to be there for you when you need them," she smiled, her warm, friendly eyes filled with tears.

"The light will return to your eyes soon, you just have to let yourself heal for the light to be turned back on to reveal everything hidden in your heart."

Tears filled my eyes as I rested my forehead on my shaking arm, blinking quickly at the grass below me. Cohen kept his hand on my shoulder as he crouched next to me, staying silent but nodding at the woman leaning towards the grave. She kissed the photo of the old man resting in the center of the long tombstone as she sighed with a large smile.

I lifted my head slowly as Cohen stood up and gently walked over to her. The old woman grabbed his burly arm as he carefully helped her stand up off the ground. I glanced at the old man's picture and felt my heart leap in my chest. *I've seen him in pictures with Mr. Keilot. They were best friends!* My heart ached as I bowed my head again as anger filled my mind.

"Oh, thank you, young man!" the old woman exclaimed gratefully, her voice immediately calming me. I leaned my head back against the wall and smiled gently as the old woman cupped Cohen's bearded face in her shaking hand with a smile up at him. Cohen trembled, leaning into her gentle, loving touch before she patted his arm and limped out of the cemetery. Cohen stood still for a moment before he turned towards me after wiping his face.

"You still don't look good," he mumbled, crouching next to me slowly. I gripped his arm tightly as I struggled to pull myself up while my head became light again.

"I didn't leave those roses," I breathed, weakly pointing to the flowers resting next to the stone. "I don't know why this is freaking me out so much…" I mumbled, angrily laughing into my arm.

"This is why I didn't want you to come back alone," Cohen snapped as gently as he could. I shook my head as I clutched my aching chest with a frown.

"Anxiety attack," I breathed, taking a shuddering breath as I began shaking. My heart began pounding in my ears as my vision blurred as I stared at my mother's intent gaze one me through the stone. "I'm fine," I weakly whispered, pulling my arm away from Cohen as I gasped for breath.

"I highly doubt that, True," Delta's voice suddenly sneered. My heart spiked in my chest as Cohen flinched, looking above us with narrowed eyes. I glanced up at the top of the wall and saw Delta standing calmly with his hands in his jacket pockets, an amused expression resting across his LED glass helmet.

"Nice job yesterday, flame boy," Delta chucked, looking disinterestedly at his metal hand. "You acted exactly how I predicted you to," he smiled, walking calmly along the brick wall.

"You're being very disrespectful right now!" Cohen hissed, glancing at the graves behind him as flames flickered by his eyes.

"Power use within a cemetery is forbidden," Delta spat. "So, I'd think *you'd* be mostly at fault if you tried setting me on fire,"

My legs trembled under me as I slid down the wall, unable to breathe again. Cohen worriedly widened his eyes at me as I let go of his arm and closed my eyes tightly with a grimace.

"What are you doing to him?" Cohen ordered sharply.

"Nothing," Delta scoffed. "Looks like he's just having an episode," he laughed slyly as Cohen narrowed his eyes. Delta leapt down from the wall, making the ground shake as his metal boots slammed into the dirt. Delta then turned and faced Cohen head on, towering over him easily. Cohen's dark eyes became filled with anger as Delta's metal hand slowly lifted and ran along his chin. "You got lucky, True," Delta sighed. "Two powerful people with fire related powers…" he smiled. Delta's metal hand then traced Cohen's jaw and his neck as he walked in a circle around him, Cohen frozen in anger and fear. "Too bad they'll go to waste with your horrible planning skills,"

Bright red flames suddenly flickered brightly from Cohen's eyes as he violently turned and swung his fist around to Delta behind him. Delta leaned slightly back with a calm expression before his metal arm shot up, gripping Cohen's wrist harshly and turning it down, twisting it the wrong way. My heart leapt in my chest as Cohen grimaced, a panicked look filled his eyes while he desperately tried pulling away from Delta's grasp. Anger filled my mind as I clenched my fists at Delta's blank mask expression staring intently at Cohen struggling.

"I'm excited to see how much of a screw up you are, True!" Delta laughed, violently throwing Cohen to the ground. Cohen gripped his wrist tightly in his palms as he hissed in pain, staring up at Delta standing over him.

"You don't just do that to someone!" I snarled. "You don't know his past!" I cried angrily, trying to push myself to stand. Something invisible from in front of me roughly shoved me back into the wall, forcing me back to the ground. Delta's glass helmet stayed completely dark as he glared over the metal patch on his left shoulder for a moment.

"You don't just swing a *punch* at someone you don't know either," Delta responded coldly, his voice distorting horribly as it became forced. While keeping his head turned towards me, Delta violently stepped forward, slamming his metal boot onto Cohen's ankle as he struggled on the ground. Cohen cried out in agony as he tried prying his foot off his leg while flames flickered out from under his jeans. Delta only slowly added more pressure as the rage in Cohen's eyes built, masked by pain. I gritted my teeth in anger as I leaned against something invisible holding me against the wall with an angry glare at Delta. He then leapt off Cohen's ankle, onto the old woman's husband's tombstone. From the stone, he jumped back up onto the brick wall with an amused expression on his face as dark mist floated away from under his helmet. With the flick of his hand, Delta jumped down from the wall, disappearing from my sight.

The ground trembled violently around us as the buildings shook. Cohen cried out softly in pain as he forced himself to stand and stumble towards the iron gate with flames shooting out from behind his eyes. I shoved whatever was in front of me away as the air shimmered quickly in two different locations, brushing past Cohen quickly. He flinched, turning over his shoulder at one of the moving air figures hitting him before he turned to me with widened eyes. I sighed in relief, as I suddenly was able to breathe again. Cohen gritted his teeth in pain as he stumbled along the wall, limping horribly with his ankle. I narrowed my eyes at his red wrist that had already begun to bruise. He knelt weakly next to me as he held my shoulder with a worried glint in his eyes.

Cohen pushed open the suite as worried and angry yells filled our ears.

"What happened to you guys?" Randy asked sharply, stepping in front of Cohen as he limped next to me.

"We'll explain later," Cohen grumbled, moving him easily out of his way. Maeve quickly grabbed Randy's arm and pulled him away from Cohen's glare as I glanced at Stella sitting on the edge of the couch next to Eela and Ryth. My heart ached in my chest as Stella kept her gaze intently on the balcony, ignoring everyone's yells of protest towards Cohen and I. Cami and Fletcher worriedly stood up off the living room floor as Cohen moved me into my room. Stretch burst through the door, mumbling insults under his breath to everyone else before he worriedly stared at me.

"What happened?" Stretch asked worriedly, handing Cohen the first aid kid.

"Delta," Cohen spat. Stretch flinched and nodded, helping me take off my jacket with a furrowed brow. "True had a weird panic attack episode, too," Cohen grumbled, limping into my bathroom and grabbing a towel. Stretch blinked quickly as he kept his eyes away from me staring at him. My head throbbed in pain as the wrap on my elbow pulsed with every beat of my heart. I watched Cohen lift his jeans and glare down at the bruise on his ankle as he ran the towel under the water before limping back over to me.

"It was someone's power," Stretch mumbled softly. Cohen glared at him as he dabbed my burning forehead with the damp towel.

"What do you mean?" Cohen snapped. Stretch narrowed his eyes for a moment before he shook his head and rewrapped my elbow.

"Giving True the panic attack,"

"How would you know that?"

"Cohen," I hissed softly, glaring up at his intense gaze on Stretch next to me. Stretch shook his head and shied away from my gaze as he rubbed his arm with a furrowed brow. My heart began to beat out of my chest as violent pain rumbled across my skull, making me grab my forehead and grimace.

"You know how I was hired to try killing you, True?" Stretch suddenly breathed. Cohen tensed, standing up slowly next to me as I turned over my shoulder at him leaning towards the door. He clenched his fists while he avoided my gaze, his brow furrowed. "I worked for Delta *and* Boss at the time. He hired me to kill you,"

"TRAITOR!" Cohen roared. He ripped his wrist out of my grasp as he shouldered into Stretch, knocking him into my desk. Stretch hissed in pain and cried out in anger as the two struggled with one another. I widened my eyes as Stretch was pinned against the wall with Cohen's flames flickering violently behind his eyes.

"Let him go!" I snarled angrily, weakly standing up towards them.

"Why? He tried killing you!" Cohen snarled back. Stretch growled in anger with a small yelp of pain as Cohen's flames brushed against the side of his neck. Stretch suddenly extended his arm down to his side, pulling out a curved, karambit knife. The sharp blade immediately struck Cohen's arm as Stretch kicked him in the chest.

"Both of you stop!" I ordered, materializing a pistol in front of Stretch's neck. I pulled my own pistol out and held it to Cohen as I slowly brought the other in the air closer to Stretch, the two of them breathing hard, glaring angrily at each other.

Cohen laid on his back, holding his hands out to me with a furrowed brow with red flames flickering from behind his eyes. A trail of blood ran slowly down the backside of his tattooed forearm as he narrowed his gaze at Stretch's glare. "I know you're upset but that was an irrational way to handle that information!" I snapped harshly, narrowing my eyes at Cohen. "And you!" I hissed, turning to Stretch. He held up the black cloth around his face with a shaking, red hand as his curved karambit knife trembled in the other. "I'll discuss this later with you! Out!" I spat. Stretch grumbled under his breath as he weakly stood up and walked towards the door with shuddering breaths. I shivered at seeing the side of his neck looking sunburned from Cohen's flames before he flicked his black jacket hood up and stalked out the door.

"What was that!" I grumbled, sitting down roughly on the edge of my bed. Cohen turned his gaze away from my angry glare as he slowly sat himself up while I lowered my pistol.

"How are you going to let a traitor keep walking among us!"

"He clearly isn't working for Delta now, it's fine!"

"He still might be! He's been lying to us this entire time!"

"Let *me* talk to him and figure this out, okay?" I half laughed, my voice becoming cold. Cohen shivered slightly as he furrowed his brow and nodded, frowning at the blood coming from his arm.

Once Cohen and I wrapped any wounds we could on ourselves, I limped out into the main room and glared at Stretch icing his neck in the kitchen. Everyone fell silent under my gaze as they widened their eyes with nervous glances at each other. I slowly inhaled with closed eyes before I narrowed them at Stretch and tipped my head to the balcony. I shivered as Stretch's eyes darkened for a moment before he nodded, setting the icepack down roughly on the counter and stalking across the room towards me.

I leaned against the railing of the balcony, staring down at the busy street as car horns and sirens blared. A chill shot down my back from a gust of wind right as Stretch closed the sliding door behind him. The air became tense as I stood with my back to him in silence. I heard him shift uncomfortably behind me. My heart spiked with anger in my chest as I tightened my grip on the metal bar below me. *How did Delta want me dead long before I knew he existed? Why is he now making himself known to the public?* I narrowed my eyes as I bit the inside of my cheek.

226

"Are you kidding me?" I laughed angrily, bringing my head down slowly before I turned and faced Stretch staring at me. "Whose side are you on?!" I demanded, stepping towards him quickly. "Are you Boss' side or Delta's side?!" I asked, clenching my fists as my heart roared in my ears. Stretch turned his gaze away from mine as he tensed. "Oh okay!" I scoffed. "You don't even know *yourself?*"

"I *do* know!" Stretch hissed softly. I shivered as Stretch clenched his fists as they began to tremble slightly.

"Tell me then!"

"Boss' side!"

"Oh, so double crossing her and working for an enemy is on her side?" I snarled quickly, stepping towards him. Stretch flinched and stumbled to the ground as he fearfully stared up at me. I widened my eyes as pure panic filled his gaze before it became emotionless again. I took several deep breaths as I furrowed my brow at him. "Are you still working for Delta?" I asked softly. "Is there anything that I might need to know about?" I added, relaxing my stance. Stretch stayed silent as he brought his gaze to the tile below us.

I narrowed my eyes as anger shot through my heart.

"Would you have any idea on why Delta want's Ryth *dead?!*" I angrily laughed.

Stretch's eyes widened in panic as he looked up at me with a furrowed brow.

"He always talked about being annoyed with her and wanting her power but never about *killing* her!" Stretch cried.

"How does he even know her?" I snapped.

"I don't know!" Stretch snapped back. "I wasn't around long enough for me to find that out!" he snarled, leaning forward quickly as I stepped away. I shook my head in disapproval at him before I turned and walked back to my room through the second sliding door.

My hands trembled as I sat on the edge of my bed in silence, staring at the painting Ryth and Eela made hanging over my desk. The bright red and yellows contrasted against the rough brick wall behind it. A gentle knock on the door made me tense as I turned my head away.

"True?" Stella's worried voice asked softly. "What happened with Cohen and Stretch?" she sighed, closing the door and slowly walking over to me. I kept my gaze turned away from her as she sat on the bed next to me. My heart began to race in my ears as I shook my head.

"Stretch used to work for Delta," I admitted, my voice wavering. Stella tensed slightly as she grabbed my knee gently in her warm hand and tipped my chin towards her with her other.

"Why would Delta say you and him are acquaintances?" she asked sharply.

"Cause we are," I mumbled. "I met him yesterday evening and earlier today,"

Stella narrowed her eyes slightly as they began to glow before she blinked quickly. I shivered under her intent gaze as my heart began to race, and I looked into her light eyes. Her grip on my chin tightened slightly before she let it go and sighed.

"Delta's the reason you've been acting weird lately, isn't he?" she whispered softly, intently keeping her gaze on me. I frowned slightly as my heart spiked in my chest. "What did he tell you?" she suddenly asked. "He told you something that hurt you. What did he say!" Stella cried angrily, leaning towards me.

I took a shuddering breath as Delta's angered warning filled my mind. The memory of the fierce cold coming from his metal hand sent a shiver down my back as I turned away from her gaze.

"You don't have to hide anything from me," Stella frowned, furrowing her brow at me.

"Delta's first move to help save the city from destruction by True Leader has been released to the public by authorities earlier this morning!" the TV in the living room suddenly blared. I quickly stood up, pulling away from Stella's gentle grasp and jogged into the main room.

I furrowed my brow as I stared at the TV showing videos of Delta and the other four people with him walking through the main lobby of the Southside Elite Headquarters. All five of them had glass LED emotion helmets that hid their faces.

"High tech security systems and small robotic guards called *Kamis* have been placed in every Elite building in the city," the reporter explained calmly. Images and quick clips from videos showed small, robotic, hybrid-type creatures that stalked the entrances to each room in the skyscrapers on their four, lanky legs. My heart began to beat out of my chest as one of the Kamis snarled up at one of the cameras before the video cut off.

"What the hell are those things?" Cami cried softly from the couch. Fletcher tucked her under his arm with a worried glance up at me as Stella sided up next to me. Randy and Maeve stood in the kitchen with furrowed brows, Eela and Ryth clinging to their sides. Cohen stared at the TV screen next to Fletcher with an emotionless expression that made me shiver. Everyone flinched as Stretch pulled open the sliding door from the balcony with narrowed eyes at the TV. My heart began to beat out of my chest as I clenched my fists at the reporter explaining more on Delta and his group.

Randy yelped from the kitchen as Ryth suddenly darted across the main room out from under his arm. Ryth roughly ran into my side as Stella stepped out of her way. I widened my eyes down at her and wrapped my arms around her as she slid to the ground, trembling uncontrollably.

"Woah, what's wrong?" I asked softly, grimacing as she wrapped her arm tightly around my scraped side. Eela slowly shuffled from the kitchen with widened eyes before she tucked herself under Stella's arm. "Ryth, what happened?" I asked again, trying to pull her in front of me. Cohen silenced the TV as we all worriedly waited for her to respond.

"He tried taking me!" Ryth cried. Everyone flinched as we all clenched our fists in anger. "He tried taking me to some place that I knew I'd die in," she cried again, her voice breaking.

"When did he try taking you?" I breathed, my voice shaking with anger as my heart roared in my chest.

"I'm sorry! I'm so sorry!" Ryth cried, keeping her face hidden from me. Her long, sleek black hair clung to her tear-filled face as I brushed it out of her eyes with a gentle grin. "He wouldn't be going after you if I would have never joined your Agency!" she sobbed.

"No, don't blame yourself," I whispered, my voice wavering as tears filled my eyes. I pulled Ryth into a tight hug as we both sat on the cold tile floor while I looked up at everyone's worried gazes. Ryth's heart beat strongly out of her chest as she continued to cry into my side. "He won't do anything to you," I promised, narrowing my eyes. "I won't let him do anything to you," I breathed, hugging her tighter. I closed my eyes as tears filled with anger and sorrow fell down my cheek, sending a chill down my back. *This lunatic is going to get it…*

CHAPTER 38

Several hours later...

My heart beat with anger in my chest as I waited for the phone to be answered. I stared intently at Delta's card in my shaking hands while I narrowed my eyes.

"Who's calling?" Delta's sleek voice suddenly hissed in my ear, making me flinch.

"You know exactly who I am," I snarled coldly.

"Why are you calling?" Delta asked calmly. "Did you finally make up your mind about your stupid plan after seeing my little show—"

"Your ass is dead, you prick," I growled sharply, interrupting him. Delta remained silent as I stood up and glared at the rooftop I met him at the day before.

"Central Park, Conservatory Gardens," Delta spat, immediately hanging up.

I forced Maeve, Randy, Stretch, and Cohen to stay behind at the entrance nearest to the gardens to keep anyone else from entering this part of the park. Everyone else waited anxiously back at the suite for any updates from us. My heart roared with anger in my ears as I glared around the empty park through the glass in my gas mask. I narrowed my eyes as I slowly stalked under the large trees surrounding the garden. My hands shook gently around my pistol in hand as I tried to calm myself down.

"I don't know who this *Delta* guy thinks he is," I whispered aloud, "but no one threatens my Agency and gets away with it,"

I lifted my pistol quickly as I moved quietly out into the small plaza surrounding the fountain. Delta laid on his back, staring up at the sky through his black LED glass helmet with no expression.

"Back for more, huh?" Delta snarked coldly, sitting up as I neared him. His dark hood covering his head waved eerily as a gust of wind casted itself around the plaza.

"Why do you want my daughter dead?" I snarled, ignoring his question. Delta shook his head at me with a small chuckle as the expression on his glass helmet seemed amused.

"Daughter?" he echoed. "So, you've raised her title to that now?" he asked, tilting his head at me. "I wouldn't know how to explain my reasoning to a guy like you," Delta sighed, leaning forward and resting his elbows on his metal knees. "Why are you so desperately angry with me? I've done nothing,"

"You know exactly what you've done!" I snarled, cocking my pistol back. "You threatened to kill Ryth. That's why I'm angry with you!"

"Mistake number one," Delta droned. "You see, True, having an emotional attachment to anyone in this dangerous business you and I are in is useless. It is sad, really," he hissed coldly. The eyes on his helmet glitched in and out between normal and angry making me shiver.

I glared at the fountain filled with water behind him for a moment as I narrowed my eyes. *You're mostly a machine. Bad choice in location...*

"I love the costume, True," Delta suddenly giggled. "So scary," he teased, the expression changing to amused. I ignored his snarky comment as I slowly wrapped myself in my pitch-black smoke and I tightened my grip around my pistol. Delta tensed slightly, gripping the cold concrete below him as the emotion on his mask went blank. My heart began to beat out of my chest as I kept my pistol aimed at him, slowly inching closer. *I don't know how much of him is metal. I can't just shoot him anywhere; it'll piss him off.*

"Sure, having emotional attachments to people in this business is useless, maybe even dangerous," I coldly admitted, "but those feelings within me are what drive me to push myself and succeed beyond everyone's expectations!" I snarled angrily. I materialized several pistols floating around me and immediately fired. Each bullet struck the concrete fountain directly next to Delta's limbs, making him yelp in panic as he flinched away from them. I narrowed my eyes as he became unbalanced and his mask glitched to an angered expression. I inhaled sharply while I fired my pistol in hand directly at his own as I charged towards him.

I used a column of smoke to launch me off the ground as I violently drop-kicked Delta in the chest, sending him directly into the fountain. The smoke column around my back caught me and lowered slowly to the ground as I stared at the frantic splashing from the fountain. Delta's distorted screams of agony echoed through the silent park as he lurched himself up out of the water. His cries of pain distorted into higher pitches before sounding completely robotic as his trembling hands raked his body in panic.

His entire mechanical body twitched violently as sparks shot from each of his limbs.

"You prick!" Delta screamed, his voice distorting horribly. Delta forced himself up onto one of his elbows as he pulled a pistol out from behind him and fired blindly towards me. A single bullet brushed harmlessly off the smoke around my arm as my vision focused on the rest, stopping them easily in the air. His glitching arm, blaring with alarms violently twitched, twisting his wrist in the wrong direction as the gun fell roughly to the soaked, cracked concrete stones below him.

With a glitching arm, Delta roughly pulled the glass LED helmet off his head, slamming it into the ground. His brown eyes were filled with blood and rage as he stared at me while ripping off his black metal mask. Both items spewed with water as they were thrown to the ground. Blood fell from Delta's once perfect eyes as he weakly forced himself to stand on his trembling legs. Small, distorted cries of pain escaped his mouth as his eyes darkened with a demented, controlled look overtaking his entire face. I widened my eyes as I stared into the dark smoke hovering directly over his eyes.

Delta blinked quickly as the smoke lifted away suddenly. He coughed hollowly into his arm, blood landing onto the sleek water filled metal.

"You're smarter than you look!" Delta laughed, his voice distorting. He smiled maniacally at me as blood fell from the corner of his mouth before he roughly wiped it away. "With amazing reaction time!"

"That's what being alone for a while does," I replied sharply, raising my pistol.

"I forgot your fancy power protects you from guns," he grumbled, glaring at his bullets laying uselessly below my feet.

My heart leapt out of my chest as a long blade extended from Delta's arm as he lunged towards me, screaming in rage. I ducked quickly under the sword, feeling the edge of the blade skimming the side of my shoulder. I fired a single round at Delta as I materialized a pistol around me and fired at it swinging through the air. The blade immediately snapped as he swung it towards me again while I jumped out of its way with narrowed eyes. The long sword retracted back into Delta's arm as he gripped his side with an agony filled expression.

Delta's legs faltered under him as he turned and tried to limp away.

"Leaving so soon?" I snarked angrily, lunging towards him. A column of smoke shot from my side, slamming Delta roughly to the ground and pinning him down. Delta cried out in panic as he struggled below the smoke restraints while I slowly leaned over him, pressing the barrel of my pistol to the box exposed on the back of his neck. My heart screamed in my chest as I breathed hard and stared down at his maniacal glint in his eye facing up towards me. "You act like you're indestructible, but you're not!" I hissed darkly, leaning down to him.

Delta's robotic body twitched violently beneath me and the smoke as I narrowed my eyes and brought the barrel of the pistol further onto the box. *You won't be a problem anymore after this.* My fingers tightened around the pistol as Delta began laughing maniacally, his voice distorting into someone else's laugh. A violent chill shot down my back as I recognized the new laugh. The same dark smoke appeared slowly over his blood-filled eyes as he stared up at me.

"Guess you'd know best, huh?" a distorted voice snarled slowly through Delta. His amused smile broke into one of pure insanity as he suddenly lurched himself forward, destroying the stones below us. His robotic arm snapped behind him, grabbing the back of my metal gas mask and violently launching me off him. Immense pain radiated from my head as my vision went black while I hit the concrete. I gasped as I gripped my chest and bleeding neck as I stared at Delta standing strongly, my cracked gas mask in his glitching robotic hand. I trembled as I felt warm blood run down my neck, soaking into my jacket as my vision blurred and ears sang.

"I want you to ask your *daughter* a very important question, True," Delta darkly laughed. His grasp on my metal gas mask tightened, crushing it easily as the radio system weakly filled with worried voices. Cold steam flew from Delta's mouth with every breath he took as he stared intently at me.

"Ryth!" he spat. "That sneakily little *brat*," he snarled, waving his twitching arms, "is my sister!" Delta beamed wildly with a prideful smirk. A wave of disbelief and anger hit me like a truck. Immense pain filled my chest as I remembered Ryth's cry of fear about Delta, her older brother. *Why didn't she tell us?*

"She just wants all the attention in the world, huh?" Delta snarled angrily. "Always forcing herself into the center of everything!"

"She isn't like that!" I breathed, gasping weakly for breath as pain struck my side. Delta nodded quickly, his metal jaw setting to the side roughly.

"Sure, she isn't..." he chuckled. "Try asking her all she did in all our foster homes to keep all attention away from me...then say that to my face again!" Delta hissed coldly, crushing my gas mask even more. "Everything was always about her! Never anything to do with me!" Delta cried, his voice distorting. "All those sleepless nights of me wondering why I wasn't good enough for our foster parents because they constantly screamed how much they hated me because of lies Ryth told them about me!" Delta cackled loudly, his stance faltering as sparks flew from his neck. "Little brat has all the attention now, doesn't she!" he snapped, glaring down at my crushed gas mask.

"You don't have to kill her!" I cried weakly. Delta's gaze darkened towards me as his body became weirdly still.

"You try having everything *ripped* away from you!" Delta suddenly cried, his voice completely normal. His blood-filled eyes suddenly switched to pure panic and fear as he widened them towards me. I furrowed my brow as I pushed myself onto my elbow and I stared at him. Delta cried out in agony as he gripped his head and fell slightly backwards, catching himself roughly on a shaking leg. *What just happened to him?*

"I have had everything ripped away from me!" I cried back. I searched the ground as I pulled myself to my feet and held my hands out to him with a wince. Delta's body jerked forward as he raised his head robotically, his eyes clouded over with a dark smoke. His glitching mechanic arm suddenly lifted and arched back like a viper waiting to strike its prey.

I widened my eyes as my broken gas mask was suddenly hurled directly at me at a dangerous speed. My heart faltered in my chest as sharp metal slammed into my face, knocking me violently to the ground. Cold concrete scraped my back roughly as I rolled into the fountain. My pain vibrated in agony as everything became distant around me. Pressure formed everywhere in my mind as my vision blurred completely and I gasped for breath. Faint memories filled with laughter filled my head as I stared up at the starry, beautiful night sky. My entire body trembled as the ground below me began to melt.

A cry of agony pulled me out of my head as I weakly turned my eyes to Delta.

"I *warned* you to stay out of my way!" Delta screamed, his voice distorting. "You sealed my stupid little sister's fate tonight by attacking me!" he laughed maniacally, his stance faltering. "She'll die now!" he screamed. "Because of *you*!" Delta beamed, stepping weakly towards me. His voice echoed around my mind as I was unable to think straight.

I gasped for air and panicked at receiving nothing. I gripped my neck with trembling hands as my vision slowly became smaller and smaller, darkness enveloping me.

Through my blurry vision I watched Delta fall halfway over as he gripped his head tightly in his hands. He violently slammed his forehead into the concrete ground before he got up completely normal, blood streaming down his face. Delta's cries of pure anger became inaudible as he fell into a crazed state of laughter, his voice distorting in and out of being normal. The same familiar laughter sent a weak chill down my back as my head became filled with pressure. Sharp pain pierced my palm, forcing me to widen my eyes and gasp for air once more.

My life flashed before my eyes as Delta suddenly surged forward, screaming. His robotic arm lifted high into the air, the broken katana blade extending from his arm. I watched the snapped blade come closer and closer towards me as I laid helplessly on the ground. Delta's entire body suddenly jerked violently side to side as his stance faltered, distant gunshots filling the air. Delta paused his stride, holding out his hands weakly as he slowly looked to the blood seeping through his clothes. His legs gave out from under him as he blankly stared at me. Arms immediately wrapped around him, the entire ground trembling as he disappeared into thin air.

Several footsteps echoed around in my head as my eyes struggled to stay open. The bitter taste of blood overpowered my mouth as I tried gasping for air. Stretch's blurry face suddenly appeared over me, his eyes wide in panic. His arms gently wrapped around me as sirens filled the air and more gunshots echoed around us. My eyes closed as pain shot through my skull, and I was quickly lifted and felt myself moving. Gunshots rang painfully loud in my head as I slowly opened my eyes to see Randy firing his gun at groups of police officers storming across the park. Cohen's bright red flames burned brightly in the distance as only dim light filled the inside of my eyelids and Cohen's raspy voice calling out my name echoed away.

CHAPTER 39

STRETCH'S POV

"We need to get him out of here!" I screamed, gripping True in fear as I widened my eyes.

"You two! Get him somewhere safe!" Randy ordered, grumbling under his breath as bullets struck the ground next to him. "

We'll hold off the police! Go!" Maeve cried; her dark eyes filled with horror at True's limp body in my arms. My heart beat strongly out of my chest as I felt blood drip from his neck onto my jacket, staining my hands. Cohen quickly grabbed my shoulder and cast a wall of flames on either side of us to create a safer path. *I should have known Delta would do something! Why did I let you come alone?*

Panic surged through my skull as the burning red flames raged on either side of Cohen and I while we ran. Memories flashed of the alley with my brothers laughing down at me in disgust. I shook the thought away as fearful tears filled my eyes and I glanced at True in my arms. I yelped as Cohen's burning palms shoved me roughly forward, my skin stinging with pain through my jacket. The flames only roared louder all around us as he continued to cast columns of them from his arms. The gunfire was drowned out by the sheer loudness of the raging fire. *Cohen, you need to calm down!*

"We can't continue at this rate!" I screamed, stopping my stride and turning to Cohen behind me. He stumbled into me with flames surging from behind his eyes. "They're putting out the fire faster than you can cast it out!" I explained. "You'll hurt yourself if you keep doing this!"

"So what if I hurt myself!" Cohen snarled, gripping my arm tightly in his burning palm. "We need to get True out of here!"

I ripped myself out from his grasp as our gaze darkened towards the other. We both flinched as the wall of raging flames suddenly disappeared by a large wave of water. *Crap the Elites are here!*

"Hold him!" I ordered sharply, forcing True's limp body into Cohen's arms. "I'll get you both out of here!" I hissed, glaring over my shoulder at the dying flames.

"Are you crazy?" Cohen cried, glancing fearfully at True's calm expression.

"Yep!" I laughed, my eyes wide with panic.

"What the hell are you doing?" Cohen asked sharply as I extended my arm around him, tightly holding him still. I shivered as my stretched skin sang in pain from the heat coming from Cohen's body as I lifted him off the ground. I ignored his comment as I searched the skyline through the roaring flames. Cohen's eyes widened as I grit my teeth in concentration to lift the two of them.

"Try your best to land softly! Aim for a flat roof!" I grimaced. I swung myself in a tight circle, letting my arm snap back to normal as I flung Cohen and True into the sky. As I let Cohen's flaming back go, at the last moment my arm cracked like a whip in the air, sending them even further away. I watched in panic as the two of them flew over the park, Cohen holding True tightly in his burning arms. My heart screamed with regret in my chest as I glanced around at the burning park surrounding me.

I grumbled in anger as police officers and Elites began charging forward after the last wall of fire around me was put out. Quick gunfire echoed over the dying flames as bullets struck the ground all around me. I grimaced in pain as violent stinging shot through the side of my leg while a bullet grazed my skin. I extended both my arms quickly from my body, knocking the wave of officers down immediately. Confused and angered yelling filled my ears as I gripped the nearest light post with an extended arm before I launched myself off the ground. *Maeve and Randy, you better get out of here! Now!*

I beamed proudly down at the Elites' angered expressions up at me as I swung through the air. I flicked myself around the light post, darting across the burnt field as my heart raced in my chest. I extended my arms to another post and yelped as bullets struck the ground directly behind me. Large grappling hooks suddenly slammed into the ground next to me as an angry voice suddenly neared. I turned fearful over my shoulder to see an Elite with several large grappling gun hooks mounted around them. *Oh you have to be kidding me—*

Violent pain suddenly surged through my body from my side. I screamed in agony as my entire body fell limp, sliding into the dampened grass from the water wave earlier. I trembled in pain as surges of electricity shot up and down my limbs, and I cried out in anger. Loud voices echoed around my head as my ears began to ring loudly. I looked up from the ground with my only seeing eye and widened it as the Elite with the grappling guns knelt over me. My arms ached horribly as my hearing shot back to normal. My shoulders were twisted painfully backwards. I cried out in pain as cold handcuffs were tightened dangerously around my wrists.

Remaining electricity in my arms sparked between the metal touching my skin as I screamed again, and pain shot up my shoulders. Cold hands wrapped around my neck, pinning me harsher into the burning ground as I angrily cursed the Elite holding me down. Panic filled my mind as I saw a sharp tazing rod lit with blue light suddenly cast towards my back by a police officer. More waves of pain and electricity coursed through my body as I screamed in agony, trying to get away. My body fell limp as the Elite punched me roughly in the head. Everything around me trembled before it became eerily silent, everything going dark.

CHAPTER 40

Cohen's POV

Violent pain shot through my body as my leg slammed into the ledge of a building rooftop. I rolled roughly along the cold roof, holding True tightly in my arms as I closed my eyes. Loud ringing filled my ears as my back hit a large transformer on the roof and I gasped in pain. My heart beat loudly in my chest as I blinked quickly to steady my vision. I laid still on my back for a moment, staring up at the smoke-filled sky as my lungs ached and my breaths became rigid.

I weakly rolled to my side, holding myself up on a trembling elbow as I widened my eyes at True lying limp next to me. I grimaced in pain as I turned to the blood gushing from my shin and narrowed my eyes at the burning park in the distance. I grumbled as I forced myself to sit up and gently pick True's head off the cold, hard concrete, wincing as his blood filled my hands and panic shot through my chest. I sat him up as gently as I could and bit back cries of pain from the flames eating away at my jeans from the gash on my shin.

I glanced worriedly at True as I forced myself to stand using the old transformer next to me. I shivered at seeing light grey smoke casting from his palm, forcing his hand to stay around his pistol. *Isn't his smoke pitch-black? What is that?* I shook my head with a frown at him as I limped across the rooftop, grimacing in pain. I shivered in pride and pain as I leaned heavily against the old concrete ledge in front of me.

Raging red flames lined a section of Central Park as I narrowed my eyes at the helicopters swarming the sky.

My heart suddenly skipped a beat as the concrete below my hand holding me up suddenly snapped. I gripped the other part of the ledge as I gasped in panic and relief and stared at the concrete pieces free falling to the busy street below. I leaned away from the edge and fell to the cold ground below me, taking several raspy breaths. I glared at my smoke filling the sky as I shivered at seeing the reflection of the flame's light slowly dying down.

I flinched as sharp pain struck me in the side of the head.

"Cohen!" Maeve cried loudly in my head making me tremble. *"Randy and I made it out, we're both injured but breathing!"* she explained tiredly. *"Where did you three go? Is True alright?"*

"I don't know where Stretch is. He got True and I out of the park," I hesitantly responded. "True is still unconscious, and we're trapped on the roof of some building." I grimaced as I dragged myself across the cold concrete, steam rising from my arms at the temperature difference.

"I can't find Stretch…" Maeve weakly admitted. *"He's either unconscious or dead,"* she spat worriedly. I shivered as I sat down roughly next to True with a worried glance at the smoke being gone from his palm. His ash-covered pistol lay ominously next to his bleeding hand sending a chill down my back once more. *"Try contacting Boss from True's phone if it still works!"* Maeve suddenly hissed, grumbling in pain. *"I don't know what she has going on, but I can't get to her either! She must have something protecting her from trackers like me!"* Maeve snapped. *"Just get somewhere safe for the time being you two, please. We're heading to you now!"* Without another word, Maeve left my head with sharp pain on the left side of my skull.

I slowly removed True's bloody jacket after feeling his burning forehead. I grimaced, gagging at my hands being covered in my own and True's blood. I searched for where he was bleeding the most.

"True, your nose is definitely broken," I chuckled sadly, turning away from his blood-filled face for a moment. His expression slowly changed, making me flinch with a worried glance at him. Discomfort and pain covering his face made my heart ache as I slowly leaned over him and looked for his phone.

I held my breath as I pulled out True's shattered phone and prayed it would turn on. My heart leapt in my chest as the screen glitched in and out of the brightness before staying on and I grumbled in annoyance as the cracked glass pierced my burning fingers while I struggled to call Boss. *I don't even think this will work… This phone is done for.* I widened my eyes as it began to ring. Almost immediately, Boss answered, sending a wave of panic into my chest. Her worried voice distorted horribly, sending a chill down my back at the memory of Delta's voice. The microphone suddenly cut out completely before it slowly came to normal.

"True? Honey, what's going on?" Boss demanded.

"True is unconscious and possibly dying," I snapped harshly into the phone.

"Who the *hell* is this," Boss suddenly snarled, her voice becoming eerily cold.

"Cohen, True's friend," I spat. "I need you to send help to my location, right now." I pleaded softly. "They're coming—what happened to True?" she quickly snapped.

"Delta and him got into a fight, both of them walked away from it with serious injuries," I explained hesitantly. *Should I wait for True to be conscious to explain this to her?* Boss grumbled softly under her breath as a loud slam echoed through the phone before she hung up.

I sat in eerie silence for almost an hour, listening to the violent sirens and loud echoes of panic surge through the city. Chilling wind howled through the buildings as they all amusedly watched the people below frantically trying to figure out what was happening. I gazed over the concrete ledge with True leaning on my shoulder, still unconscious and barely breathing. From what I could see of the Conservatory Gardens, everything had been fully burned by my flames. *This will all be fixed back to brand new soon… People can do anything nowadays when they have the right power.*

Loud rumbling suddenly filled the stairwell to my right, making me wrap my arms around True fearfully with widened eyes. Two tall people in all black with huge guns suddenly burst through the door, forcing it off its hinges.

"They're here!" one of them yelled. A herd of footsteps loudly echoed up the stairwell as a group of people came flooding out the narrow door. One of the girls darting across the roof towards us pulled a small metal ball out of a bag on her side. Everyone immediately paused as she held it up to the sky. I shivered as it became invisible in her hand before she dropped it to the ground.

A large metal rod slammed into the concrete, locking it in place as it extended upwards, groaning softly. The large group of frozen people quickly began moving again, ignoring the sheet of thin metal folding open over us in a dome. The metal slowly became thinner and thinner as it disguised itself as the sky above us. It roughly slammed down on every corner of the roof top as small LED white lights illuminated the dark dome. Quiet whispers of worry filled the air as everyone closed in on True and I.

"The other two are being taken care of, they're safe," one person explained gently.

"Boss is sending more people to the rest of the Agency back at the complex as well," another quiet voice murmured.

"All of you are going to be brought to the Underground hospital at HQ, and for safety reasons, *no one* is allowed to leave once you're all there until further notice," someone else snapped. I shivered as I was pulled gently away from True. My heart throbbed in my chest as he was carefully laid onto a stretcher. *Safety reasons? Isn't Boss the reason why True is in danger in the first place with someone breaking into her files?!*

CHAPTER 41

STRETCH'S POV

I coughed hollowly through the smoke-filled air as I was kicked harshly in the back. Elites surrounded me completely, shoving and pulling me forward with zero empathy. Every step I took was countered by an Elite hovering around me.

"Let me walk! Assholes! I'm not doing anything!" I hissed loudly. *No wonder everyone hates you guys so much!* I glared over my shoulder at the Elite behind me as I smirked softly. I suddenly slammed the back of my head into their face, sending them to the ground. Loud angry yells filled my ears as a small taser rod was smacked into my side.

I screamed in agony as the eclectic current shot down my legs, making them buckle under me. The Elites roughly held me up as the one in front of me moved out of the way. Another Elite suddenly darted towards me, slamming a metal rod into my stomach. I grimaced and coughed horribly, leaning forward as I gasped for breath. I then spit the blood in my mouth from being knocked around directly onto him with a smirk. I wiped the rest of the blood from my lip on my shoulder as I narrowed my eyes at the Elite glaring down at the blood covering his badge.

"That's enough!" a commanding voice bellowed. "Police will take him from here!" the same voice growled, prying the metal bar out of the Elite's hand with a pitiful glance at me. Gentler hands suddenly took the place of the Elite's harsh grasps as police officers guided them away from me. I only laughed at the curses escaping their lips as they all angrily glared at me and walked off. My legs gave out completely under me as I fell to my knees. The officers holding me up yelped in alarm, crouching next to me for a moment with worried glances at each other.

"Almost to the car, c'mon," one of them winced.

I weakly gasped for breath inside the police car as I glared at the flames still scorching the park. I shifted uncomfortably from the heat building up in the car as the fire slowly inched closer. I suddenly yelped in panic as something violently wrapped itself around my neck. I was shoved roughly into the seat, pinned down against the damp leather. The air shimmered quickly as if something was struggling in front of me. The invisible grip tightened on my neck as I coughed hollowly with narrowed eyes.

I suddenly slammed my face into the air in front of me. An invisible figure quickly fell into the metal chain wall guarding the front seat as blood began to roll down their face, floating in the air. I stared intently at the shimmering, bleeding air in front of me with darkened eyes as I gasped for breath, grimacing at the heat filling my lungs. The air shimmered away from me as something stumbled into the seat moments before the entire car trembled. Dark arms wrapped around the invisible air and disappeared.

Rage filled screams escaped my mouth as I frantically threw myself around the backseat. I kicked everywhere in the air that could reach by staying still.

"Funny trick, Dusk!" I snarled, slamming my foot into the metal chain wall. I swung my legs over to the seats next to me, kicking the door multiple times. "You already pulled that trick on me prick!" I angrily laughed. "Get some new ones!" I dared, glaring over my shoulder as I breathed hard. My chest ached as the cold, metal cuffs on my wrists stung my burning skin.

"Am I getting arrested or slow-cooked! What the hell!" I exclaimed, shouldering into the door. I suddenly bent over coughing wildly as the air inside the car became extremely hotter. Sweat and blood beaded down into my eyes causing me to hiss in pain as they stung sharply. I grimaced as I activated my power, extending my arms further behind me before slipping out calmly from the cuffs. *The taser stunned me from using my power for a bit… Too bad these cops have never met me before, so they don't know normal cuffs don't work on me! Stupid bastards.*

I rubbed my sore wrists slowly, frowning at the small electric current scars along them before I glared outside the window. I struggled with the lock on the door for a moment before I was able to pull it up and push open the door. I staggered outside of the heated car and gasped for breath, immediately grimacing as smoke and ash filled air entered my lungs. I shut the door immediately, bringing my arm to my face as I coughed hollowly. I tightened the black bandana around my face for a moment before I flinched at an officer turning to look at the car. They stared worriedly at me before they turned and continued talking to the officer next to them.

I took a deep gasp of clean, burning air inside the car before I pushed the heavy door open. I carefully kept my gaze intently on the officers as I slid down to the steaming, damp grass before shuffling underneath the car. As I held myself up on my hands and knees, the once cool dirt under me began to heat up quickly as a loud roar of flames surged through my ears. I widened my eyes and turned over my shoulder to see flames falling dangerously closer to the car as a loud groan from a tree echoed over the distant fire. I yelped and rolled out from underneath the vehicle before leaping out of the way of a burning branch as it slammed down onto the car.

Panicked screams from the officers filled my ears as I hissed in pain, kicking the ground and batting out the flame climbing quickly up my leg. I gasped for breath again and rolled to my feet, sprinting quickly across the burnt field.

"He's out! Get him!" an angry voice ordered. I launched my arms from my body, gripping an old light post and flung myself off the ground away from the bullets.

"Fuck you guys!" I screamed, flicking the Elite's storming across the field towards me with narrowed eyes.

I roughly fell onto the concrete street outside the park before I quickly darted through the confused crowd. Yelps of panic escaped the civilians' mouths as I shoved everyone out of my way while more police charged towards me through them. I extended my arms up quickly to a balcony of an apartment building and leapt into the air, glancing down at the angry officers swinging to grab me. I pulled myself onto the balconies high above the street, startling people watching from their windows in curiosity at the burning park. My heart raced in my ears as

I shoved someone into the metal staircase along the building and leapt over them, continuing to the roof.

I breathed hard as my heart frantically beat out of my chest. Helicopters began to swarm the sky as I narrowed my eyes and ducked under an old table and chair resting calmly on the roof. I quickly darted across the rooftop as the searchlight passed over and wrapped my arm tightly around a metal pipe. I held my breath as I stepped off the edge, allowing my arm to continue extending as I lowered myself down back towards the street into the back alley of the building. I pulled the black cloth off my face as I coughed again into my arm and winced while I dropped roughly onto the trash littered ground below. I quickly scampered away from the street, my breaths becoming quick with panic.

I slid to the end of the alley as I turned fearfully over my shoulder and narrowed my eyes at the crowded street. I quickly took out my cracked phone and called Boss.

"I made it away from the police! I'm ducked in a back alley hiding from Elites and authorities," I breathed tiredly.

"Glad to finally hear from you, Stretch! I'm glad you're safe!" Boss whispered softly. "I'll send a pin for a pickup location back to HQ, alright?" she continued. "It's too risky to send anyone to go get you where you are,"

"I'll head that way to the pin ma'am," I sighed, shivering as a chill shot down my back.

A high-pitched hiss suddenly echoed through the alley. I widened my eyes and slowly turned over my shoulder. *What the hell?* A small robotic, hybrid creature with glowing red eyes was stalking silently down the alleyway towards me.

"Stretch!" Boss cried worriedly as I let the phone fall away from my ear. The metal gears on the machine's joints moved smoothly as if it wasn't even real. The long, sharp claws tapped the cold concrete as its narrow beak opened, revealing a row of small, sharp teeth. The same high-pitched hiss rang through the air. *What is a Kami doing here outside of an Elite building?*

The small robotic machine suddenly roared, its voice distorting. It violently slammed into me, knocking me roughly into the brick wall. Violent sparks shot from the Kami's body as I pulled my karambit knife out and held it in front of me. The curved blade pierced immediately through the sheets of metal as it screamed in agony. The claws of the Kami locked into the brick wall behind me as it snarled in my face, revealing a rotating blade deep within its throat. I yelped, letting my legs give out under me as the rotating shredder blade destroyed the bricks right where my head once was.

The Kami roared weakly in confusion as I struggled to pry my knife out from its underside as bricks fell onto me, hitting me in the face. The claws locked into the wall suddenly released, the Kami leaping backwards and flipping midair. The ground shook as the small machine grumbled in annoyance, glaring down at my knife sticking out near its chest. I shoved the heavy bricks lying on my shoulders off as I widened my eyes at the machine staring at me. A deep growl filled the air as the rows of small, reverse hooked teeth were revealed again.

The Kami snarled angrily, its beak dropping open completely. A smaller chain lined with small hooks suddenly shot from its mouth, wrapping violently around my leg. I cried out in agony as I was forced out from under the pile of bricks and dragged across the alley, my hands desperately trying to grip the concrete. The Kami ripped my knife out of its chest as it stood on its hind legs and grabbed my shoulders with its long claws. The machine lurched me to my feet before a giant metal rod extended from its chest, slamming directly into me and launching me back to the ground. I gasped weakly for breath as my vision immediately blacked out. Flashes of the Kami stalking closer and closer to me filled me with panic as I lay helplessly on the ground. The machine let out a blood chilling screech of anger that echoed around my mind until everything became silent.

CHAPTER 42

DELTA'S POV

"Dammit!" I screamed, falling to the ground of the old warehouse building. My entire body twitched violently as I struggled to pull myself onto my knees with gritted teeth. The building shook and groaned as Bourbon dropped Nerve and Clou roughly in the middle of the warehouse room before disappearing again. Dusk appeared out of thin air moments later as Bourbon came back, the room trembling again. Warm blood ran Dusk's face as she crossed her arms and glared at all of us staring at her.

"Have you tried putting yourself in rice?" Dusk snarked coldly, wiping the blood from her nose as she stalked across the room. Nerve and Clou burst into laughter as I slowly turned my twitching head to the side, glaring at her from across the room. Bourbon rolled his eyes, an amused smirk on his face as he light skipped across the entire room, startling Dusk sitting on the couch. He crouched next to the old couch and pulled out a singular dark box with a glare at Nerve and Clou laughing and walking towards him. Both fell silent under his glare before he suddenly appeared standing over me as the room trembled.

"Very funny, *chameleon*," I spat, my voice distorting. Dusk grumbled under her breath from the couch as Nerve and Clou sat on the tile floor below us with worried glances at each other.

"I told you to stay away from that ridiculous fountain!" Bourbon snarled, smacking the back of my head roughly. My metal legs gave out from under me as I fell to the floor and grimaced in pain. My arms trembled below me as I stared angrily at the water dripping from my body. *I didn't expect him to do anything! Looks like he has a sense of humor when it comes to fighting as well.*

Bourbon rolled his eyes as he flicked the box away from his hand and held out a circular dark object with a grumble of annoyance. I glared up at him as I slowly lifted my metal arm behind my head and extended the rod from my finger and unlocked the box on the back of my neck. I inhaled sharply as I pressed the small button hidden on the side as my vision immediately went black. I shifted uncomfortably in my mind as I was suddenly forced to be floating in suspended animation inside my head.

Small, teal light illuminated from my chest as I curled myself into a ball and stared at it softly, darkness surrounding me. Pain struck the back of my neck as I grimaced, feeling Bourbon remove the battery in the box and place the new one in. I sighed in relief as the darkness all around me faltered, slowly becoming light again. I widened my eyes in panic as dark smoke clouded over the teal ball of light in front of me, a red hue being visible through the smoke around it. *Get out! You've done enough for now!* I was violently thrown back into my body.

I laid on the cold floor inside the warehouse room as I gasped for breath, clutching my chest tightly. My robotic limbs immediately began resetting themselves as I rolled to lean against the wall, a surge noise filling the air while my body twitched. Each limb disassembled itself, staying intact and attached to my body as droplets of water fell from each crevice, metal rods, and wires and boxes sealed themselves shut again. I shivered at being able to see through my metal arm for a moment before it sealed back to normal, forcibly staying sealed in waterproof mode.

"It sucks to do that," I breathed, coughing hollowly into my arm.

"I would think so. It's basically activating your own power on yourself," Clou called nervously from across the room. I glared sharply up at him as I rested my elbows on my knees in front of me. Bourbon stood over me, a disapproving glint in his eyes. I took several deep breaths as my metal limbs surged once more, waterproof mode deactivating calmly. A chill shot down my back as pressure formed inside my head, and I frowned, remembering the red hue to the teal orb through the smoke.

"True really screwed me good, didn't he?" I breathed, grimacing as Bourbon pulled me to my feet easily. I frowned at him and turned to the mirror behind me as I sighed at my reflection. I blinked quickly, squinting at the dark smoke hovering over my eye as I narrowed it at myself. *I said get out!* I violently slammed my metal fist into the brick surrounding the mirror as I grumbled angrily under my breath. The smoke seemed to falter slightly, teasing its departure before it finally floated off. I leaned closer to the mirror and clenched my fists as I narrowed my eyes.

"He dented my *face*!" I hissed, glaring over my shoulder at the others gathered at the furnished corner of the room.

"If you would have let us come, none of what just happened to you would have happened," Dusk snapped. Bourbon nodded once, his gaze turning to Nerve sitting anxiously next to Clou. My heart ached slightly in my chest as Nerve's eyes became panicked as he stared at everyone looking at him. I shook the feeling of empathy away as I frowned at them.

"Nerve needs to remain my little secret for now," I chuckled calmly, staring directly at him. His frantic light eyes widened as he cowered away from everyone, falling over onto his elbow as his fluffy white hair trembled on his head. *Let's just hope Stretch hasn't chickened out already and told them everything.* I grumbled as I stalked across the room, staring intently at the four glaring at me. Each of them slightly tensed as I neared them with a scowl on my face. "I warned True, so whatever happens next to him, and his Agency is his fault!" I growled, glaring over my shoulder at the sirens echoing through the street.

"The Kami you sent after Stretch found him," Bourbon suddenly spat. My heart spiked in my chest with anger and slight pity as I frowned down at the ground.

"Good," I sighed. "That idiot needs to know what happens to someone who switches sides against me," I hissed, clenching my fists. *I can't let this happen again. I can't have another one of us leave for True.* I narrowed my eyes down at the four staring at me before I closed my eyes. *Maybe it's time to go see him again and get some upgrades for myself…* "If True wants to play dirty, I'll be fine with it." I chuckled coldly, shivering as I felt the dark smoke cloud over my eyes as the four leaned away from my glare.

CHAPTER 43

COHEN'S POV

My vision blurred several times in the ambulance ride to HQ. I watched brightly lit skyscrapers shoot past the windows on the back doors of the vehicle as people surrounded me, whispering quietly to each other. My heart lurched in my chest at the image of watching True get put onto oxygen and forced out of my sight filled my mind. I narrowed my eyes slightly as I saw a large metal door pass over us, bright LED lights illuminating the inside of the vehicle from the concrete columns above the car. The back doors of the ambulance suddenly swung open as the car slowed to a stop.

I was quickly pushed down out of the car as I squinted up at the bright lights blinding me. I lifted my head at the distant cries of Eela and Ryth and widened my eyes in sorrow as I saw the two of them step out of a car and collapse to the ground sobbing. Stella knelt next to Eela, holding her tightly in her grasp as the two of them watched True get pushed passed me on the stretcher, the nurses surrounding him, yelling angrily. Fletcher leaned down and held Ryth back as she screamed for True and tried running to him while he disappeared through swinging metal doors. My heart sank as Cami stared worriedly at me while she rested her hand on Stella's shoulder.

My heart spiked in my chest as I saw Randy being rolled past me, tied down harshly to his stretcher. His amber eyes were wide with panic as his curls flew in front of his face as he screamed, throwing his head up and desperately trying to get out of the restraints. *No, no, no! Randy calm down! This isn't the asylum!*

"Don't tie him down!" Maeve's distant voice screamed angrily. "You have no clue what people have done to him in the past!" she cried, her voice breaking. Randy's panicked screams and struggle to escape the restraints only made the people above him force him further onto the stretcher as he wildly resisted. Angry comments from everyone else being held back at the cars by guards filled my ears as they began to ring slightly before everything became silent, darkness enveloping my vision.

CHAPTER 44

SEVERAL HOURS LATER...

Sharp pain radiated around my head as I weakly opened my eyes, blinking at the large room in front of me. I lifted my head slowly and glanced down at my leg and grimaced before closing my eyes as my vision blurred. I opened them once more and saw Cami and Fletcher sitting at the opposite end of the large room watching something intently on their phones. I blinked several times before I turned and saw Maeve lying in a hospital bed next to me, Randy on the other side of her facing the wall.

"Welcome back, Cohen," a calming voice suddenly whispered, making me flinch. "Dr. Machada, I work here at the HQ hospital," an older man explained, leaning slightly over me from my right. "I was just coming to check on your vital signs." Dr. Machada sighed, tapping a screen in front of him quickly while his dark eyes softened into pity while looking at me.

"Cohen!" Fletcher cried weakly, standing up and quickly darting across the room with Cami right behind him.

"I'll go get Stella and the girls," Cami whispered, holding Fletcher's shoulder for a moment before turning to the door on the left side of the room.

"Are they going to be okay, Dr. Machada?" Fletcher asked nervously, siding up next to me with a furrowed brow.

"Once Boss' new healer gets here all of you will be completely fine," Dr. Machada answered bluntly. "You all just have to stay alive until she gets here," he sighed, frowning down at the screen in front of him before grinning happily at the two of us.

"Is True awake yet? Have they found Stretch?" I asked as Dr. Machada jogged quickly out of the room. Fletcher frowned at me for a moment and nodded, his dark eyes filling with tears as he gripped the side of my bed.

"I know nothing about Stretch, but True is still unresponsive," he mumbled softly. I sighed, leaning my head back on my pillow as my heart ached in my chest.

"I'm sorry! My brother is too dangerous! None of this should have happened to you!" Ryth's weak voice suddenly cried. I opened my eyes wide and saw Ryth and Eela dart across the room towards me. I sat up quickly, grimacing as my hip popped abnormally loud, and I leaned over and brought both girls into a hug. Eela latched onto my arm as Ryth leaned into my shoulder, and they both began to sob. I held them both tightly under my aching arms as I watched Stella jog into the room behind Cami with widened eyes.

"You *knew* Delta was your brother?" Cami hissed sharply, narrowing her eyes at Ryth. I glared at Cami's angered expression for a moment as Ryth trembled under my arm. Fletcher shook his head, staring intently at Cami as he frowned at her. Stella sighed softly, standing at the edge of my bed with crossed arms as she glanced at Cami·leaning into Fletcher's side while we all looked at Ryth and Eela beneath my arms.

"They've both been a mess," Stella gruffly commented, her voice wavering slightly as she looked away from everyone. *Obviously. They don't know what's going on other than True is dying, and Delta had something to do with it.*

I inhaled slowly as Ryth and Eela began to hold the other as they slid out from my arms and sat on the floor. *Don't blame yourself Ryth; this isn't your fault.*

My eyes filled with tears as Stella slowly walked over and sat on the ground next to the two of them as they cried. I flinched as Maeve suddenly sat up in the bed behind Stella and the girls, making them all yelp. Maeve's dark eyes were wide with panic and anger as she glared at the IVs sticking out from her arms with her breaths quickening. She hissed in anger, ripping the chords from her body as everyone in the room tensed. Randy rolled over in his bed as he slowly pulled himself up and held his hands out to Maeve, speaking quickly in Spanish to her as multiple doctors frantically ran into the room.

"Maeve calm down!" I sighed, sitting up straight in my bed. Maeve grumbled angrily as she shoved the doctors surrounding her away as she held out her hand to them, bringing her face into her arm. Her hand trembled violently in the air as she slowly was able to calm her breathing down, keeping her eyes away from everyone.

CHAPTER 45

A TENSE HOUR LATER...

"This crazy *motherfucker!*" Maeve screamed angrily, waving her hand at Randy laying on his side in his hospital bed. "Was just going absolutely crazy with his gun then gets *nailed* with a bullet and goes *flying* past me like he was a piece of plastic!" she cackled. No one in the room could hold back their laughter as Randy nodded quickly, a maniacally smile on his face. "Then he just *stands up* like nothing happened to him, yells 'I'm good!' and continues shooting at people!" Maeve wheezed, letting her face fall into the pillow below her. *Sounds about right, Once Randy gets fired up, his adrenaline gets so high that he basically turns into a machine.*

Randy continued to wheeze into his arms, clutching his stomach tightly as he hit his hand on the bed below him. Everyone in the room, even the doctors, were uncontrollably laughing at the two of them explaining what happened. *Thank you guys for doing that, we all needed an emotional break from all this.*

"Cohen!" Randy cried softly from under his arms. "I just saw you shoot through the flaming air like a *missile!* When did you turn into some kind of frog?" Randy asked sharply, his face immediately becoming serious. I wheezed into my hand as I was caught off guard by his immediate expression change.

"I was like 'Woah?! What did I just see!'" Randy exclaimed, a forced accent overtaking his voice before he snorted into his arms again, breaking into a coughing fit while holding his stomach. Maeve nodded quickly, holding her bruised hand to her face as she continued laughing. Everyone in the room sighed with relief as our laughter slowly died down.

"You're all absolutely crazy," Stella mumbled, rolling her eyes and holding back a smile.

"You're just noticing this now?" Randy asked sharply, a heavy Hispanic accent taking him over. Stella snorted into her hand, sending everyone into another laughing spree.

Maeve and Randy continued explaining everything that had happened to them in the park. Their stories ranged from intense to pure comedic ones. It had gone from seeing a police officer fall on their face to Maeve getting hit with rocks thrown by Elites and any other weird occurrences in between. *These two were made for each other, that's for sure... Both are a little mentally screwed up, and both have an amazing sense of humor that compliments the other while also protecting each other with everything they possibly have to offer.*

"Stretch has been found and is being taken into emergency surgery," a doctor suddenly exclaimed. Everyone in the room silenced themselves as reality began to weave its way back through our happy hearts, crushing the life out of them.

"What happened to him?" Randy asked sharply.

"Didn't he get arrested?" I breathed softly.

"We don't know what happened him, but he has horrible blunt force trauma to his chest with remnants of metal inside his wounds," the doctor snapped quickly, darting back around the door. The nurses in the room all immediately dropped what they were doing as they all charged out of the room, yelling frantically at one another.

A chill shot down my back as everyone's eyes widened at each other.

"There is no way Delta could have attacked him!" Randy hissed.

"He was too destroyed from the water..." Maeve trailed off nervously. Cami and I suddenly gasped softly as we locked eyes.

"What if it wasn't him?" I quickly offered.

"Didn't Delta have those metal machine things at the Elite headquarter buildings?" Cami cried anxiously, wrapping her arms around herself. An uneasy chill settled across the room as the air suddenly became heavy. *If a single machine was able to take Stretch down, what does this mean for the safety of the entire city? Delta has them pretty much everywhere…* My heart lurched in my chest at the thought of Delta using them to destroy the city.

"Ryth, what's wrong?" Stella suddenly gasped. I widened my eyes as everyone turned to Ryth leaning in the corner of the room, her arms wrapped tightly around herself.

"He's angry," Ryth cried softly, a single tear falling from her eye as she blankly stared at the floor. Her long, black hair fell in front of her dull eyes as she trembled, shrinking in on herself.

"Who's angry?" Stella asked worriedly, crouching on the floor in front of her as she pulled her dark hair out of her face and held it in her hands.

"Delta…" Ryth breathed as she blinked several times. "He's coming for me!" she gasped, her arms tightening around herself as she began to shake uncontrollably.

"No one can get into this facility, Ryth," I frowned slowly.

"Delta can! He already has!" Ryth screamed, her voice lined with panic and rage. "You don't know my brother!" she laughed; her eyes wild with fear. "He'll stop at nothing to have me killed!" she sighed anxiously as Stella pulled her closer with a furrowed brow.

"How did he get into a place like this?" Randy grumbled. Ryth shook her head, a sad smile filling her face as silent tears streamed down her neck.

"He went crazy in that lab," Ryth whispered quietly, her voice wavering. "They did something to him,"

"What lab? Who did something to him?" I asked worriedly.

Ryth began rocking back and forth slowly in Stella's arms as she began laughing silently, her laugh forced and filled with panic.

"He signed up for some government power testing trial run when I was five," Ryth explained gently. "His power is like mine in the sense that it can destroy something. For him, he can destroy digital commands on anything," she chuckled weakly. "I didn't see him for another five years, and when I did, he looked like he does now."

"Do you know anything about the other people working with him by chance?" Cami asked sharply. Ryth nodded slowly with a shrug.

"I know their names and what they can do, but that's really it," she frowned.

"If Stretch were awake, he would know," I whispered.

"Excuse me," Maeve hissed. "*Why* would he know?" she snarled. I widened my eyes as I bit the inside of my cheek and looked away from Maeve's dark eyes. *Jeez True! You really didn't tell them?*

"Bourbon has light speed," Ryth suddenly spat as everyone began asking angry questions. *What the…* They all fell silent as we turned towards her expectantly. "Dusk can camouflage herself and other things with Clou being able to go into people's dreams," she continued, her voice monotone. "Nerve has some kind of emotional manipulation power…" she shivered. My heart fell in my chest as everyone shifted uncomfortably. *He must have been at the cemetery giving True that panic attack…* I clenched my fists angrily as I narrowed my eyes down at my ankle in a cast. *He could have killed him, and I wouldn't have been able to do anything!*

"Nerve is the one who's the most dangerous," Ryth added nervously.

"No shit!" Maeve hissed sharply at her.

"He killed 30 people at once by making them commit suicide," Ryth sighed. Everyone's face fell with horror as we stared at Ryth laughing softly under her breath, her hands running quickly along themselves. My heart beat strongly out of my chest in panic as we all slowly looked at each other. Randy clutched his chest slowly with a frown at Maeve's narrowed eyes while Eela hid under Fletcher's arm next to Cami.

"A person can do that?" Randy asked softly, her voice breaking in fear. Ryth nodded, a fake smile against her emotionless eyes.

CHAPTER 46

STELLA'S POV – SEVERAL HOURS LATER…

"Why didn't True tell everyone that Stretch was a traitor!" I hissed sharply, glaring at everyone quickly. "Plus, why didn't *Stretch* tell us himself that Delta was going to be a problem?" I asked angrily, clenching my fists as the corners of my eyes began to glow. I took a deep breath as I closed my eyes and stood still for a moment while I crossed my arms again. I frowned as I blinked my eyes open and saw Cami waving her hand at me before glancing at Maeve, Randy, Eela, and Ryth sleeping. I sighed and nodded at her as I turned towards the door, staring down the hallway to the ICU rooms.

Why do you push yourself so hard, True? Look where it's gotten you this time! I huffed angrily as I shook my head and turned away from the ICU door, and my heart began to ache. *I can't keep letting you do this to yourself… My heart can't handle this.* A gentle hand on my shoulder caused me to flinch with widened eyes. I turned and saw Fletcher staring down worriedly at me with a gentle grin. He hesitantly lifted his arm towards me and pulled me into a gentle hug as he began to tremble.

"True will be okay," Fletcher whispered softly. "He has to be, right?" he asked hesitantly. "He's the strongest man I know," he whimpered quietly as his heart began to beat frantically in his chest. I pulled myself out from under his arm and looked up into his dark eyes filled with fear. *True was right, someone's eyes can tell a lot about them.* I whimpered softly as I tucked myself into his side once again and held me as I suppressed tears with angry mumbles under my breath. His grip only tightened around me as his heart leapt out of his chest while he shuddered softly. My own heart spiked out of my chest as I looked under Fletcher's arm. Cohen sat in his hospital bed with his face in his hands, red flames flickering from behind his eyes. I squeezed Fletcher tightly before I pulled myself away from him again and slowly jogged across the room to him.

I slowly sat next to Cohen as he turned and hid his face from me. I gently rested my shaking hand on his burned arm as I bit the inside of my cheek, holding back a whimper. My heart lurched in my chest as a soft cry escaped Cohen's mouth, and he brought his arm to his face again. I grabbed his wrapped hand tightly, tipping his chin to me, and shivered. We stared intently at each other in silence, understanding everything we needed to tell each other. My own heart began to race as tears filled my eyes at seeing tears stream down his face. I blinked tears out of my eyes quickly and pulled him towards me, wrapping my trembling arms around his burning back. Cohen immediately melted into my grasp as we both let out a quiet sob into the other's shoulder. *You've been through hell and back with True and I; not once have I ever heard you complain.* We only held the other tighter as we continued to cry as our best friend was battling for his life down the hall, and there was nothing either of us could do to help him.

CHAPTER 47

TRUE'S POV

Agonizing pain shot through my skull, pulling me awake. I lay still, grimacing in pain as a headache pulsed around near my neck. *Where am I? Where are the others? Did Delta escape?* My breaths quickened as I began to panic from eerie ringing filled my ears. Distant voices frantically argued with one another as I felt gentle nudges along my arms and short sharp pains. A small heart monitor began to beep wildly, sending more painful echoes around my skull. I grimaced in discomfort as I forced my eyes open. I immediately pushed my head deeper into the pillow behind me as immense dizziness smacked me in the face from seeing the blurry room spin around. *Who are you people!*

"True, we're glad to see you awake, but you need to calm down," a gentle voice echoed softly. "Your Agency is safe," the same voice reassured me. A shaking, warm hand rested on my shoulder as I slowly opened my eyes again. An older woman with steel gray hair that fell well past her shoulders smiled calmly at me, her dark, tan face filled with wrinkles. The woman lifted her other hand to the earpiece on the side of her head with a sigh. "He's awake," she gently explained, leaning away from me and walking slowly to the counter next to the bed.

After a few minutes of puzzled silence, a group of doctors came rushing into the room holding clipboards.

"You're lucky to be alive, True," one of the doctors breathed. "With a level three concussion and a cracked skull, all of us are astounded on how you don't have permanent brain damage," the older woman with steel gray hair sighed. I widened my eyes as I frowned down at the IV lines attached to my skin while I squirmed uncomfortably.

"How long have I been unresponsive?" I asked softly, my voice wavering.

"Two days," one of the doctors winced. I widened my eyes as I rested my head gently on the pillow behind me and I blinked quickly to steady my blurry vision.

"True! Baby! I'm so glad you're awake!" Boss' loud voice suddenly cried, making all the doctors in the room flinch. Boss pushed through the door in front of the room with a furrowed brow and eyes lined with worried tears. "My healer is here, thank goodness!" she exclaimed. Multiple doctors' comments of protest were silenced by Boss' glare towards them as she waved them out of the room. "Meet Lyasu Kumi," she beamed, turning over her shoulder to the woman in the doorway. I flinched as her warm eyes stared intently at me before she set her bags down and slowly walked towards Boss leaning over me.

"She came all the way from Japan, and I'm so grateful that she accepted my offer so quickly!" Boss exclaimed, grabbing Kumi's hands in her own for a moment before letting them go and smiling at us. Boss' sleek black hair shimmered under the bright lights as her dark blue suit lined with golden accents did the same.

"Another healer?" I rasped softly, cleaning my throat with a wince. "Aren't those kinds of powers rare?" I winced. Kumi nodded, tying her long, dark brown hair in a low bun behind her head before she closed her eyes with a deep breath.

I watched her intently with a shiver as Kumi's hands moved out in front of her as if she were holding something. Her eyes remained closed as she gently began hovering her hands over my body, sending a wave of panic through my chest. The pain radiating from my body slowly subsided everywhere her hands passed, and I widened my eyes worriedly at her. A weird, familiar warmth rested along my body as Kumi shivered with a frown before gently opening her eyes. The warmth slowly retreated, making me grimace in pain.

"His wounds are too unstable for me to heal," Kumi frowned. "He needs to be awake and responsive for a few hours with medication already in his system to help me out," she sighed. "I can't heal what's not present in his body," she continued, tapping her chin thoughtfully. Kumi suddenly walked briskly across the room and began looking through a cabinet resting above the countertop. Her sleek hands brushed against many boxes before taking a single box down and resting it on the counter. "I need to go evaluate the others. He will have to be healed last," Kumi sighed, frowning at me slightly. I tipped my head to her with a thankful sigh as Boss nodded, flicking her hand to the box and staring intently on the steel haired old woman standing next to me.

The old woman sighed and nodded at Boss as she turned to the counter. Boss gripped my aching hand gently in hers as she stared at me intently for a moment. Her ice blue eyes sent a chill down my back as she frowned at me, running her fingers along my chin before quickly darting out of the room after Kumi.

"This medication will make you groggy, but I know it will help you," the old woman sighed, opening the box slowly. I frowned at her for a moment and nodded with a glance at the IV lines sticking into my arms. *I really hope no one is too badly injured. I can't believe I let myself be caught so off guard!*

I flinched as a cold pad was placed on my skin from the old woman. She rubbed the underside of my wrist several times before sticking the long needle into it. I grimaced as extreme heat began to flow up my arm as I shifted uncomfortably.

"Try your best to stay awake, if you have any negative drawbacks to this medication, please say something, okay?" the old woman sighed slowly. Her long hair suddenly moved around her shoulder, holding down a cotton pad harshly on my wrist as she walked away and threw the needle into a trashcan. I widened my eyes as I stared intently at her long steel hair holding the cotton ball down and shivered as it retracted back to her head. "If you need anything please call," she sighed, throwing the ball into a trashcan. I nodded, rubbing my aching arm for a moment with a wince of pain.

CHAPTER 48

An hour later...

I flinched as the large door in front of me swung open. Kumi calmly walked into the room with a gentle smile at me as Boss quickly followed behind her.

"How are you feeling, True?" Kumi asked softly, holding her hands in front of her for a moment.

"Anxious and tired," I replied softly. Boss frowned at me over Kumi's shoulder and rubbed her hands together worriedly. Kumi nodded, closing her eyes gently.

"The medication I had the doctors give you is working then," she whispered. "My power will make you even more tired, so don't expect to be up and moving after I heal you," she mumbled. I nodded with a frown at her hands as I shivered.

I widened my eyes in shock as Kumi suddenly inhaled and blew thousands of small, glowing butterflies into the open space between her hands. The butterflies stayed closely compacted together in a tight ball hovering under her fingers before she gently angled her hands downward, allowing them to roll calmly away. The butterflies slowly retracted away from each other, immediately hovering towards any wound on my body. Boss and several doctors in the room watched in amazed silence as I shifted from the warmth of the butterflies.

I blinked quickly as several butterflies hovered over to my face and crossed my eyes slowly while I stared at the butterflies landing along my nose.

Everyone in the room suddenly flinched as the golden butterflies suddenly jerked in the air. Their warm, golden glow faltered as they shrunk into small, dark specs. Once the butterflies turned into the dark specs, they immediately began to gravitate back towards Kumi's hands. I shivered in discomfort as the ball of darkness in front of her only grew larger and larger as her brow furrowed. I widened my eyes as Kumi's skin on her hands began to dull and shivered as her fingertips suddenly wilted into a dark, cracked stone before it began climbing up the rest of her arms and forming on the tip of her nose. I gasped in sudden relief as all pain was gone from my body.

"You need to stay in bed and rest," Kumi grimaced, opening her eyes worriedly at the ball of darkness enclosing around her chest. I nodded furrowing my brow at her with a frown.

"Doesn't that hurt?" I asked softly as she turned away.

"Not for long. Nothing is permanent, and pain is only temporary," Kumi replied calmly, a loving grin coming across her face. My heart spiked in my chest as I nodded once at her and sighed as she awkwardly limped out of the room with one of her feet completely stone.

"She's pretty cool, huh?" Boss breathed proudly. I nodded, rolling my neck around and taking a deep breath as I suddenly felt exhausted.

"Is everyone alright?" I asked softly, clenching my fists.

"They all are physically fine since Kumi has healed the ones who are injured," the old woman with the steel-grey hair sighed gently. Boss stood up fully with a thoughtful nod down at me as she frowned. I brought my shaking hands to my face and rubbed the back of my tense neck as I shook my head, blinking in confusion in feeling no physical pain at all. I stared down at my hands for a moment before Boss chuckled softly.

"Her power has an interesting feeling that it leaves on the body, huh?" she smiled. I nodded, shivering at not feeling pain I never knew I had until I realized it was gone.

"Kumi is going to be working under me permanently for now," Boss sighed worriedly. "Let's just hope you all stay safe enough to not have to use her power often," she mumbled, frowning at me for a moment. I nodded, shifting anxiously in the bed as I pushed myself up.

"Why are you doing so much for my Agency and I?" I suddenly asked, looking intently at Boss. The old woman widened her eyes and nervously stepped out of the room quickly without looking at either of us staring at the other. My heart began to race in my ears as Boss stared blankly at me for a moment.

"I'll discuss this with you at a later time," Boss explained softly. "Get some rest," she whispered, holding my shoulder worriedly for a moment before she left without another word.

CHAPTER 49

DELTA'S POV – A WEEK LATER...

Cold air brushed against my back as I stared with disdain out of the large glass panel in front of me. I scanned the city skyline with a frown for a moment before I sighed at the building trembling violently.

"I don't need to hear your stupid opinion again, Bourbon," I spat sharply, glaring over my shoulder at him standing silently behind me.

"Well, you're going to hear it anyway," he replied calmly, bringing his hands behind his back with a frown. We stared blankly at each other for a moment before I narrowed my eyes at his gaze and turned back to the window. "These changes in upgrades will kill *you*, Delta." Bourbon snarled angrily.

"But they'll make me stronger," I countered calmly.

"Stronger?" he laughed. "You're already strong enough!"

"This isn't about my own plans anymore, Bourbon," I warily hissed, turning towards him slowly. Bourbon's brow furrowed as he leaned slightly away from my intent gaze at him. A chill shot down my back as my vision blurred slightly as I felt darkness envelope my eyes. "True is who I'm focusing on," I explained coldly, my voice distorting. Bourbon shook his head as anger and guilt filled his eyes.

"I don't know what have going on, but whatever it is, it's stupid and irrational!" Bourbon snarled. "Why waste your time on a lunatic like True? He's not worth it!" he laughed softly. "That poor bastard wants to end himself already, doesn't he?" Bourbon asked harshly. "Just give him time, and he'll eventually solve your problem himself," he sneered, bringing his hand to his head as if it were a gun and smiled darkly. A shiver shot down my back as my vision became unclouded and I blinked worriedly at Bourbon's glare towards me.

The door in the back of the room suddenly swung open causing us both to flinch. Bourbon immediately disappeared, causing the entire building to tremble. The woman in dark scrubs worriedly looked up from her clipboard to me before glancing up at the ceiling. I blinked at her for a moment before she waved her hand and turned to hold the door open. I shook my normal arm out with a frown at my metal one as it tensed slightly while I walked across the room and ducked under the low doorway.

"Dr. Briner had you down for a few upgrades, correct?" the woman asked softly, walking briskly past the glass panel in front of the main desk. I followed behind her calmly and nodded once, shivering as I glanced at all the doors on the left wall of the long hallway. I shook my head as fierce lavender struck my nose and grimaced at the overwhelming scent. I focused my attention on the white walls and dark grey floors to distract myself as the woman in front of me slowly began writing in her clipboard.

"Briner wants to try something different this time around with you," the woman explained worriedly. I shifted slightly as I frowned at her intent gaze towards me in the corner of her eye. "He found a new student who is apparently brilliant like you," she continued. "He's capable of doing something pretty interesting, so I guess Briner wants to see if it'll work for you," she beamed, scratching something out roughly on her clipboard. I shivered as I glared down at my robotic hand and shrugged.

"Whatever he thinks is best for me I'm fine with," I lied, biting the inside of my cheek as my heart spiked in my chest.

"He should be here to see you shortly," the woman sighed, frowning at her watch. "He got caught up with working at another client's property and needed a little extra time to work on something away from the office,"

"Sounds like him," I awkwardly laughed. The woman nodded with a gentle smile at me before she tucked the clipboard into a plastic container on the wall and closed the door. The room immediately felt several times colder as I glanced worriedly at the scuffed paint near the door. *Why change what we've been doing so last minute without notice ahead of time? That's not like Briner…*

CHAPTER 50

TRUE'S POV – LATER THAT EVENING...

"Isn't it a weird time for her to call us down to her office?" Cohen asked softly, glancing nervously at the armed guards surrounding us. I nodded with a frown and shivered at one of their tense glares down at me.

"It may have something to do with a question I asked her last week," I sighed hesitantly.

"Oh great, what did you do to piss her off—" Cohen immediately snarked. I held back a smile as several guards suddenly began snickering under their breaths with amused glances at one another. My heart spiked out of my chest with worry as I shivered slightly from the elevator doors opening.

"I've done a lot of thinking, True!" Boss' excited voice suddenly boomed, causing Cohen and I to flinch. The guards all around us immediately silenced themselves, standing tall and still as they stared intently out at the dark room. Boss sat at her desk in the center of the back wall of the huge room with her hands folded calmly in front of her. Cohen shivered slightly as her gaze slowly turned to him while we slowly walked across the large room.

"Thank you two for coming," Boss sighed happily. "Now, onto what I called you here for, get comfy!" she exclaimed, waving her hand behind us. I raised my brow slightly as Cohen tensed his arms with a frown. People suddenly emerged from the darkness, pushing large chairs into our legs, forcing us to sit down.

"Did we do something?" Cohen grumbled softly, glaring at the person retreating into the darkness. Boss let out a cold, genuine cackle as she leaned her head back and clenched her hands together.

"Oh honey," Boss sighed. "If any of you screwed up, I don't think we'd be having a friendly conversation right now!" she sneered through gritted teeth. Cohen and I shivered with worried glances at each other as Boss pridefully smirked. "I think your Agency should move into HQ," Boss suddenly admitted.

I widened my eyes and blinked a few times as I stared blankly at her intent gaze on me. I cleared my throat and sat up in the chair with a nervous chuckle.

"Excuse me?"

"You'll be much safer if you move into this tower," Boss gently began. "Think about it, True," she continued. "The Elites are getting more and more help from authorities and *Delta*, and they're getting too relentless in their search for you," she explained. I nodded, frowning at her as Cohen shifted in his seat. "That complex building you're in is just an open invitation for you and your Agency to be arrested or killed on sight," she sighed, shrugging her shoulders quickly. *You have a point, but why are you doing this?*

"Do other clients of yours live here at HQ as well?" Cohen asked softly. Boss chuckled as she shook her head.

"No, only my staff lives here with me," Boss replied gently.

"Is there a reason why you're giving us all this extra treatment then?" I asked worriedly. Boss blinked quickly as she turned her eyes away from the both of us staring expectantly at her. She sighed softly with a small chuckle as she began shaking her head. Cohen glanced worriedly at me as I kept my gaze on her and I furrowed my brow.

"With Delta making more violent moves around the city and proving his threat level to be high against True, I need to make extra precautions," Boss spat. "That was way too reckless for you to go alone!" she snarled, pointing roughly at me.

"I didn't know he would react that way, ma'am," I gently explained, shivering under her harsh gaze. "Ryth is in danger! I couldn't just sit back and do nothing!" I huffed. Boss raised her hand up to me as I inhaled to continue. Cohen frowned at her gaze before turning away from her sharp glare towards him. My heart began to beat out of my chest as she sighed at me.

"I know how you feel, True, but you *need* to make sure you stay alive. If you die, this entire operation will be for nothing," Boss snapped, her voice wavering. "I know how difficult it is to have a stranger threaten to kill your child," she whispered quietly, averting her eyes. My heart spiked in my chest as Cohen shifted uncomfortably. Boss' dark acrylic nails shakily ran over her hands as she kept her gaze away from us. *I never knew you had a family…*

"Maybe 10 or so years ago, I was basically sitting in your shoes, True. I had a dream, a goal, a plan," she breathed with a faint smile. "Everything was going so smoothly for me and my family until some lunatic killed my husband and 15-year-old son," she spat. My heart fell in my chest as I clenched my fists, and I furrowed my brow. Cohen shivered slightly as white flames flickered from behind his ears, and he gave her an apologetic look. Boss stayed silent as she rested her chin on her still hands, her gaze intently resting on the dark desk below her.

"True, you remind me of my son," Boss suddenly sighed, looking sharply up at me. I widened my eyes as my heart spiked in my chest. "A bright young mind who struggles within themselves but always finds a way to keep others safe," she breathed softly. "I won't let the same thing that happened to my son, or my husband happen to you; that's why I'm doing so much extra for you and your Agency."

"Thank you. I'm so sorry for your loss," I gently grinned. Boss lifted her hand as she sat up fully in her chair.

"I don't need your condolences, but I appreciate them." Boss strongly stated. "I will do everything in my power to make sure that your Agency stays *safe*," she promised, leaning over the desk towards me.

"Yes ma'am," I smiled, looking worriedly at Cohen.

CHAPTER 51

LATER THAT NIGHT (3:00 AM)…

I suddenly felt myself falling out of a dreamless sleep as distant flames began to echo around my head. Hot air blew roughly past my face as I opened my eyes worriedly to see a large prison cell on fire far below me, coming closer each second. I flinched with a yelp of pain as I landed harshly onto the burning concrete of the cell floor, and I coughed hollowly into my arm. Roaring, bright red flames towered and climbed up the walls as screams of panic filled the air from a large door across the room.

I gasped softly as my eyes focused on Cohen sitting in the middle of the cell, the large flames hissing with delight as they circled around him.

"Cohen?" I called out weakly, coughing hollowly into my arm. Cohen turned over his shoulder with a panicked expression as he saw the roaring fire latch onto my arms.

"What are you doing here!" Cohen cried, standing up quickly. A loud bang on the door caused us both to flinch as more flames began falling from the ceiling. We both quickly stepped towards each other as the fire suddenly wrapped itself tightly around us, pulling us forcibly out of the cell and through the ceiling.

"Yeesh, what a hellish nightmare," an oily voice suddenly sneered loudly in my ear from the darkness. "I'd hate to drag my dear best friend into it, huh?" the voice asked rudely, shaking Cohen around quickly. I narrowed my eyes and yelped, and my stomach flipped over itself as the flaming arm slowly burnt out. Pure darkness began dragging Cohen and I through open air as an uncomfortably cold wind brushed against our skin. My skull vibrated roughly as we slammed into cold concrete ground that loomed out of nowhere. Cohen coughed softly into his steaming arms as I groaned in pain, holding my side tightly in my shaking, burnt arm.

"I'm so sorry, True," Cohen breathed softly, his voice echoing eerily around me. "Are you alright?" he asked nervously. I grimaced in pain as I pushed myself up on my elbow slowly.

"Sure,"

"Gosh, do you two ever stop asking how the other is doing or what?" the same oily voice sighed, bored. I flinched as a small spurt of flame shot up from Cohen's palm as he sat a few yards in front of me. The voice echoing around us chuckled softly as I slowly pulled myself to my feet and limped over towards where the flame disappeared.

"Where are we?" I asked anxiously, tapping Cohen's steaming arm gently after I bumped into him.

"I can't see anything," Cohen snapped. I snickered into my hand and nodded, squinting out at the pure darkness surrounding us.

"You two are in a holding place," the voice answered calmly. "It's where I bring people to wait when I haven't decided on what I'm going to do with them yet,"

A small flame suddenly appeared in front of us once more as Cohen held his palm out. The white flame cast an eerie glow to the darkness surrounding us. I flinched as a large, metal arm loomed out of the surrounding darkness, barely visible by the flame. The sleek, metal reflected slightly against the white flame as Cohen, and I shivered with worried glances at each other.

An eerie scrape of metal suddenly echoed around the room. Small sounds of something tapping on the concrete began scurrying in circles around us, sending anxiety wrapping around my neck. One moment, the small taps were on our right; the next, they were in front of us and to the left. A small, high-pitched growl pierced the awkwardly silent air as the flame on Cohen's palm went out. A violent chill suddenly shot down my back as the entire room seemed to tense. Whatever had been moving around in the darkness had gone completely still.

"No, no, screw this," Cohen suddenly hissed, his raspy voice echoing. A short, bright spurt of red flame suddenly shot from his wrist in front of us. My heart leapt out of my chest as the fire coming up from his wrist illuminated the space in front of us. Two dull eyes along with a large, bird like, mechanical machine stood over us silently. It's dead eyes and small sharp teeth resting in its half open beak made my heart lurch out of my chest in fear. The large machine suddenly let out a deafening screech as its long claws swiped towards us, knocking Cohen and I away from each other.

I slid harshly across the concrete ground as I grimaced in pain and clutched my stomach. The large mechanical machine screeched again as Cohen's flame went out and angry snarls filled the air.

"What is that thing!" I asked angrily, coughing into my arm. "It looks like a huge version of the Kamis Delta has!" Cohen yelled sharply. "The damn thing won't stay still long enough for me to look at it properly!" he snarled in annoyance, as a bright column of white flames shot from his palm. The large machine angrily screeched, darting away from the light coming from the flame and disappeared into the darkness.

I pushed myself up onto my elbow to sit up right as a heavy metal boot slammed down on my chest. The entire floor below me trembled as I gasped in pain and gripped the cold metal in my shaking hands while I widened my eyes. Delta's LED emotion mask suddenly powered on weakly in front of me, slowly leaning down. The expression glitched in and out between angered and joyful as the pressure only increased down onto my chest and I grimaced.

"Delta?" I breathed softly, lifting my head gently with gritted teeth. The metal boot slowly slid across my chest, pushing more pressure onto my shoulder as I struggled to pull myself away.

"Feels nice to finally get to stand over you like this," Delta's sleek voice chuckled, distorting slightly. The entire room around us suddenly trembled again as Delta flinched, the expression on his mask briefly flashing worried. He turned robotically over his shoulder as I squinted my eyes slightly past his leg. Cohen knelt on the ground with the flaming machine laying helpless behind him. Its robotic claws twitched angrily towards him as he stared blankly at the ground. My heart spiked out of my chest as I saw his eyes filled with regret as he clenched his fists slowly in front of him.

Delta's heavy metal boot suddenly forced all his weight onto my shoulder. A violent *crack* filled my ears as agonizing pain shot up my neck and side. I cried out in agony as Delta only began to press harder onto my shoulder while I frantically tried getting away. Cohen suddenly leapt up from his feet, a ball of red flames surrounding his wrist as he stared at Delta with pure hatred. Delta only stared blankly back as Cohen darted across the cold concrete towards us, my vision blurring from the pain in my shattered shoulder.

The air shimmered gently behind Cohen from the light of his flames as a loud *clang!* echoed around the room. Cohen slumped over to the ground as he cried out in pain, gripping the back of his head, spurts of white flame flickering from his neck. The giant flaming machine laying behind him suddenly was dragged silently into the darkness as Clou stalked back in his place. His cold eyes rested intently on Cohen lying on the ground helplessly as I grumbled up at Delta and he leaned off me. I immediately shoved his leg away from me and pushed myself further away from him with my trembling legs as I gripped my shoulder. After two short claps from Delta standing over me, bright LED lights suddenly flashed on all around us. I brought my hand above my squinted eyes as my vision blurred with a grimace escaping my sore jaw. *Where the are we?*

The large warehouse room loomed ominously over all of us. Tall ceilings lined with sturdy metal beams made up the skeleton of the room as railings on the roof allowed giant cranes to hang from simple chains. Each space against one of the four walls had metal skeleton structure with distorted figures and shapes looming around them. I suddenly flinched as I turned my head to see two people wrapped in dark smoke and light grey smoke standing in front of a more completed metal structure. Anxiety shot up my neck as I widened my eyes at the two people standing with their backs to me as the burn on my palm suddenly began spewing smoke. I quickly waved the light grey smoke away, drowning it out with my pitch-black smoke as I narrowed my eyes at the two figures. Delta moving away from me made me flinch once more and turn my blurry gaze back to him.

My heart beat out of my chest in panic as he stalked over to Clou leaning over Cohen, who was lying on the floor, his hands covering his head. I quickly pushed myself up onto my other elbow as I grimaced in pain with narrowed eyes. The air suddenly shimmered in front of me as something forced me back down roughly to the cold concrete below me. I gasped for air as something tightened dangerously around my neck. I kneed whatever was leaning over me multiple times, hitting them with my free arm.

I widened my eyes as light grey smoke suddenly peered its way into my blurry vision. The smoke gently hovered around what was holding me down before striking at it like a snake. The smoke tightened swiftly around a narrow part of the invisible person holding me down as the pressure over my neck faltered. I violently kicked the solid air in front of me as I saw the air shimmer as something reached towards the smoke. The camouflage disguise hiding the person faltered as fiery-red hair briefly shone through. My heart leapt out of my chest. Dusk immediately disappeared into thin air as Clou jogged quickly over towards me. I shivered as I watched the light grey smoke filter gently up into the air and disappear.

"What's the point of all this Delta!" I asked angrily, glaring up at Clou's intrigued gaze down at me. Delta slowly turned over his shoulder from staring at Cohen below him as he chuckled softly.

"You made a very idiotic mistake, True," Delta snapped coldly. "This doesn't concern him," he whispered, waving his hand at Cohen struggling to stand. With a wave of his hand, Clou suddenly sent Cohen into the air, disappearing through the dark ceiling above us as he yelped. A chill shot down my back as I slowly pushed myself away from Clou and furrowed my brow at him.

"You made the decision to try and fight *me*," Delta snarled. "This is a battle you will not win, True. I've made sure of it." His voice echoed around the room oddly as it distorted into someone else's. I widened my eyes as I quickly glanced over my shoulder to see only one smoke figure remaining, their back still turned towards me. Darkness suddenly enclosed around me as the giant warehouse lab faded away silently. Delta stalked forward out of the darkness as he gently took off the glass helmet over his head and narrowed his eyes at me. "Sweet dreams," Delta sneered, his voice distorting once more.

I flinched myself awake as I quickly sat up in bed, breathing harshly. I blinked my blurry eyes at the open room lined with beds and sighed in relief as I gripped my sweating head gently in my hands. Distant tremors of pain shot up my neck from my shoulder as I rolled it slowly with a frown, my heart beating strongly out of my chest. I exhaled slowly as I glanced at Cohen leaning up on his elbow in the bed next to Stella and I. His dark eyes were wide with worry as he stared at me with a frown, flickers of flame coming from behind his ears. The bed shifted slightly as I flinched and widened my eyes, turning to see Stella staring sadly up at me. She closed her eyes slowly with a sigh and turned the other way, staying silent as my chest ached.

CHAPTER 52

A FEW ODDLY CALM WEEKS LATER, EARLY IN THE EVENING...

"Thank you again for taking us out to dinner, Boss," I breathed gratefully, rubbing the back of my neck with a grin. Everyone nodded in agreement behind me with soft giggles and warm smiles.

"Oh, don't worry about it!" Boss chuckled calmly. "Obviously getting the Elites name list completed is worth celebration!" she beamed, turning on her heel swiftly. "I'll begin to have my people work out a plan for you all to follow to get the job done," she sighed. "For now, you all rest up and relax for a little bit," she ordered, raising her brow sharply at me. I shivered under her cold, loving gaze and nodded.

Eela, Ryth, and Cami raced swiftly down the hall, their laughter echoing loudly against the white tiled floors. Stella and Cohen walked alongside me, struggling to hold back their smiles as they watched Fletcher dart after the others, tripping Cami as he passed her. Maeve rolled her eyes as Randy protested against her arm, and the two of them began to bicker softly under their breaths in Spanish. I shivered as a chill shot down my back from passing the swinging doors of the hospital wing of HQ and glanced at Stretch walking silently behind us. I nudged Cohen and Stella forward, pausing my stride and waiting for Stretch to walk up beside me.

"Are you alright?" I asked him softly, elbowing his arm gently as I walked alongside him. Stretch kept his hands in his jacket pockets and his dull gaze resting on the tile floor below us.

"Yea, I'm fine." Stretch sighed reluctantly. I furrowed my brow at him and shook my head, turning back to the others ahead of us waiting at the end of the hall for the elevator.

"You sure?" I asked again, looking intently at him in the corner of my eye. He shrugged, glancing up at the others and tensed. "You've been awfully drawn back these past few weeks," I mumbled softly, looking down at the tile. Stretch tensed again as he looked up at me sharply for a moment. "You don't have to act tough with me, Stretch," I chuckled softly, holding back a smile. "You also don't have to act like an outcast when you're with us," I continued, looking back to him and grabbing his arm. Stretch paused as I held him from walking on, and he turned over his shoulder to look at me with his seeing eye. "You're part of the Agency now. You are allowed to be happy and be yourself," I beamed, furrowing my brow slightly at the flash of anger in his eye. Stretch blinked quickly and nodded, pulling away from my grasp. I stood in shock for a moment, my hand hovering awkwardly in the open air as Stretch continued walking down the hallway, his gaze resting on the floor.

I jogged slowly to catch up with the rest of the group and frowned at everyone still waiting on the elevator.

"What's taking it so long?" I sighed, shaking my head at Stretch's quick glance at me.

"It's jammed," Fletcher grumbled, kneeling in front of the panel with the buttons on the wall.

"Why are you glaring at me?" Randy suddenly hissed, narrowing his eyes at Cohen. Stella giggled softly as Cohen amusedly continued glaring at Randy. "I don't use my power in the elevator!" Randy continued harshly, stepping towards him. Maeve sighed and held up her arm, pulling Randy back and rolling her eyes at Cohen's smug gaze at her.

Fletcher glanced back at all of us, silencing our amused smiles for a moment. He ran his lanky hand along the panel for a moment and flinched as a single spark shot from under the metal sheet.

"It's been tampered with," Fletcher mumbled, pulling the panel from the wall and sighing at the frayed wires.

"How do we know *you* didn't do that?" Maeve snapped.

"Oh, come on!" Cami laughed angrily. "He obviously didn't do it!"

"I was *joking*, Cami,"

"Maeve?" Stella spat. "Joking? Since *when*?" she continued, widening her light eyes at her. Eela and Ryth snorted into their arms as everyone began laughing softly while Maeve's cold face flushed.

"We'll just take the stairs up to a different floor that has elevator access to the suite," I sighed, rubbing my aching head after laughing. Everyone sighed in disappointment as I rolled my eyes and let my hand fall to my side. "Either we take the stairs, or we wait for the Boss to have someone fix it," I spat. Soft grumbles of annoyance echoed softly from everyone as we all began walking towards the stairwell door around the corner of the opening. "I know you're tired, but let's just walk up to the next floor and see if the elevator panel there is working." I sighed reluctantly as I shivered, glancing at the destroyed wires hidden behind the panel hanging from them.

Stella, Cami, and Maeve's voices echoed loudly through the metal stairwell as they had begun arguing about a news headline they saw on the TV at the restaurant. Randy and Fletcher talked quietly behind me about a song they were trying to remember as Eela and Ryth walked beside me. I shivered as I glanced over my shoulder to see Cohen trailing behind Fletcher and Randy silently. I suddenly widened my eyes and paused my stride with a furrowed brow. Fletcher knocked into my side gently and yelped before stepping back down a few steps.

"Where's Stretch?" I asked softly. Cohen glared over his shoulder behind him and shrugged with a frown.

"I saw him come into the stairwell," Randy whispered, pursing his lips as he leaned over the railing and gazed down at the staircases lining the walls below us.

"Has anyone noticed him acting a little bit off lately?" Cami asked gently.

"It's *Stretch*," Maeve suddenly spat. "Isn't he just off in general?" she snarked. Stella and Cohen snickered under their breaths as Eela and Ryth giggled. I rolled my eyes and frowned at them as I also leaned over the railing and blinked at the stairwell below us.

"We'll worry about Stretch later, let's hurry up out of this stairwell. It's hot," Maeve snapped.

"It's because I'm in here," Randy mumbled hastily, raising his brow at her glare.

"Shut up," she called over her shoulder as she jogged up more stairs. Ryth and Eela laughed softly as Randy began angrily whispering under his breath in Spanish from behind us. Everyone scoffed softly and rolled their eyes from his comment as we all continued up the stairs to the next floor.

After waiting patiently up in the suite on the top floor of HQ for Stretch to return for a little bit, I had decided to call Boss. My heart spiked out of my chest as I waited for her to answer as the noise in the phone glitched slightly.

"True? Is everything okay?" Boss suddenly asked, her voice wavering in and out.

"Yes, I'm fine," I quickly began. "Do you know where Stretch is?" I hesitantly asked. Boss remained silent for a moment as I furrowed my brow.

"No, I thought he was with you guys," Boss grumbled, her voice glitching through the phone. I shook my head as she began talking again with the phone distorting her voice.

"I can't understand what you're saying," I replied gently. "My phone's acting weird,"

"It's not—" Boss echoed. "Sending someone—" she quickly stuttered. "Find—" her voice distorted once more before a high pitch ring echoed into my ear. I blinked several times as a low static noise began to come from the phone while I brought it away from my face and frowned at the normal screen. Moments later, the call ended abruptly as I scoffed. *That was interesting, to say the least.*

I furrowed my brow again as I rolled my neck out and glanced out at the bright colors covering the sky from the setting sun through the sliding door in my bedroom. I cycled my phone's power before I mumbled under my breath and tried calling Stretch. Each time, I was sent to voicemail, my heart began to beat stronger in my chest with worry. I rolled my eyes and began to message him to see if he would reply. I widened my eyes in annoyance as I blinked quickly and squinted down at the phone for a moment.

"You read the messages at least," I grumbled softly. I frowned as the three dots in the corner of the screen came up and disappeared time and time again.

"I'm in the bathrooms on the gym level, I didn't feel well. Be up in a bit,"

Stretch finally responded. I shivered as I furrowed my brow at his message and shook my head.

A series of quick and frantic knocks on my door sent a spike of panic through my chest. Eela burst through the door as tears were in her eyes and she mumbled under her breath, her voice wavering.

"Hey," I gasped softly, standing up and walking towards her. "What's wrong?" I asked, holding her shoulders gently in my hands as my heart began to beat out of my chest.

"Something's wrong with Maeve," Eela cried softly, leaning roughly into my side. I wrapped my arms around her as I furrowed my brow and stared out of my open bedroom door into the main room of the suite. I held Eela's hand tightly in my own as I quickly jogged out of the room and across the living room, pausing in the hallway leading to the other bedrooms.

Cohen stepped out of Maeve and Randy's room with a furrowed brow at me and a gentle glance at Eela clinging to my side.

"Clou must be doing something to Maeve," Cohen whispered softly, leaning near my ear. "She won't wake up," he continued, his voice wavering. My heart leapt out of my chest as I leaned away and turned towards him with a frown.

"Where's Ryth?" I asked Eela gently.

"In our room," she softly whimpered. I held her tightly under my arm as I nodded and looked into the room, shivering at seeing everyone else worriedly looking at me. "Go with Ryth, okay?" I softly sighed, rubbing her shoulder slowly.

I flinched as Fletcher and Cami suddenly darted through the doorway towards the kitchen, arguing softly with one another.

"Are we sure she's just not in a deep sleep?" I began softly. I immediately silenced myself as I widened my eyes in panic at how pale Maeve was while she laid lifelessly in bed. Randy sat on the bed next to her, his entire body trembling with panic as his eyes were wide and frantic.

"We've done everything we can to wake her up!" Randy cried sharply, moving his shaggy curls out of his eyes as his voice wavered.

I glanced at Stella frowning at me in the corner of the room and slowly walked over to Randy's side, shifting uncomfortably at Maeve's exhausted expression. I quickly leaned down and grabbed Randy's lanky wrist roughly in my hand and held it up to me as I stared intently into his frantic amber eyes.

"Breathe for a second," I gently told him, furrowing my brow as he slowly began to stop shaking as badly. I let go of his wrist and turned over my shoulder as Fletcher and Cami came jogging back into the room with worried glints in their eyes. Cohen's gaze met mine from the doorway as I shivered, glancing to Stella staring at Maeve blankly.

"I thought that emotion kid could only use his power if he saw them with his own eyes," Stella mumbled worriedly.

"Well, obviously Clou must be doing something to her if she can't wake up," Cami snapped, setting a rag on Maeve's forehead as Fletcher gently sat her up.

"Can't we get Kumi or someone up here to help her?" I asked sharply, trying to mask the panic in my voice.

"The elevator isn't working! Neither are any of our phones!" Fletcher grumbled, glancing at Cami next to him for a moment.

"Stretch said he wasn't feeling well," I began softly. "Do you think Maeve ate something that she was allergic to at the restaurant?" I asked, raising my brow at Randy.

"This is *Maeve* we're talking about," Stella sighed with a small chuckle.

"She's not allergic to anything, let alone anything food related!" Randy snapped worriedly. Cohen nodded from the doorway and slowly stepped inside with flames flickering from behind his eyes.

"Why would Delta even be taking out our tracker—" I suddenly snapped. Everyone in the room flinched as the entire building violently trembled, the light flickering quickly above our heads.

All of us froze with widened eyes and intent glares at each other as we remained silent. Suddenly quiet footsteps began to scurry across the main room, sending a jolt of panic through my chest.

"The girls!" I cried out worriedly, stepping towards the door. Cohen turned to the open door quickly as the air shimmered slightly. The door immediately slammed shut as Cohen reached for the doorframe. He yelped and cried out in pain as the door nicked his knuckles while he stumbled backwards, gripping his bleeding hand tightly. "No!" I roared angrily, lunging across the room.

I gripped the handle fiercely in my shaking hands and struggled to pry the door open as panic shot through my chest. Eela and Ryth's screams from their room only made the panic in my heart grow as I angrily began to slam my shoulder into the door.

"Move!" Cohen snarled sharply, grabbing my arm and pulling me away from the door. I flinched as a wave of flames surged past my and set the door on fire. The hinges immediately melted away from Stella's flames as she continued breathing fire towards them.

Cohen darted away from me and violently kicked the door down, gipping the burning door frame in his hands as he turned quickly to the main room. I widened my eyes in horror to see Eela's bedroom door widely open, the room destroyed. I leapt over the burning door as something under it struggled to move and ran into the main room with clenched fists. Cohen and Stella followed right behind me, stepping purposefully on the door as something growled loudly in pain. My heart fell from my chest as I slid to a stop in the main room with widened eyes.

Bourbon and Clou stood near the elevator in the suite with dark glares in their eyes. Ryth and Eela were under both of Clou's arms as he calmly held two sharp knives towards them, staring directly at me. Panic surged through my chest as I stared into Bourbon's dark, angry eyes as he towered over Clou ominously. The brief memory of being pinned down in the alleyway by Bourbon's strong arms with my pistol aimed at my head sent my heart leaping out of my chest as it roared loudly in my ears.

"Take one more step, I dare you," Clou sneered sharply. I shifted uncomfortably as his oily voice slithered around my ears like a snake wanting to strangle its prey.

"Get your hands off them you creep!" I angrily snarled, clenching my fists tightly as I glared at Bourbon's amused gaze. *I can't risk shooting Clou; he'll use the girls as a shield. Bullets don't work on Bourbon with his light speed...* I glanced over my shoulder at Randy holding his gun to the person struggling underneath the burning door as Cami and Fletcher crouched down on the other side of the corner, their gazes resting on Cohen and Stella next to me. "What do you want with them?" I asked calmly, holding my hands out harmlessly as my voice wavered.

"They would be great bargaining pieces, don't you think?" Clou cooed softly, looking down at Ryth and Eela staring fearfully at me. Ryth's cold eyes darkened as she quickly glared up at Clou, and he tightened her grip around her neck, bringing the knife closer to her face.

"They have nothing to do with whatever is going on between Delta and I!" I snapped, clenching my fists as I furrowed my brow. Clou chuckled softly as he glanced up at Bourbon standing silently next to him.

"Oh really?" Clou smiled. "So, either of the girls don't have a single relation to Delta?" he asked, tipping his head slightly at me. Stella shifted angrily next to me as her eyes began to glow like lava. Smoke and flickers of flame shot from her nose and mouth. Cohen's eyes had red flames coming from behind them as he stood tensed with clenched fists and an angry gaze on Clou. "I think we're done here," Clou mumbled, winking at me calmly.

Anger shot through my chest as I narrowed my eyes at his smug gaze and my heart seemed to slow itself. In the corner of my eye, Fletcher suddenly dropped to the floor, both his palms resting quickly onto the white tile. Immediately the tile in the entire suite shifted into a Jell-O-like state, throwing all of us off our feet. Everyone stumbled around in panic as Clou yelped, dropping both knives but keeping his grip on Eela and Ryth. The ground below Stella, Cohen and I became solid again as the three of us sprinted across the room with narrowed eyes. My heart leapt in my chest in panic at seeing a thin line of blood falling down the side of Ryth's face as her eyes filled with rage up at Clou.

Bourbon suddenly fell backwards with a dark look in his angry eyes. Cohen lunged towards him with a concentrated ball of flames. In an instant he was gone as the room trembled violently. Bourbon appeared directly between Cohen and I as I widened my eyes. I was roughly shoved away from him as Bourbon's dark arm swung towards Cohen in an arch. Cohen flew over the kitchen counter swiftly as the walls in the suite trembled again.

Behind me, Bourbon appeared directly in front of Fletcher and Cami with a grumble of annoyance. Bourbon roughly picked Fletcher up off the floor and launched him down the hallway. Loud glass shattering filled our ears as Fletcher fell through the glass table at the end of the hall. Cami screamed angrily as Cohen dragged her out of the hallway by her hair as he lunged for Randy. In one swift motion, Bourbon forced the pistol from Randy's hand and violently struck him in the face. Randy stumbled backwards quickly, blood running from his face as he fell to the floor inside of their room, fearfully staring up at Bourbon.

Cami suddenly lunged up from the floor, with bright red paint flying from her palms. Bourbon screamed in agony as his skin began to hiss softly from the pain hitting it before he punched her back down to the ground. Randy was on his feet again and lunged up at Bourbon. The door on the ground suddenly flung itself up as Dusk shimmered into the air and disappeared. Randy was suddenly launched off his feet as Bourbon disappeared and Cami frantically shouldered into the solid air pinning Randy by his neck to the tile.

As Stella and I neared Clou still stumbling away from us, Ryth and Eela both began to try and force themselves away. I widened my eyes in horror as Ryth's shaking hand suddenly latched onto Clou's wrist, and a violent *crack* filled the busy, tense air. Clou screamed in agony as he shoved Eela violently into Stella, knocking them both over. His grip around Ryth only tightened with his other hand as her arm swung up to hit him in the face. She pushed herself away from him again, kicking him roughly in the shin before she darted over towards me.

Ryth's eyes were wide with panic and fear as she reached for my hand. The walls of the suite suddenly trembled violently as Bourbon's dark arms wrapped around Ryth's neck.

"No!" I cried out hoarsely. In an instant, Ryth had disappeared into thin air. The suite trembled repeatedly as I seemed to fall in slow motion towards the floor. My hand closed around the empty air where Ryth's shaking hand once was. Agony and grief suddenly surged through my chest as my shoulder roughly slammed into the tile. Everything around me became distant as harsh; ringing filled my ears, and my vision blurred with panic, my breaths slowed.

I blinked quickly, leaning up weakly on my elbow and turning over my shoulder at the suite. Stella held Eela tightly in her grasp as they sat on the floor, both sobbing as they held one another. Cami knelt over Randy, holding his chest as he lay on his back, and Fletcher limped quickly out from the hallway. Blood ran down his side as he winced and knelt next to Cami, and they looked worriedly at Randy's bleeding face. I flinched as Cohen slowly pulled himself up using the wall in the kitchen and held his bloody hand to his face.

"No, no, no!" I screamed, my voice breaking. I slammed my fist into the tile as I bowed my forehead to the floor as panic surged through my chest. "Take me instead!"

"PLEASE!" I roared, clenching my fists tightly, grimacing as my nails dug into my skin.

The room suddenly trembled once more as everyone gasped. I flinched and held my hands over my head while I heard a wave of flames shoot over me from Cohen in the kitchen. An angry hiss filled the air as a quick *zap* stung the air. Cohen cried out in agony as something pierced the wall behind him. I quickly picked my head up and widened my eyes in panic as he stared at the blood running down his arm. A sleek dart glinted dangerously through his blood dripping calmly down the side, the dart pinning his arm to the wall. His eyes boiled with rage as he stared at the air looming over me.

I slowly looked away from Cohen and felt my heart drop in my chest. Dusk suddenly materialized out of thin air; her hand still closed tightly around an invisible object in her hand. Her sharp green eyes glared at everyone momentarily before they landed on Cohen as he ripped the dart out of his arm and the wall and grimaced.

"Try that again, flame boy, and I'll shoot him," Dusk hissed, bringing the solid air towards me. I shivered as a pristine dart gun was suddenly resting in her hand as she smirked proudly at Cohen's glare. "Aren't you all just so interestingly weird?" Dusk chuckled, crossing her arm over herself as she kept the dart gun aimed at me. "You can have a chance to get Ryth back," she taunted. "Central Park at the Conservatory Gardens," Dusk beamed, a wicked smile spreading across her face. "I wouldn't recommend you going though," she laughed. "That's a battle you'll lose; and plus, some heart-wrenching truths will be found out if you go," she sighed calmly, her eyes scanning the room once more. In an instant, she disappeared into thin air as it shimmered. The walls of the suite trembled once more as we stared at where she once stood in shock. *Ryth...*

CHAPTER 53

CLOU'S POV

"You're going to pay for that you little prick!" I snarled angrily, gripping my broken wrist tightly in my shaking hand. I glared at Bourbon holding her tightly in his grasp as he wrapped a zip tie around her wrist while she frantically tried getting away. I flinched slightly as Bourbon violently threw her to the ground as she cried out in pain from landing awkwardly on her arm.

"You won't get away with this!" Ryth hissed angrily. "True will come get me!" she snapped, glaring up at Bourbon and I as she pushed herself to sit up slowly.

"She's a little brat, isn't she?" Delta's voice suddenly laughed, making everyone flinch. I tensed as I saw Delta slowly loom from the dark hallway in the back of the room. I narrowed my eyes as a chill shot down my back from his new fully mechanic body as he stalked across the warehouse room. My gaze drifted to Nerve sitting by the furnished corner of the room, his eyes wide with fear and his fluffy white hair trembling on his head. *Did he do something to you when we were gone?*

"True won't be doing anything good enough to save you, Ryth," Delta spat gruffly, tucking his sleek metal arms behind his back as he stared coldly down at his sister. I furrowed my brow and leaned away slightly as I saw a dark haze over both of his eyes as he stared too intently at her. *What's happening to you?* His hazy eyes suddenly shifted over to me manually as I frowned at him and glanced worriedly at Bourbon staring at him. Bourbon shook his head with a sigh before he disappeared into thin air. My skin began to crawl with unease as Delta's gaze towards me became too intense, no sign of movement anywhere in his face.

Ryth flinched as Delta suddenly turned back to her quickly. The room trembled as Dusk suddenly stood next to me with Bourbon stalking away from her. I glanced at the burns all over her skin and shivered at the dart gun resting calmly in her hand.

"She's powerful for her age," Dusk spat.

"You think?" Delta laughed angrily, standing up fully. "Ryth is the reason my entire shoulder was metal,"

"Now you're *all* metal!" Ryth snarled, spitting at Delta as he narrowed his eyes down at her.

"I've been fixed fully," he hissed coldly. "You're nothing different than you were a few years ago!" Delta laughed, stepping towards Ryth quickly. "Scrawny, weak, and helpless!" he snarled, leaning down and grabbing her roughly. I shivered as he pulled Ryth to her feet and slowly ran his pristine metal hand along her bloody chin. He tucked her dark black hair behind her ear as he grinned slightly at her for a moment. Ryth's eyes darkened into hatred as she leaned away from his hand with a frown. She suddenly lifted her leg and strongly kneed Delta in the stomach.

Delta grunted in pain as his shirt followed the newly bent metal hiding under the fabric. He cried out softly in annoyance as his grip around her arm tightened dangerously. Ryth cried out in panic as she was easily lifted off the ground, Delta's hazed eyes stared maniacally at her as he held her in front of her. "This is *payback*." he suddenly hissed with gritted teeth. I widened my eyes as Dusk gasped and stepped forward. Delta's new, strong, metal hand violently closed fully around Ryth's arm.

A clean *crack* echoed through the tense air as Ryth began screaming in agony. Delta's grip only tightened around her arm as his eyes lost all sense of humanity, my heart leaping in my chest.

"Delta!" Bourbon snarled. "What are you doing!" he sharply asked, raising his burly arm.

Delta ignored him as he lifted her higher off the ground and she frantically swung her legs to get away from him. His metal arm moved back and forth slightly as she cried out again in agony, tears streaming down her face. Delta's eyes suddenly widened as he stared lifelessly at Ryth sobbing in front of him.

Delta's hand immediately opened, dropping Ryth roughly to the floor as he stood over her in silence. I tensed to move towards her as Bourbon suddenly shook his head and glared at Dusk and I.

"What is wrong with you, man!" Bourbon angrily snapped, walking quickly across the room towards him.

"Nothing." Delta beamed, turning robotically towards Bourbon. The two of them came chest to chest as they tensed and stared intently at each other, both radiating with rage.

"She's a child," Bourbon hissed. Delta remained silent as the dark haze over his eyes faltered slightly before becoming prominent again. I worriedly glanced at Nerve and frowned at him, tipping my head towards the two of them staring at each other. A chill suddenly shot up my back as my heart beat strongly in my chest.

"Delta!" I snapped sharply. Bourbon widened his eyes slightly as he turned over his shoulder and stared at me. Delta kept his gaze glued to Bourbon like a possessed hawk before slowly turning his head towards me. "I need to talk to you." I hissed, clenching my fists. *Come on. You're still in there somewhere...* I furrowed my brow as I intently stared at the haze over his eyes. *I don't know who or what that is, but my best friend is still there.*

Delta's eyes softened for a moment as I tipped my chin up at him and frowned. He blinked quickly a few times as his entire body made a quiet surge noise. He glared worriedly at Bourbon standing so close to him and stepped away from Ryth laying on the floor grimacing in pain and fear. *There you are...* He remained silent as he shoved Bourbon out of his way and walked calmly across the room towards me. I turned on my heel, avoiding his direct gaze, and trembled as he walked up beside me. Fierce cold radiated off his metal arms as he kept his blank gaze staring ahead of us.

I glanced over my shoulder to see Nerve dart across the room and slide to his knees next to Ryth as Bourbon and Dusk glanced at each other and stood over them. I shivered as Nerve gripped Ryth's shoulders for a moment before she went limp immediately in his arms. He blinked several times with a frown as the skin under his eyes darkened significantly before fading back to normal as he hugged her gently with closed eyes.

Cold wind ripped through the open sky as we stepped out into a destroyed part of the warehouse. This small area had only three walls and no roof. One wall was halfway broken-down, having fallen into the other levels of the building. The opening extended up the rest of the floors all the way up to the roof. The old warehouse swayed in the wind and groaned from everything shifting around it. I shivered as I kept my back to Delta as he gently closed the door we walked through behind him.

"What is wrong with you!" I suddenly cried, turning to face Delta sharply. "You're changing!" I hissed, pointing roughly at him with my non broken hand.

"So is the rest of the world, Clou," Delta replied sadly, keeping his gaze on the city looming through the darkened sky. His new metal arms shifted and glinted in the distant light bouncing off the skyscrapers as he slowly rolled his shoulders out with gentle surge noises. "You've changed, too, you know!" Delta hissed after we stood in silence. "You've become sympathetic and a coward!" he snapped. My heart lurched with anger in my chest as I clenched my fists tightly.

"I've changed because I don't know what is going on with you!" I snarled. "What was *that* back there?" I cried, waving my hand to the door behind him. I breathed hard as panic filled my chest and Delta stared blankly at me. "What is happening to you? You're completely ignoring the city about helping to keep the Elites safe!" I snapped. "Why are you so focused on killing True all of a sudden?"

Delta did not respond; a simple, forced grin slowly spread across his face as his eyes became clouded with the dark haze over them.

"Are you even there anymore?" I asked softly, my voice wavering. Delta's fully robotic body twitched as his eyes flickered closed for a moment.

"Physically, yes, but," Delta cooed calmly, "mentally is debatable,"

"I'm asking—pleading at this point!" I snarled, stepping towards him. "I need to see *Delta*, the *human* who is my best friend!" I breathed worriedly. Delta remained silent as the dark mask over his eyes faltered again. *You're fighting something. What is doing this to you...?*

"A man?" Delta echoed angrily. "No, the man has been dead," he spat, his voice distorting horribly. "All that's left is the machine," he beamed in a forced tone, a maniacal grin spreading across his face again. A moment of panic and agony flashed through his eyes as the dark screen faltered again. I widened my own eyes and stepped away from him with a frown as my heart spiked out of my chest. I no longer saw Delta standing in front of me. A complete, dangerous, stranger loomed malevolently in his presence.

CHAPTER 54

Delta's POV

I slammed the door closed behind me roughly and stumbled back into the warehouse room. I gripped my head tightly in my hands for a moment as I gasped for breath. *You need to stay out of my head...* I narrowed my eyes and shook my head, glaring up at the others sitting around Ryth in the furnished corner of the giant room.

"What are you doing, Bourbon!" I snarled, pushing myself away from the door and weakly stalking across the room towards him leaning over Ryth on the couch.

"Making sure she's still breathing!" he hissed sharply.

I sharply stepped towards Bourbon, grabbing his wrist tightly in my metal hand and quickly pulled him away from Ryth. Bourbon turned immediately and faced me head on again as his eyes darkened in anger. In the corner of my eye, I saw Dusk quickly pull Nerve away from our reach and shove him to the floor next to her. His light eyes glared at Dusk but softened into fear as he looked back up at Bourbon and I. *Why are you thinking you're free to do whatever you want after I got those upgrades, huh?*

I suddenly lifted my arms and violently shoved Bourbon away from me. Bourbon grunted in surprise as his back slammed into the metal breaker mounted on the wall as the lights all around us flickered. Bourbon lunged away from the wall as his eyes suddenly filled with rage. I ducked under his arm before I shouldered into him roughly. Bourbon quickly disappeared out from under me as the room trembled. I stumbled forward, catching myself against the brick wall as I breathed hard and stared down at the metal tin holding my batteries for a moment.

"Real coward-like, Bourbon!" I snarled over my shoulder. I suddenly gasped in pain as severe pressure struck me in the side of the head and I grimaced. I tightly wrapped my hands around my head as the presence filtered back into my skull, filling every corner of my mind. I cried out in agony as it tightened itself around my mind and strangled me as I gasped for breath. *I told you to stay out! I promise I'll go! Give me a second!* My legs immediately gave out from under me as I held my hand in my face and struggled to breathe.

"Wake Ryth up," I grumbled weakly, rolling over onto my elbow as I grimaced in pain. The pressure inside my head slowly released itself as I gasped and rested my forehead on my hands. The presence inside my mind also relaxed as it chuckled in delight before fading away. I blinked harshly and lifted my head, glaring at Nerve with narrowed eyes. His trembling white hair stilled for a moment as his gaze focused on Ryth laying on the couch behind me while Bourbon stalked towards us silently. "You know where I need to go," I sighed, frowning up at him. He nodded once and sighed before reaching down towards me. Suddenly pure white filled my vision with neon streaks of color shooting past me.

My vision slowly blurred back into focus as I blinked quickly while leaning against the cold wall. I glared over my shoulder as the hallway trembled and Bourbon appeared, holding Ryth in his grasp. I narrowed my eyes and quickly forced her away from him and began briskly stalking down the dark hallway with a frown. Ryth struggled in my metal hand as I kept my gaze on the glass doors at the end of the hall, ignoring Bourbon and Ryth's cries of protest.

"Delta!" Ryth cried, making my heart spike out of my chest. "Please! Let me go!" she pleaded weakly. "I won't tell anyone what happened! Just leave True and everyone alone!" she continued, her voice wavering in pain.

"Shut up," I snapped out of habit. I widened my eyes as I turned towards her and stopped walking. Ryth looked up at me through her long, dark hair and shook her head.

"You're not my brother," she whimpered. "I don't know who you are," she continued, her voice breaking.

I inhaled to speak to her as the presence suddenly shot back into my head. I immediately let go off Ryth's arm as I fell into the wall, holding my head tightly in my shaking hands. *Get out! I wasn't doing anything!* My vision blurred heavily as I felt the dark smoke begin to filter over my eyes again.

"*Make me,*" the voice sneered coldly, pressure forming dangerously close near the base of my neck. "*See what happens if you try,*" the voice hissed, echoing around my head for a moment as I grimaced in pain. I stayed silent as the voice chuckled pridefully and slowly faded away.

My vision slowly focused once more as I slowly turned my head to Bourbon holding Ryth tightly in his grasp. My first instinct was to get her away, but my metal arm wouldn't move. I was frozen in place as rage built up inside my heart as I wistfully stared at Ryth's fearful eyes. "*You wanted her dead, so I'll give you what you want. Quit trying to help her,*" the voice suddenly snarled. I gasped in pain as violent sparks shot from my arm as I tried lifting it to reach for Ryth.

I don't want her dead anymore! I need her alive! Don't make me do this! Please! The voice only laughed darkly in response.

I suddenly pushed off the wall again and began walking down the hallway again, Ryth's shaking arm in my cold, metal hand.

"Where are you taking me?" Ryth asked softly, her voice wavering. I roughly pushed open to heavy metal doors behind glass panels and ignored her. I quickly let go of her arm and moved her away from me as I lifted my right hand to a sensor mounted on the wall. I widened my eyes in panic as Ryth suddenly lunged at me. She turned and shouldered harshly into me, knocking me backwards into the wall. I gasped in pain as I felt more sheets of metal bend and compress in on themselves. I howled in agony as my vision blurred and a quick warning shot through my ear.

I held myself up with the wall and violently kicked Ryth across the small room we were in. She hit the wall and slid to the floor coughing hollowly into the tile and taking rattling breaths. I widened my eyes in horror as I stared at small droplets of blood splattering onto the floor from her coughs. *I'm sorry, sister…*

Violent pain suddenly slammed into the base of my skull, making my vision go completely dark. Loud alarms rang in my ears as the sensor on the wall failed to read the symbol on my metal palm. I took several gasping breaths as my vision slowly came back and I leaned heavily against the wall.

"Look what you made me do!" I hissed, my voice distorting horribly. I grit my teeth in pain as I hit the back of my head against the wall and clenched my fists tightly. The glass door to our left suddenly opened as the alarms stopped. My heart fell out of my chest in panic as I met *her* cold eyes staring angrily at me, no emotion on her face.

CHAPTER 55

TRUE'S POV

My mind raced frantically in circles as I jogged calmly through a back entrance into Central Park. Angry flashes of the conversation everyone had while we waited for Boss to fix the elevator to the suite rang through my head. I clenched my fists tightly as I narrowed my eyes in disgust. *I can't believe Stretch told Delta and his group the exact location of HQ…and betrayed us, again.* My heart ached slightly at the glint in Stretch's eyes earlier today, then I remembered Ryth's terrified eyes as I frowned glancing over my shoulder at the others. *I'm glad Cami will at least be safe back at HQ with Maeve.*

My heart leapt out of my chest with anger as I suddenly locked eyes with Delta as he stood in the rebuilt Conservatory Gardens. I chill shot down my back as I gazed at his fully mechanic body with narrowed eyes. *When did you become fully mechanic?*

A large, pristine spear extended out strongly from one of his metal arms while a pistol glinted dangerously in the other. Bourbon, Clou and Nerve all stood over Ryth, kneeling on the ground in front of the fountain in silence as I took a shuddering breath at seeing her defeated state. Someone else was kneeling next to her with a dark cloth wrapped around their head as it hung low in front of them.

"Look who decided to come see the shit-show!" Delta laughed loudly, his voice distorting and sending an eerie echo through the silent park.

"Do what you want to me. Just please," I began loudly, "let Ryth go," I pleaded, narrowing my eyes at Delta's blank LED mask.

"Oh?" Delta chuckled calmly, the mask becoming amused. "Just Ryth? What about…?" he continued amusedly, turning his gaze to Bourbon next to him briefly. Stella and Cohen tensed next to me as I heard Randy and Fletcher grumble under their breaths while Eela whimpered behind me.

Bourbon leaned down quickly and pulled the dark cloth off the head of the person kneeling next to Ryth. Everyone tensed behind me as I gasped softly and widened my eyes. Stretch's dark hair fell from his head as he kept it bowed, his gaze away from all of us. Bourbon chuckled darkly as he leaned down and roughly grabbed his head, forcing him to look up. My heart sank in my chest as I looked at his bloodied and bruised face. His seeing eye was filled with guilt and anger as he stared directly at me, taking shuddering breaths. Blood dribbled from the side of his mouth as dark bruises lined his jaw, his seeing eye was almost swollen shut.

"What did you do to him!" I asked sharply, tightening my grip around my pistol.

"Are you kidding me?" Delta laughed, leaning back his head slowly. "Still worried about a *traitor?*" he scoffed, stepping slowly past Ryth. "I wonder how far you'll go with trusting anyone, regardless of what they've done to you," Delta droned softly, his voice distorting horribly as he stalked towards Stretch. Delta extended his arm towards Stretch, tipping his chin up with the end of the sharp blade coming from his arm. Stretch grimaced as the tip of the blade dug slowly into his skin and Delta stared ominous down at him. I trembled slightly as Stretch's eyes darkened into hatred. He glared at Delta while blood slowly ran down his neck.

"I sadly wasn't able to get what I needed done with Ryth completed in time," Delta sighed, his voice completely altered. Clou's light eyes slowly peeled themselves away from Ryth to Delta as a worried glint filled them. *Why do you sound like that? What's wrong with you?* A single spark shot from the back of Delta's neck as he removed the blade tip from Stretch's neck and slowly walked back over to Ryth, the black glass helmet on his face completely blank.

"Just let her go," I pleaded weakly, my voice wavering with anxiety. "Do what you want to me! She's done nothing!" I cried, stepping towards the group swiftly.

"Oh really?" Delta suddenly snarled, turning sharply towards me. "She's done *nothing?*" he echoed angrily.

"I don't care what she's done to *you!*" I hissed darkly, slowly wrapping myself in my pitch-black smoke as I slowly inched towards them, my eyes resting intently on Ryth. I trembled in anger at seeing her arm and shoulder bent at an unnatural angle, bruises and blood lining her neck and face. "She's just a kid!" I cried. *I don't want to hurt any of you, I can't just shoot you all and take Ryth either. Bourbon will for sure get her away from me again.* "She's scared, Delta!" I continued, slowing my stride before I stopped completely. I glanced warily at Delta who had gone completely still. "She's your sister! Don't you see how terrified she is right now!" I asked, waving my hand gently at her as Clou slowly stalked towards her.

I glanced over my shoulder at Stella and Cohen with a wistful gaze at Eela cowering under Fletcher's arm while Randy scanned the surrounding area. *Why did I let you come? Delta could take you and hurt you... Eela, I know you're worried about your sister, but I need you safe...* I glared back over my shoulder towards the fountain as my heart began to beat strongly out of my chest while a gust of cold wind swept across the stone platform.

"Please," I pleaded gently, staring directly into the darkened glass mask. I flinched and stepped back as a single wisp of dark mist slowly lifted itself out from under the helmet, disappearing into the air.

Delta's body trembled slightly before his robotic arm suddenly lifted and fired a single round directly at Ryth as his entire body surged dangerously.

"No!" I cried, lunging across the stone with tears filling my eyes. Ryth cried out in agony as she slumped over next to Stretch as his eyes widened with horror. Eela's screams of anger made my heart lurch in my chest as I sprinted towards Delta with my pistol raised.

"Now!" Delta suddenly ordered, his voice completely being different. Bourbon smiled darkly before roughly shoving Stretch over into the stone and disappearing into thin air, making the ground tremble.

A dark arm roughly knocked into my shoulder, spinning me around towards the others as I widened my eyes. Bourbon appeared directly behind Cohen as he leapt in front of Stella with a raised fist of fire. Bourbon's burly arms easily wrapped around Cohen's neck, and the two of them disappeared into thin air and the ground trembled. My heart lurched in my chest as I spun myself around, materializing several pistols floating around me and firing at Delta standing ominously over Ryth. In the corner of my eye, I saw Clou dart across the stone platform towards Randy as Dusk materialized out of thin air and lunged towards Stella. Bright red flames suddenly illuminated the sky behind me as agonizing screams filled the air, and I fired again at Delta.

"Careful!" Delta laughed darkly as the bullets bounded harmlessly off his metal body. "Wouldn't want to strike Ryth, now, would you?" he called out harshly, turning out of the way of another bullet. "I think I'm the least of your worries True!" he yelled angrily, leaping out of the way as I lunged towards him. I roughly slammed my side into the concrete fountain as I angrily cried out in pain. Delta was on the other side of the stone platform, Nerve and Ryth being held back behind him as the black glass helmet was filled with pride. *Where did Stretch go? He was just right here!* I widened my eyes as everyone froze while a blood chilling screech filled the air.

A metal creature suddenly slammed roughly into the stone next to me after being dropped out of the sky as the ground shook. The concrete below us shattered as the Kami snarled up wildly at me, rotating metal teeth revealed behind the beak. I leapt out of the machine's reach as it lunged towards me, slamming its huge, front metal claws into the ground. Two more Kamis were dropped out of the sky over Stella and the others quarreling with Dusk and Clou. The three mechanic creatures wildly snarled and attacked anything that moved, including each other.

"They're a work in progress!" Delta's voice chuckled loudly, sending a chill down my spine. I glanced quickly over to where he once stood and trembled at not seeing him, Ryth, or Nerve there. I backed quickly away from the Kami stalking silently towards me as its eyes widened slightly, tipping its head back and forth. I flinched as Ryth and Nerve suddenly appeared out of thin air, leaning against the fountain as the ground trembled. Delta's dark, distorted laugh echoed eerily through the air as the Kami hissed proudly. *I knew something was up with these machines!*

"True! They're not fireproof!" Stella's voice cried out loudly against the Kami's screams. The Kami in front of me suddenly turned completely around and charged at her, its metal jaw flying open and a rotating chain shooting from its mouth.

"Stella!" I yelled, stepping after the machine as my heart dropped in my chest.

"I don't think so!" Delta snarled, suddenly standing next to me as the ground shook. I yelped and ducked under the sleek blade on his arm as I felt the tense air glide over the side of my head. A single gunshot echoed through the air as my vision tunneled on the bullet flying towards me and I narrowed my eyes. I immediately returned the bullet back with a wave of my hand as I extended a column of my smoke towards Delta darting out of my reach.

"Coward!" I snarled angrily, lunging towards him as Bourbon's dark arms made them both disappear while the ground shook. I casted out two columns of smoke behind me as I turned on my heel through gritted teeth. "You're playing a dangerous game without a single *glimpse* into the rulebook, True!" Delta's voice angrily yelled. A cold, metal boot suddenly slammed into my back, sending me to the ground as I coughed hollowly into the stone. I yelped and quickly rolled away from the sleek, metal blade from Delta's arm as it struck the concrete where my head once was.

I materialized several pistols in front of me and fired repeatedly as Delta cried out in agony. The bullets began piercing the metal covering his body with violent sparks shooting from the impact. He fell out of my view as I rolled back to my feet, my heart beating out of my chest as my vision blurred slightly and my feet swayed under me. Violent pain suddenly struck me in the side as I cried out in pain and thickened the smoke around me. I glanced quickly over my shoulder to see Clou charging towards me with bloodied hands and a dark glint in his eyes. I backed away quickly from him as his fist swung towards me, a blade on the end of a brass knuckle wrapped around his hand, slicing the side of my face as my stance faltered.

The ground under us all suddenly vibrated as it turned into a liquid state. Clou stumbled around weakly as we both yelped and fell to the moving concrete. My vision blurred as I hit the back of my head on the ground behind me. I saw Fletcher crouching with his palms in the dirt guarding Randy laying on the ground behind him. My heart leapt in my chest as I saw Eela dart away from Stella's side across the stone platform towards Ryth and Nerve by the fountain. Stella suddenly stood up from kneeling next to Randy and sent a knife across the open space with a growl of anger.

My ears rang loudly in my head as I struggled to my feet under the steadying ground and widened my eyes. Cold metal hands suddenly wrapped around my neck as I was violently shoved back to the ground. Clou steadied himself on the hardening concrete and quickly raised his pistol towards Eela dragging Ryth away from Nerve who was holding his bleeding side with shaking hands. His eyes were wide as he stared at Eela crying as she stared down at Ryth limp in her arms.

"Eela what are you doing!?" I cried angrily, desperately trying to stand up from under Delta's cold metal hands pinning me down.

A loud gunshot echoed through the silent, tense air. Eela's slow stride faltered as the bullet struck her in the leg, the two falling over. I cried out in pain as I gasped from a quiet *crack* echoing from behind my ears as my head was pinned harshly into the cold concrete. Stella and Fletcher's cries of anger sent my heart leaping out of my chest.

"Sorry, True!" Delta laughed darkly from leaning over me. "Looks like it's game over from here on out," he beamed, leaning slowly over my shoulder to stare directly into my eyes. I widened my eyes as I gasped for breath while I stared up at Delta's bloodied and cut face as he narrowed his once perfect brown eyes at me. "If people can't die for what they believe in and love," Delta whispered, his voice distorting as he added pressure onto my neck, "then there is no reason for death at all."

CHAPTER 56

COHEN'S POV

Everything became oddly silent around me as pure white light filled my vision. My heart spiked out of my chest in panic at the thought of being dead but was relieved as neon strings filled the white space. A darkened street suddenly appeared all around me as I smacked harshly into an old light post and slid to the ground. I coughed hollowly into my arm as I blinked to steady my blurry vision and widened my eyes up at Bourbon towering over me with a blank expression. I tensed, pushing myself away from him as I frowned with a furrowed brow before he scoffed at me and disappeared. The ground and buildings trembled violently as I shivered with a worried glance around me.

I quickly leapt to my feet as Stretch suddenly appeared out of thin air, falling roughly onto the roof of an old taxi and rolled to the street. The taxi's alarm began to blare loudly through the abandoned, silent street as my heart roared with anger in my chest as I clenched my fists. I jogged down the sidewalk with narrowed eyes as I stared intently at Stretch kneeling weaky on the ground, clutching his stomach and coughing hollowly into his arms. His coughs echoed eerily underneath the car alarm as my heart spiked out of my chest with brief pity.

In one swift motion, I roughly kicked Stretch in the back, sending him to the street before I grabbed his jacket collar and lifted him to his feet. Stretch yelped in panic as he gripped my hand around his neck with his bruised arms behind his head as I turned him around and slammed him into the glass panel of the building next to us. I held his collar and shoulders tightly in my hands as I pushed him multiple times into the building and flames flickered from behind my ears.

"I should have gotten rid of you the moment you admitted to working for Delta!" I snarled, flames flickering out from my palms holding Stretch against the glass. His eyes widened in panic as a hatred-filled glint flashed across them, and he extended his arms violently towards me. His rough and bloodied palm quickly wrapped around my neck as he swiftly shoved my hand off him. A sharp pain suddenly struck me in the chest as Stretch lifted both of his legs and kicked out at me, extending them at the last moment and sent me into the taxi behind us. The taxi and I skidded roughly across the deserted street, crashing through a glass window of another building as I fell to the glass filled ground.

The building's alarm and the taxi's alarm began blaring loudly in my ears as my vision blurred and pain radiated from my chest. I gasped weakly for breath as I watched Stretch waver across the street towards me, hitting the flames latching onto his neck and jacket out slowly. His head hung low as his blank gaze stared at the glass on the ground with a disappointed frown across his face.

"I had to!" Stretch cried angrily, clenching his fists as he quickly looked up at me, his eyes filled with regret and rage.

I shook my head as I gasped in pain and widened my eyes down at myself. My raspy breaths faltered as I stared at the small knife sticking out of my chest. My shaking hands covered over it for a moment as my head became light at the sight of blood seeping through my dark shirt. I narrowed my eyes as my heart spiked weakly in my chest with anger. I suddenly lifted my hand, sending a wave of white flames surging through the room towards Stretch standing in the street. He yelped, extending his arms into the air and pulling himself over the flames moments before glass shattered from above and shards fell in his place.

After weakly forcing myself up the stairwell exposed by the taxi destroying the wall, I burst into a large office room as the building's alarm stopped. Cubicles and computers lined the entire open space with several papers floating gently off desks from the draft shooting through the stairwell from behind me. I breathed shallowly as I leaned against the doorframe and glared at the small knife in my chest with a hiss in pain before glaring back up at the room.

"You want to play dirty now, huh!" I screamed angrily, opening my hands slowly.

Red flames spurted quickly from my palms, latching strongly onto the dark carpet below me and immediately began spreading and climbing the cubicle walls. I coughed hollowly into my arm as I pushed away from the doorframe and stalked slowly through the rows of office stations with grumbled of pain and annoyance. Flames licked and clawed their way through the entire room as thick smoke began to hinder my sight sending flares of pain down my throat. I glared over my shoulder at a large filing cabinet engulfed in flames suddenly toppling over, sending more waves of roaring flames to the tiled roof.

"Is this the end, Stretch?" I asked hoarsely, my voice echoing softly over the screeching flames. "After everything the Agency has done for you! This is how you break things off?" I laughed angrily, glaring over my shoulder at something darting across the room. Flames brushed against my skin, gently sending warm chills up my body as I shuddered from the smoke beginning to wrap its way around my neck. *If I would have used my normal white flames, there would be less smoke.* I coughed hollowly into my arm as I gripped a burning cubicle wall and grimaced at the flames happily latching onto my flesh.

My heart leapt out of my chest as a large filing cabinet was suddenly launched across the room directly at me. I yelped in panic and turned out of the metal box's way before it knocked me roughly to the flame-filled carpet. I cried out in agony as my recently healed ankle became trapped under the heavy metal and I struggled to pull it away. Panic shot through my chest as Stretch suddenly leapt up onto the cabinet and stared down at me blankly. I gasped weakly for breath and coughed hollowly as I fearfully looked up at Stretch, pain shooting up my leg.

"If you want to call it the end, go ahead," Stretch spat gruffly, his wavering voice barely audible over the roaring flames.

I narrowed my eyes and quickly grabbed a burning office chair next to me and launched it up at Stretch. The flaming chair knocked into him roughly, sending him off the cabinet and into a flaming cubicle. His screams of agony filled me with panic as I cried out in pain from the filing cabinet slammed fully onto the ground while I pulled my ankle out from under it. I struggled against the burning carpet and slowly forced myself to my feet as I coughed hollowly into my arm.

Panic surged through my mind again as Stretch cried out once more. The distant memory of being surrounded by dead bodies in my old prison cell overcame my mind as anxiety began to strangle every other thought out of my head.

Stretch suddenly leapt over the filing cabinet, shouldering into me roughly. I yelped in surprise and struggled arm to arm with him as we knocked each other into different walls of the flaming cubicles. Stretch suddenly kicked me in the knee, sending me to the ground as he grabbed the knife sticking out of my chest and pushed it harshly deeper into my skin. I cried out again in pain before I smacked my head directly into Stretch's face as we both stumbled away from each other, both of us gasping for air and taking wheezing breaths.

"Why Stretch?" I cried weakly. "We all trusted and accepted you!" I snarled angrily, stepping towards him as he tensed and clenched his fists.

"I know you did!" Stretch snarled back, his voice breaking as he suddenly leapt backwards out of the way from a falling, flaming beam from the roof. Stretch stared intently at me through the wall of flames before a curtain of smoke let him disappear.

I yelped and darted away from the collapsing ceiling as desks fell through the charred tiles above us. My lungs screamed in agony as my vision wavered while I put pressure on my chest and widened my eyes at the knife being gone. My legs faltered under me as I weakly made my way near the open window Stretch had broken through and fell to the ground, gasping for breath.

Burning smoke filtered its way steadily out of the open, shattered window as I held my sleeve in front of my face and coughed into my hand. My heart sank in my chest as Stretch slowly stalked out of the flames towards me.

"He *forced* me!" Stretch cried out, his voice rasping horribly. His blind eye and seeing eye were both filled with tears as he clenched his fists and continued directly towards me. My heart beat loudly out of my chest as I stared at his black jacket being almost completely burned off, patches of his skin completely mangled from the flames. The blood on his face had become caked on like scabs from the flames drying them as he grimaced. "Tell me, Cohen," Stretch laughed sadly, his stance faltering. His shaking hands twitched with panic as tears streamed down his face and his eyes narrowed. "How many times do you think a heart can break and still function normally?" he asked sharply, stopping in front of me and standing over me ominously.

I widened my eyes as I stared at his completely broken, defeated and guilt filled gaze down at me as he remained silent.

"Don't know the answer, huh?" he snarked, rolling his eyes and glaring around the flame filled room. "Think about it!" he hissed, lunging towards me.

Stretch extended his arms violently towards me and shoved me through the large glass panels behind me. My stomach fell awkwardly as my vision blurred while I watched the flaming window slowly loom farther and farther away. My entire body shook with agony as I slammed roughly into a dumpster and rolled onto the glass filled street. I lay on my back for a moment, blinking weakly up at the blurry, burning building in front of me. Red and blue lights slowly flashed brighter and brighter from behind me, reflecting off the glass. My ears sang loudly, echoing ringing screeches around my head as my heart began to falter in my chest from the pressure forming in my lungs. My heart weakly leapt out of my chest as I turned and saw Stretch leap from the burning building as a roar of flames shot out from both broken windows on either side of the glass skyscraper. *Stretch! What are you doing!*

CHAPTER 57

TRUE'S POV

Several consecutive shots fired through the air as sparks shot from Delta's metal body and he cried out in pain. He had been knocked barely enough off me, relieving some pressure off my neck as I gasped for air. I quickly shot columns of smoke up towards him, wrapping him tightly and throwing him off me roughly. His mechanic body smacked into the concrete fountain next to us as I weakly pulled myself to my feet and stumbled over to Stella, Fletcher, and Randy while Clou lay on the ground, staring at Delta with fear in his eyes.

Randy dropped his gun as he leaned his head back on Fletcher behind him and I fell to the ground in front of them. Stella fell to her knees next to me and worriedly grabbed my hand as she glared at Clou and Delta sitting by the fountain. I breathed weakly and glanced at Randy smiling at the ground with Fletcher's gaze resting intently on Eela, Ryth, and Nerve on the other side of the fountain. My heart fell out of my chest as I stared at them as tears filled my eyes. *No…*

Stella's grip on my hand tightened slightly as she rested her forehead on my shoulder, and I pushed myself up onto my elbow with gritted teeth. Grief lurched violently through my chest as I stared at Ryth's lifeless body lying in Eela's arms while she leaned her head gently against the fountain. The skin under Nerve's eyes had darkened significantly as he worriedly stared at the two of them, putting pressure on his bleeding side with gasps of pain.

I glanced over to my left and shuddered at seeing the three burned Kami bodies lying helplessly in the grass, their dull eyes and sharp beaks forever frozen in screams of rage and agony. *Why try to use machines to fight us but make them killable with fire? Delta knows I have Stella and Cohen's fire power to help us.*

I shook my head and glared over at Clou's gaze resting intently on us. I shivered with a quick glance over my shoulder at Dusk's body laying still in the grass with gentle flames flickering from the charred ground around her. The entire ground suddenly trembled as a warm, angered filled gust of air shot across the entire courtyard.

"Now you tell me one thing, True!" Bourbon ordered sharply, lifting a pistol directly at me as Stella tensed and widened her eyes. "How have you survived this long!" he snarked, a wicked grin spreading across his face. My heart leapt with anger in my chest as I clenched my fists and narrowed my eyes at Bourbon's raging glare.

"I've been asking myself the same thing," I glowered darkly, tipping my chin up at the barrel of the pistol coming closer to my face. Stella trembled slightly next to me as her grip tightened around my shaking hand. Bourbon's glare darkened down at the two of us before he slowly glanced at Stella with an amused scoff before narrowing his eyes back to me.

Fletcher suddenly lunged passed me as Stella leapt to her feet. Bourbon yelped in panic as Stella shouldered roughly into him, and Fletcher pried the pistol from his hand. A single shot echoed through the air as Bourbon cried out in agony moments before Fletcher's palms latched tightly onto Bourbon's arm. Stella was violently shoved to the ground as Bourbon easily shook Fletcher off him. I tensed and forced myself to stand as I stepped towards Stella holding herself up on her elbow on the ground. I widened my eyes as Fletcher seized up with Bourbon again, gripping his burly arm once more.

In an instant, his entire right arm disappeared into thin air. Bourbon's scream of agony echoed eerily through the park sending a jolt of panic through my chest. Stella's eyes widened in horror as Fletcher was shoved to the ground, and he cried out in pain and clutched his side. Bourbon gripped the cleanly-cut part of his shoulder as he doubled over onto his knees, and blood poured quickly onto the broken stone below him. His cries of agony continued, becoming raspy while more blood fell from his shoulder as his other hand gripped the open wound tightly. His dark eyes were wild with rage and panic as he glared at all of us before screaming in agony once more. The ground suddenly trembled, and he was gone, his cry of pain echoing through the silent park.

"I didn't sign up for this, Delta!" Clou's weak voice suddenly cried, breaking the tense, shocked silence. I flinched and looked up at Clou standing next to Delta struggling to stand himself up by the fountain. "I didn't sign up to watch you destroy yourself over someone else's plans you're being forced into!" Clou screamed, his voice breaking as he stepped towards Delta.

"Who told you that?" Delta demanded; his voice completely altered. An uneasy chill shot down my back as I widened my eyes at them.

"I only said yes to helping you so you wouldn't be alone!" Clou snarled. "I know how dangerous it is for you to be alone with yourself!" he hissed, pointing roughly at Delta as he stared blankly down at him. "Stop listening to them!" Clou ordered, waving his hand at his own head. "Whatever they're telling you is a lie!"

"Quit trying to change who I am!" Delta snarled, his voice distorting back to normal as he gripped his head tightly and fell onto his elbow on the fountain ledge. His bloodied eyes widened in panic as the concrete gave in under his weight and part of his elbow was splashed with water.

"*You* aren't this!" Clou cried angrily, stepping towards Delta again. My heart began beating out of my chest as the two of them fell silent with one another as Randy pulled himself next to me and widened his eyes. Stella and Fletcher turned back to us with furrowed brows before we all looked back to Delta and Clou staring at one another.

"You don't understand!" Delta suddenly cried, his voice completely normal and breaking. "I don't want to do this!" he continued. "I didn't sign up for this either!" he screamed; his voice lined with pain. "*She's* making me; I can't stop her, no matter what I do!" he screamed once more as he gripped his head tightly in his metal hands with widened eyes in pure panic. "She's *in* my head, and she won't get out!" he snarled painfully, his voice distorting as sparks shot from his neck.

"Who's in your head?" I asked sharply. Delta suddenly went eerily still as his face became emotionless, sending a chill down my back. *He's being controlled! Who's doing this to him?*

Delta's head slowly turned back to Clou as all the life was drained from his blood-filled eyes. His entire body trembled violently back and forth as sparks began shooting out of his metal limbs. Both of his metal arms slowly began to snap and rebuild themselves in front of our eyes as Delta began taking shuddering breaths, his stance faltering before he fell onto the side of the fountain behind him. Clou's eyes were wide with horror as he stared at Delta making horrid gurgling noises as we all watched in fear. A gagged and distorted cry of agony suddenly escaped Delta's mouth right before he went completely limp, blood dripping from his metal hand.

Clou and Nerve looked intently at the other, eyes wide with horror before slowly turning to us staring with mouths wide in shock and confusion. My heart beat strongly out of my chest, roaring in my ears as I stared at Delta's limp body. *This isn't good…* A loud surge noise suddenly echoed through the tense air from Delta's body, making everyone flinch. Delta quickly rose to his feet, his head hanging limp from his shoulders and his eyes dripping blood onto the water filled stones below him. *Yea. Totally not good…* Delta's eyes slowly blinked open, a dark, ominous, red glow hovering over them.

His entire body shuddered as Clou struggled away from him with widened eyes. Delta let out a distorted, sudden cry of anger as his metal arm trembled, and he lunged towards Clou. "No—" I cried loudly, forcing myself to stand. Delta's metal arm violently slammed directly into Clou at full speed, shoving him into the concrete stones below them. Nerve cried out in panic, his grip around Eela and Ryth in his arms tightening as Stella and Randy gasped in shock from behind me. I slid to a stop as I widened my eyes in horror at Clou's blank expression. He was staring at the ground next to him as Delta stood over him, completely still.

Fletcher angrily cried out under his breath as he quickly forced himself to his feet and sprinted across the stone platform towards Eela and Ryth being guarded by Nerve. He slid to his knees roughly towards Nerve's outstretched, shaking hands as tears streamed down his panicked face, and he leapt away from Eela. Fletcher shook his head at him and quickly began helping him move Eela and Ryth further away from Delta, who was still frozen in place as he stood above Clou's still body below him his eyes wide. My heart ached in my chest as I limped over to Delta's tense mechanic body as tears filled my eyes.

"No!" Delta whimpered weakly, his voice distorting back to sounding normal. "I'm sorry! I'm so sorry!" he cried, falling to his knees and immediately lifting Clou's limp body up slightly. "She made me do it! I promise!" Delta screamed, his voice breaking. "Get out of my head!" he ordered angrily, his metal hands setting down Clou's body as he gripped his head tightly. His metal fingers dug into the sides of his skull as he forced himself to stand, and he doubled over screaming in grief. His entire body suddenly jerked forward, his cry of grief getting cut off immediately.

Delta stood up manually and quickly turned over his shoulder to Nerve and Fletcher dragging Ryth and Eela further away. He then violently lunged into a full sprint from a stand still as his metal blade extended back from his arm and his pistol in his hand raised. His metal boots pounded strongly into the earth, sending tremors to my feet. My heart leapt out of my chest as I suddenly began sprinting across the concrete platform as more tears filled my eyes.

"FLETCHER! GET OUT OF THERE!" I screamed, my voice breaking in panic.

"Run!" Stella cried weakly from behind me.

A large metal rod shot from Delta's arm, slamming into Fletcher's head as he shoved Eela down the hill. He fell over roughly, holding himself weakly over Ryth's limp body as he coughed hollowly into his arm. Nerve leapt up to his feet and forced the rod away from Fletcher before it retracted back towards Delta's arm. The skin under Nerve's eyes suddenly darkened to almost pure black as his light eyes filled with hatred and rage as he stood strongly between Delta surging towards Fletcher.

Delta's heavy metal arm swung in an arch towards them, forcing Nerve directly out of his way as Fletcher picked Ryth's limp body up in his bleeding arms and struggled to stand on his feet to run. Delta quickly lifted his other arm and fired consecutively at Fletcher as he finally had begun to make it further away from him.

"No!" I cried angrily, tears streaming down my face as I watched the bullets pierce Fletcher violently in the back repeatedly before he fell limp to the ground next to Ryth. Stella and Randy's angry sobs echoed through the air from behind me as my vision blurred with panic. *Cami, I'm so sorry… I can't make it there in time. They're both gone—*

Burned, outstretched arms suddenly wrapped around me and shoved me roughly forward as I widened my eyes. In the corner of my eye, I saw Stretch lying on the ground with Cohen kneeling over him, both covered in burn marks. I materialized several pistols around me as I fired them all towards Delta standing over Fletcher and Ryth's bodies. Bright sparks shot from his metal body as he had no reaction to the bullets hitting him as I wrapped my smoke around myself with pure rage boiling through my aching heart. Panic surged through my chest as Delta's head suddenly snapped towards me and he began charging at me.

"We're not done yet!" Delta's distorted voice roared.

I braced myself as I extended a column of smoke towards Delta as he neared me before he shouldered me violently to the ground.

"True!" Stella cried in a panicked tone as everything around me became silent and dark for a moment. Immense pain shot down my body, sending a wave of adrenaline through me as I gasped for breath and wrapped more smoke around Delta's neck. He pinned me roughly to the ground. My heart leapt out of my chest as his metal fist suddenly roughly hit the side of my head, causing my smoke around myself and his neck to falter before he picked me up and leapt into the sky as a surge of flames flew under us.

My vision blurred horribly as cold wind shot past the both of us. Delta began laughing maniacally as he pinned me in front of him. The sky above us was beginning to turn pale orange as sirens echoed through the air over my racing heart. *He can fly now?! If he keeps going higher, we'll both die from falling from the height—*

Without thinking, I suddenly fired my pistol several times as my arm was pinned under me against Delta's metal body. I cried out in agony as I felt each bullet strike my left knee, sending waves of pain and heat throughout my entire body while my vision blacked out with each bullet. Delta's grip on me loosened as I felt the air brushing past us slow significantly.

"It'll take more than a few bullets to kill me!" Delta snarled angrily, his voice distorting horribly as the pressure on my back became stronger. His other metal arm suddenly whipped around and latched onto my shoulder, squeezing it tightly between his fingers. I cried out in agony as Delta slowly began to pull it slightly further and further away from me. "I'll rip you limb from limb and scatter you throughout the entire *city* if I have to!" Delta hissed coldly, a strangely familiar voice echoing into my ears as I widened my eyes in panic. *What—?*

"I'm sorry!" Delta suddenly cried, his voice distorting back to normal. Delta let out another cry of agony as a surge shot through his entire body, and the dark haze covered both his eyes again. I blinked as my vision blacked out and felt my stomach turn over several times, and I widened my eyes in panic.

Delta's eyes were calmly closed as we fell swiftly back down towards the gardens. Right before we hit the fountain, Delta's eyes were forced open and completely normal. I felt him throw me roughly away from him right as the tip of the fountain pierced through his metal body and loud ringing filled my ears, everything becoming silent for a moment. My heart beat strongly out of my chest, echoing around my skull as the only thing I could hear. Pain shot from every inch of my body as I tried to focus on breathing, as no air would enter my lungs. The pressure forming in my chest was becoming unbearable while I cried out softly in agony.

I slowly opened my eyes and breathed shallowly as I gripped the soaked soil below me. I blinked several times and weakly pushed myself up onto my elbows, gazing at the risen earth all around me and shivering at seeing Delta laying on the other side of the opening in the ground, the tip of the fountain directly through his metal body. I stared at him for a moment before I slowly pulled myself out of the crater and lay on the soaked concrete while glaring up at the sky becoming brighter. I forced myself to roll onto my elbows as I squinted and searched the ground for my pistol as my vision blurred and my chest screamed.

My shaking hand slowly lifted out towards my dented pistol laying on the ground, and a thin column on my pitch black-smoke extended from my palm and dragged the gun towards me as I threw myself to my feet. I gasped in pain as my leg's immediately gave out under me as violent pain shot down my left hip.

"How are you still alive?" I weakly asked, gritting my teeth as I narrowed my eyes at Delta's gaze towards me. He remained silent as he stared blankly at me. I lifted my pistol at him with a frown. I struggled up onto my feet once more, leaning all my weight onto my right leg as my vision blurred. Right before I pulled the trigger, extended arms suddenly slammed into my side, knocking me to the ground and causing the bullet to strike the ground next to Delta's head.

"Why would you do that?!" I angrily screamed, coughing hollowly into my arm as I glared at Stretch lying on the ground in front of me.

"He's lost enough!" Stretch cried, his voice breaking as he let his head fall to the concrete below us. "Look at him!" he continued, his voice rasping. My heart spiked out of my chest as my vision blurred. Cohen weakly jogged over and pinned Stretch to the ground with his hands forcibly held behind his back. I shook my head slowly at him and turned my gaze to Delta laughing softly in the bottom of the hole from the caved in fountain.

"If you think I'm the real threat," Delta chuckled wearily, "then you're dead wrong," he spat, his voice wavering. I narrowed my eyes at him as I shook my head with a scoff.

"Funny joke, you lunatic," I snapped weakly, trying to get myself to stand and failing. Pain surged through my body from my knee as I felt warm blood gush down my leg. Delta's head twitched sideways back and forth several times as an empty smile filled his face.

"Your mother, True, she's *alive!*" Delta suddenly cackled, his voice distorting. My heart immediately fell in my chest as it faltered, my brow furrowing slowly. *No...*

"She's alive, well, angry—and searching for your blood!" Delta screamed, his voice breaking as his smile twitched into a forced frown as his metal body surged. "She *planned* everything that has ever happened to you! Including the death of your father and Mr. Keilot, all the way to tonight!" he beamed, his voice wavering. He let out a pain filled laugh as his metal hands weakly gripped the sharp point of the fountain sticking out of his body. I shook my head slowly as my vision faltered and the ground below me swayed.

"How...?" I rasped, my voice barely a whisper. Cohen and Stretch stared at me with widened eyes as flickers of flame came from behind Cohen's angry eyes. *She...planned...Dad...Mr. Keilot...?* My entire body trembled as the world around me seemed to cave in. Pits of grief surged through my entire body as I gasped repeatedly in panic, gripping the ground below me tightly as I widened my eyes. Delta only let out a maniacal cackle that constantly distorted as his entire body surged multiple times, his laugh slowly dying away.

An angry scream of agony and grief suddenly echoed from my left. I widened my eyes in panic as Eela leapt down into the large crater with

Delta and placed both of her palms on his destroyed metal body. Delta immediately began screaming in agony as I watched the metal sheets, bolts, wires and gears begin to distort, bend and break out of shape as Eela pressed harder into his body. Delta's body moved back and forth violently before a final surge echoed through the air, his head falling backwards completely limp with blood falling from his eyes like tears. Eela fell back off him, screaming and sobbing into the air as she kicked his metal leg, her cries lurching my heart each time.

Stretch slowly reached down into the crater as Cohen stepped off him and lifted Eela out, setting her down next to me. Eela fell into my side sobbing as she held me tightly in her shaking arms. I held her tightly under my arm as I stared blankly at Delta's lifeless mechanical body lying in the bottom of the destroyed fountain. My eyes drifted to his right palm, weakly laying open with a burning rose symbol engraved into the metal. I lifted my hand and stared at the burn on my palm with a frown as my eyes blurred with tears.

Randy and Stella slowly limped over from where Ryth and Fletcher lay with Randy, shoving Nerve forward with his hands tightly behind his back. Nerve's eyes were filled with panicked tears and the skin under his eyes stained dark as he stared at Delta lying lifelessly in the crater. Distant sirens echoed through the city as we all blinked in shock. My heart roared in my chest as every noise became muffled, and light grey smoke gently filtered from my palm, wrapping gently around my hand. My hearing suddenly shot back to normal as a cold voice suddenly filled our ears after moments of distraught silence.

"What Delta speaks of is correct..." a voice from Delta's still body hissed.

My blood ran cold.

My heart faltered in my hollow chest with panic and grief.

"True, my son; I *am* the one behind this all," my mother's malevolent voice chuckled. "I hope to see you soon my little, *innocent, rose.*"

Epilogue

True and the rest of the Agency were swarmed by guards from HQ minutes after the voice of True's mother came from Delta's dead body. Being so overcome with emotion, and pain, True had fallen unconscious as guards separated everyone and escorted them away from the park individually. Stretch, Dusk, and Nerve were all arrested and escorted to the hospital wing of the HQ Prison on the outskirts of the city to be treated for their injuries. Once recovered, they would be sent to the prison after various trials. Bourbon, however, was not found by any investigation teams after searching the city for him for weeks. The Agency had lost Ryth and Fletcher. Clou paid the ultimate price for defying the one in control of Delta with his life. Delta was dead.

Sneak Peek at 'Behind the Devil's Lie' Book 2 of "Burden of the Innocent Rose"

True's mother... *The Estate*

The darkened room surrounding me sent waves of calmness through my body, helping ease my intense headache. My hands shook gently with disappointment as I thought over the fight Delta had put up against True and his Agency. I blinked quickly as the pitter patter of rain surrounding the room brought me out of my own head and I sighed. *I'm deeply annoyed that I spent so much of my time and money to perfect Delta, only for a little ball of sunshine child True loves, to kill him... He at least gave me the upper hand, for now.*

"My little rose surprised me today," I beamed slowly, staring down at the desk below me. "This just means everything is going according to my plan."

I chuckled, rubbing my forehead gently and felt the raised burn on right my palm brush against my skin. A chill briskly shot down my back as I slowly raised my head and stared up at the dark room.

The walls surrounding me suddenly trembled as I gripped my desk tightly.

"Arthur? You and your stupid bird better not be playing any tricks on me," I grumbled softly, trying to mask the irritation in my voice as I squinted at the darkened room. "You know Mother needs her alone time after dealing with True."

I folded my hands in front of me as I furrowed my brow. I rolled my eyes and slid my hand across my desk, flicking the lights on in the room all at once. White marble floors contrasted the deep mahogany walls, two giant doors staring at me opposite my desk.

The tall, muscular man called Bourbon was kneeling in the center of the room with his head bowed in front of him, his locs covering part of his face. Blood ran swiftly from his right shoulder where a clean cut ran straight across his flesh while he breathed heavily.

"Oh, there he is!" I called out cheerfully, standing up. The room's walls shivered as I kept my gaze glued on him while his stance wavered, using his normal hand to steady himself. The blood from his fingers streaked the floor, my eye twitching in annoyance.

"My wonderful replacement for Delta, who I know won't give up."

I sighed, smiling wickedly at him as he slowly lifted his emotionless face towards me. His dark eyes were empty other than bursts of rage breaking through their calm demeanor against his warm brown skin. *True, you and your Agency are in for a pleasant surprise.*

Imposter Clone Disorder
(ICD)
ICD Explained

What is it?

Rumored to be hereditary mental disorder that is extremely rare to be passed onto children, ICD has the ability to create a "clone" of the host. The possibly first, brief mention of this disorder was found in a journal by a mental institute nurse in 1757, which stated a patient was being followed by an "odd, undocumented twin" around the halls, until the patient was found dead in his room one morning.

With rising stress levels in the population of New York City, and the entire world, this disorder has become slightly more common, raising questions from scientists everywhere. In most cases, the host has the mental choice of passing on the genes responsible for the disorder to their children. No known cases of the disorder being passed on *purposefully* are reported, most hosts were only unaware of the disorder until first contact with the clone, long after their child was born.

Very little is known about this disorder. Most documented cases are difficult to research due to the host's choice to not answer questions for "safety reasons," quoted from Skye Morgan. Another host has also mentioned briefly that the clone itself told her to refuse any questions researchers ask for reasons the clone would not state. She then asked to remain anonymous to journalists when they would publish that information to the public. The only set in stone fact on the clone's purpose is to attempt to take the place of their host, either with consent or by *force*.

The Clones

The clones have been described to be an "altered" version of their respectable host. They are "born" at the exact same time as their host and grow up living a similar life to one another. If the clone prefers to move faster, their life will speed up and their reality will fluctuate depending on how the host lives when they encounter the situations already passed by the clone. In a way, the two follow the same, slightly altered timeline. This allows the clone to choose the speed at which it lives and how their reality will be for a short period of time. However, the clone will end up on the exact same timeline as their host the closer the "merging event" gets.

Let's make this clear, these clones are **not** human. They have no ability to understand or feel human emotions, have a human mindset, or have human mannerisms. They are simply entity extensions of their host that have limited free will. Very few cases of documented ICD have stated that the clones have the ability to learn how to feel human emotions after the merge and with lots of time, depending which spectrum their merging event falls. The spectrum's full reach is still unknown, but the difference between both ends is drastic.

Attributes of the Clones

All clones' physical appearance resembles the host's power or look the exact same as their host with minor differences that are difficult to spot. Their mental attributes, however, are almost always the exact opposite of their host.

> *Stages of the Disorder…*
> Birth
> Life
> First meeting
> Relationship building
> The Merge
> Conflicted Merge*

*Stage 6 is extremely rare with only two documented cases containing it in the entirety of the disorder's history. Both cases have no authorization to reveal details to the public eye other than

that stage 6 is more life threatening to the host in *every* aspect.

Can This Disorder Be Cured?

No, all attempts to cure the disorder have been unsuccessful. Outside influence by medical treatment only causes discord between the host and clone, making the situation even more dangerous. The only known way to "rid yourself" of this disorder is to let the stages play out naturally and *hope* your case doesn't evolve into a **Stage 6**.

Though the normal death rate of this disorder is 50 percent, allowing the stages to carry out with no outside influence and under heavy medical observation and assistance to injuries given to host by clone, the death rate decreases to a 35 percent chance.

It is recommended that if you know of anyone who may have this disorder to let the local medical authorities know immediately. For the safety of the possible host and those around them, it's best to catch the disorder early to give more preparation time to keep all those involved safe.

If the disorder plays out with no medical observation and without minor assistance where it's needed, the clones are known to become more violent and pushy with the host; the presence of those under government rule smooths out the rough edges...for the most part at least. The clones may not be human, but they're smart enough to stand in line with the presence of those in authority watching.

Newspaper Article Excerpts mentioning ICD

ICD strikes again: A heart-wrenching murder of an ICD victim in Lower-Class Sector

Amy Keilot was murdered by her own clone in the middle of night, leaving behind her husband and young daughter. Authorities are reporting that Amy's ICD is the second known case of "Stage 6" the final, most lethal stage of the mental disorder that is highly uncommon. Through interviews with her husband, researchers were able to find out more information on this mysterious stage regarding the disorder.

Keilot stated, "Her outward behavior began to change in the oddest ways, in the ways that are almost impossible to catch if you're not paying enough attention. It started in her morning routine! She began changing the order she put her shoes on…" Though this information seems vague, it's one step closer to pinpointing ways to save hosts from the twisted demise of Stage 6. More information was shared regarding this case, but it cannot be seen by public eyes.

Government power-testing lab terminated following accident: The unexplained, fatal explosion

Patient #008571, known as Delta Navarro, one of the hundreds of victims from the explosion, lost several limbs and his own life, but was somehow resurrected due to his own power called Override. Given immediate medical attention and emergency surgery to remove the limbs heavily affected by radiation and injury, #008571 miraculously improved in a short period of time, even showing better performance levels than ever before. The cause of the explosion and the unexplainably high radiation levels existing solely the day of the event, is still unknown to this day.

Patient #997525, known as Asterin Hall, was rumored to carry ICD due to the "second" entity present during procedures shortly before explosion (dismissed as power reacting to strict testing conditions). #997525 has been labeled as a possible reason behind the explosion due to a power malfunction that happened at the same exact time, injuring a respected lab worker, Dr. Skye Morgan. No charges have been pressed, and no concrete proof is available. Investigations into the facility were compromised during an Elite Headquarters security breach, and the case was immediately dropped following the lab grounds becoming a restricted area, its location removed off all search engines.